Bread & Joy
The Paths of Plenitude

Marcos H. N. Rossi

Bread & Joy
Copyright © 2020 **Marcos H. N. Rossi**

All rights reserved. No part of this book may be used or reproduced by any means, graphic, electronic, or mechanical, including photocopying, recording, taping or by information storage and retrieval system without the written permission of the author except in the case of brief quotations embodied in critical articles and reviews.

Stratton Press Publishing
831 N Tatnall Street Suite M #188,
Wilmington, DE 19801
www.stratton-press.com
1-888-323-7009

Because of the dynamic nature of the Internet, any web addresses or links contained in this book may have changed since publication and may no longer be valid. The views expressed in the work are solely those of the author and do not necessarily reflect the views of the publisher, and the publisher hereby disclaims any responsibility for them.

Any people depicted in stock imagery provided by Shutterstock are models, and such images are being used for illustrative purposes only.

ISBN (Paperback): 978-1-64345-907-3
ISBN (Ebook): 978-1-64345-908-0

Printed in the United States of America

Preamble and Thank-You Notes

During the winter of 2013, after publishing *Flowers on the Balcony* and receiving positive feedback and words of encouragement from friends and family, a new idea started to brew in my mind, more in the form of questions than an actual action or motion. Would I be ready for something bigger? Could I actually write a novel? Would I be up to such a huge challenge?

That idea (or just a questioning at that time) would be wandering in my mind for a few months, but would be placed in the back seat as something secondary, since those were days filled with uncertainty. I was fighting for the survival of a small business with my wife, Vania, a fight that we ended up losing, and the most pressing issue became the need to find a job, in order to take care of our family.

However, serendipity would play a favorable role on pushing this project forward. The Brazilian edition of *Flowers on the Balcony*, launched in June 2013, ended up reaching beyond my circle of family, friends, and acquaintances, and some feedback received from people whom I had never seen before were so overwhelmingly positive that suddenly the answer to my own question became clear in my mind. Yes, it was time for a new and bigger challenge; I was going to write a novel.

But allow me to step back in time for a moment. The attentive reader must have noticed the use of the word *project* in the previous paragraph. Well, this is exactly what it became, with phases, a timetable, resources, a mission, a vision, and a draft of a storyline that was born after a small little push, received in the form of some innocent questions asked by a child.

During my days of home business (and later, job hunting), I had the opportunity to enjoy taking my youngest son, Gianpietro, to his piano classes. One day, while I was driving him to class, he turned to me and asked, "Dad, are you going to write another book?"

My answer to him was more a doubt than a resolution. I said I would like to, but wasn't too sure. Then he went on asking questions, such as, "What would it be about, and where would the story be?" He carried a curiosity that ignited something inside me, and as I started elaborating on my answers, it became evident that I actually had something. That day, instead of distracting myself with my iPad while listening to his delightful music, I started to draft the backbone of a story right there and then, and at that very moment, *Bread & Joy* was conceived. So my first thank-you note goes to you, Gianpietro, my adorable little one, for making me understand that I actually carried something that needed to flow from my head to a piece of paper (or iPad).

But although the drafting of a story line, the definition of a theme, and the choice of a place in time and space for the story to happen all came to me as part of a natural creative flow, the project of writing a novel posed some challenges that were quite new and different from writing a blog (that eventually materialized into a book).

First, the blog *Flowers on the Balcony* brought along an inherent process of feedback. I would write a text and post it, and people would read and comment about it, would become followers, suggest themes, and suddenly the whole thing created its own motion, retro-feeding itself. And I got used to it. But that motion does not apply to a novel, and its absence got me stuck, asking, "How can I possibly write something without a feedback process? How can I even evolve without such addictive mechanism?"

After writing my first pages, it became clear to me that I needed to come up with an alternative. I needed to receive some criticism to give me a sense of direction and would reassure me that I was heading the right way.

So in August 2013, I decided to engage a few people that are very dear to me and had been faithful followers of the blog, and asked them for a favor that only real friends would say yes to. I requested them to use part of their valuable personal time to read what I was writing and provide me with their candid feedbacks. And proving that they were real friends, after some slices of pizza and a couple of beers, they enthusiastically accepted.

This group met with me four times in a year and provided me with invaluable inputs, suggestions, and recommendations. Without this feedback process, I would never find the motivation to finish the job and most likely would lose my sense of direction. So my next thank-you goes to this group of wonderful people: Rogério Fagondes, Angélica Konrad, Paulo and Josiane Pressi, Nelson Gonçalves, and Lúcia Maria Machado (Grandma Lúcia, as we all call her); without you, this book would simply never happen.

But the absence of a feedback process was not the only challenge I would face on my journey of writing a novel. As I made the choice of placing the story in a historical moment (World War II in England), I needed to make it realistic. Getting the historical events and dates with precision became a necessity, so a vast research on WWII was done, and as the most relevant facts of those difficult years were inserted into the narrative, it brought along to readers the benefit of refreshing their memories of such facts (at least from the European front perspective) while they read the story. However, that was not enough. I needed the name of real places (neighborhoods, cities, counties). I needed a local knowledge that my few visits to England just proved to be insufficient to generate. That was when a name of a dear person came to mind: Shoa Abedi, who provided me with much-needed information and also revised the veracity of names and facts in a way that only a British citizen would be able to do, so another thank-you note is needed here. Without your contributions, my friend, Shoa, this story would probably not feel so realistic.

As I was reaching the end of the creative writing process, I thought it was time to really put the story to test and decided to engage someone who lives with books in her hands; Estela Lutero has been a great friend for almost thirty years. She is a PhD and has read more books in her life than I would probably read in ten of mine. I called her and said, "Would you read this and provide me with your candid feedback?" She not only accepted, but read the whole manuscript in record time. Her feedback was quite encouraging, and the change suggestions were so few that I finally felt confident enough to go ahead and publish the work. Estela went a step further and engaged her daughter, Ana Clara Tavares, a college student who was raised in Canada, to do the translation to English. The translation phase took six long months, but made the publishing of the book in English a reality. So, Estela and Ana Clara, thank you for your priceless contribution.

But most importantly, I need to thank those who sacrifice themselves along on my writing journeys. For me to be able to find the time in my morning hours to keep up with the challenge of writing one page a day, I have to go to bed early, and such routine pushes me to a different time zone inside my own home, sometimes sacrificing valuable hours of family time. So to you, Vania, Gianlucca and Gianpietro, I say thank you for being so patient and for understanding that this is much more than a hobby, it's a passion, and in order to materialize this passion into a published book, it demands its share of sacrifices. And please remember that without having you as my ultimate motivation (after all, what I want most out of this writing journeys is to leave you a legacy), I simply wouldn't find the strength and discipline to do it.

And finally, I would like to thank my readers. To everyone who read *Flowers on the Balcony* and provided me with positive feedback in person, by phone, emails, and messages on my social network pages, thank you. You became my fuel to continue and made me realize that there is no turning back on this journey. I hope you enjoy *Bread & Joy* just as much.

Part 1
Paths That Cross

The Accident

THE WALL CLOCK WAS SHOWING almost eleven o'clock at night, which was the usual time for the last round of alcoholic drinks to be served.

Without giving it much of a thought, Frank stood up from his table, which was hidden in a darkened corner of the pub, and stumbled his way toward the counter to order another couple of beers.

Albert, the barman and owner of the place, looked over Frank's right shoulder and noticed that the beer mug he had just ordered was still there, half-full on his table. Through a defiant and serious glance, he confronted Frank and without using a single word, brought him enough discomfort to redden his face. Frank lowered his head and feeling the world spin slightly around him, complied, reducing his order to just one more, to what, although a bit concerned, Albert consented.

Just as Frank was served, the clock struck eleven. Albert then went on with his usual routine and made the final call for the last round of drinks before closing doors. There weren't too many people at the Great Lion on that cold night.

The number of companions on Frank's table had now doubled. Instead of just one beer mug, there were two. His already full stomach was starting to reject each swallow, as the half-full mug was emptied.

He then looked at the last mug with a mix of disgust, shame, and greed. Disgust because his body couldn't withstand another sip.

Shame, for he knew he shouldn't be spending the little he had left from his army retirement pension on drinking. And greed, because he also knew he was just a few sips away from a complete blackout, one that would help him sleep for hours on end, anesthetized from all his pains. This last feeling led him to an instinctive reaction, declaring greed the absolute winner over disgust and shame. In a single lift, he brought the mug to his lips and without breathing, drank half of its contents.

He took a brief pause to release some of the ingested gas and to take a breather. He rested the mug over the table and looked around. The bar was now almost empty, and Albert flashed a bothered look from the corner of his eyes as he wiped down the tables and placed chairs upside down on top of them, anxious to close and finish the night. Somehow that condemning look reminded him of his father, in a not-so-distant past.

With a fixed glance on some point on the wall, he remembered his family, the incompatibilities, the losses, the goodbyes, and the defeats collected over the years in his yet young but troubled life. He thought of all the emotional confusions, his difficult temper, of his inability to live intimately with anyone, and then took another long sip.

Still with a lost glance, he thought his life had always been a long search, but he was not too sure what he was searching for. There was this constant perception that, for whatever reason, he was continuously choosing the wrong paths in life. It felt like there was always a storm around him, and no matter how hard he would try to get away from it, it would follow him and would again consume him in winds and thunders. It wouldn't make a difference on how hard he would try to move away from the storm. It was always there.

Then suddenly, he heard an old familiar voice whispering in his ear, "Stop running from the storm, Frank. The storm is inside you. For it to go, you will have to confront it."

In shivers, Frank turned around looking for the owner of that voice, for it was someone he knew very well, but found himself facing a blank wall.

This last reverie was all he needed for his hand to move the mug to his lips and empty it until the last drop.

He stood up abruptly and stumbled to the counter. Leaving the money in his regular spot, he said good night to Albert, who responded with a worried gaze. Indifferent to Albert's concerns, he turned around and made his way to the door. In the blink of an eye, he was out on the streets, where the cold winter winds made him try to close up his coat, but his numb fingers struggled, so intoxicated was he.

The skies were calm that night, and there was no apparent risk of new German bombings. On that February of 1943, things had shifted, and England was the one to heavily bombard Germany. The Soviet Union began to impose severe losses on the Germans in Eastern Europe, winning the Battle of Stalingrad, this being the first time the Nazis would recognize a significant defeat. In Africa, the battles were one by one being won, as in El Alamein, which lead General Rommel, the Desert Fox, to withdraw toward the countryside of Tunisia, allowing the Allies to regain control of Libya. On the other side of the world, in the Pacific, the United States had won in Guadalcanal, initiating an important offensive move. There was this feeling in the air that the war was at the beginning of its end.

In every step Frank took, he could feel the sidewalk move. The distance between the light posts and the walls seemed to increase and decrease without any sense, and at times, he couldn't tell if he was heading up or downhill. Probably it was neither.

He wrapped his arms around one of the light posts and stopped for a moment to check location and make sure he was heading in the right direction. As he looked around, he saw a typical London scene of those days, with buildings semi-destroyed by the war, roads poorly lit, and cloudy skies that kept a full moon hidden. That was when he recognized his corner, not too far away. Now all he needed to do was to cross the street and turn right. In just a few more steps, he would be arriving at the boardinghouse where his messy and dirty room awaited, with promises of a warm bed and hours of sleep without interruption. There he would rest from his emotional pains and would get away from his personal storm, at least for a few hours.

In an act of bravery, he took a long breath, looked to both sides of the road, and did not see a single soul. He let go of the light post and stepped down the sidewalk, deciding to make the crossing. His first three shaky steps proved he did not need that last mug of beer. In a fraction of a second, the world spun in an irresistible way. His right leg, which had been fractured some time ago, weakened and allowed his heavy body to fall backward without any reaction that could help him turn and absorb the impact with the ground. He then felt an immense pain on his head and a strong discomfort in his neck.

In a last moment of consciousness, he realized he had fallen, hitting the nape of his head on the street gutter. Now his head rested against it, curving the neck in a very uncomfortable angle. On bringing his hand to the back of his skull, he felt it damp and thought he had maybe fallen over a puddle, but on checking it, realized it was covered in blood.

He tried to look around to see if there was anyone who could help him, but the intense pain in his neck prevented him from doing so.

Now with intolerable physical and emotional pains, he felt pathetic. Looking at the ground, he felt a deep sadness as a tear rolled down his face, and he started wondering if that would be his final scene, a scene so ridiculous and depressing that it made him doubt if he really wanted to be found by anyone in such state.

As his eyes slowly closed and he lost consciousness, he was able to notice a figure approaching, but there was not enough time to recognize a face.

Unexpected Aid

As Frank opened his eyes, he felt as if he was still in the same place and situation of when he lost consciousness. He was still lying down, felt deep pains throughout his neck and head, and could see the shape of a person not too far from him. But he soon realized that the fresh-smelling sheets and comfortable pillow resembled nothing of the street and drain-hole from his last memories. He also had a bitter taste in his mouth and was extremely thirsty, sensations that were all too familiar and that were unfortunately recognized as evident signs of a hangover. At that moment, he heard a female voice say, "Doctor, he is waking up."

Slowly recovering his vision, for a brief moment, Frank thought he had recognized a familiar face. "Jennifer?"

As the image became clearer, he could then realize that the woman was, in fact, not known to him. She was a nurse, who approached with a concerned look on her face, saying, "No, Frank. My name is Elizabeth. Please don't move too much, as you have hit your head quite hard and twisted your neck in a concerning manner. This is why you are wearing a brace around it. How do you feel?"

Frank wasn't sure exactly how to answer such question. He was disappointed, since for a split second, he thought he had found again his teenage love, someone he hadn't heard about for a long time and feared had died in one of the German bombings.

He took a few seconds to self-evaluate, but all he could answer was, "I'm thirsty, very thirsty."

Frank then realized there was another person in the room, who quickly came forward to introduce himself. "Hi, Frank, I am Dr. Philip. You are in luck, since we're only here in passing. You hit your head quite hard, but with no fractures. The cut has been properly stitched and will soon heal. Your neck will take at least a few more days to regain its movements. Please relax and be patient with it. But what really complicated your situation was the high level of alcohol in your system. For a brief moment, we thought we were going to lose you. How many mugs of beer did you have? Well, that doesn't matter anymore. What matters now is that you will be in this room for only a few more hours and soon will be taken to the common area, along with the others. Elizabeth will take care of your thirst."

While Elizabeth lifted the upper section of the mattress by turning a noisy crank handle, Dr. Philip made a few last recommendations and hurried out the door.

Now seated upward on the bed, Frank was able to better evaluate where he was.

The room had poorly painted white walls without a single window. The bed, despite the chipping paint on the frame, appeared to be in good condition and was more comfortable than the one he had in his boardinghouse. He noticed a bedside table to his right, but couldn't properly see it, since the brace around his neck kept him from turning his head.

While Elizabeth made her way to a dresser in the corner of the room to pour a glass of water, Frank could better observe her. She seemed to be around his age, was thin and lean, but appeared to have a nice figure. Her white and freckled face looked tired; however, she carried a calm and delicate smile. Her light straight hair fell down to her shoulders, and her movements were calm and harmonic. However, what really caught Frank's attention was the tenderness of her green eyes.

Elizabeth served him water, which was quickly downed with the typical eagerness of someone who had a hangover. When finished, he took a deep breath and asked, "Where am I? Who brought me here? And how do you know my name?"

Elizabeth glanced at him with the corner of her eyes and smiled with joy, since she knew now that her patient was slowly recovering his senses, and said, "Discovering your name wasn't easy, since you carried no documents with you. The owner of the bar you were drinking at, first carried you to a local medical center. Apparently he noticed that you had drank too much and decided to follow you after you left. When they were changing you out of your bloody clothes, they found a veteran medal hanging around your neck, and this is why they transferred you here to the military hospital. You probably wouldn't have made it if you were left out there on the open, considering the amount of alcohol you ingested, along with the almost freezing temperature we had last night. The owner of the bar probably saved your life."

Elizabeth briefly paused and noticed that Frank held a distant stare, fixed at some point on the wall. He seemed to be embarrassed from all of it. She decided to break the silence and holding a smile on her lips, went on, "I need to ask you a few questions, given the injuries on your head, just to make sure that everything is okay. Are you ready?"

Coming back to himself, Frank consented with an almost unnoticeable facial expression. Elizabeth then started with the questions:

"What is your full name?"

"Francis Farrow."

"Where were you born?"

"I was born in a farm called Bread & Joy, in the county of Lincolnshire, on November 7th 1921. I am twenty-one years old."

"Do you have anyone? Where is your family?"

This last question caused Frank to pause for a moment. He took a deep breath and with a grave glare, responded, "I don't have anyone. My parents died in a bombing in October of 1940. My older brother went out to fight in Africa, but he hasn't responded to my letters for quite some time. I don't know if he is dead or alive."

Elizabeth tried not to demonstrate any emotions; after all, she wasn't in a situation much different than his. This was the reality of many people in London during those days. She followed with her inquires. "What do you do? What is your occupation?"

Once again, Frank took a moment to pause. The level of discomfort with the questions was increasing. He again looked away to a point on the wall and said, "I have done nothing more than get drunk since I was dismissed from the army in June of 1941."

"And why did they dismiss you?"

Frank felt as if the questionnaire was getting a little too personal and reacted by responding, "Isn't it clear by now that my memory is well and that my head is working fine?"

Elizabeth realized that she had let curiosity make its way into the conversation and apologized.

"I am very sorry, Frank. You are right."

Frank quickly noticed the change of expressions on Elizabeth's face and the embarrassment he had caused with his response and felt the need to explain himself.

"Please, don't feel bad about this. It's still difficult for me to talk about these things."

"I understand. But if you would allow me a comment, this may be part of the problem. Not speaking about your pains won't help you process them or better understand them. This leads you to live in a permanent state of flight from yourself. If you don't face your ghosts, they will never go away."

Unexpectedly, Elizabeth's comment brought to mind the voice he had heard the previous night, which told him that the storm lay within him and that he would have to face it sooner or later. He then responded, "You may be right, but unfortunately I don't have anyone that I could do this with."

Elizabeth could more and more understand Frank and his ways, his need for alcohol, and his emotional fragility. Without really knowing why, since she was not supposed to become more intimate with patients, she offered him help. "Look, you will be here for a few more days before you fully regain your strength and movements. If you would like to talk, please feel free to do so. I would love to hear you and to know more about you. You can count on me, okay?"

Frank was surprised by such offer. It had been years since he was last offered such heartfelt support. He looked into Elizabeth's eyes and felt for her feelings foreign to him, different than anything he had felt before. In fear, he coldly responded, "Thank you, I will consider it."

Elizabeth then turned toward the door and closed the conversation by saying, "Do you need anything else? I have many other patients to look after."

Frank responded negatively with a quick hand sign. Elizabeth then excused herself and told him she would be back shortly with medication and to help relocate him to the common area of the hospital, as he was no longer in need of special care.

As he found himself alone again, Frank went back to his thoughts. He remembered the previous evening, the loneliness he felt in his room, which led him to the bar, the countless mugs of beer, the difficult walk until his fall, the physical and emotional pains, and the oncoming figure that approached him as he lost his senses.

"Albert…what a good man he is. I must return to the bar and thank him when I get out of here."

After whispering these few words, he felt lucky, at least in that moment. The owner of the bar was kind enough to worry and care about him, and had saved him. Thanks to his military past, he was taken to a good hospital, which wouldn't cost him anything, and was being looked over by an attentive and pleasant nurse. What else could he want? For a second, he thought about God and how he had drifted away from him. He felt thankful, despite of all he had gone through, and came to the conclusion that something needed to change. If he continued on this path, a tragic and melancholic ending was sure to come. He felt as if he needed to do something, something drastic and radical. But do what? He wasn't able to fight in the war anymore. He no longer had a family. He couldn't find a job.

He decided to calm down and resign himself to the fact that, at least for a few days, he would be confined to a bed and would have lots of time to think. He then remembered a thought that had been shared by someone who was very special to him and whom he missed truly. It was the owner of the voice he had heard the previous night in his drunken state. This person would tell him that sometimes, destiny imposes on us a sort of punishment, like adults do with children when they misbehave. It places us in a corner, looking at nothing more than a wall for an undefined amount of time, to think of the things we have done and reevaluate our actions.

That's it, I am being grounded in order to rethink my life, he thought.

Suddenly his thoughts were interrupted by the door, which swung open. Elizabeth, along with two other nurses, arrived to begin his relocation.

At the common area of the hospital, he realized that his punishment was soft in comparison to what others were going through and that he was truly fortunate. He then experienced once again the sufferings of war, seeing the agony of other soldiers gravely injured—some missing whole limbs and others who would not make it past that day. He felt guilty for occupying a bed for a reason so vile, when others could be in need of such space. He then realized that Elizabeth was observing him. She approached and gave him his medication with water and said, "Don't worry. You will not be here long. In a few days, you will be able to go home. I will return in the evening to see how you are doing. If you would like, we can talk for a bit then."

Her words brought a mixture of relief and agony to Frank—relief for he would not be occupying the space on that bed for long and would not need to witness the suffering of the wounded soldiers around him indefinitely. However, the simple thought of returning to his solitary room in the boardinghouse was somewhat painful. In that very moment, he decided he no longer wanted to live there. Where he would go, he still didn't know.

Lost in his thoughts, he caught himself willing that Elizabeth was still there and noticed he was anxious for her promised visit, later that evening. He then closed his eyes and fell asleep once again.

The First Conversation

Frank slept for hours, and when he woke up, it was already nighttime. He thought that his constant state of drowsiness was most likely the effect of the medication. While trying to move around to a more comfortable position in his bed, he felt his distressed neck and thought, *Oh, oh, this is going to take some time to heal.*

Soon after, a nurse passed by and asked if he was in need of anything. He simply asked for more water and for her to help him raise his mattress so he could better view his surroundings, to which she responded promptly. The nurse informed him that soon, dinner would be served. Frank then realized he hadn't eaten anything in nearly twenty-four hours.

It was only when the food arrived that he noticed how hungry he was. The meal was a luxury for those difficult days and consisted of mashed potatoes, some rice, and vegetables, which he quickly devoured. The sensation of the warm food in his stomach was invigorating. He felt stronger and primed.

At that very moment, he noticed Elizabeth's presence on the opposite side of the room as she cared for other patients. The air was heavy, and the strong odor of medications bothered him. The infirmary room he was in was quite large, but he could still easily see what was going on in his surroundings. The room was about twenty-five meters long and eight meters wide, where twenty beds fit with ease. All beds were occupied, and Frank was on the opposite end to the entrance facing the entry door, from where he could observe the whole room. On the bed beside him, a man somewhere in his midthirties lay unconscious. He had been like that since Frank's arrival, and for a moment, Frank wondered if he was still alive at all.

Frank started following Elizabeth with his eyes, hoping that she would see him, but apparently she was doing her last round before going home. She was passing by each bed, and Frank had the impression that she had looked after him already while he was sleeping, since she was moving toward the opposite direction. He felt frustrated, thinking that she would not fulfill her promise.

However, as Elizabeth finished looking over the last patient, she turned and started walking slowly to his side of the room. Frank then felt something similar to a chill in his stomach, and a wave of joy took over him. She was coming after all.

As he watched her walking toward him, he noticed she was not exactly what could be defined as a woman of singular beauty, but there was something extremely beautiful about her, something that he simply could not express in words.

"Hi, Frank," she said as she approached his bed.

"Hi, Elizabeth. I am glad you came. I thought you were ready to head out."

"And I would be, in a regular day. But today, I have a conversation scheduled. I left you last on purpose. How are you feeling?"

"A little better, but my head and neck are still in a lot of pain."

Elizabeth then reached out for her purse. From inside, she took out two makeup mirrors and positioned them in a way so that Frank could see the back of his head. She showed him the deep cut and the large bruise he had on the right side of his nape. It was only then that Frank realized that his hair had been nearly entirely shaved and only a top was left. He looked like a soldier again.

"Wow, what a huge cut. And the bruise is quite noticeable."

"Yes, Frank. This is why it's just normal for you to feel such pain. It's good to know that you are feeling a little better. But I am not here to talk about your head or your neck. In two days or so, you will be feeling much better and ready to go home. I am here to talk about your other pains, to understand what really brought you here, because you may rest assured that it was not for the cut in your head or the twist in your neck."

Frank took in those words like a punch to the stomach. Elizabeth was right and had read between the lines. For a moment, he wished she was a little less direct and would simply sit there and keep him company. However, she had a sharp look in her eyes, one that would dive deep inside, and that made him realized it would be difficult to escape.

He then made an effort to look at his surroundings. Noticing his concern and discomfort, Elizabeth assured him that the patients around him were asleep, or were about to fall asleep, due to their medications. Frank calmed down a bit, but his mouth would not move. He looked at Elizabeth with frightened eyes, showing that he was in a new and uncharted territory. He was not used to talking about himself and barely knew how to do so. He felt an incredible discomfort and feared that he would be opening a Pandora's box, having no idea what would come out of it.

Once again interpreting her patient, Elizabeth said, "Frank, I know this is difficult, but you can trust me. As soon as you start talking, it will become easier, and soon enough, you won't want to stop. You need to take this out of your chest, or chances are that from here, you will be returning to the bar, and soon enough, from the bar you will be back here. And that will be if you are as lucky as you were this time."

Frank avoided eye contact and looked away to a distant point. He kept his stare there for a few moments without saying a single word.

Elizabeth then stood up and, in a kind but firm tone, said, "Frank, on any regular day, I would already be on my way home. My shift ended ten minutes ago. I am here to help you when I could be on my way to rest. Are you going to benefit from this or not?"

Frank did not move. Something much stronger had frozen him like a statue. Elizabeth then reached for her purse, put it over her shoulder, and said, "Very well, Frank, the choice is yours. Have a good night."

Elizabeth took three firm steps toward the door, and that was enough for Frank to panic. He begged in a hesitant but desperate voice, "Wait…come back…please."

Elizabeth halted and stood still for a second. She turned her head and looked toward Frank with the corner of her eyes. Frank then realized what she had that was so beautiful—her eyes. They were sweet and yet penetrating, delicate but at the same time sharp. It was the type of look that carried something addictive, and that would stay for a while, even after she had left.

Elizabeth slowly made her way back, placed her purse where it was before, pulled out a chair, and sat herself next to Frank. She glanced over at him with an open expression and said, "I'm all ears."

Frank could feel deep inside that her words went beyond just an expression. Elizabeth had positioned herself in a way that showed she was truly ready to hear him with both body and soul.

"Okay, Elizabeth, I don't know exactly how to do this, since I'm not used to this kind of exposure, but I'll do my best."

"Why don't you start from the beginning? At what part of your life do you feel things went off track? And please don't tell me it was from the moment you were born, because I know that can't be true."

Frank chuckled and took a moment to think. This was an interesting question, one that led him to briefly look at his life in retrospect. He then said, "You are right. It wasn't. It was in my teenage years that I began to feel that I was different. I had a hard time fitting in."

"I understand. Let's start from there then. Tell me about that time in your life."

"Okay, I will. You are about to meet a Frank that very few people truly know, but one that is still part of me. It's like the spring of a river. Very few people know it. However, it's part of the river just the same, and it has a strong influence over its course. But prepare yourself, this can take some time."

"Don't worry, Frank, when I can't take it anymore, I'll let you know, and we can continue tomorrow."

Tomorrow? She'll be back tomorrow? This is wonderful. She will be back tomorrow, thought Frank. He still didn't understand why, but that new information filled him with joy and encouraged him to speak.

"All right, Elizabeth, let's begin. Are you ready to be bored to death?"

And they both smiled as their eyes met.

School Rules

Frederick Farrow rushed through the staircases of the neighborhood high school. It was just ten thirty in the morning, and he still had lots to do in that particular day. He had left his work at the factory to attend an urgent meeting at the principal's office.

He no longer needed to ask for directions to get to his destination. After all, this was already the third time in that August of 1936 that he had to meet the school's principal, always for the same reason.

His teenage son Frank, nearly fifteen, had committed another act of indiscipline and Frederick, as usual, was summoned for another lecture. Times were difficult. Nazi Germany was starting to bother their European neighbors. It had reoccupied its lost territories in the borders of France along the Rhine River in May, violating the Treaty of Versailles signed at the end of the World War in 1919. The threats of a new war rose to the air, and that brought a new concern to his mind, for he had two sons, one already old enough to be a solider and another who would soon reach such age.

A reclusive man, illiterate, and of few words, Frederick could not understand what was going on with Frank, his youngest. It had been thirteen years now since they left Bread & Joy, a potato farm in the countryside of Lincolnshire, looking for better fortune in the factories of Croydon, in the outskirts of London. When they left the farm, Frank was only a small playful baby. But at the age of thirteen, he seemed to have lost his ways. His disdain for studying became evident, and little by little, the situation became intolerable. Beyond skipping his classes, when he did attend them, he would madden the whole classroom, defy teachers, bother the girls, and harass the studious ones. This time, he had confronted his religion teacher, putting him in an embarrassing situation questioning the virginity of the Holy Mary openly in front of the other students.

"This time he crossed the line, Mr. Farrow. Where have you heard of a child questioning the Virgin Mary? What will the other parents think when their kids bring up the incident? You must take some form of action, or we will be forced to expel your son from this school," said the principal firmly.

"You are absolutely right, ma'am, I will talk to him."

Frederick was impatient and wanted to quickly resolve the situation and go back to work, after all, he feared losing his job. Those were complicated times, and it would be difficult to find another one.

"Speaking with him will no longer suffice. He is in need of some tough corrective measures."

Understanding what the principal was suggesting, Frederick was quick on the answer. "Madam, tell me, how can I apply the measures you are suggesting on a kid that is now bigger than me?"

Obviously, the question was left without an answer.

As he arrived home that evening, Frederick was no longer as calm. With sharpened eyebrows and a look of disappointment in his face, he walked by Frank without saying a single word. He told his wife, Charlotte, about the incident at school, argued that he would not know how to handle it, and asked her to intervene.

Frank, perceiving what was soon to follow, made his way to his room, where he could be alone since his older brother, Peter, worked the night shift.

Charlotte entered without knocking and with fury in her eyes, said, "Can we talk?"

"Yes, and I think I know what this is about. I didn't really do anything, Mom, I just said what I thought. Am I not allowed to do that?"

In anger, Charlotte raised her tone of voice.

"How do you dare to think anything like that of the Holy Virgin Mary? You know that I'm devout to her. I always ask you to pray for her, and she has always taken care of us. How could you dare offend something so sacred? You have changed, my son. Sometimes I don't even recognize you. What is happening to you? Tell me, I am your mother. Maybe I could help."

Frank remained silent and looked away, with his eyes fixed on a point in the wall. He seemed distant, looking for an answer to his mother's questions. Deep inside, he didn't really know what was going on with him. He didn't like rules, he didn't like being told what to do, he wanted to know why things were like they were, he hated hypocrisy and wanted hard answers. How was it possible for a woman to become pregnant without having sex with a man? Divine miracles were not well-supported explanations for him. Everything was supposed to have plausible, scientific answers.

The classes bored him. He could not stand being there looking at the teachers as they vomited information without any care for their students. He wanted to participate, question, speak, but all this was against the rules, and he hated them.

The perception he had was that he was different, that he did not fit in. And for this reason, he didn't have any motivation to be there. He simply did not want to study.

Finally he responded to his mother, who was quickly growing impatient to his silence. "I don't know, Mom. It's been a while that I feel strange. I don't even understand myself."

"Well, you better begin to. I will no longer accept any kind of offensive behavior to the Virgin Mary. I always knew that these teenage years would be difficult, but you are crossing the line. We need you to finish your studies so you can start working and help with the expenses. If you don't fix this, things will only get harder for you. If a new war comes and you are not studying or working, you can be sure they will be sending you to the battlefield."

His mother stood up and made her way to the door, then quickly turned back to Frank and offered her final words of advice, "And don't forget, this Sunday when you go to church, you will be confessing for all your sins. Ask to be forgiven for your tongue, my son, or God will punish you."

This was another thing that Frank just could not accept. How was it possible for God to be a synonym of suffering? God should be good, kind, loving with his own creatures. After all, was God love or punishment? He also didn't have an answer to these questions. His head was burning in confusion, wondering if it wasn't just easier to simply accept everything as it was and not question anything at all. At least this would bring him peace and surely less trouble. But he just couldn't. Questioning things was so natural to him, and since no one else he knew was like that, he felt as an intruder, as someone who would always generate chaos and confusion.

He would confess himself after all. He resigned to the fact that he was a sinner and that on Sunday at church, he would redeem himself. But his resignation would not last very long.

Church Rules

THE ELEVEN O'CLOCK MASS HAD long started that Sunday morning when Frank entered by the side entrance of the church. As he made his way in near the altar, his nostrils were inundated by the strong scent of incense that the priest had just spread.

He wasn't quite sure why they had that ritual, since no one had ever taken the time to explain it. What upset him the most was the fact that he couldn't just raise his hand and ask, "Dear Father, why do you do this every Sunday?"

Other similar questions also spun through his mind. Why would people sing in such sad tones at church? Why couldn't a priest get married? He considered being a priest when he was a child, but the thoughts of celibacy were just intolerable. Why couldn't women become priests? The fact was that no explanations were ever offered for any of these questions. Everything had to be accepted as indisputable. Things had always been this way and would always be.

The priest's voice interrupted his wandering thoughts. He was running the homily, a word that Frank also ignored the meaning, only knowing that this was the moment when the priest would give orientations to the followers on how they should behave. Most times he didn't pay much attention, since when he did, he would hear things like *women's submission, the one and only church, virginity, chastity, wrath of God, penance,* and other things that would make him yawn and lose interest. He would tell himself in these situations, "God can't be only this, it just can't be."

But he was there to confess himself. For a split moment, he had forgotten his main objective. However, in listening to the priest and the things that were being said, more doubts came through his mind, and he began to feel less and less guilty. The idea of confessing was becoming less appealing as well. Acting on an impulse, he rushed to the confessional box, realizing that if he would think a bit more, he would simply abandon his intent.

As he kneeled, his joints crackled, and without thinking much, these words came out of his mouth;

"Forgive me, Father, I am confused and disoriented. I no longer know what to say or do. I have a mind filled with doubts and questionings, and I am hurting my family with this attitude. I need help."

He exhaled in relief. He had done it. He had said everything he needed to say with only a few words. The feelings of relief were overwhelming. He had confessed his sinning confusions and questionings; now all he had to do was to wait for the priest's wise words and advice. Certainly, he would leave church with some guidance. And then he heard a trembling and tired voice coming from within the confessional box, saying, "Pray, my son. Pray a lot and ask for protection, for the devil acts in many ways. You could be disturbing your home because of him. Pray three rosaries and light a candle. I absolve you from your sins in name of the Father…"

The priest went on speaking, but it didn't matter, since Frank was no longer listening. His frustration reached its peak. Was that everything the priest had to say? That he was "possessed"? All he had to do now was pray the rosary three times and everything would be okay? That didn't make any sense to him. And on top of it, being judged and absolved by someone who seemed to offer such a limited and narrowed perspective brought him the feeling that he should keep questioning things and consequently sinning. He felt an even stronger need to defy what seemed to be pure hypocrisy.

The priest's words seemed to spin around his mind, "the devil acts in many ways." He then began to question if his thoughts were really coming from him, if his thoughts were really his own, if it was possible that these thoughts were actually the devil's work and impulses.

In that moment, he decided to separate within him what was his own thinking and what would come from to the devil. If things were aligned with the rules of church, school, his family, then these thoughts would be his own. But if things were in conflict or simply questioning all these things, then it would be deemed to be the devil's work, and it should be banned from his mind. This would be the only way to fit in to his surroundings and not cause any more problems.

This was it. He had finally found the formula. From then on, he would no longer be a troublemaker. He would be a good example, and the devil would no longer dominate him. He would no longer feel so unwanted and abandoned by the ones he loved.

Lost in his thoughts, Frank did not notice that the mass had come to an end. He remained seated there for a long time, trying to convince himself of the conclusions he had reached.

Suddenly, a few feet away from him, the door of the confession box opened with a harsh shrieking sound. Frank observed with sadness the figure of his "judge," Father Walker, leaving the confession box, dragging himself to the vestry.

Father Walker was the oldest priest he knew in the parish and represented what was most traditional and conservative in the church.

Frank had no sympathy for him, and in his hands, he had placed the power to be judged and forgiven. The thoughts in his head became even more confusing than before. Although it seemed absurd, he apparently felt a greater identity with the ideas and questionings that he had just attributed to the devil and almost none to the ideas and behaviors he longed to incorporate.

Could it be that he has really "possessed"? An unbearable identity crisis began to fill his thoughts. At the end of the day, who was he really? The person he believed to be until that moment or someone influenced by destabilizing devilish thoughts, placed in his mind by some maleficent entity?

Then he questioned out loud, "Or could it be that they want me to believe that I am not who I think I am so that I stop being someone that they don't want me to be?"

This last thought terrified him, but he no longer had time to ponder upon it as the church was beginning to close.

He had a lot to think and elaborate about, so he decided it was time to go home. However, he would soon realize that his home would not be the best place to try to organize his ideas.

Family Rules

FRANK MADE HIS WAY HOME through the streets of Croydon with slow unpretentious steps, without any rush to arrive at his destination.

On Sundays, lunch was normally served later than usual. His mom was probably leaning against the stove, and his father most likely would be listening to the news on the radio. Nothing really interesting would be happening there that would justify a greater urgency in his pace.

While walking, he tried to place his thoughts in order, looking for reference points and searching for his own identity. He wanted answers and needed to go beyond what he saw or felt, but he couldn't go really far. He only knew that his life was filled with questions and that he was tired of them. He ended up rejecting the ideas of any evil possession. Maybe that wasn't what Father Walker meant after all. Maybe there was another explanation. But if there was, why didn't he give it to him? Why couldn't he be clear and objective?

Parables. He had learned their meaning in school recently. In his current moment of questionings, they didn't help much, only thickening the haze that floated around his mind.

When he finally arrived home, the clock in the living room marked just past one thirty in the afternoon, and everyone was waiting for him to have lunch. As he opened the door, he was received by angry faces and fulminating stares. His mom was first to ask, "Frank, where were you? Didn't you see the time?"

His brother, Peter, followed with more complaints. "What is wrong with you? Do you have any consideration for us at all? We're starving to death here."

Frank then tried to defend himself. "I needed to think a little, so I walked home slowly. But why didn't you start without me? I could eat alone later."

Up until that moment, Frederick was sitting quietly at the corner of the living room. He then stood up and addressed his son harshly, "Listen to me, you brat, I had enough from you this week. You made me go through the humiliation of listening to your principal lecturing me at your school, given your questionings of what is holy. Now you want to change our Sunday lunch? Don't you know that Sunday lunches are meant for the family to eat together? Get to your seat right now. We are all going to eat. Charlotte, please serve lunch!"

Frank shut his mouth and obeyed almost instinctively, for he knew that when his father would go out of his usual passivity, the situation was serious. But he wasn't hungry and barely touched his food. Again, he was the target of further criticism. After all, everyone had waited for him, and he just wouldn't eat. Irritated, he left the table and went to his room.

Then he heard his mom's steps on the hallway and intuitively knew he would be punished for his disrespect. Charlotte said with a monotonic angry voice, "You are not going out to see your friends today. You are grounded and will stay home."

"But, Mom—"

"I don't want to hear a single word from you. I can't take any more of your evil acts."

Charlotte shut the door behind her, putting an end to the discussion. This was too much for Frank to swallow. Spending the Sunday away from his friends of the neighborhood was humiliating. He was furious and could not agree to it.

In his mind, he was questioning all these traditions. Every Sunday was the same, and he could no longer stand such routine. He would get even more baffled when his mom, every now and then, would ask him to say the prayers. To him, he didn't need to be thanking God but his father, who worked hard for the food to be on the table. But if he would say this to his mom, she would seriously condemn him.

And she had used the word *evil*. Could this all really be the devil's work?

Frank could not understand how he was capable of creating so much trouble so quickly and without any effort. Just an attitude outside what was normal, an observation contrary to what was classified as common sense, and that was it; he would be lashed and filled with rejections.

He was feeling quite disoriented, but one thing was certain, he needed to be with his friends. After all, he didn't have much more left. Only with them would he feel comforted, being near the ones who were just like him.

He decided that he would sneak away from his punishment, but unfortunately this new form of disobedience would not bring the benefits that he was hoping for.

The Growing Distance from Friends

Frank had been out of the house for a few hours already. Sneaking out through the window wasn't so complicated, since after Sunday lunch, it was routine for everyone to take a short nap. But his feelings of guilt were overwhelming, for although his parents didn't notice him sneaking out, it would be quite difficult to return without getting caught.

But the objective was achieved. He was out with his group of friends discussing football, talking about motorcycles and cars, flirting with girls, and smoking some cigarettes. He had been smoking without telling his parents for a few months now.

But things just didn't feel right. Something just wasn't fitting. No matter how hard he tried to get distracted, his questionings from the past few days were still hanging around in his mind. Over and over, he found himself lost in his thoughts, drifting away from the conversations with his friends, which at this point, were on topics completely parallel to his own. He thought about school and his difficulty evolving with his studies, his troubled family life, the church and how uncomfortable he felt there, and finally, his relationship with himself.

He simply didn't know who he was anymore. He did things that hurt others, ran away from home, smoked behind his parents' back, and searched for God in a different and silent manner, in a way that no one else around him did. The conversations with his friends were no longer that interesting. He knew he was far from being an adult, but strangely he no longer felt like a kid.

He was deep in his thoughts when Jennifer arrived, beautiful as usual. She had long blonde hair that fell past her shoulders, always well arranged. Her light pale skin stood out on that sunny afternoon, and her deep blue eyes would call the attention even from a distance. Tall and slim, she made her way in her nicest dress and quickly brought to Frank the typical hormone reactions of his age. He stood up and made his way toward her to talk. But as he approached her, he felt avoided. And that would happen again, and then a third time. Growing impatient, he pulled her by her arm and asked her abruptly, "What is going on? Why are you avoiding me?"

The girl looked back in fear and to avoid further embarrassment, pulled him aside a few steps away so they could talk in private.

"My parents came to know about your problems at school, Frank. They don't want us to be close to each other anymore. They don't even want us to talk. They threatened to move me to another school. I'm really sorry, Frank, but we can't be together anymore. You better look for another girlfriend."

As she finished talking, Jennifer stood up and walked back to the group she was before being unsettled by Frank.

It all happened so quickly that Frank just stayed there, feeling a bit dizzy and confused.

He lit another cigarette and smoked it down in fury, feeling miserable. The emptiness he felt was greater than his chest could handle and would fill the streets, the town, and his whole world.

How many other girls would avoid him? Would he lose his friends as well? In that moment, he felt a strong urge to talk, to just speak to someone and vent. He needed a way to open up and liberate all his feelings, talk about the questionings that fogged his mind and until that moment, had found no answers.

Then in his mind, he started analyzing his friends one by one. His cousin Paul had just turned thirteen and was too immature; he wouldn't understand. Jennifer was already out of the equation. With the rest of his friends, he had never really had a truly serious conversation. His mom and he were not speaking the same language, and his father would be even less understanding. His brother, Peter, was always emotionally closed off and had never given him a chance to talk about anything like that. The church had already had its chance.

Each possible option was discarded until he felt completely alone, without any real friends or anyone who would understand or accept him as he was. Actually, at that point, not even he would understand or accept him. He didn't want to go home, he didn't want to go to church, he didn't want to stay out on the streets, he didn't even see a reason to exist. Lost in those thoughts, he walked away from his friends. With his mind in a haze of sadness rising up from deep within, he barely realized how many street blocks he had wandered.

Resigned, he decided to head back home. It was still relatively early, and that could give him an opportunity to get back in without being noticed, avoiding any more troubles with his family.

When he climbed back through the window, he noticed that everything was just as he had left it. It was a miracle, but no one had been there to notice his absence. He went to the bathroom and washed himself to get rid of the cigarette smell. His parents were still asleep, and his brother had gone out.

He made his way back to the bedroom and locked himself in. Little by little, his pain came back in full force. He could no longer hide away from it. The first few tears slowly filled his eyes, and he began to cry. And then he cried a lot and for a long time, until he fell asleep.

When he woke up, it was already dark. His parents had gone to the evening mass, and soon he could expect them back for dinner.

He walked around the house aimlessly. Never in his life had he felt so alone. Never had he felt so distant from everything and everyone, including God, and he began to question the existence of God. He looked to his mom's bedside table and saw the Holy Bible sitting there. He picked it up in disdain and flipped through the pages, stumbling on the following words:

> Ask and you shall be given; seek and you shall find; knock and it shall be opened.

The reading of those words in such a moment of hopelessness touched him deeply. It couldn't have been a mere coincidence. He continued to read until he quenched his curiosity. Who would have said that? He then realized that it had been Jesus himself.

He then filled himself with all humility he could gather in his heart and asked God to help him find a path, a direction, a point of reference in his life.

After finishing his little prayer, he laughed at himself, as if such gesture made absolutely no sense. After all, he didn't have much hope that it would be answered.

But it was too late now. The message had already been sent.

A New Friendship is Born

Frank woke up from his afternoon nap still a bit groggy from the medications. He had already become used to feeling a bit doped, after three days of treatment.

He was no longer using the protection around his neck and little by little, felt that his usual movements were coming back, free from pain. The cut on his head was healing into a scar, and the size of the bruise had decreased significantly.

Although satisfied with the healing process, Frank also felt a bit agitated, for he knew what this meant. Soon he would be sent home, and that was not a pleasant thought. This would mean a return to his solitude and most likely to his corner table at the bar. But more importantly, it would deprive him from the company of Elizabeth.

She had kept her promise with remarkable loyalty, visiting him every night since he was hospitalized to hear him talk about his troublesome teenage years, his blunders, and he had become used to that delightful ritual.

When he noticed that dinner was about to be served, his heart filled with joy, for he knew that it was just a matter of time until Elizabeth would come to see him.

Right on schedule before the end of her shift, she walked into to the infirmary to do her evening round the same way she had done over the past few nights. Leaving Frank for last, she approached him with her usual smile and warm glance. She quickly began the conversation by asking, "How is my troublesome adolescent doing?"

With a smile that carried a bit of embarrassment, he responded, "Much better, Elizabeth, fortunately and unfortunately."

"What do you mean?" asked Elizabeth, not understanding his response.

"Nothing. Never mind," responded Frank, still surprised with his own comment.

Elizabeth stared at him, a bit puzzled, but at the same time, she had a feeling she knew what Frank meant by those words. To break the ice in that awkward moment, she asked Frank to return to his story.

"Okay, Frank, in the last few days, you told me about your difficult teenage years and the problems you had fitting in, but to be honest, I still don't see anything that serious. Many teenagers go through these phases, and sooner or later, they find their way out. Didn't it happen to you as well?"

"Yes, it did, my dear friend. And it was a fortunate moment in my life."

After three days of talking, both had given room for some intimacy in the way they treated each other. Calling her his friend was something they had grown comfortable with. Frank realized in that moment that talking about his teenage years was starting to bore Elizabeth and decided to fast-forward to a later time in his life.

"A few years later, something unexpected would happen that changed me forever. Someone new would come into my life, becoming an everlasting influence. But unfortunately, even this would turn into suffering."

"Really? Another girl?" asked Elizabeth with renewed curiosity. This reaction made Frank feel confident that he had won back the attention of his listener.

Frank chuckled at Elizabeth's question and said, "A girl? No. At that point in my life, no girl would want anything to do with me. Well, to be honest, in that sense I don't think my life has changed very much." He laughed at his own bitter humor and continued,

"No, Elizabeth, something really unexpected happened. Once, I heard this person say that we should always expect the unexpected. At the time, I didn't really understand what he meant, but I am starting to think that he may have been right all along."

"Expect the unexpected? How do you do that?" Elizabeth responded with a slight laugh.

Frank began to love more and more not only Elizabeth's smile and eyes, but also her sweet tone of voice and her controlled and timid laugh, as if she didn't want to call much attention on herself.

"To be honest, I still don't really know. But as I relive those moments while we talk, I am slowly realizing that it could be a true thing. From a given point on, my life was a sequence of unexpected events. Sit down. I'm going to tell you about Benedict. Oh, what a great character he was."

A Loss in the Family

August of 1939 began with threats of an invasion of Poland by Nazi Germany and the Soviet Union, who had signed a pact of nonaggression dividing Eastern Europe in zones of influence. Both had agreed to divide Poland in half. Since France and England had promised to protect that sovereign country in case of an invasion, war seemed to be just a matter of time. Everyone was worried.

It was a hotter than usual Saturday afternoon, and Frank hoped to run away from his problems and emptiness by reading. He tried not to think much about life, but his reflections were inevitable.

He thought about the studies he had dropped nearly two years ago and his lack of an occupation. Since he left school, he hadn't been able to stay at a job longer than six months. He couldn't adapt into anything. His past jobs were dull, without any greater meaning and any real perspective. Worst of all, he had discovered the darkest sides of human nature. He had discovered pure materialism, scrooge souls who demanded from him to be like them and have the same aspirations, to be greedy and work for money just for the sake of having more money.

Now close to his eighteenth birthday, Frank found himself in a new situation where most of his time was being spent alone at home. Peter, his father's declared favorite because of his docile and mature character, had found a job in a factory on the north side of London.

Given the long distance and the late work shifts, he had decided to move to a boardinghouse close to the factory. Now he would only come home on his days off, which would come in the most erratic order. But despite having the chance of being a kind of only son, the distance between Frank and his parents had grown wider. He had nearly no communication with them anymore. Frederick wandered around the house mournful, quiet as usual, just waiting for his retirement to come. Charlotte had given up arguing with her youngest son a long time ago. Different from Peter, who was quiet, focused and able to execute his tasks and responsibilities with devotion, Frank was irreverent and challenging. She felt incapable of answering to his doubts and questionings. With a broken heart, she began to see him as a lost cause.

Since the confession incident with Father Walker, Frank had never returned to church. He no longer prayed, read the Bible, or talked about God. In fact, he had never felt as distant from him, but deep inside, he had never stopped seeking and still nurtured a hope to find him. He just had no idea how to do it.

He felt alone, but was starting to get used to such feeling, and that was a scary thought. He was afraid to accept solitude and the bitterness in his heart. He longed for a new path, a new direction, and as everyone else, deep inside he just wanted to be happy. But then again, he felt skeptical and could not contemplate any better future to his life.

The doorbell suddenly interrupted his moment of reflection. He stood up and made his way to answer the door. It was the neighbor telling him that there was someone on the phone who wanted to talk to Charlotte. Frank called his mother, who quickly made her way to the house next door to answer the call.

When she came back, Charlotte was in tears. Her oldest sister had passed away suddenly, and she had to make her way immediately to the village they used to live at, near the Bread & Joy farm in Lincolnshire, to attend the funeral and address some family matters.

Frederick tried to comfort his wife without success while Frank watched her with pity, but no grief, since he didn't have many memories of his aunt.

His father suggested that Frank stayed behind to watch the house, which he gladly agreed to; after all, he didn't see a purpose in traveling so far away to attend a funeral of someone he barely knew. Plus, Frank appreciated the moments where he could have the house to himself to do whatever he wanted whenever he pleased.

His parents left that same night, and Frank was able to be completely alone. Or almost, for his loneliness had become his greatest companion and friend.

There, in the silence of the empty house, he scavenged the depths of his soul, searching for some light in the midst of his personal darkness. He remembered the years when he used to go to school and his inconvenient behavior, his visits to church, his inconsistent relationships, and family discussions. If his life seemed unhappy and empty then, at least he had things to do, to question and discuss. Now he didn't even have that.

He remembered the day that Jennifer left him—his despair in searching for someone to talk to, the loneliness he felt at home, and finally the prayers he made after reading a few lines in the Bible.

He didn't clearly remember the words, but he knew it had something to do with asking and being answered to. After three years, it seemed like something stupid and senseless, done in the peak of his despair, and he was certain that he wouldn't receive any answers to his prayer. Besides, he judged himself unworthy of being answered. According to his mother's teachings, only those who acted within God's laws and commandments were to be given his forgiveness and blessings. Frank knew he wasn't exactly a prime candidate to such profile.

Given the loneliness that his life had fallen into, Frank questioned what the future could possibly bring him. Suddenly a possibility came to mind that left him in panic. What if his parents suffered an accident on their trip? What would become of him?

Such thought sent goose bumps down his spine and a bitter taste rose in his mouth. He had nothing to fall back on. He hadn't finished his studies, didn't have a job, the house was rented, and his brother was living far away and certainly wouldn't want him around, since their personalities were much too different.

"My god, what would happen to me?" he questioned.

For a moment, he regretted many things and saw his parents in a different light, less conflictive, more caring. He depended on them and had never given them anything other than aggressiveness and pain. If he were left alone, he would be nobody, without anyone to take care of him.

He came to the conclusion that he needed to change and take a different path, rebuild himself as a person, but he didn't have a single idea on how to start. He didn't approve of his parents' ideals, and the selfishness of society and religion made no sense to him. He felt like an alien left behind on a strange planet to live out of his own luck. It was quite difficult being so different.

His prayer from three years ago returned to his mind. Was it really that difficult to be answered? Was it possible that God would be such a merchant, only attending to prayers if something had been given to him first? Could it be that the only way to reach God was to pass through the guardianship of a religion? He didn't believe in any of those things. Deep inside, he still thought that one could find God through other paths. But which paths would those be?

He decided to skim through his mother's Bible once again, but this time, he didn't find it. She had certainly taken it with her to pray at the funeral. He felt stupid, since once again in a moment of suffering, he was looking for the Bible to comfort him. Why would he only look for it when he was suffering, if the Bible was always there? Why wasn't he more consistent? Either he simply stops seeking it in moments of despair, or he should always go to it. But the truth was that the absence of the Bible left him with nothing. In that very moment, he really longed for it.

Lonely and tired of thinking, he decided to go to bed. He knew that the following day would be just a repetition of this one. It would be more or less the same, with nothing new, without any twists or answers to his questions.

Just before falling asleep and without knowing if it was truly him speaking or his soul calling for help, he said, "Please, God, help me. Show me the way."

Before he could put much thought into what he had said, he fell asleep.

On the following day, things wouldn't be the same as he thought it would be. The unexpected was expecting him.

The Arrival of a Stranger

Frank spent most of the following day not doing much. He slept until noon, had lunch, listened to the news on the radio, and in the afternoon walked aimlessly through the streets of the neighborhood.

By the end of the day, he was feeling bored and became a bit more mindful of the time, since his parents were to return before dawn, which was already upon him.

Lost in his thoughts, he heard the screeching of a car in front of the gate. He looked out the window, and there was a taxi, with Frederick and Charlotte already working on taking their personal belongings from the back and also a piece of luggage that Frank did not recognize. That was when he realized there was a third person getting out of the car.

It was an older man, probably in his seventies, with a calm and serene look in his eyes and an attitude that fostered his resigned acceptance of everything that was happening to him. The long gray hair that fell below his shoulders and the thick goatee borrowed him the looks of a medieval Celtic wizard. With the help from the taxi driver, Frederick removed from the car a big heavy wooden chest that was placed on the sidewalk.

Confused, Frank tried to identify who could be this weird figure. But one thing was certain. That extra piece of luggage belonged to that man. He then heard his dad calling his name, asking for help to carry the chest inside the house. He quickly ran outside where he could get a more detailed look of the old man. He was thin, but seemed to have good health and, despite his age, was agile and lucid.

Noticing that Frank had fixed his eyes upon him, the old man returned the attention and said, "You certainly don't remember me. I am your grandfather Benedict. How is life, my son?"

Jaw dropped and without much thought, Frank responded, "Confusing!"

The old man smiled with candor, as if he completely understood Frank's reaction. He immediately knew that his grandson's confusion went far beyond that current situation, and holding the smile, responded, "Great, that's how it's supposed to be. I think we will get along quite well."

Still confused, Frank felt those words in a way he had never experience before. With a deep look, his grandfather's eyes seemed to see the meaning beyond the words. Although he could not yet make sense to it, that old man had made an impact on him different from everyone else. He felt as if that man already knew him for a long time.

Suddenly, his trance was broken by his father yelling in his ears, "Don't pay attention to him, Frank. He doesn't make much sense. Now come help me. We need to get this chest in the house."

His mom, noticing her son's confusion, whispered in his ear, "Help your father and then come talk to me in my room. I'll explain everything."

Frank proceeded in helping his father carry that heavy chest into a little room in the back of the house. He then realized that in that small room was everything that old man had in life—a suitcase that carried a few clothes and the chest. He had no idea what it contained.

Frank sat down on it to rest a bit and used the break to ask, "What do you carry in here that is so heavy?"

"In that chest, my son, I carry my greatest treasure. Much of who I was and who I am is inside this chest. You are sitting on top of what is most precious to me. And this treasure could be yours one day."

In listening to his response, Frank stood up immediately, embarrassed for sitting on something so precious. Frederick quickly wanted to know what kind of treasure was inside the chest, which he had just carried in his hands and could be passed onto his son.

The old man then got the key to the chest and opened it.

The disappointment that Frank and Frederick felt was hard to hide. Inside the chest, there were books and more books of all sorts—old, new, small, big, thin, thick.

Frederick looked at Frank, said the old man was crazy, and left.

Frank had the same impulse, but controlled himself. He didn't want to seem rude with his new guest and tried to demonstrate some interest. He skimmed through a few books, but his gesture did not have the impact he was hoping. His grandfather spared him the effort.

"Don't worry, my son. They won't have much value for you today. But one day they will. This is why I keep them like a true treasure. Now go talk to your mom. I have lots to organize. This place is a mess."

It was only then that Frank realized that his grandfather would be staying in the small room at the back of the house, which they also used for storage, and to him that didn't make much sense, as his brother's bed was vacant.

He ran over to his mother's room looking for explanations. She seemed to anticipate all his questions and was readily waiting for him. "I had no other option, son. As you know well, he became a widow very early, since your grandmother died quite young. He was living with my sister, who was single, and there was no one else to care for him. So I had to bring him home. I know this is a big change for you, but you are going to have to get used to it."

In all honesty, Frank was yet to have an opinion on the whole situation, but after giving it a quick thought, he decided he didn't have anything against it.

When he asked about the use of the room in the back, she had as a response that it was under his grandfather's condition to accept moving in. He wanted to stay in a room where he could be alone, not bothering anyone. He also asked to work the land in the back of the house to plant vegetables. He didn't want to be a burden.

Charlotte finished by saying, "Son, my father is a very good man, but he is also very lonely. Nobody really understands him. But at the same time, he is always searching for ways to understand and give advice to everyone. The problem is that most people do not understand his advice. Your father thinks he has lost it, but in all honesty, he was always like this, different, saying things that seemed not to make much sense. Get close and make friends with him, but try not to take everything he says too seriously. It would be a waste of your time."

Now everything was clearer. Frank's grandfather wasn't just a guest. He was there to stay. And through it all, Frank wasn't shocked, scared, or worried about the whole situation. He was curious. He was excited for the new relationship that was about to begin. He didn't understand why, but he felt some connection with that old man. He wanted to know him better, even if according to his mom, it wasn't really worth it. Something attracted him to his grandfather, and he intuitively felt that his influence could actually be of a good sort.

He would get closer to him to find out what was behind his intuitions.

One Last Conversation?

On the fourth day at the hospital, Frank was feeling much better, and it was of no surprise when Dr. Phillip dismissed him to go home.

It was eleven o'clock in the morning, and Elizabeth was still an hour away from starting her shift. Willing to see her one last time, Frank used lunch as an excuse and asked if he could stay a bit longer, since it was certain he would have nothing to eat at home. Dr. Phillip agreed and let him stay.

Frank felt a mixture of emotions when he saw Elizabeth walking in. He was happy to see her, which had become the norm, but at the same time he felt sad. He had become emotionally attached to her and didn't want to say goodbye.

Different than her normal routine, this time Elizabeth made her way to Frank first and said, "Congratulations! Today you are finally going home. Are you happy?"

Despite the positive tone in her voice, her facial expression wasn't showing the same excitement. Frank looked into her eyes and shook his head, insinuating that he was less than pleased to go.

"What's wrong, Frank? Are you still not feeling good enough to go?" asked Elizabeth.

"No, that's not it. I feel great. The problem is to go back to that dirt-hole that I would not dare to call home. Also, I'm really going to miss our conversations in the evenings. I wasn't even able to tell you about my grandfather and all his life lessons. I really wish we could continue."

Frank's response brought a change in Elizabeth's expression. She thought for a moment and said, "Okay, let's do the following then. You don't need to leave just yet. There isn't anyone else waiting for admission today. This way you can stay until the end of the day. We can chat one more time. What do you think?"

Frank's smile expanded from ear to ear, and he agreed with her plan immediately.

That same evening, he would continue his story.

The First Contacts

On the following day, life seemed to go back to its usual rhythm. When Frank woke up, his father had already left for work. His mom was in the kitchen preparing lunch and at the same time was cleaning up the mess he had left behind the night before. The clock already marked ten forty-five, which was a bit beyond his usual wake-up time, making it a little too late to look for work in the morning.

Charlotte thought about condemning him for another lost morning in his job search, but opted to keep her mouth shut and just kept doing her things. She was tired of fruitless discussions with her son.

Frank appreciated his mom's silence. After all, he knew everything that was going through her mind and already felt guilty for his own deadweight, guilty enough to understand that his mom's silence was speaking more than a thousand words.

He drank his glass of milk and ate some bread without any rush. He stayed seated at the table with his glance fixed at a point on the wall, almost as if he wasn't there at all. He thought about his short but at the same time confusing path, the problems at school that offered no appealing reasons to attend, the tedious church, which in his perception only offered rules and punishments without any spiritual appeal or greater meaning, his friends, whom he no longer had anything in common with and who at the end only offered him a false sense of security, and finally he thought about his family, who were seemingly lost in another space and time despite being so close to him.

That was when he heard a weird hum in the backyard, and it took him a couple of seconds to remember the new figure who had arrived there the previous evening.

"Aren't you going to say good morning to your grandfather?" asked his mom, noticing her son's reaction.

Frank finished his glass of milk, stood up, and slowly made his way to the backyard.

Once he got there, he realized that his grandfather had probably woken up quite early, since a good portion of the land in the backyard had already being cleared and was little by little being prepared to be cultivated.

They acknowledged each other's presence through a timid yet fraternal smile, and Frank stayed there for a while, observing his grandfather. With a special care and heart, Benedict was putting to use a piece of land that until that moment had been good for nothing.

After a while, his grandfather broke the silence and asked, "Why didn't you guys make use of this area before?"

And Frank replied, "I don't know really. When we were kids, we used to play here. Then, after we grew up, it was forgotten. And then, all these weeds started to grow over it."

"Well, the same thing happens with people," responded his grandfather.

Frank didn't understand what he meant by it, but in a way, he felt as if such comment was for him. Although a bit worried of what he was about to hear, he decided to ask for an explanation, to which his grandfather responded, "It is quite simple, my grandson. God gives us innumerous abilities and talents, qualities and potentials. It's what I call our garden of the soul. If we don't use them, weeds start growing within us, and little by little it takes over everything until our garden disappears completely. The only ones who can cultivate these internal gardens of our souls are us, ourselves. How is your garden, my son? Is it being cultivated, or is it full of weeds?"

Goose bumps rose up throughout Frank's body, and he felt as if an invisible knife had cut through his belly. That question echoed within him, right in his core. Looking back at his grandfather, Frank noticed Benedict smiling from the corner of his lips, as if he knew precisely the impact of his question. Leaving the question unanswered, since it was absolutely unnecessary, Benedict turned to his grandson and said, "Do you want to cut some of the weeds off?"

And then he offered to Frank the second hoe, which was resting useless in a corner. Frank accepted the offer and awkwardly started removing weeds.

After a few minutes, his face was covered in sweat, but in a way, that exercise was doing him good, as if he was removing the weeds from his own soul.

For a moment, Frank went into a sort of trance as he frantically removed the weeds, then slowly he returned to reality and started thinking that what he was doing was just ridiculous. He left the hoe behind to the side and slowly left.

Benedict didn't show any reaction. He knew he had left his grandson a little confused with the unexpected questioning.

Frank was lost in his thoughts as he made his way into the kitchen.

Charlotte, noticing her son's change in expression, immediately asked what had happened. Frank mechanically responded, "Grandpa said that my soul is filled with weeds."

"What? Didn't I tell you that he sometimes says things that just don't make any sense? Don't pay attention to him, son. Oh, my father sometimes…"

Charlotte continued in her rambling without giving much room for Frank to better explain what had really happened. His grandfather hadn't actually used those words. But in a way, he had made Frank understand it as such, and gotten him thinking.

He couldn't understand how it was possible that no one ever realized the usefulness of the land in their backyard. He, who spent the whole day inside doing absolutely nothing, hadn't noticed the potential that was right there in front of his eyes. Yet his grandfather, on his first day in their backyard, had made it into something productive.

And what about his potentials and abilities, could it be that they had already turned into nothing more than weeds? After all, he could no longer notice them. His self-esteem had never been so low. But now he was questioning if any potentials or abilities existed but couldn't be seen, as his soul was so filled with weeds that his entire internal garden was completely suffocated.

He decided he would try to claim back the garden of his soul. If it still existed, he would find it, even if that meant cutting through all the weeds that were growing there. Suddenly he realized he had forgotten a small detail and asked aloud, "How do I do this? Removing real weeds is easy. All I need is a hoe and I can start cutting it. But the weeds of the soul, how am I supposed to get rid of them?"

He would need to talk to his grandfather again and ask. He should have a formula for this. He would look for him that same evening with more time.

Once again, the answer to his inquiry would surprise him.

Benedict's Request

As the night came, Frank was feeling a bit eager to speak with his grandfather Benedict. Right after dinner, he made his way to the small room in the back of the house where he noticed the door left half opened. When he walked in, he saw his grandfather lying on the bed with his chest facing up and his arms extended comfortably at his sides. He wasn't moving at all. He wasn't showing any sign of life. Frank was starting to get worried when Benedict took a deep breath and with his eyes still closed, asked his grandson to relax and assured him that they would talk in a few minutes. Frank calmed himself down and took a seat. Then he noticed his grandfather waking his way out of his trance, slowly moving his arms, his legs, his neck, until he finally opened his eyes and sat up on the bed.

"Sorry, I didn't know you were sleeping," said Frank.

"I wasn't. I was meditating in deep relaxation. It's great for the mind, for the body, and spirit. One of these days I'll teach you."

Frank didn't show much interest, for he had never heard of such thing, much less of the benefits he could have from meditating. Noticing his grandson's lack of interest, Benedict asked, "What brings you here, son?"

Benedict's paternal way of talking had a double impact on Frank. Initially it bothered him; after all, he barely knew that man to receive this kind of treatment. However, it was also very pleasant, since it was offered in such a disinterested way. That almost stranger wasn't asking for anything in return. He had never seen such spontaneous and unconditional caring, and that was delightful.

Frank went straight to the point.

"I want to talk to you about the weeds in my soul. This morning, you asked me how my internal garden was doing, and I think the answer is that it's filled with weeds. I don't know where it came from, I don't know how it started growing, I just know I feel like everything is covered with it. How can I cut it? How can I find my garden, if it still exists?"

Benedict looked right into Frank's eyes and said, "You have already completed the first step, son. You looked within yourself and had the humility to see that things aren't going so well. Admitting to a problem is the first step in solving it. Looking within you is not an easy thing to do. It requires a large amount of humility and courage. You only took notice that your garden is completely filled with weeds because you know that once, it wasn't as such. You stopped cultivating it somewhere in your past, son. You need to find it and start cultivating it once again."

Benedict paused so Frank could take in his response and then continued, "The answers to your questions are very close to you—where these weeds came from, how they grew so fast, how to cut them. Think a little about this. But to begin, wake up tomorrow around seven in the morning and come help me work the land in the backyard, and we can talk more about it. How does that sound? Now let your grandpa get some rest. I think I'm getting old. The work done today completely exhausted me."

Frank agreed and said good night, making his way out. But he was feeling quite disappointed, for he was hoping to get a more concrete answer from his grandfather. Like almost every other boy his age, he didn't want to spend any time looking for answers. He wanted everything to just be given to him, ready to be acted upon. But the response had been given to him in the form of another question, rather than a straight answer.

He hated when others answered his questions with another question. But what bothered him the most was his grandfather's request.

Frank, after so many disappointments, had created the bad habit of mistrusting everyone. He would think that others were always trying to take advantage of him or to use him. In that moment, he hesitated to trust his grandfather. He thought that maybe old Benedict wasn't so unconditionally caring after all, that maybe he did want something in return. Maybe he was acting this way just to make his grandson work for him in the garden.

That thought began to grow inside his mind. It was so obvious. His grandfather was definitely trying to fool him. He decided that he was not going to wake up early next morning. He would stay in bed, sleep until late, and keep doing the same things he had always done. He would not be used.

He headed to his bedroom lost in these thoughts when he ran into his father in the hallway. Frederick was having financial difficulties, and in those situations he would become even grouchier. When he spoke, he did it with few words and went right to the point.

"Frank, did you go out looking for work today?"

The answer was negative, but Frank remained elusive to avoid any complaints. His father didn't question much; after all, he had slowly given up on his youngest son and no longer expected much from him.

As he rested his head on his pillow that night, Frank was irritated and disappointed with his grandfather and thought, *Tomorrow, I am going to surprise that old man. He's going to be there waiting for me. When I wake up, he's going to lecture me, and I am going to tell him that I am not stupid. He won't fool me.*

When he was about to close his eyes, he felt guilty. An inner voice was telling him that his perceptions were wrong. He quickly brushed off this voice, turned to the other side, and tried to fall asleep, but the feeling that the weeds were growing and taking over his garden was inevitable.

The following morning, he woke up even later than usual. After breakfast, he made his way to the backyard, ready to listen to all that his grandfather would say to him and confirm what he suspected. He would then tell him he wasn't stupid, that he was never easily fooled by others, and that his grandfather would have to do everything himself.

But as he made his way to the backyard, Benedict just smiled and greeted him good morning, like he had done the previous morning, to which Frank responded coldly.

What would follow left Frank completely surprised—absolutely nothing. Not a single word. Not a single complaint. Not even any questionings, just a big languid smile from someone who already expected that kind of behavior from his grandson and so was not upset at all.

Frank stood there for a moment longer and then left. He went to the streets to distract himself, giving the false impression that he was out looking for work.

He tried not to think about what had just happened. He met up with his friends, smoked a few cigarettes, and walked around the streets, only returning home near dusk.

In getting back home, Frank couldn't control his curiosity and made his way to the backyard to see what his grandfather had done all day.

In looking at Benedict's work, which showed a great deal of progress from the day before, he couldn't avoid the feeling of failure and envy toward that old man. He was seventeen years old, was strong, but produced absolutely nothing. On the other hand, his grandfather worked hard without a single complaint at seventy-plus years of age.

When he walked into the house, there was Frederick and Charlotte heatedly arguing over the home finances, the bills to pay, the monthly installments. Frank wanted to walk in without being noticed, but it was impossible. His parents stopped talking, and both looked in his direction. There was an awkward moment of deep silence when nobody said anything. Without saying a word, Frank circled around the dinner table where they were arguing and made his way to his room. In reaching the hallway, he heard his parents restart their discussion exactly from where they had left it.

Nobody asked him anything or made any demands, not even a single comment was made, and that brought him an awful feeling.

Old Benedict didn't ask or demand anything, but looked at him with affection and hope, while his parents asked nothing probably because that was exactly what they expected of him.

He took a shower and made his way to the dinner table. There was a bad feeling in the air, for his parents' discussion about the finances hadn't come to a very positive conclusion. Frederick was getting himself deeper into debt. The money he made from work was little, and there weren't many options available. The only way out was to cut expenses, but now he had another mouth to feed. Benedict broke the silence saying that the garden was progressing quite well and that soon he would be cultivating vegetables, which they would no longer need to buy at the market.

Frederick thanked him, but questioned if the results would really come so quickly, since he worked alone. Benedict responded calmly and confidently, "They will, Frederick, they will."

In finishing the response, Frank and Benedict exchanged glances, and Frank could notice a slight smile in the corner of his grandfather's lips.

Frank went to bed a little earlier than usual. He thought about talking to Benedict, but he figured he would probably be tired and eager to get some rest.

Feeling bad, with guilt eating him inside, Frank started to believe that he was wrong about Benedict and that maybe there was no second intention to his invitation. Maybe he truly wanted to help him. With this last string of hope, he set his alarm clock to wake up at seven. He would wake up early and help his grandfather. After all, he didn't have much to lose.

In closing his eyes that night, he felt as if he had taken the first step on cutting off the weeds from the garden of his own soul.

A Change of Attitude

THE ALARM CLOCK ECHOED LOUDLY and scared Frank for a moment. After all, he was no longer used to that sound beaming at his ear so early in the morning. Getting up was harder than he expected, but something stronger kept him going.

In getting to the kitchen so early, he was faced with shocked stares from both his parents, who right away started asking him if everything was okay.

He said he was fine, took a bite to eat, and made his way to the backyard, where he found Benedict already working.

Frank greeted him and quickly started asking for instructions on what to do. Benedict greeted him back and said, "Welcome! I knew you would come."

He proceeded in giving instructions to Frank, who followed them right away.

From a distance, both parents observed everything with puzzled stares, not really knowing what to think. Frederick turned to Charlotte and said, "Let it be. At least he is doing something."

Then he turned and made his way out to work. Charlotte observed them a little longer, but headed back in shortly after to continue her housework.

Frank and Benedict worked in silence for a while. Frank quickly started feeling the impact of the lack of exercise in his soft hands, not used to manual labor. Benedict, already expecting such difficulties, quickly offered him a water break. They sat under the shade of a tree, and Benedict decided to break the silence.

"So how are things, Frank?"

Frank looked to the side while he drank his water, thinking on how to answer such question, and then decided to be direct.

"Pretty bad, I think. I left my studies behind, I can't find a job, I don't get along with my dad, and my mom doesn't understand me too well, I can't adapt to church, and finally, my friends are one by one finding their place in life, and I'm staying behind. I don't know, Grandpa, but I am starting to think that I might be the problem."

Benedict looked at him for a moment without saying a single word, as if using silence to let Frank think about his own comment. The strategy seemed to work, and Frank continued, "It's like nothing seems to go right in my life, and I feel really bad. I feel like a complete loser. I am seventeen years old, and I don't have any meaning or purpose in my life."

His grandfather then spoke, "Frank, no river finds the ocean right at its spring. It needs to follow its path, which is never just a straight line. Almost all the rivers start with turbulence and torrents, but eventually they calm down and find their natural rhythm. What sometimes looks like a dead end is just a change in course. It's just a matter of time before a new path shows up. You are still just in your spring. Your path is just starting to define itself. Be patient."

Frank loved that analogy. Although it sounded a little weird, it seemed to make so much sense.

Benedict continued, "What's important in times like these in our lives is to have eagerness to learn. I like to call this the sponge attitude towards life."

"Sponge? What do you mean?" asked Frank, a little confused.

"Oh, this is a fantastic concept Frank, where nothing is lost in life. If you can adopt it, nothing in your life will be negative. It's quite easy. Everything in your life happens for a reason. Nothing is by chance. God is always placing in your life the people and the experiences you need for your spiritual growth. Therefore, everything that happens in your life has a meaning, has a lesson to be learned. There is always something that you can take advantage of."

"Even the bad ones?" asked Frank in suspicion.

"Especially the bad ones, since those are the ones that teach us the most and the ones that make us stronger and wiser. It's especially the bad experiences, the difficult times in life, that make us grow and become better human beings. But everything depends on how you see them. If you position yourself as a victim of circumstances, someone born with no luck, believing that nothing will go right, you are not taking advantage of these experiences, and everything will become negative in your life. It becomes a habit, a very dangerous habit, by the way, to think that everything is going to go wrong. But if you look at these experiences as if they were life lessons, as something that is simply preparing you for better times, if you extract the essence of such experiences like a sponge, you will become someone stronger every day. Nothing bad that happens in your life will be able to keep you down for long because you'll be able to transform it into something good and positive. It becomes a change of attitude towards life, where you can only win. You just told me you feel like an absolute loser, for which I tell you, that's great! That is absolutely excellent! For every loss, every mistake, every defeat will make you grow and will make you become a winner one day."

Frank listened to every word in silence and began to rethink each of his own experiences. His grandfather was totally right. He didn't learn anything from what had happened to him. He always placed himself as the victim, as if the world was against him. If he adopted the so-called sponge attitude, what would he have to lose?

"You see, Frank? When we change the way we see things around us, the world around us changes completely. Are you ready to go back to work?"

With that last thought, Benedict stood up and returned to his duty. Frank took a few moments longer to react, but quickly followed his grandfather. He was fascinated by his grandfather's words and was curious as to where he had gotten so much wisdom. So he asked, "Where did you learn all of this? It couldn't have been at Bread & Joy in Lincolnshire. And where did all your books come from? You brought so many with you in your big chest."

"Come to my room this evening after dinner. I'll tell you a little bit more about my story. And before I forget, you said that your life has no purpose. Well, the purpose of life is to have a life of purposes."

Frank didn't really understand this last statement from his grandfather, but agreed to go visit him later that evening. Lost in his own thoughts, he just continued working. He had lots to process and think about.

The Story of a Pilgrim

When Frank arrived at his grandfather's room that evening he was exhausted, however, he was also feeling much better about himself.

Working had made him feel useful, a feeling he hadn't experienced in quite some time.

The door was slightly open, and he could see that his grandfather was doing the same relaxation routine he had done a couple of nights ago. He already knew what to do and waited in silence until Benedict got out of his trance and opened his eyes.

"Do you do this every night?" asked Frank in curiosity.

"And every morning as well. I wake up at five, prepare my tea, and go meditate while it cools down a bit."

"Wow. This is that important to you? Why?"

"Because it helps me calm my soul, my emotions, quiet my mind, and organize my thoughts. If today I am serenity, once I was a storm. Once we were very similar, you and I, Frank. The difference is that I was blessed with experiences and mentors who guided me on how to process such experiences and changed my way of seeing the world."

Frank was surprised with this last comment.

"Similar to me? How could that be? You are calm, easygoing, optimistic, hardworking. I am nothing like that. Honestly, I think I am the exact opposite."

"Remember that analogy about the river? You see, my spring also wasn't the calmest."

From then on, Frank remained silent and listened, because everything his grandfather was saying was really starting to interest him.

Benedict continued, "In my youth, I grew up in the same farm of Lincolnshire where you were born. I was a difficult young man. I didn't accept rules imposed by the family, by the school, or by the church. When I reached my early twenties, my parents arranged a marriage for me. I married your grandmother, and with her I had two daughters, but I still felt unhappy. I felt stuck and jailed. As a nation, we were living very prosperous times, with dominance over a large part of the world, and there was the possibility of joining the army and serve in foreign places. So when the opportunity presented itself, I didn't think twice. I enlisted and ran away. I went to the other side of the planet, leaving my family behind with the promise of a salary that would keep them living well, and that I would return as soon as my term of service ended. But at the end of every term, I would ask for another, and the years just kept passing. I served in China, India, Africa, and Middle East. I lived like a runaway. When I finally came back, I wasn't the same person. I had been transformed into somebody completely different. Your grandmother also wasn't the same young lady I left behind, and my daughters were already teenagers. It took some time for us to readjust, if we actually ever did. Like I said, I returned much different and came back with a baggage that was never truly understood by anyone."

"What do you mean, Grandpa? I don't understand what baggage you are talking about."

"I am taking about two types of baggage, Frank, the spiritual and physical ones. The spiritual baggage is inside of me. The physical one is right over there."

He pointed to the chest tilled with books.

Frank stood up and opened the chest once again, but this time he took the time to examine them with more attention. There were dozens of books that talked about Oriental culture from both China and India, books about Islam, African religions, Judaism, Christianity, and books about Greek, Roman, and even Celtic mythology.

Frank then started to understand the type of baggage that his grandfather had brought after so many years of pilgrimage around the world. In curiosity, he asked, "Have you read them all?"

"A few times," Benedict responded with a proud smile.

Frank was surprised with his response, since he didn't have the habit of reading, and all those books looked like enough reading for someone's whole existence. He continued in asking, "And because of these books, you came back different?"

"Oh no. Not at all. The books came later, so that I could better understand what I had lived."

"What do you mean?" asked Frank, confused.

"Frank, having the opportunity to live in all these different places was truly a blessing. As you probably already realized, I am not really classified as a normal person."

He said that making a funny face, causing the both of them to break down in laughs.

Then he continued, "In every place that I lived, I made good use of my free time and tried to understand the local culture, experiment with new foods, new customs, and even their religions. I attended temples, mosques, met Hindu masters, Buddhist monks, shamans, priests, wizards, and all other sorts of spiritual leaders. Each of these encounters influenced me in a way or another, and from then on I always searched to understand these religions and sects, their origins, their rituals, and I learned from each of them."

"Which one did you choose to follow?" asked Frank.

"All of them!" said Benedict with a heartwarming laugh.

Frank's jaw dropped completely at this response, and he thought that maybe his parents were right. Perhaps Benedict really wasn't in his best mental state.

Noticing his grandson's reaction, Benedict added, "You used the right term, Grandson—*choose*. The spiritual path is a choice, one that is unique, individual, and non-transferable. And the religion one follows is only secondary. People confuse religion with God, paths with destiny, and the language with the message. You see, religions aren't

God. They are masks invented by humans to try to understand him. Since God is much beyond our comprehension, we create religions, which are protocols of communication with what is divine. They are ways of humanizing what isn't human, to turn it into something understandable, manageable, and to a certain point, controllable. But all of this is nothing but illusion. We will never understand God in his entirety, and we need to stop searching for him in religion. He just isn't there."

"Then where is he?" asked Frank, eager for an answer. After all, he had been searching for an approximation with God for years, but the church seemed more like an obstacle than a path. This time, the answer didn't come in the expected manner. Benedict, in a soft and caring way, added to the question, "Where is he, Frank? Where is the only place he could be?"

Frank stopped, thought for a moment, and responded, "In heaven?"

"No, Frank, it's not in heaven. You are allowing abstract concepts to cloud your vision."

"I don't know the answer then. But I know he's not at the church. That place is awful, filled with rituals I don't understand and people that say words without much meaning."

His grandfather's look turned into a smile of serenity. He looked deep into Frank's eyes and said, "Do you remember the conversation we had earlier this morning? You came to the conclusion that the problem was you, not others. The same applies here. The problem is not your religion, your church and its rituals, or what people there tell you. The problem is that you still haven't made enough effort to understand them and to take away everything that suits you and make it useful to you. They are not going to tell you what you want to hear, Frank. They will say what you need to hear. It is your role to translate the message. It's not always easy, but nothing in life is."

Again, surprised with his response, Frank tried to argue. "For a moment I thought you believed religion was bad and unnecessary."

"Oh no, my grandson, much like the opposite. Religions have a fundamental role in helping people transform God into something they can understand, and with that, bring them closer to him. It's important to understand, Frank, that religions are just a means, not an end. They are a means for you to get to God and evolve your spirituality. The problem is that many people confuse the means with the end, and they begin to adore the religion rather than God."

"Why do you think this happens?"

"Because we still are tribal beings. We are primitive, and we divide in tribes much like our ancestors. We need a family tribe, a tribe for the neighborhood, for church, a tribe for our football team, and even for our country. Being part of tribes makes us feel less alone, as if we belonged to a group of people similar to us. There is nothing wrong with this. The problem is that this creates antagonisms. It creates the idea of 'us and them,' which is a step closer to 'us against them,' and this causes disputes between groups, in many cases even wars, like the one we are about to witness. Do you understand now, Frank? There is nothing wrong with following a religion. It can and will help you get closer to God and develop your spirituality. You just can't make it an end in itself, but instead look at it as a means."

"But there are so many things there that don't make any sense that I have a hard time accepting."

"Did I say at any moment that the religions I got to know were perfect? All of them, without exception, were human creations. And humans are imperfect. Because of this, none of us can create perfection. Expecting perfection from any religion is, at minimum, unfair."

Frank stopped for a moment to process all that was said. That last argument seemed to make all the sense in the world, but he still didn't know how to react to it. Benedict then concluded, "When your body is hungry, you need to feed it, right? And what do you do in that situation?"

"I eat something," answered Frank.

"Exactly. But is food always there, ready to be eaten? Do you just need to take it and bring it to your mouth?"

Frank thought for a moment and understood what his grandfather was trying to say. In reality, anything to feed his physical body required some kind of work, like washing, cooking. Even fruit, cultivated right from the tree, needed to be washed and sometimes peeled.

Benedict continued, "It works the same way when you're feeding your spirit, my grandson. It needs treatment, cleaning, peeling, even before you can ingest it. In any religion, we need to learn how to separate what is useful for us and what we should ignore. When you eat a banana, don't you need to peel it first? With religions, it's exactly the same. You need to throw out what is human and imperfect and focus on what is divine and feeds your spirit. Throwing it all out, as if all is bad, and not feeding yourself not only is unfair but also leaves your spirit in a state of starvation. And that's when the weeds we talked about the other day start growing and taking over everything."

When Benedict finished, Frank went into a sort of trance. He had never heard so many wise words. His grandfather had come full circle, going back to the talk about internal weeds, which now made more sense than ever.

"You still haven't told me where God is. If he's not at church, nor in heaven, where is he then?"

"I'm not going to tell you, Frank. This is something you will need to find out on your own. Now let's rest. We have a lot of work tomorrow."

With a tap on his grandson's shoulder, he closed the conversation.

Frank made his way to his bedroom lost in his thoughts and with a lot of information to process. He had learned so much about his grandfather that night, but he had learned much more than that. He still hadn't understood it all, but he did know that the more he learned, the more he wanted to know.

Without any second thoughts, he fixed his watch to wake up early once again and quickly fell into a deep sleep.

Nonetheless, Frank completely ignored at that point that the days ahead would bring some really sad news.

One Last Walk Together

THE CLOCK ON THE HOSPITAL wall was already marking almost 9:00 p.m. Without noticing the time, Elizabeth had heard Frank talk for more than two hours. When she realized how late it was, she stood up abruptly and said, "Frank, we need to go. Listening to the stories about your grandfather was so interesting that I completely lost track of time. Come on, get up and wash up. I want to check you up one last time before we leave."

Her commands brought Frank back to reality and made him remember that his friend in confidence, before anything else, was still his nurse. He stood up and followed her request without arguing.

Once he was back, Elizabeth measured his blood pressure, heart rate, and took another look at his head, which was much better, and she asked him to move his neck around a little more. Everything seemed to be well, except the expression on Frank's face. The time to leave had finally arrived.

"Are you okay?" asked Elizabeth.

"Yes, just a little dizzy. Probably because I've spent so many days in bed…I think."

"Hmmm…," responded Elizabeth, showing some concern merely in sympathy to her patient. And then she suggested, "Let's leave together. I will accompany you to the train station. I am heading there anyways. You should put on your coat since it's quite cold outside."

Frank accepted Elizabeth's offer immediately and felt a bit better, for he would be able to spend a little more time with her. Also, he knew that the moment he walked out of the hospital, he would no longer be her patient and would be stepping into a whole new world of possibilities.

He put on his coat, which was still filled with poorly washed-off blood at the back, took care of the paperwork, and the two of them walked toward the hospital exit.

As they stepped out, the cold wind brought Frank back to the reality of February in London. He closed his coat, and both of them began to make their way to the train station, which wasn't too far away. Although unintentional, the cold made the two of them walk closer to each other, and that pleased Frank, who thought, *I am enjoying this woman's company more than I should, and saying goodbye will be much harder than I thought.*

In arriving at the station, Frank remembered that he had no money, and Elizabeth offered to pay for his ticket home. Although feeling a bit embarrassed, he had no other alternative than accepting her offer. Elizabeth asked Frank for his final destination so that she could pay for his ticked, and in that moment, they noticed that they would be taking the same train. The only difference was that Elizabeth would get off three stops later.

"What a coincidence!" said Elizabeth with a smile that Frank had already learned to appreciate.

Yes, what an unpleasant coincidence, thought Frank, smiling at his own irony.

They sat side by side on the train, which quickly began to move.

Frank began to think that these were probably the last moments he would spend with Elizabeth, which made him feel distressed. He started to think about something to say that could make this moment last a bit longer or that could justify seeing her again. So he asked, "I know it's a little late, but would you walk with me to my place? It's not too far from the station."

Elizabeth was caught by surprise by his request and hesitated. "I don't know, Frank, it's already quite late."

Frank remained silent, looking into Elizabeth's eyes, his glance almost imploring for a few more seconds of attention.

"Okay, okay," agreed Elizabeth, smiling as if showing that her gesture was of pure kindness.

As they left the station and started to walk, Frank stopped suddenly and changed directions. Without understanding what was happening, Elizabeth asked, "What's going on? Did you hit your head so hard that you forgot where you live?"

Frank laughed at Elizabeth's joke and responded, "Oh no. I just want to quickly stop by a place first. Let's go to Albert's bar."

"Are you serious? Frank, you just got out of the hospital," said Elizabeth with a concerned look on her face.

"Don't worry. I am not going there to drink. I just want to thank him."

Finally understanding what was happening, Elizabeth immediately smiled. She was going to meet the person who had saved Frank from a much less fortunate fate.

After a few blocks, Frank stopped and pointed to the other side of the street. There it was, the Great Lion, another typical London pub that had survived the difficulties in times of war. He turned to Elizabeth and said, "Welcome to my second home."

Elizabeth didn't like his joke very much, but followed Frank in crossing the street, which at that time was nearly empty.

They made their way into the bar, and the smell of beer filled both of their noses. There were very few people there, which was not the norm for a Friday night, so it wasn't hard to find Albert behind the counter washing beer mugs. When Albert saw Frank, he quickly stopped and went to meet one of his most regular customers.

"Frank, it's so good to see you. I like your new haircut."

The two laughed at Albert's joke and exchanged a strong handshake. Albert noticed Elizabeth, whom Frank quickly introduced. "Elizabeth, this is Albert, the man who saved my life a few days ago. Albert, this is Elizabeth, who took care of me for all of these days."

Albert shook Elizabeth's hand and quickly said, "Sit down. What would you like to drink?"

"Nothing today. I just came by to thank you. You probably saved me from a tragic fate. I am very thankful to you, Albert."

"Please don't mention it. I did my obligation, for I saw that you really weren't doing too well that night. You went over your usual share."

That observation made Frank fill a little embarrassed in front of Elizabeth, who also pretended to be distracted and looked the other way. Noticing the effects of his comment, Albert tried to fix the situation. "Look, sit down. Are you hungry? Let me serve you something to eat. Today it's on the house to celebrate your recovery.'"

Elizabeth and Frank looked at each other, and they were quick to agree that they were both hungry. And besides, Albert's invitation was a luxury in times when food was rationed, and refusing it would be offensive. To make things worse, Frank would have nothing to eat at home. So, they accepted the invitation.

"Let's sit anywhere except at that table, please. It brings me bad memories." He pointed to the table where he used to sit to drink and numb his pains. Elizabeth consented, and they picked the table farthest away from the other customers that were still around.

An awkward moment of silence followed; after all, they were in a new territory, more personal, which had nothing similar to what they had experienced until then. Trying to break the discomfort of the new situation, Frank started talking. "Until today, we only talked about me. Why don't you tell me a little bit about you, Elizabeth?"

"There's not much to say to be honest, Frank. I was born and raised in London. I studied nursing and started working as soon as I graduated and still do this till today, since with this war there's been plenty of demand. I am an only child, and my parents died in one of the first German bombings at the end of 1940. I was only eighteen years old, and it was a really difficult time for me. But I survived. Today, I live alone, in hopes that the war won't last much longer."

Frank felt sorry for Elizabeth's short yet painful story and tried to show her some comfort and sympathy.

"I am so sorry for your parents, Elizabeth. It seems to be the story of many people these days."

Trying to change the direction of the conversation, he decided to enter into a more personal territory and asked, "What about a boyfriend, do you have one?"

Elizabeth laughed at his question and said, "A boyfriend in times like these? Are you crazy? Dating someone when you don't even know if he'll be dead or alive the next day? And besides, all the interesting guys of my age are fighting in Europe or Africa. You are an exception."

Interesting? Did she just let it slip that I am interesting? thought Frank with an enthusiastic smile.

Elizabeth, realizing what she had said, blushed and tried to disguise it by asking, "Why aren't you there, Frank? What happened to you?"

With a sad glance, Frank responded, "I broke my leg during a preparatory training in September of 1940. The fracture took over six months to consolidate, and I never again was fully able to recover my agility and movements. Since I hadn't finished my studies, they concluded that I would be of no use for administrative work. They dismissed me in May of 1941. They opened an exception and pay me a kind of compensation for hurting myself during training, which I'm not even sure I deserve, but it's enough to pay for my room, my food, and my beer."

Noticing that this topic was unpleasant for Frank, Elizabeth changed subjects. "I love hearing about your grandfather and his life experiences. It seems that he had a strong influence over you."

"He really did, Elizabeth. It's just unfortunate that I am so far from putting his lessons into practice."

The food arrived with a delicious aroma, bringing another moment of silence between the two while they ate, but the feeling of discomfort between them was no longer present.

It was already getting late, and as they finished eating, they thanked Albert once again and left. On their way to Frank's boardinghouse, they passed through the same corner where Frank had fallen a few days ago. The whole scene returned to Frank's memory, which he deflected immediately. He just didn't want to think about it anymore.

Bread & Joy

As they approached the boardinghouse, Frank realized that he could not invite her in under any circumstance. His room was all dirty and messy. It was so awful that she would be sure to never return. When they got to the door, he turned to Elizabeth and said, "Here we are. I wanted to thank you for everything you did for me these past few days, not only for the medical treatment but more importantly, for taking the time to listen to my story. You helped me a lot. I still have a lot to tell you, but unfortunately, we just ran out of time. Also, thank you so much for accompanying me here. You didn't have any obligation at all to do this."

"It was a pleasure, Frank. It's great to see you recovered. And I even got a free dinner."

The two of them laughed, but quickly became silent and looked at each other with a sad expression.

"Goodbye, Frank. Be well."

"Goodbye, and thank you so much once again."

As Elizabeth turned and started making her way down the sidewalk, a voice inside of Frank said, "Do something, Frank. Don't let her go like this. Do something now!" And then, without thinking much further, he yelled, "Elizabeth!"

His scream echoed through the empty streets and scared Elizabeth, who turned around immediately. The look in her face clearly showed that she was hoping for that call to happen. But Frank didn't really know what to say. A few seconds went by until he finally asked, "Did you like Albert's food?"

"Yes. It was great," answered Elizabeth, not really understanding where Frank was going with his question.

"Do you want to meet me there again tomorrow for dinner? This way I can tell you a bit more about the things my grandfather taught me."

The expression on Elizabeth's face changed immediately to a big smile that covered her face.

"I would love to. I think I'll be able to get there at around seven thirty."

"Sounds perfect. I'll see you there tomorrow then."

Elizabeth waved, turned around, and walked quickly down the street. Frank watched her until she reached a point where he could no longer see her and felt his heart tighten. He was already missing his nurse, confidant, and friend. In fact, he didn't really know how to define her. That was when he realized what he was truly feeling.

Uh-oh. Red alert. Frank is in love, he thought.

When he walked into the boardinghouse, he was floating in the clouds. What he was feeling seemed to be bigger than his chest, and it filled his surroundings. Once he had admitted the existence of his feelings, they appeared to have grown to gigantic proportions, in a way that it scared him. All these feelings were so new, that he didn't really know how to deal with them.

However, his emotional trance was broken the moment he entered his room. The pile of dirty clothes, the messy bed, and the papers thrown around his tiny desk reminded him of his difficult and lonely reality.

As he took off his clothes, he realized that it wasn't only his room that needed cleaning. He also needed a good shower.

He lay down and said to himself, "Tomorrow is cleaning day, inside and out."

Thinking about Elizabeth, he closed his eyes and fell asleep. But he was happy, for tomorrow he would see her again.

Tea for Two

THE CLOCK ON THE WALL of the Great Lion showed seven fifteen, and Frank was already sitting at the same table where he had sat with Elizabeth the previous evening. He was so anxious that he exaggerated on his haste and arrived a bit too early to their meeting place.

It had been a busy day cleaning up his room, washing his dirty clothes, and most importantly, taking care of himself. He took a good shower, shaved his beard, cut his nails, and before leaving, did something he hadn't done in a long time—put some cologne on his face.

His exercise of cleaning his room and himself had brought an invigorating effect, and he felt really great about himself, a feeling he hadn't experienced in a long time.

Despite being at a pub table, he wasn't drinking. He had turned down the beer that was offered to him, which shocked Albert and provoked an observation such as, "Wow, somebody seems to have changed." And that was exactly how he was feeling that day. He didn't understand exactly what was so different, but he felt uplifted and thought about returning to his search for work the following day.

When the clock showed seven thirty, he began to feel really anxious. *Could it be that she is not coming?* he asked himself.

At seven forty, he could barely control himself, so agitated was he, and at seven forty five, he was beginning to feel down when finally Elizabeth rushed through the door. She had her usual tenderness in her eyes, but couldn't hide a bit of guilt for her tardiness. Frank's heart skipped a beat when he saw her, and a great feeling of joy filled his chest.

In arriving at the table, Elizabeth quickly started to explain herself, "I am so sorry for being late, Frank, but new wounded soldiers arrived today, and I had to work until a bit later than my usual shift."

"No worries at all. I also just arrived," responded Frank, trying to hide his own anxiety.

He lifted his arm and made a signal to Albert, who attended immediately, bringing over the menu. Since the place was a pub and they were in times of food rationing, there weren't too many options, and they made their choices quickly.

"The same as yesterday, Albert. It was delicious," said Elizabeth.

"Make it two then," completed Frank.

Albert didn't need to take any notes. He wiped his hands on his apron and asked, "And to drink?"

Frank and Elizabeth looked at each other, and before Frank could say a word, Elizabeth responded, "Tea for two, please."

Albert looked at Frank in surprise; after all, it wasn't the type of drink that he was used to serving. Frank returned the glance and with wide-open eyes, lifted his shoulders as if saying, "Find a way and do what she is asking."

Albert, with a resigned look on his face, said to Frank, "You owe me another one. I will get the tea in the back. You guys are in luck since I keep some for me there, but I will gladly share it with you both."

It was only after Albert left that Elizabeth took better notice of Frank, on how his appearance had changed and how neat he was.

"Frank, you don't even look like the same person without that beard. And here between us, your new cologne smells way better than the one from yesterday."

Frank awkwardly laughed at Elizabeth's joke, for he had hoped that she hadn't noticed his awful smell from the day before, and thanked her for the compliment. Elizabeth then returned to the conversation. "So, Frank, from what I understood, your grandfather made you rethink religion and your disagreements with it, right?"

"Yes, he did, Elizabeth. But he also made me rethink a lot of other things."

"Really? Tell me, Frank. I am curious."

Happy with Elizabeth's interest, Frank returned to his story and would soon share with her new life lessons he had learnt from his grandfather.

A Leader?

On September 1, 1939, Poland was invaded by Nazi Germany. The following day, the British government would declare the mandatory enrollment of all men between the ages of 18 and 41, which would leave Frank and Frederick out, but Peter would have to enroll. The state of imminent war left the vibes in the Farrow family quite down.

The sun was beaming high on September 3rd when Frank and Benedict finally decided to take a break for a sip of water. The piece of land had already been completely cleared, plowed, and fertilized. It was ready to receive the seeds.

Somehow, Frank also felt the same way, almost as if the weeds in his soul had been trimmed, for he was doing something useful with his time and was also in the company of someone who cared for him in a way that he had never experienced before. It was the type of care and attention that carried no interest on getting anything in return and that was focused on what he brought inside him. As he was getting ready to ask a few questions to his grandfather, Benedict broke the silence.

"So your mom told me that you didn't finish your studies. Is there anything you would like to share with me about this?"

Frank, at first, felt a little uncomfortable with the topic. After all, this was just one of his many unfinished and unresolved situations, but the way Benedict had approached it wasn't so invasive and made him feel like opening up.

"I was always a troublemaker. I would argue with my teachers, I would question their rules and their authority. Most of them didn't really care about me. In class, I couldn't just sit there and listen. I wanted to ask questions, debate about everything, but they wouldn't let me, and that was so revolting. They would say that I was disturbing their classes. I started so many fights with my teachers that I ended up getting expelled."

"Expelled," mumbled Benedict, widening his eyes in mock surprise. He then became fully quiet, creating an empty space for Frank to fill.

The grandson then continued, "Yes. Soon my reputation became known to other schools in the neighborhood, and none of them wanted to accept me. My dad didn't try much either. I think he got tired of all the complaints. The fact is that I don't think school was made for me. I didn't get anything there except a whole bunch of punishments and bad treatment."

"It wasn't made for you. Interesting. And do you think that it should have been?"

Benedict's question caught Frank by surprise, which made him stop and think for a moment on what he had just said. Finally he responded, "No, of course not. It's just a way of saying that school and I don't go well together."

"Oh, I see. So then you started working. Were things different?"

"No," responded Frank saddened. "To be honest, it was even worst. I wouldn't accept the orders of my bosses without asking questions that they were not willing to answer. And they were always demanding things from me without giving me anything in exchange. And worst, they wanted me to be more ambitious and to look for ways to make more money by doing overtime. But I would refuse. If they wanted something from me, they would have to give me something first. Eventually they would end up letting me go. I also don't think that a factory is the right place for me."

"Oh, I see," responded Benedict, once again using his silence as a space for Frank to keep talking.

"I don't know, Grandpa, but the way I see it is that none of these places are right for me. All I saw was a bunch of negative things, which would only bring me down. And now I am here. I can't go back to school, and I can't find a job. I've hit rock bottom. I have no enthusiasm or purpose."

"Okay, so let me see if I understand. You think neither the school nor the work environments were made for you. They don't allow you to express yourself, and what you appear to get from them is nothing more than bad treatment, punishment, and demands, making you feel as if you were being used. All of these things make you feel down, and you are feeling as if you've hit rock bottom. Is that it?"

"Yep, that's it. Thanks for the summary," said Frank.

"Well, you are right in one of these things, Frank. Neither the school nor the factories were made for you in particular. Schools were created to fulfill the collective needs of millions of people, and factories maintain a necessary hierarchy so that they can function and prosper. After all, someone took the risk to invest time and money in a company that not only brings profits but also creates jobs for many people. But that's not what I am trying to focus on. What I am trying to say is, where did you get the perception that the world needed to adjust to you? In your perspective, neither school nor the factory fit you. But what kind of effort did you make to adapt and make sure that you would fit in the school and the factory? So the world is not perfect and was not designed to fit you, but how did you contribute to make them better than they were when you first found them?"

While his grandfather was talking, Frank began to close himself, crossing his arms and legs, getting into a more defensive position.

However, he knew that what Benedict was saying was true. He had always looked at things from an egocentric perspective, waiting always for the world around to adjust itself to him and not the opposite. But Benedict still hadn't finished talking.

"And understand one more thing, Frank, the world works with an ongoing dynamic of actions and reactions. What you give to the universe is what it gives back to you. What goes from you comes back to you. I understand that you only got from these institutions things that hurt you somehow, but what did you give them in the first place?

Nothing. Only questionings and aggressions. So they responded with the same form of energy. Want to question us? We will also question you. Want to be aggressive on us? We will be aggressive on you."

Frank now was not only completely closed on himself, but he also had his head down. It seemed like all those things that his grandfather was telling him were hitting him hard. So he burst out, "Grandpa, do you think it's easy? It really hurts when you feel like you don't belong anywhere."

Benedict's face and stare changed immediately and became filled with compassion and tenderness.

"Son, I know exactly how you feel. I was just like that as well, remember? And this is why I'm telling you all this. And you say that all these things hurt. Your pains can be your greatest allies if you learn to listen to them. They can be your greatest masters. What are they trying to tell you, Frank? What are they teaching you?"

Benedict finished his inquiries and headed back to work, for he knew that he had left Frank a little surprised with his questions. For that same reason, he didn't say anything when he noticed his grandson hadn't returned to his activities and kept himself seated on the ground with his eyes fixed on a random point, as if he was in a different time and space.

Frank reflected on the words of his grandfather, for he had never looked at his sufferings from this angle, as if they were his masters, as if they were trying to teach him something. His reactions were always of revolt and of rejection of such feelings. He reacted like a child that in experiencing pain, would cry, complain, and search for immediate relief, not always in the most adequate way. But now he was starting to see things in a different light. He felt as if he had been so egocentric and childish. Suddenly Benedict's questionings led him to a whole new perspective. For a brief moment, he began to feel esteem for his mistakes and for his pains. They could offer him an infinite number of teachings that could be useful to him. But there was still a fundamental question to be answered.

"But why I am so different?" asked Frank to his grandfather.

Benedict brought his attention back to Frank, looked him in the eyes, and said, "Because, although you don't know it yet, you are a leader. There is nothing worse than a person who is a leader and doesn't know it, for rather than contributing, he creates disturbances. Rather than adding, he divides. You think with your own head, you have your own ideas, your own initiatives, all of which are characteristics of a leader. But if these attributes aren't properly worked and developed, they transform into insubordination, indiscipline, and misalignment."

Frank again was surprised by his grandfather's response. He remained there, seated with his mouth open, not knowing how to react. After a long pause, he said to himself, "Me? A leader?"

"Yes, my grandson, a leader. Unfortunately the majority of people don't know how to recognize a young leader when they see one, and for this reason, they don't work on their personality traits. On the contrary, they actually feel disturbed by them. But this isn't only their fault. You also need to take a role in making yourself become a true leader."

"Really? And what would be my role?"

"Let yourself be led. Be humble and understand that before you can lead, you need to first be led by someone else. To be followed and have followers, you need to follow someone first. If you don't dress yourself in humility and let yourself be guided, molded, and led, you will never be able to transcend your current state. You will never be able to transform your impulses into a leadership that transforms the world around you into something better than how you found it. On the contrary, you will focus solely on questioning and challenging the status quo, without proposing anything that would represent an improvement. Rather than creating value, you depreciate things. Rather than generating light, you only generate heat, like an old lamp that burns energy but doesn't illuminate. You are expecting perfection from your teachers, your bosses, your priests, your parents, but you aren't able to put yourself in their shoes. You don't try to understand that they are human beings like you, filled with fears and questions, but they have also lived much longer than you and carry a lot more scars from their own battles that can really be helpful to guide you and orient you. Try to understand yourself and others as imperfect beings, including the leaders that life brings to you. Learn from their experiences and wisdom, but also from their imperfections and mistakes. Being imperfect isn't a problem. It's the norm. Not trying to be in constant evolution, that is the real problem."

Benedict's words hit Frank deeply, for that was exactly how he felt. He was creating disturbances, disruptions, and for the first time in his life, someone was making sense to all this, and he no longer saw his personality traits as something so bad. Perhaps it was just a rough diamond that needed to be polished up. But his grandfather was still far from finished.

"If you feel as if you've hit rock bottom, that's excellent."

"Excellent? What do you mean, 'excellent'?" asked Frank in disgust.

"Of course it is. From here you can only go up. There's nowhere else to go. Now it only depends on you to climb up. There is no better place to start transforming your life than when you've hit rock bottom. Make this your main purpose in this moment of your life. You said you didn't have a purpose, right? Well, now you've found one."

Benedict looked over to Frank tenderly and shot him a wink. It was almost as if he had given him a little gift.

Frank was touched by his grandfather's kind look and gesture. In just a few minutes, his wise words had made the greatest difference in the world. He felt different about himself and wanted to start a revolution right there and then. Only in very few moments of his life had he felt so motivated to go and try a fresh start. So he said, "It's a shame you took so long to come into my life. If you had showed up earlier, I would have avoided so much damage. I have too much to fix. I feel as if there is a long road ahead for me to work through. Will you help me?"

"When the disciple is ready, he always finds his master. Don't worry, for everything happens when it is supposed to. Of course I will help you. But you need to want to be helped first. If not, there is nothing I can do."

Benedict stopped talking for a moment, left the hoe, and made his way slowly toward Frank. He placed his right hand on his grandson's shoulder and said, "Frank, beware, for in reality we never know if the bottom we've hit is really the bottom. You might still have a lot in front of you until you really hit the rock bottom, so you will need to be much stronger than you think."

Frank laughed at his grandfather's observations and said, "I don't have any friends, I don't have a girlfriend, I don't have school, I don't have a job, I'm far from God, my family no longer believes in me—how could this possibly get any worse?"

Frank and Benedict didn't have any more time to keep talking. They heard a scream coming from inside the house and recognized Charlotte's voice. They ran inside to find her in the arms of her husband, in tears. When both asked what had happened, Frederick told them what they had just heard on the radio. England had just declared war against Germany, and Peter would certainly be drafted to fight. In a matter of months, it would be Frank's turn to go. The world was changing and changing drastically.

A Powerful Lesson

They could no longer find the energy to keep working on the land that day. Benedict and Frank dedicated themselves to comforting Charlotte and listened to the news about the war on the radio. With the invasion of Poland, England and France didn't have any other option than to declare war on Germany, and the mobilization was already underway.

Peter had left work and was home, packing his bags to present himself to the army recruitment. At one point, he turned to Frank and said, "Prepare yourself, little brother, for in November, you'll turn eighteen, and then it will be your turn."

That observation sent chills down Frank's spine. Benedict seemed to have been right one more time. Apparently, rock bottom was still pretty far down.

Guessing his grandson's thoughts, Benedict placed his right arm over his shoulder, looked him in the eyes, and said, "Be strong, for your toughest journey is yet to begin, but something tells me that you will be very fortunate throughout this difficult path."

Frank felt encouraged by his grandfather's comment and went in to help his brother.

At the end of that day, after lots of tears and farewell hugs, Peter was gone, with fear in his eyes and a tight heart. Charlotte was desperate and wouldn't stop crying. Frederick tried to be strong and not demonstrate the pain that he felt himself, looking to console his wife by saying that the war wouldn't last long and that before they knew it, he would be back home. Evidently, even he didn't believe in the words he was saying.

Frank went to bed early that night, but he couldn't fall asleep. He was worried about his brother, he was worried about his family, but most of all, he was worried about himself. In only two months, he would also have to enlist and offer his services as a soldier to defend his country, and he didn't feel one bit prepared for the challenge. And that was when he realized there would be very limited time to spend with his grandfather and that he would need to take the most out of such healthy influence.

The following morning, he went to Benedict very early and said, "Grandpa, please help me. I need you to prepare me for what's to come. I am terrified."

Benedict hugged him tightly and said, "Grandson, what you are asking of me is way above my capacity, for time is so short, but I will do my best to help you."

"How much time do you think I'll need to feel wiser, self-assured, balanced, and spiritually evolved?"

Benedict chuckled with the side of his lips and responded, "About two years."

Frank thought for a moment and said, "What if we work harder? What if we double the amount of time we spend together? Maybe we can talk more in the evenings and on the weekends. How much time do you think I would need then?"

With irony in his eyes, Benedict responded, "Well then, that would make a lot of difference. With all this effort and dedication, it would take about four years."

Frank looked at his grandfather with a look of someone who didn't understand his crazy math. Benedict laughed at his grandson's puzzled face and explained, "Frank, forget time as a factor. If you only focus on the end of the journey, you won't pay attention to the path and will certainly get lost, or will get distracted from what really matters. Each experience, each lesson, each moment of reflection needs to be lived intensely, always focusing on the here and now, for that's all you really have. Yesterday is gone. The past can't be altered.

And tomorrow is a mystery we don't control. You need to live in the present and focus on what it brings to you in every moment."

"I understand, Grandpa. But the fact is that we only have two months together until I have to enlist, and apparently this won't be enough time for much."

"Well, let's make use of the time we have. And besides, nothing guarantees that we will have two months. I repeat, the future is a mystery we don't control."

Noticing the anguish in his grandson's eyes, Benedict decided that he needed to do something immediately to alleviate his tension.

"Let's start with an exercise that you'll find useful for the rest of your life. I am going to teach you how to relax, to meditate and pray, and I will ask you to do this exercise every day until your birthday. Shall we begin?"

"Yes. What do I have to do?" responded Frank, a bit surprised, since he wasn't expecting his grandpa's teachings to start with something so practical such as an exercise.

"Well, first go to the washroom, empty your bladder, clear your nostrils, and return. When you are back, remove your shoes, lie down on my bed, and lay your arms out on your sides."

Frank stood up and proceeded as his grandfather requested. Although he couldn't see any sense in what had been asked, he had learnt to trust that man. When he finally lay down comfortably on the bed, Benedict asked him to close his eyes and to breathe slowly and deeply. He did this for about two minutes until once again his grandfather broke the silence. "Let's begin by relaxing your muscles little by little. Focus first on your feet. Relax each muscle on them, then make your way up to your calves…legs…knees…thighs. Now think in your hands and feel them relax…now your arms. Now pay attention to your face and relax each facial muscle, your forehead, let your jaw fall. Now think of your shoulders. Notice how they are tense. Let them relax."

As Benedict was slowly orchestrating the exercise, Frank was relaxing each part of his body and was impressed with the level of tension that he was carrying, especially when he felt the stiffness of his jaw and his shoulders.

"Now pay attention to your chest and your abdomen. In this area, we concentrate a lot of tension, and it will require a lot of your focus to relax it. Let's take it easy. Keep relaxing, little by little."

Frank suddenly became aware of something that he had never noticed. He felt a kind of knot in his stomach area, as if a tennis ball was inside of him, and that was dissolving as he breathed and relaxed.

"Once you relax this area, go back to focusing on your shoulders and neck, which may have tightened again."

Benedict was right. As Frank relaxed his plexus area, his shoulders had contracted again. Frank realized then that relaxing was not something as simple as he had imagined. He also understood why he needed to have cleared his nostrils and his bladder; only then he could breathe deeply and relax the abdomen without urinating all over himself.

"Very well, Frank. Now I want you to imagine that in front of you there is a sun, which is your own. This sun emanates a light that is your source of vital and spiritual energy, a powerful energy that comes from your creator, and it's loaded with everything you may need to go through all difficulties in your life. This source of divine energy that we choose to call God is there, in front of you, at your disposal. Absorb its powerful energy. Feel calm and strengthened at every moment. Feel the warmth of its light and its power. And mentally, talk to it. Talk to your divine source of energy. Ask what you want from it. Strength, balance, love, protection, and care for those you love. Enjoy it and feel one with this energy source, because this energy and you are one. Think for a moment of all the blessings you have been already receiving from this wonderful divine power and be thankful for each of them: your home, food, family, bed, warm clothes, water for drinking and bathing. Things that we take for granted but that are denied to so many less privileged souls. Feel loved by this divine energy."

While being guided by his grandfather, Frank began to feel a peace and power that he had never experienced before. He felt so close to God and loved by him that he hoped this exercise would never end. Mentally he spoke with that "sun" and thanked his creator for everything he had. He also asked for help, protection, and strength to face what was yet to come.

Benedict then told him to stay there, in that state of prayer and meditation for as long as he wanted or felt necessary. Silently Benedict left the room and went to care for the land.

Forty minutes later, Frank awoke from a deep sleep in the same position that he had begun his relaxation and found himself alone in Benedict's room. The perception was that he had slept for hours and felt rested, with a renewed energy he hadn't experienced for a long time. He left his grandfather's room still somewhat wobbly and covering his eyes, which took some time to get used to the brightness of the day.

Without looking at his grandson or interrupting his work in the garden, Benedict asked, "How do you feel, kid?"

"I'm sorry, I fell asleep and slept deeply. My apologies, I think I ruined the exercise."

With a smile on his face, Benedict immediately corrected his grandson's perception.

"Absolutely not. You did not ruin anything. It is natural for someone to fall asleep when they are in deep relaxation. Not only your body but also your mind rests. And your spirit, in connecting with your divine energy source, also strengthens. As you repeat this exercise every day, you will begin to feel drastic changes in your life in all areas: physical, mental, and spiritual."

"About the spiritual aspect, this way of praying is very weird. I didn't do a single prayer that I had learned at the church, and you made me see God as an inexhaustible source of light, warmth, and energy. I used to pray imagining a bearded old man I once saw on a painting. This is all so different."

Benedict consented, nodding positively, and realizing his grandson's confusion, explained, "This is how we are taught to imagine God when we are young, since in order to understand it, we need to humanize it. And then we use it as humanizing instrument. We say that if we don't do things this or that way, we will be punished by it. Around God, we created a code of conduct and behavior to govern our society. Forget all of that, Frank. Goodness is not a religious issue. It is an ethical issue. It's a choice. God does not need to take a human form to make sense. God actually doesn't need to make sense. Our human minds are too limited to understand God in all of his dimensions. We just need to feel him within us. The rest comes naturally. Kindness, love, charity all naturally emanate from those who have this kind of energy in their hearts. Abandon the need to understand God, Frank. You just need to have faith. Faith is the way to win over all your fears. Those who have faith do not fear."

"So do you think I should stop going to church? Should I stop doing all those prayers I learned?"

"No, Frank. Don't get confused by what I am saying. Any method you use to get closer to God is worth it, including attending the mass and taking part in their usual prayers. For example, despite following my own communication protocol with God, I have never ceased to pray the 'Our Father.' Prayers do have powers, Frank. What I am suggesting is that you develop your own way of communicating with all that is divine, with devotion and faith, and open the channel of connection with this divine energy. Let it in and let it occupy your being. Divinity is also part of the human being. Go to church, pray their usual prayers, but do not create in your head the perception that God is way over there and that we are all the way over here. When doing your communion, for example, do just that. Get in communion with God. Let him in your pores, in your being, feel the divinity within you. These rituals are powerful, but we end up repeating them mechanically, without experiencing them in its entirety."

Frank listened quietly and then realized something important and quickly changed his face, as if he had discovered something completely new.

"Wait a minute. You said we have to feel God and his divinity within us. Would this then be the answer to the question I asked the other day? God is within us?"

Benedict just looked at his grandson with an expression of love and happiness, since Frank had reached that deduction on his own.

"That's it, Frank, you found the answer. God is within us, and when we find him here inside us, we understand that he just happens to be everywhere. We start seeing him in everything—in a sunrise or a sunset, in a flock of birds, when a child is born, and even in the bad things that happen to us, since we know that he is orchestrating everything in his infinite wisdom."

"Okay then. I think I'm beginning to better understand your ideas. But where did you learn all of this?"

Benedict stood there for a moment looking at a distant point in time and space, trying to come up with an answer to his grandson's question.

"India, China, the Middle East, and so many other places. I don't remember anymore where I learned what and how. I think I'm getting old, my grandson."

They both laughed at this last remark, but Benedict's look was slowly becoming more serious, which worried Frank.

"What happened, Grandpa? Why did you suddenly get so serious?"

Benedict approached him and looking into his eyes, said, "Frank, saying that I am getting old is not as funny as it used to be a few years back. I'm really starting to feel old. I do not think I will live to see the end of this war. So I think it is time to share a secret with you."

Frank felt a shiver down his spine. Benedict's words brought him deep emotions. He had become inexplicably so attached to his grandfather that the idea of losing him was almost unbearable.

Benedict then continued, "After traveling through so many countries, discovering so many religions and many different philosophies, and having read so many books and listened to various religious leaders, I found a master who finally made sense to it all, that brought together the pieces of this huge puzzle. He appeared in my life by surprise in the form of a wise old man and has never left me. In fact he's here now, in this moment with us."

Frank immediately took a look around, searching for such person, but saw no one. He looked at his grandfather, making the face of someone who was not understanding what was being said.

Benedict continued, "You won't be able to see him, Frank, at least not yet. But I am sure that one day he will appear to you when you least expect. And if you allow yourself to be guided by him, he will have all the answers you seek. He brings all the wisdom in the universe and will never abandon you as long as you do not abandon him."

For the first time since meeting his grandfather, Frank began to have real doubts about his mental health. His father and mother had said several times that he wasn't right in the head and that he said things that made no sense. Now he stood before him, talking about an old man who nobody else could see. Not knowing what to say and how to react to this, Frank just nodded and asked, "And where did you find him? Where should I search for him?"

With a serious and tense glance, Benedict turned to him and said, "No, do not search for him. Searching will be the worst thing to do in order to find him. He will find you when you least expect it."

"Oh, okay. Got it. I think. Well, I believe I've had enough lessons for today. I'm going to check if my mother needs any help."

Noticing his grandson's confusion and knowing he needed some time to process everything he had just said, Benedict let him go.

Once inside the house, Frank thoughts raced through his head. He had so much to think about and so much to review in terms of his beliefs and his way to interact with God. He now also had a new daily task that he still didn't understand very well. He was concerned about his grandfather, with his health and his sanity. Benedict had talked about the possibility of having little time left to live, which caused him distress. But what really made him confused was his grandfathers' secret: the wise old man that only he could see. Did he really exist? Or was it nothing more than a delusion of someone who was already losing his mind?

He decided then that he would not let these doubts impair the short time he had left with Benedict. If the wise old man would be mentioned again, he would ask him more questions, but for now he would forget the subject. He sat next to the radio and started listening to the news about the war. His concerns about the future were growing more and more each second.

Crossing the Line

As the clock hit ten o'clock, Elizabeth apologized to Frank and asked to be excused so she could leave. After all, it was already getting late and the Great Lion was beginning to empty.

Frank was caught by surprise. He had completely lost track of time, which was becoming a habit when Elizabeth was around.

It was already the third night they were meeting for dinner, and for the past couple of nights, he had accompanied her to the train station, but today he had a different plan. He would offer to follow her home. When the train arrived and Elizabeth was preparing to say goodbye, Frank asked her to wait and said, "Today, I will keep you company all the way home, if you don't mind."

Elizabeth was taken by surprise by his request and had no reaction. In a split second, the two were already inside the train and on their way. They sat side by side on a wagon that was almost empty, and a somewhat uncomfortable silence occupied the space between them. Frank thought, *Am I moving too fast?*

Elizabeth then broke the silence, "Frank, you shouldn't have bothered. I appreciate the care and attention. If you don't mind, I'll wait with you until your train back home arrives."

Frank smiled and thanked her for being so kind, but deep inside, he was not too happy with her offer, since he wanted to go a bit beyond her train station. As they got there, Frank decided to open his intentions at once.

"Elizabeth, I'd like to walk you home if I'm not asking too much. You've done it for me once when I was not well, and I never had the opportunity to return the favor. May I?"

Elizabeth was a little reluctant, but consented in the end, showing him the way. She was a little surprised with that change in his attitude and didn't know for sure how to react. But the fact that Frank had followed her until that point brought her a mix of fear and excitement.

"Is it far?" asked Frank.

"No. It's right around the corner. Why? Are you already having second thoughts?" Elizabeth asked him mockingly, and they both smiled tensely.

After walking for a few minutes, they stopped in front of a small apartment building, which had only four floors and an appearance of neglect and poor maintenance typical in times of war.

For a moment, Frank felt sorry for Elizabeth, for her hard routine as a nurse in difficult times and for her humble situation. On the other hand, he was also aware that other women of the same age were even less fortunate.

He looked at the sky, which was less cloudy than usual, and saw the moon shinning with a peculiar intensity of winter nights. He took a deep breath and thought to himself, *It is now. It has to be now.* He approached Elizabeth and with shivers in his stomach and trembling hands, risked a fond touch above her left ear. She was immobilized, not reacting negatively but not giving anything in return as well. Her startled look made Frank hesitate for a moment, but he was determined to go all the way with his intent. Then he came a little closer and made a move forward to kiss her. That was when he felt Elizabeth's hand on his chest, holding him back, preventing him to finish his affectionate move. Frank stopped and looked at her, not understanding the reason for such rejection.

"Frank, we need to slow down. I have lost many people I loved during this damned war, including…"

Suddenly her eyes were filled with tears, and Frank then realized that the war had taken away someone else, other than just her parents. "You don't need to talk about it if you don't want to," said Frank, sensitive to the pain he could witness in her eyes.

After a few seconds of silence, Elizabeth put herself together and continued, "I was engaged, Frank. I was getting married. My fiancé was then recruited to fight in Africa. He never returned. He was killed in combat."

A gloomy silence fell between them, and Frank did not know what to do or say. He stood there silent for a moment and then said, "I'm sorry, Elizabeth. I didn't know. Are you okay?"

"Yes, I'll be fine. Please don't take it personally. I like you. But that is precisely the problem. I'm afraid to get emotionally attached again. I'll need more time. I would like us to just continue talking for a little longer. Do you understand?"

Although frustrated by the rejection he had just gone through, Frank was happy with what he heard. There was hope after all.

"Of course, Elizabeth. I love your company, and I would not give it up for the world. I just would like to have the privilege to continue to walk you home from now on. When you feel more secure, you will invite me in, and everything will be different. I'm sure it will."

After a brief pause, he continued, "Tomorrow is Sunday. Isn't it your day off? What if we did something different? How about a walk in the park? Should we meet at Hyde Park Corner station at eleven?"

Elizabeth then gave him a tender and grateful smile, nodded, said good night, and left.

Frank then began a slow return toward the station. Although he still felt some level of discomfort in long walks, when he was halfway, he decided to walk home instead of taking the train. He had much to think about and a rejection to digest.

As he was making his way back, he thought of Elizabeth's words, "Fight in Africa…killed in combat." He then remembered that he was to be sent precisely to Africa when he had his accident and broke his leg, being then sent to treatment and later released from his military services. He also remembered all his revolt and succumbing to alcohol when he saw himself with no family, no job, and unable to fight for his country. Hearing about the tragic fate of Elizabeth's fiancé made him see things from a different perspective.

While he was slowly walking through the dark streets of London, words once said by a familiar voice came back to his mind: "He, who wins, loses and he, who loses, wins. Everything is relative. Nothing is totally bad, and nothing is totally good. When you lose something, something is being earned, and to earn something, you will have to give up something else."

Then he said out loud for anyone to hear, "Wise words, Benedict. Wise words."

As he heard his own voice echoing throughout the London night, he looked around to see if he was heard by anyone else but him and felt relieved when he did not see a living soul.

It would be a long and lonely walk back home.

The Walk in the Park

That Sunday of February 28th wasn't as cold as it should be, considering the time of the year, and Frank was already waiting at the agreed corner fifteen minutes earlier than scheduled. Suddenly he realized that he could have brought some flowers to Elizabeth. He looked around to see if there was a florist nearby, but found nothing that could fix the situation quickly. He then noticed Elizabeth making her way toward him, coming from the other side of the street and said to himself, "Great job, Frank, another missed opportunity."

However, as he thought of Elizabeth's reaction the night before when he tried to kiss her, he quickly comforted himself thinking that it was probably better that way.

He stood there, watching her as she made her way across the street. She was dressed in a more formal way than usual, all in gray, with a skirt that fell a bit below her knees, a slightly thicker vest to confront the low outdoor temperatures and a hat that hid her trapped hair. But the makeup she was wearing, albeit discreet, lent a glow to her face that Frank hadn't yet appreciated, and he saw her prettier today than in previous occasions. As she approached, he thought to himself, *Behave, Frank, you don't want to ruin this up, do you?*

Elizabeth smiled and greeted him with a kiss on his cheek and said something about the favorable weather. A little surprised by the new form of greeting, he smiled, nodded, and offered his right arm so she could hold it as they walked.

They soon found a bench to sit on, with a privileged view of the park. Even in times of war, London was still able to maintain its aristocratic charm. Both sat quietly and enjoyed that rare moment of relative peace and beauty, until Frank broke the silence. "I'm sorry about yesterday. I…"

Elizabeth reacted immediately by putting her delicate perfumed hand on his lips and said, "Shhhhh…let's not talk about yesterday. Just enjoy this beautiful moment. Tell me how the story with your grandfather ended. I understand that he had a very strong influence on you, but I want to understand particularly how such a positive energy could possibly give room for you to get in such bad shape. Can you explain this to me?"

"Of course, Elizabeth. You will soon understand everything. The pieces of the puzzle will all come together in a bit. If the war made some serious damage in your life, it also made in mine. I'll tell you."

The Pebbles in the Bucket

THE MONTH OF OCTOBER 1939 began with more aggressions between Germany and the Allies. The invasion of Belgium, Holland, and Luxembourg by the Nazis was expected to happen any time now, so British troops were mobilized to the Belgian and French border, and that was where Peter was sent to.

The Sunday mass had just finished, and Frank began walking toward the front door of the church when he decided to stay there a while longer. He waited for everyone to leave, sat on the back row, and began to look at the decor and architecture of the temple that he had attended for so many years but had never taken the proper time to admire.

Since he had had those conversations about spirituality and religion with Benedict, he had learned to separate the two things in his head and in his heart and had made peace with the fact that not everything had to make complete sense or be perfect in any given religion. Now he finally felt at peace during the mass and enjoyed all the good it had to offer. And he decided to simply ignore or dismiss what he did not like or approve, as one discards the peels of a fruit. He would just absorb the spiritual nourishment he needed, and that was enough for him.

He said a few more prayers for his family, for the end of the war, for his brother, and for himself. He thanked for all he had and also for everything he didn't have and went home.

As he made his way into the streets, he regretted not bringing a thicker jacket as the cold October air was beginning to show its claws. He walked quickly, hoping there would still be time to have a quick conversation with his grandfather before lunch was served. After over a month of interactions with Benedict, he felt more calm and serene, but he still could not quite understand why he would attract so much negativity to himself.

He entered home without being noticed and soon found Benedict at the backyard contemplating his garden, which was already quite green and full of vegetables almost ready to be harvested.

"Good morning, Grandpa. Your garden looks beautiful. Congratulations!"

"Our garden, my grandson, our garden. You also worked on it and deserve as much credit as I do. How are you today?"

Frank felt proud about his grandfather's comments. He really had put many hours of hard work there, and to be recognized for it made him feel good about himself.

"I'm fine, but I wanted to ask you something. The relaxation, meditation, and prayers you taught me are having an amazing positive effect on me. Now I feel more centered and balanced, less angry about certain things. But with only those, will I stop being a misfit? Will they prevent me from finding so many negative things in my life?"

"Hum…that's a great question, Frank. I'll tell you a little story that may help you find the answer. Let's take a seat in this shade."

Interested, Frank quickly obeyed and sat with his grandfather.

"An old fable says that a wise man used to sit on the shade of a big tree at the entrance of a small medieval village. There he received many people who wanted his advice and words of wisdom. One day, a man who was moving to the village came to him and asked, 'Since I am new here, I would like to know if I made the right decision to come to this place. Could you tell me how the people in this village are like?'

"The wise man thought for a moment and replied with another question, 'How were the people of the village from where you came?'

"Surprised by the question the man changed his face. He became somewhat irritated and said, 'They were terrible people. They would fight each other for anything, always with frowns on their faces, never willing to help each other. Each would take care of their own lives and showed no interest in knowing about the lives of others. I felt very isolated and lonely. And whenever I would approach someone, I would get in some kind of trouble. So I decided to leave, since I was quite unhappy.'

"The wise man looked at him with pity and said, 'I am so sorry, my friend. The people of this village are exactly the same. Good luck.' The man then became very disappointed and left.

"Later that same day, another man approached the wise man, coincidentally with the same questions and restlessness. The wise reacted the same way and with the same question. Only this time, the answer he got was different.

"This second man replied, 'Oh, they were wonderful people, always greeting you with enthusiasm, helping you when needed, celebrating your victories and comforting you in your defeats. We would sit around a bonfire telling our stories and singing until the late hours. We loved each other very much. I only left there because I had to, but I already miss my friends.'

"The wise man smiled candidly and, with a look of compassion, said, 'You can be at peace, my friend. You came to the right town. People here are just as such.' The man felt really happy and embraced his counselor and left."

"I don't get it, Grandpa. Wasn't the wise man talking about the same village? How could he give such two different answers? Had he lied to one of them?"

"Absolutely not, my grandson. Each of these individuals carried within their own answer, so no matter where they were, they would find exactly what they experienced in their respective villages. What we take within us is what we find. What we give, we receive. Wherever we are, the world around us reflects who we are and what we give to it."

A long uncomfortable silence prevailed between the two, and Frank began to think about the story he had just heard. He thought about his difficult and aggressive attitude that he had had until then toward everything and everyone and how the world around him had reacted exactly the same way. Breaking the silence, he said to himself, "I would like to erase all my past mistakes. I would like to be wise, just like you are."

His grandfather laughed at his remark, which made Frank confused.

He had no idea what was funny about what he said, so his grandfather tried to explain. "Frank, if I could erase all my past mistakes, I would also be erasing all the wisdom of my present. It does not work like that, son. If we learn how to make use of our mistakes, they will become our greatest masters, remember?"

Yes. His grandfather had already told him that.

"When we become wiser, we make better choices and better decisions. But to come to that, we need to have a lot of experience, which only comes through bad choices and bad decisions. There is no other way, Frank. You cannot become a well-travelled sailor through other people's travels, can you? Or get to know the taste of the dishes of a restaurant by licking the menu?"

Frank laughed at this last analogy, but it had hit the target as it helped him understand his grandfather. He needed to be more open to new mistakes and learn from them, and there was no reason for regrets about his past. What mattered was to start from that point and on. He needed to change his attitude toward people and life.

"Frank, there's something I need to tell you, and you may not like hearing it. We have only about a month to go before you have to report yourself for military service, and this war is giving every indication that it will last for quite some time. Soon you will be separated from your family and all your points of reference, and you will go on to live some hard times. I guess what I mean is that things will get worse a little, maybe a lot, before they get better. It is very important that you live one day at a time, with the spirit of an apprentice, until you come out on the other side. At times, you will believe that you have already arrived there on the other side, but it will be just an illusion. When you get there, deep inside, you will know. Do not lose faith in your life and in your future, no matter what happens to you.

Keeping a positive mental attitude can make all the difference in the world, so you will not only trespass the difficulties, but you will leave them behind stronger and evolve, as a human being and as a spirit. And remember, one day you will find a wise old man who will guide you. Just be alert and one day he will come to you."

Once again his grandfather mentioned the wise old man that would appear out of nowhere, and again this disturbed him. Why would he need another master? However, this did not take up much of his attention. Benedict had mentioned an important point, and he did not want to lose it. For quite some time, he had noticed himself to be a very negative person, always thinking about the worst that could happen, focusing on the bad of each situation and on how people could possibly harm him. He also saw himself as someone who carried a lot of negative energy, thinking little of himself and not believing in his own qualities. He decided that it was time to address this issue.

"Grandpa, how can I have a more positive mental attitude? I have a hard time with that. I'm always seeing the negative side of everything, preparing for what might go wrong. I'm always seeing an unhappy ending to things, and so I prefer not to start them."

Benedict stood still, looking at Frank in the eye with an ironic smile. Frank felt that look like a command to stop for a moment and think about what he had just said, a command he obeyed instinctively. Somehow, he and his grandfather began to communicate in a way where words were not necessary.

"I'm always seeing an unhappy ending to things, and so I prefer not to start them."

Frank was scared by his own confession. He had been setting an unhappy ending for himself. His expression of surprise said it all. It was as if a lamp had lit right above his head. Seizing the moment, Benedict said, "I did not know you had that power to predict the future, Frank. Why have you never told me anything about it?"

Frank smiled at the joke, but the tender and deep look of his grandfather made it clear that it was much more than a joke.

"Frank, think thoroughly about what you are doing with yourself. Without having any idea of what life may bring you, you are limiting yourself, predicting your future as something bad and as if something will go wrong. How can you tell if you haven't even allowed yourself to try? If you think of yourself as defeated, there will be no other possible outcome. You will fulfill your own prophecy. In fact, you should want to bring more adventure to your spirit, my son, and start with an open end, always thinking about succeeding. But if it doesn't happen, that is just wonderful. One more experience. More experiences, more growth, more self-development. In this approach nothing is lost, nothing is defeat. You become a sponge of positivism that absorbs everything that happens to you as something that is making you better and stronger, day after day after day, experience after experience."

Frank listened to all that, impressed with the philosophy of his grandfather, but within himself he remained incredulous.

"When you talk like that, you make it sound very easy, Grandpa. But I don't know how to change my attitude like that. I don't think I'll be able to."

"So you will not. Simple, isn't it? And if it's that simple to the downside, it is as well for the upside. Do you know what the missing ingredient is on one side that is abundant on the other? Faith. If you believe that you will not succeed, you won't. Now if you use your faith in God, knowing that you will not live anything that you are not supposed to live, knowing that whether things work out or not, you will only grow and that you will be fulfilling your spiritual prophecy and not your own pessimistic prophecy, then what could possibly stop you?"

Frank made a face, showing he hadn't fully followed his grandfather's reasoning. Benedict then took a step backward, in order to take two steps forward.

"Frank, your faith in God is what is missing. I'm speaking of the faith of those who put their own destiny in the hands of someone who is superior and loves us in a way that we will never understand. You came to this world in this place, at this time, and in this family to live a series of experiences that aim to develop you as a spirit. Forget Frank. Frank is just a character that your spirit is wearing right now. It is a material vehicle for your spirit to live the experiences, good or bad, that it must live to follow the path of light. If you hide yourself from the world and deprive your spirit of these experiences, it will be stagnant and will not evolve. It will not grow. It will remain away from the divine light as a spirit that still has much to learn. Do not imprison yourself, Frank. Believe that God has a plan for you and live an adventurous life. Let your spirit live. Do not keep it captive. Have faith. Live your life with courage and an open heart. The rewards are unimaginable."

Frank looked at a lost point in the horizon, as if everything that his grandfather was saying was making him see the world under a totally different light. It was almost as if he was going through a process of recreating himself.

"And remember, son. To the spirit, there is no victory or defeat, there is only growth and development. From the moment you start seeing life from this perspective, everything will be worth it."

"All this sounds wonderful, Grandpa. But I feel that I don't have a north to follow. I don't know what the next step is or which direction I should go."

Benedict then got up, asked Frank to follow him, and started doing things that didn't seem to make much sense. He took a bucket and put it on the ground. Then he gathered ten pebbles and positioned them in the center of the garden at a distance of about five meters from the bucket. When everything was set, he called Frank and said, "Frank, this is an easy exercise. Take a pebble, one at a time and throw it, and try to hit them into the bucket."

Frank felt somewhat ridiculous doing what, to his eyes, looked like a childish play without any sense, but as he had learned to trust his grandfather, he obeyed him.

He threw the first stone and missed by a large distance, so bad that he even blushed. He took the second stone and better measuring the effort, threw it a lot closer to the bucket, but missed again. He looked at his grandfather with a confident look as if saying, "I'm getting the hang of it." The third stone hit the rim of the bucket. The fourth finally hit the target, and Frank celebrated as if he was a child. He no longer felt ridiculous and started to have fun with it. Benedict, at a distance, merely observed.

Of the last pebbles thrown, only one, the seventh in the series, missed the target. For having hit the target with most pebbles, Frank ended the exercise with a proud look, as if saying to his grandfather, "See? I hit the target with most of them."

Benedict then collected each of the ten stones and took them back to Frank's feet. Frank bent down, took three of the stones in his hands, and was ready to repeat the exercise, when Benedict said, "Hang on. This time we'll do something different. You will close your eyes."

Smiling, Frank reacted like a child who was having fun.

"No problem, I know where the bucket is. I think I will hit it a few times."

With an ironic smile, Benedict completed, "But there is just one important detail. I'll move the bucket, and you will not know where it'll be."

Frank's face changed dramatically. Outraged, he said, "What? And how do you expect me to hit the target even once if I do not know where the bucket is and have my eyes closed?"

"Have faith," said Benedict, who just looked at Frank, waiting for his grandson to close his eyes.

Frank took a deep breath, closed his eyes, and muttered, infuriated, with a low voice, "He really is crazy."

When Benedict commanded, Frank began to throw the stones, each in a different direction. Each pitch had a distinct strength, always trying to guess the direction and the distance where the bucket could be. One after the other, the stones would hit the ground, and Frank started getting frustrated. When he launched the last stone, he opened his eyes, feeling angry. He still had time to see the stone hit the ground, about ninety degrees from where the bucket was. All shots missed the target, and he felt ridiculous again, as if he had wasted his time.

Benedict gave him a stern, serious look, as if that had been an important task, then made a sign with his right hand, calling Frank back to his room and to there he went. As a good disciple, Frank followed. He was eager for an explanation.

"How did you feel in the first exercise?" Benedict asked.

"At first I felt ridiculous, but then it was fun. It took me a while to get the hang of it, but gradually I better measured the strength and direction and soon got confident. In the end, I had more right hits than wrong ones."

"Hum. Interesting. And in the second exercise?"

"Oh, that was terrible. I didn't know where to shoot. I started to throw stones to all sides, and even having faith that I could hit the target with some luck, it didn't happen. Faith didn't help me at all. If this was an exercise to learn to have faith, it had the opposite effect."

"But it was not, Frank. You will soon understand. What did the bucket represent to you?"

Frank stopped to think, because he knew that from this moment on, the teachings would come. He had already grown used to the style of his grandfather of questions and responses. Then he said, Well, I think the bucket became my target. My objective became to hit the pebbles in it."

"Very well. And what happened when you focused on the objective?"

"Well, at first I missed badly, but then I got better and started hitting the target, and I had fun with it."

"That's perfect. But what happened when you did not know where the target was? What happened inside of you when the objective was not clear?"

"I started to throw the pebbles in all directions, hoping I could hit one with the help of faith. But after a few wrong shots, I started throwing the stones at random, without any care or hope to hit the target.

"Okay. Do you see any resemblance to the current moment of your life?"

Frank felt that question differently. It caught him by surprise, and he did not know what to say. But soon he began to understand the point his grandfather was trying to make. He had no objectives in life. There was no target. His life goals were not clear, so he went on shooting to every side and was now tired and without hopes that he would hit something.

Again, his grandfather made use of an absolute and long-lasting silence, letting Frank fulfill it when he was ready.

"Of course, there are similarities. I'm starting to understand the exercise."

"That's right, Frank. In the first part, as you had a clear goal in your mind, you immediately sprang into action. A little awkward at first, but soon you figured it out and gained confidence. However, when you became too confident, you did not try as hard and missed again. You realized that, corrected the route, and hit all the others. And that's how it is in real life. When we start pursuing a new objective, the first actions are erratic, until we figure things out and start doing it right. So we get confidence, and we go on. New mistakes will happen, but the objective is still there. With minor adjustments, we get it more right than wrong. All we need to do is persevere. Now when we do not have a clear goal or objective, we begin to take actions wildly, shooting to every side, hoping to hit something. We can even hit the target, Frank, but we will only know what we hit after shooting. We may have hit something that we did not even want to hit at first. One of your stones almost hit my forehead."

Frank laughed at his grandfather's comment but soon fell silent, knowing that he was not finished.

"The last stones you threw, you did out of obligation. You had lost the will to do it, just like you are now in your life, right? If I offered you one more stone, you probably would refuse throwing it. In such a situation, Frank, faith can do very little for you. It also needs direction. It also needs a target. In short, you need to develop goals and objectives for your life, as this will give you new energy, and soon you will move into action. A person without goals or objectives does not know where to go and soon loses the will to keep trying, because it does not know exactly what to try, do you understand?"

"Well, I guess now my goal is to enlist and fight for my country."

"Yes, Frank, this may be your new goal. But beware, because this is a goal that came from the outside, and it may not be fully aligned with your true self. When an egg is broken from the outside, it only serves you to make an omelette. But when it is broken from the inside out, the result is a new life. Try to find your own goals, your own targets in life. Try to break from inside out, Frank. Do not live your life based on other people's objectives and goals. It is very easy to be seduced by external goals, because they often come ready, packed in beautiful ideals that are just illusions. Our society also sells us dreams and ideals for our lives. But if we stop to coldly analyze them, we will notice that they are not necessarily ours. They never were. Remember, Frank, it's your life. Not anyone else's."

After his explanation, Benedict once again made use of silence to allow his grandson to reflect. After a few minutes of quiet reflection, Frank got up and slowly walked toward his room without saying a word, moving as if he were in a trance. He had a lot to think about himself, about his fearful and negative attitude, but mostly about the lack of targets and goals. He felt the need to review and realign everything. But he had no idea how to do it.

Part 11
Paths That Separate

The Storm

A FEW DAYS PASSED BY UNTIL Frank returned to Benedict for another round of conversations. He had been following his relaxation and meditation exercises and had been praying as taught, always imagining a huge sun emanating divine light from the creator in front of him. He had been attending church without the old defenses and was coping with the world around him in a much more harmonious and positive way. However, something was still missing and got him feeling frustrated.

He felt as if he could only partially use what his grandfather was teaching him, so he decided to take a break from their conversations, since he felt as if he couldn't absorb much more.

Charlotte and Frederick had already accepted for some time now, the closeness between Frank and Benedict. After all, such connection seemed to be doing well for their son. And with the imminent arrival of the military enrollment, they stopped putting more pressure on him to find an occupation. The time now was to wait and make the most of the presence of their youngest child at home.

With two weeks missing for his birthday and consequently to his enrollment, Frank was already involved in preparations. He searched for information on where to enroll and what he needed to take with him. He was already beginning to prepare himself emotionally for the separation with his parents, his grandfather, his room, and all homely comforts such as homemade food, the living room couch, his clean blankets, and all the free time that came as part of the absence of a formal occupation.

This set of changes and separations brought along an emotional pain that he had never experienced before in his life. It felt like something was dying, but he couldn't exactly tell what or who. But at the same time, there was in him a sort of excitement, a strength building from within, an energy that he still didn't know for sure what it was, but that made him feel like a child that is about to get a gift and can hardly wait to open the package.

Whenever a storm of emotions and feelings would come and confuse him, Frank had made it a habit to consult with his grandfather. When he knocked at the door, which was slightly open, Frank couldn't help noticing that Benedict was writing something that he quickly closed and subtly tried to hide. Respecting that gesture, Frank turned his head, looking elsewhere, and waited for Benedict to give him permission to enter. However, his curiosity was such that he could not help asking, "What were you writing? A letter?"

"Not exactly. One day you will know. What can I do for you, son?" His grandfather's caring manners always eased him to open up and talk about his feelings and emotional distresses. Leaving aside the curiosity about what his grandfather was writing, he went straight to the point. "I'm feeling confused. As usual, I should say. Can we talk a little?"

"Of course, my grandson. But first you have to get that sad frown off your face. There should be no guilt in feeling confused. After all, you are only eighteen, or almost, and being confused is normal at this age. Well, actually I think we go through different stages of confusion throughout our whole lives."

Frank felt like his grandfather had opened up the opportunity for him to ask for clarification on another point, before getting to the real reason why he was there.

"Since you mentioned that, I would like to say that not everything that we have talked about I feel I can make sense of, or use. An example would be having my own targets and goals. I could not see clearly what they are. I still don't know where my own bucket is."

"I understand that, Frank, and it's normal to be that way. Many of the things that I am telling you took years for me to organize in my head and begin to make some sense. I'm sure that for you it will not be different. And you certainly will use this knowledge one day, maybe in a different way than what I used it for. Each one of us is unique in this universe. And everything has its time. One day this information will come to you in a more organized way and easier to understand, and you will also be more prepared to make better use of it. You should see our time together as just an initiation of all that is yet to come. And never forget to be open to find the wise old man. He will only appear to you if you are open to it. And when you find him, he will help you in times of confusion."

Once again Benedict mentioned the wise old man. As their time together was getting shorter each day, despite the discomfort that this apparent delusion from his grandfather brought, Frank decided to explore the subject a bit further.

"Grandpa, you already spoke of this old man a few times. How did you meet him for the first time?"

Benedict was silent for a few seconds, looking away to a point in the wall, as if the question had brought back very old memories of not-so-happy moments. When he broke the silence, his eyes were glazed, as if he was in a trance. His tone was grave, and he spoke in a slow pace.

"Those were hard times in my life, Frank. I was a little over thirty and felt very lonely in a strange land of different habits than my own. It was in India where I began to have the first teachings of spirituality, meditation, and the power of the mind. But my inner conflicts were still too strong. I felt homesick and hated the army and the things that I had to do on behalf of British sovereignty. It was a confusing time in my life. I used to drink heavily to numb my pains, and little by little, my body began to feel the effects of the abuse I imposed on it. I reached a point where I thought I was going to die, slowly and miserably. One day I woke up with a tremendous hangover and went to a lake near my camp where the water was pure and crystalline. I was craving fresh water. When I got to the lake, he suddenly appeared, out of nowhere. I looked around, and there was nobody else there. It was just me and him. He scared me at first, and I was afraid. I closed my eyes and almost ran. But something told me to give in to that vision. I took a deep breath, opened my eyes again, and there he was looking deeply into my eyes."

"And then? What happened?"

Frank was mesmerized by his grandfather's story and was curious to know how it would end.

"From the moment I conquered my fear and accepted his presence, we began to talk. We talked for hours, and for a reason I don't fully understand, nobody else came by. Our first conversation was not interrupted at any time. Since then, whenever I want or need, I summon him, and we can have long conversations. He brings within him all the wisdom of the universe."

"Can you summon him now? Can't I talk to him?"

Benedict suddenly left the trance and looked at Frank with a smile and tender glance, and said, "It doesn't work like that, Frank. The condition for him to come is that I have to be alone. When you find him, you will understand."

Frank did not like that answer. It seemed too convenient that such wise old man would only appear when Benedict was alone. He became convinced that this story was just his grandfather's reverie and decided to return to the subject that had brought him there in the first place.

"Shall we talk about my current confusions? For now, I have you, and you are my wise old man, ha, ha, ha!"

Without laughing much at his grandson's joke, since he felt disbelief in the air, Benedict turned to Frank and devoted his full attention to him. "I have been feeling very strange. All these changes that are about to happen are making me feel a deep sadness that I do not quite understand. But then at the same time, there is a new sensation, as if I were eager for all these changes to happen. They are two feelings so different from each other that I don't think they should be happening at the same time."

With his usual calm and quiet look, Benedict responded to his grandson's remark, "Welcome to the world of humans, Frank. We are beings filled with dualities. To have extremely different feelings at the same time or in a matter of minutes is part of our humanities, so don't feel bad about it. We are all like that. But let's talk first about your sadness. Close your eyes and tell me what comes to your mind when you think of it."

Frank followed his grandfather's request. He closed his eyes, forgot any other feeling, and turned fully to the sadness he felt. It did not take long for the words to start coming out of his mouth. "The first thing that comes to mind is my mother. I will not see her for a long time…and it hurts. I think about my father and the fact that we do not understand each other…that I'll leave without addressing this issue. I think that I will lose you and our conversations that have helped me so much. I think of my house, my bed, my mother's cooking…and especially I feel scared at the fact that…"

Frank took a long pause before he continued. There was a surprised expression on his face, as if he'd just had a moment of discovery. Then he proceeded, "I will no longer be able to…be a child anymore."

At this moment, Frank could not hold the emotions and began to cry. Tears ran down his face, and there was nothing he could do for it to stop. He tried not to cry, but was immediately warned by Benedict not to do that; he told him to let it all out of his chest.

Frank cried for a few minutes, with his hands covering his face, until those emotions finally eased. As he was calming down, he felt much better and lighter. Finally he had the courage to face Benedict and found him looking back with tenderness and empathy, as if he knew exactly how he was feeling.

"Okay, Frank, let's leave aside these emotions for a moment. Are you ready to talk about your excitement with the upcoming changes? When you are, close your eyes again and just think about that. Tell me what comes to your mind."

Frank still took a few seconds to stabilize the intense moment he had experienced; he took a deep breath and followed his grandfather's request. Again the result didn't take long.

"First, I am a little afraid…afraid of the unknown…afraid of how I will be treated by others…afraid of suffering…afraid of dying…but behind this fear, I am very curious about what I may find—what I'll learn…the adventures that I will live…people I will meet. There is this will to live new things…to rediscover myself… to find out who will be this new Frank in this new life that is soon to start…I want to live all that is to come, despite of all these fears."

Both remained silent for a moment, until Benedict ordered Frank to open his eyes. He looked at him tenderly and asked, "What have you learned in this exercise Frank?"

Since Frank was expecting that an interpretation was going to be provided by his grandfather, he was caught off guard by the question and had to stop and think for a moment.

"Well, first, it became much clearer why I feel so sad at this time. Soon I will be leaving behind everything that keeps me protected and taken care of. I'll be leaving the people who, each in their own way, love me. All my points of reference will be changing."

"And how do you see all this now?" Benedict asked.

"In a very different way. I feel a gratitude to my parents that I had never felt before. I have love and respect for everything that surrounds me. Never before had I realized how much I have. It seems I had to feel the loss of all these things to understand their value."

As in other moments of discovery like these, Benedict allowed the silence to fill the room and let Frank elaborate his thoughts and emotions for a moment. Then he asked, "What about the other reason of your sorrow?"

Frank was silent for a long moment. That emotion was a bit more difficult to articulate. With a voice filled with emotion, he said, "I felt a very strong thing about not being able to be a child anymore, Grandpa. It is as if something in me was dying, and that makes me very sad. Why does it have to be that way? Why does my child side have to die? Becoming an adult is very hard."

Benedict's expression suddenly went from candid to serious. With a piercing gaze, he involved Frank's face with both hands and said, "Yes, Frank, to mature is very difficult, and this is a process that will never end. Your old grandfather is still maturing right now. And these experiences are always accompanied with changes, pain, and frustrations. And they all can be very hard, so hard, that you should never allow the child inside of you to die, Frank. Your childhood may be ending, but your inner child shall not die. Never. It will always be within you. Do not suffocate it. Do not repress it. In fact, you should always rescue your inner child in difficult times."

The puzzled look on Frank's face made it clear that he needed more information on that. Realizing this, Benedict asked, "When you were a kid and something made you sad, how did you react?"

"Well, I would cry a little, would get angry, but as soon as a friend would come by or I would get a new toy, I would forget everything and I would go on to enjoy myself again. The pain wouldn't last very long. All I wanted was to have fun."

"Exactly. This is the summary of what I'm telling you, Frank. Be sure to play, be sure to have fun, and when a new pain comes to visit you, feel it, learn from it, but do not get caught in it for a long time. Go back to play, have fun again, find a new toy. Go back to being a child whenever possible, Frank. This child within you is who will carry you through the difficulties many times in life."

Again silence filled every space of the room. Realizing that this subject had already been exhausted, Benedict made the transition to talk about the other half of Frank's feelings.

"What about your excitement and anxiety. What did you learn?"

"That I'm about to live a new adventure. That despite being afraid of the unknown, I will have the opportunity to experience new things. I will be able to travel to distant lands, meet new people. I'm feeling like I am five years old and getting a new toy."

"Aha!"

Benedict's loud scream got Frank a bit scared, since he did not understand his grandfather's reaction.

"Did you realize what you just told me, Frank? From what you just said, I can tell that the child in you is far from dying. It seems very much alive to me. Your inner child is right there Frank. It's this excitement about novelties, about new discoveries, about the opportunities to recreate and reinvent yourself that you should never lose. Always allow this child to be alive and strong, making your life something more adventurous and picturesque. Being an adult all the time can be very boring, Frank. Surf on this wave of excitement, my grandson, and let it guide you in times of transition. I guarantee that you will enjoy your life much more and much better and everything that comes in terms of change and novelty. The new always comes, Frank, and the more you are open to it, the less you will suffer from unexpected life changes. This is the true art—to expect the unexpected."

Suddenly Frank felt much better. He could perfectly understand what his grandfather said and felt how important it was to keep his inner child alive.

"Thank you, Grandpa. Once again I feel that you were able calm me down. I do not know what I'll do without our conversations. Sometimes I feel that the confusion is so great within me that I'll go crazy. As if around me there was a storm and a raging sea that does not subside. I cannot wait for this storm to go away."

Frank then realized that Benedict was not looking into his eyes this time, and he had a kind of an ironic smile on his lips. So he could not contain his curiosity.

"What? What are you smiling about?"

Benedict then slowly turned to him and said something that would stay in his memory for many years, "Stop running away from the storm, Frank. The storm is within you. For it to go, you will have to face it. One day you'll understand that. As for our conversations, do not worry. When you find the wise old man, you will be in excellent hands. And my intuition says that you'll find him much earlier in your life than I did. Now let your grandfather work a bit. I bet you also have some preparations to work on, right?"

Yes, Benedict was right. Frank had a lot to do, but his mind was in something else at that moment. As usual when he had long conversations with Benedict, he felt a little puzzled and needed to digest all that. So he left the house to walk through the neighborhood and think for a while. He took the opportunity to bid farewell to the places that were familiar to him, as his old school, the market, and finally the church.

Seeing the door open, he decided to go in and confess, but found no one to do it with. Then he sat on the first seat and stood there looking at the picture of the crucified Christ, which was in the center of the altar. For a moment, he felt compassion for such pain and suffering that the image conveyed. Jesus had sacrificed himself for those who loved him. Then he felt an incredible identity with that image and said in a low voice, "Yes, Father. I'm also about to sacrifice myself for my country and for those I love. Give me your protection. Do not let anything bad happen to me. Give me the blessing to return as soon as possible."

He cried a little and then got up, made the sign of the cross, and began his way back home. It was time to start the final preparations. The day he would leave was approaching.

Happy Birthday, Frank

NOVEMBER 7TH, 1939, ARRIVED AT the Farrow family with a mixture of joy and sadness. After all, Frank was turning eighteen, reaching the age of adulthood, but at the same time, it was time to enroll and serve his country in a cruel war, a war that was beginning to cost many lives, and for that family, it was already taking away the second member in a short period of time.

Although the main stage of the war was for now on the other side of Europe, rumors that France and other neighboring countries would soon be invaded worried everyone. At that moment, British soldiers were being recruited as a precaution, but everyone knew that once their great ally would be the victim of an aggression, British forces would be called to act. It was all a matter of time. Not to mention that air attacks between Britain and Nazi Germany had already begun and the feeling of insecurity grew each day.

There was no consolation for Charlotte and Frederick, who struggled to hide their concern for their children.

Frank did not expect much of a celebration. After all, those were difficult times, and there was little to celebrate. He left home early and headed to church to pray and ask for protection for what lay ahead.

But his mother prepared him a surprise. While Frank was out, she made a cake and at the end of the day gathered everyone at the dinner table to sing "Happy Birthday" so each could give him a small gift.

His father was the first. It was not much of his nature to show affection, but today he broke that rule. He gave Frank a hug, looked into his eyes, and said, "Congratulations, son. You are already a man. Take this with you and write your memories. It may worth you something when you come back."

When he finished speaking, his eyes were reddened, and he could barely contain his emotions, perhaps for the absence of a greater conviction that he would actually see his son returning from the war. He walked away, quickly trying to hide his feelings since in his old-fashioned mentality, that was an embarrassing sign of weakness.

Frank opened the package and was surprised by a brand-new diary that his father had bought him.

Charlotte came soon after with a similar package as the one from his father, and Frank thought for a moment that, by coincidence, both could have given him the same gift.

"Son, it is with great joy that I have noticed you closer to God again. It seems that the conversations with my father were not a bad thing after all."

Charlotte smiled at her own ironic observation, winked at her father, and kept talking. "So I want to give you this. You will need its power very much."

When he finished opening the package, Frank was surprised and emotional. In his hands was the Bible that he had borrowed in past times of distress. His mother was giving him her own Bible.

"But, Mother, this is yours. How will you go on with your readings? I cannot accept this."

"Do not worry about me, Frank. It will certainly be more useful with you. In addition, it will serve to remind you of your mother in your most lonely hours."

It was getting harder and harder for Frank to control his emotions.

Finally, Benedict approached him. Suddenly, Frank remembered the first time he saw him months ago and realized that his grandfather's beard and hair were now even longer, further strengthening his aura of a medieval Celtic wizard. Benedict then handed him a paper rolled up in the form of a straw, tied with a red ribbon. The old man positioned himself in front of the boy, placed both hands on each of his arms, looked him in the eyes as he was used to doing, and said, "Frank, you know I'm a man with no possessions, so I prepared something for you myself. In this piece of paper is a collection of phrases and thoughts that will be of great use in difficult times. I want to give you as your last task—to read them and mentally practice them daily. Choose a time of the day, and every day at that time, read three of them, think them through and memorize them. Little by little, they will have a powerful effect on you and your thoughts."

The words *last task* had a strong impact on Frank, who now was fighting to hold the tears that were threatening to spring from his eyes. He didn't want that relationship to end. He had developed a special attachment to his grandfather.

Trying to change a little the vibe and the farewell mood that had taken the room, Charlotte said, "Enough with the crying. Now take your gifts to your room, put them at once in the suitcase, and let's have a piece of cake."

Frank then wiped his eyes with his fingertips and did as his mother suggested. Despite being very curious to read Benedict's phrases, he put the straw with the red ribbon between his clothes in a way that the Bible and the diary would not wrinkle it and returned to the kitchen to enjoy a piece of cake that his mother had already cut out for him.

As they ate and savored their pieces of cake, Frederick and Benedict started telling their stories of friendship and camaraderie lived in the previous war, trying to reinforce the fact that not only they had survived it, but they also had experienced good times and had grown as men and as persons. That almost orchestrated attempt to raise Frank's morale, along with Charlotte's surprise and the gifts received, all had a positive effect, and he now felt much better.

Later that night, when he stood up to retire to his room, Benedict embraced Frank once again and said, "It is important that you live these times, which will be difficult to everyone, one day at a time with the spirit of an apprentice, until you come across on the other side."

Frank remained silent for a moment and then asked, "And how will I know that I came across?"

"Ahhh, you are learning to ask great questions. This is very good. Many times in our lives, good and new questions are more important than old and obsolete answers."

Benedict then walked slowly to the kitchen door, already making his way toward his room. Before leaving, he turned to Frank, gave him a wink and said, "No worries. You will know."

Once in his room, Frank opened his suitcase and searched for the gift that his grandfather had given him. He removed the red ribbon carefully and unfolded the sheet of paper. On it, he found carefully listed fifteen phrases that had been written with a very neat handwriting, which clearly showed Benedict's affection and dedication on preparing such list.

Acting more out of curiosity than anything else and without really reflecting much about the words, Frank began reading the phrases one by one:

1. I am becoming a better and stronger human being each day. I will overcome one by one the obstacles that life brings to my path. I will persevere, and I will win.
2. I will convert errors or mistakes made by me into learning experiences, not guilt.
3. I will use every opportunity that life gives me to help others. I will treat others as I would like to be treated, even when I am not.
4. I will always seek to learn something new. I have different qualities and strengths, but many of them are yet to be discovered.
5. I will put focus and energy on the things I can control and in the hands of God, with all my faith, the things I cannot. He'll know what to do.

6. I will always exercise forgiveness toward those who do me wrong. I will use pardoning as an act of love toward those who hurt me and toward myself.
7. I will make the best out of my present time, because it's all I have. I will make of my past a source of learning experiences, and of my future, a sea of possibilities.
8. I will build a better world myself, being the agent of the changes that I want in it.
9. To understand my neighbor, I will put myself in his place and will feel his pains and joys.
10. All that is good or bad one day will pass. I will take the best out of each experience and move on. What does not kill me makes me stronger.
11. I will create my own positive thoughts. A positive attitude begins within me and does not depend on what is around me.
12. To love your neighbor is a matter of choice and attitude, not of feelings. I will choose to love, and I will do it through my actions every day.
13. Fears and limitations are generally fruits of imagination. They are not facts, only beliefs. I will not allow these beliefs to limit me. I will seek to be all that I can be.
14. My future is a blank page, and the pen is in my hands. I will write what I want, and I want for myself the most beautiful story that I can create.
15. I will thank God every day for all I have and for all that I don't have. After all, he knows better than anyone what I really need in my life at this moment.

With tired eyes, once he finished reading, Frank turned aside and fell asleep. He had no time to reflect on the sentences, but deep inside, he knew that they were not only for times of war. His grandfather's gift was something to be carried with him for the rest of his life.

Farewells

Frank woke up to a cold gray morning and thought that there could not be a better scenario for his farewells. He took a good shower and had a strong breakfast; after all, he was not sure when he would do both things well done again.

As planned the day before, at 10:00 a.m., he was ready and Frederick would accompany him to the station, where he would then take the next train toward his new life.

At the doorway, everyone waited for him with gloomy faces, but Charlotte soon tried to disguise her most painful feelings. She hugged her son, told him she was proud of him, that everything would be fine, and that soon they would see each other again at Christmastime.

Benedict soon followed. He pulled him into a corner of the room, hugged him with affection, and whispered in his ear, "This isn't the end, okay? Our paths will cross again, maybe in a slightly different way. But we'll be together again. I promise you."

Frank found his grandfather's words quite weird, but he was too overwhelmed to question him at that particular time. He headed slowly out the door, where he saw his father waiting for him at the sidewalk. As usual, Frederick had moved away, since witnessing emotional moments was not on his list of favorite things to do.

After taking a few steps, Frank sighed deeply and clenching his fists, turned back toward his home. He looked at his house one last time, looked at his mother and grandfather, gave them a final wave, and holding back his tears, went on, walking side by side with his father, who remained silent the whole time.

Lost in his thoughts and emotions, Frank did not see the time and the walk pass, and suddenly realized he was already at the station, ready to get in the train. He looked at his father, hoping for a hug and some kind of fraternal moment, but he just put a hand over his shoulder and without looking into his eyes, said, "You'll be fine, Frank. We'll see each other soon, okay? Take good care of yourself, son."

Frank consented silently and boarded the train, which quickly began to move.

Already in his seat and with the suitcase on his lap, Frank stretched his neck and looked out the window, searching for his father for one last glance, but he could not find him.

Suddenly he had a terrible feeling, as if he had wasted a unique opportunity to hug his father and tell him he loved him. He thought for a moment about his mother, grandfather, brother, his home, and all that he was leaving behind.

Then he looked around him and did not see a single familiar face, and a cold feeling in his stomach made him realize that the dreaded moment had arrived. He was on his own, and from that moment on, his life would never be the same. The unexpected once again was expecting him.

The End of a Phase, the Beginning of Another

"And that was the last time I saw them," Frank said, finishing his narrative. He had a sad look on his face and was staring at some distant point out in the park.

Elizabeth was in total silence and stared at him with eyes of pity and compassion. She almost couldn't hold her tears.

"But how come, Frank? You did not return home for Christmas? Couldn't you go back home anymore?"

Frank smiled ironically and replied, "Darling, that's another long story, since my life in the army was much harder and complicated than you think. But I have already bored you too much with my misfortunes. Are you hungry? I am. Shall we look for something to eat? I think we will have a hard time finding something tasty and at a good price these days. I should have thought of that yesterday when I invited you to walk in the park."

Elizabeth agreed with the suggestion immediately. Smiling, she held up a finger, asking him to wait, and started looking through her bag. She took two carefully wrapped sandwiches out, that she had prepared herself.

Surprised, Frank smiled back and said, "Wonderful. I did not know we were going to have a picnic. You really are full of surprises, Elizabeth."

"I'll take that as a compliment, Frank. Should we eat and then walk for a bit? I'll let you breathe for a few hours, but then I want to know what happened during your time in the army, until the day our lives crossed at the hospital. There are many missing pieces in this puzzle. My intuition says that there is much more there than a broken leg."

Frank chewed his first bite of the sandwich in total silence and kept staring at some distant point in the park. Elizabeth was right, but to talk about that chapter of his life would not be fun. On the other hand, Elizabeth's curiosity intoxicated him and pointed in a direction that pleased him very much. He would have more time with her. Lots of time. He would tell her all about his time in the army. He still had a lot to reveal. But before that, he remembered that he had something more to share about old Benedict. He got up and took from his left pocket a small object and showed it to Elizabeth.

She peered at it curiously and asked, "What is this, Frank, a key? What is it for? What does it open?"

"I have no idea."

"What do you mean, you have no idea? Why are you showing me this?"

"When I arrived at the army training camp and unpacked my bags, I found a sealed envelope with nothing written on the outside. I thought it was a short letter from my mother, but it was not. Inside the envelope there was just a note from Benedict and this key."

"And what did the note say?" asked Elizabeth, increasingly curious.

"'Keep this key carefully. One day it can be very useful.'"

"That's it?"

"That's it. Nothing else."

"It did not say what it was for?"

"Nothing. Just one more of the many mysteries of Benedict."

Elizabeth was silent for a few moments, savoring her sandwich and thinking about everything she had heard until then. After a while, she came back with another question that had been on her mind for quite some time.

"Have you ever found the so-called wise old man?"

Frank gave a restrained laugh, but full of irony. Elizabeth soon realized that the answer was negative, but she continued with the subject, "All right, you have not. But do you think you will ever find him? That he exists?"

Frank pondered a bit before reacting, since he was not very sure of his answer. After a few seconds of silence, he said, "Yes and no. I think it is possible that he exists, but only in his mind. I do not think I will find an old man who knows everything, who is just mine, and whom I can call whenever I want to. There's something else in this story that Benedict did not tell me."

"Yes, I agree with you. What an interesting person your grandfather was. It is really a shame he died in the bombings of 1940."

Frank looked at Elizabeth with a face of someone who had yet another startling revelation. Elizabeth immediately understood that there was something else to come and quickly asked, "What? Why are you looking at me like that?"

"I told you when I was at the hospital that my parents died in the bombing raids. I never said that Benedict died."

"What? Benedict is alive? And where is he?" Elizabeth responded, totally surprised by the news.

"I'm not sure. Before the bombings started, I received a letter from my parents saying they were alone. Benedict had decided to return to the Bread & Joy farm in Lincolnshire and left. When I was dismissed from the army, I wrote to the farm asking for information about him. A man named Carl, an employee of the farm, answered me saying that he had once disappeared, leaving behind all his personal belongings. He also said that he had the habit of taking long walks through the fields early in the morning, before starting his daily chores, and that he had never returned after one of these walks. There were several searches, but he was never found, dead or alive. I replied, asking them to advise me in case they ever find him, but I never got any answer. However, my intuition tells that one day I will meet again that unique character."

Elizabeth was stunned by this revelation. Benedict could still be alive.

They finished their sandwiches, and the afternoon sun brought along a much more pleasant temperature, perfect for a walk. Frank stood up and offered his right arm to Elizabeth, who promptly responded favorably to the invitation. Then they walked through the park in silence for a long time. The sense of peace and harmony between the two grew by the minute, as they enjoyed the flowers, the birds, and the beautiful sights and smells that the park was providing. And then, Elizabeth surprised Frank once again.

"Frank, I want you to come with me to my apartment. I will prepare some tea, and you can keep telling me about your adventures in the army. What do you think?"

Frank felt a wave of happiness invade his chest and wanted to go out leaping like a child. But with an inhuman effort, he was able to hold his composure and serenely said, looking into Elizabeth's eyes, "I would love to. It will be an honor."

He then positioned himself facing Elizabeth, placed both hands around her neck, thumbs lightly touching her ears, and again made a deep eye contact, asking permission for the next step.

This time there was no negative reaction from her. Her eyes not only gave him the expected permission, but practically asked him to go ahead. And the long-awaited kiss finally happened.

After a few seconds, amid the picturesque landscape of the park, they turned and went arm in arm toward the train station. For them, the day was just beginning.

The New Life

Once seated comfortably on the train, Frank put his right arm behind Elizabeth, embracing her, and in return, she rested her head on his shoulder. Frank felt a sense of peace and harmony that he had never experienced before. Still a little dazed and confused with her unexpected change of attitude, he could not control his curiosity. "Elizabeth, what made you change so fast about—"

Before he could even finish the sentence, Elizabeth again gently placed her delicate hand over his mouth and made a very characteristic sound, "Shhhhh."

He immediately fell silent and thought to himself, *Very nice, Frank. There you go again almost ruining everything. Thank God one of us thinks for both.*

However, while reflecting for a moment over Elizabeth's change of attitude, he thought that she could be lowering her defenses, and that would be a good thing. But the fact that she didn't want to talk about it worried him, raising doubts about this being a lasting change or just a momentary thing, and without fully understanding the reasons, he felt afraid of what it all could mean.

His thoughts were soon interrupted. Elizabeth suddenly pulled away her head and said, "Why don't you take advantage of the fact that we will be on the train for a while and tell me about your experience in the army? I'm curious to know what was so bad about it.

After all, your grandfather had given you a good initiation and great tools for you to face the challenges that were ahead."

The curiosity she had for his life and his experiences inebriated him. Her devoted attention made him feel like the most important person in the world. Her questions also made him think and reflect about his life, which greatly helped him to better understand his own experiences.

"That is very true, Elizabeth. He just forgot to warn me that such tools would not help me much in the army."

Elizabeth looked at him with an expression typical of someone who did not understand the remark; he then went on to explain it.

"When I arrived at the training camp, I was soon brought to my dorm. They showed me where my bed was and where I could keep my things. I was told that my training would begin that afternoon and was asked to wear my uniform. Then I went through a series of physical tests, and later that week, I received the news that I did not meet the minimum conditions for combat. My physical condition was so bad that they sent me to another division in another camp in Exeter, where I met other recruits in bad shape. It was there that I met Sergeant Dixon, and from that point on, my life would never be the same."

Elizabeth attentively listened and felt like asking several questions, but with a supreme effort, she remained silent, not willing to interrupt Frank, who continued, "In this new camp, there were many others who, in one way or another, were like me—being either sedentary people, overweight, or too thin. In other words, they were all people who still needed to work hard to be called soldiers and be in conditions to fight defending the country in a battlefield. And Dixon seemed to be there to make our lives a living hell. Don't worry. Soon you will understand everything."

Arriving at the New Training Camp

THE LONG TRAIN RIDE HAD caught Frank by surprise. Just when he was beginning to get used to his bed and the training camp located south of London, he received the news that he would be sent to Exeter in the far west of England, where he would spend a long combat preparation period.

November had ended with the news that the Polish government was exiled in London, as the country had been occupied and divided in two by the Soviet Union and Germany. The cold of December, which was beginning to dominate and shorten the days, along with Frank's homesick feelings, seemed to bring on him a heavy and depressing vibe.

For the first time in his life, he was experiencing a December without the Christmas spirit, so he could hardly wait to get his holiday leave to return home, even if for just a few days.

Upon arriving at the new training camp, he went through a ritual similar to the one experienced in the previous camp, being introduced to his dorm and bed. The accommodations were very similar to the other camp, but there was something different in the air and face expressions. Something heavy and negative could be felt there. As he passed by some of his future training mates, one of them looked at him in irony and said, "Welcome to paradise, Private Farrow."

Frank just kept walking silently, preferring not to answer, but thought that such phrase, said in such tone, could not be a good sign.

Once he found his bed, he was about to put his briefcase beneath it, but before doing so, he took out the diary that had been given to him by his father. He thought it would be a good moment to document his thoughts and put it up to date before dinnertime, so he began to write. That was when he noticed a stir in the dorm, with all other soldiers hiding magazines and other readings hastily. Someone then passed quickly by Frank and whispered, "Put that away. Dixon is coming."

A bit surprised by the situation and not really understanding the message that had been whispered to him, Frank was slow to react. Suddenly he realized he had over him a huge shadow, cast by the weak lighting of the dorm. He looked up and found a figure, rather frightening, looking at him with an expression of fury. On the left pocket of the uniform, he could read a name that would be in his memory forever: Sergeant Dixon. Frank then stood up to greet his superior and left his diary over his bed.

When he rose and stood at attention, he could then see the height difference that existed between him and Dixon. The sergeant was very tall, at least six inches taller than him, and had a huge body full of muscles. If that was not enough to form a very intimidating figure, his face carried a closed expression that seemed to have never known a smile.

The sergeant then approached face-to-face with Frank, looked him in the eyes, and began to inspect him from top to bottom. Frank felt an awful chill and a knot in his stomach. Dixon then started to smell Frank in a way that everyone could hear him. Then he said loud and clear, "Hmm, the smell of mama's boy."

The other soldiers started laughing, and Dixon looked again in Frank's eyes. By now he was beginning to tremble with a mixture of fear and indignation. Dixon then looked at the bed and found what he was looking for. He changed his face expression, showing even more anger in his eyes, took Frank's diary and shouted in his left ear, "What is this, Private Farrow?"

Frank was already unable to breathe properly and answered with a trembling voice, "It's only my diary, sir."

Frank then started to worry when he heard giggles around him. Something was not right. Dixon raised Frank's diary and started showing it to all, saying, "Only a diary, gentlemen. Only a diary. Let's see if this is true."

Dixon then preceded scanning the journal, looking for something. Frank was disgusted with such invasion of privacy and had the urge to jump into the sergeant's direction in order to take the diary from his hands, but fear held him back. Suddenly Dixon stopped flipping through the journal and looked at Frank with a look of mockery, as if saying he had found what he wanted.

"Listen to this, gentlemen: 'I have just arrived at my camp in Exeter, where I will be taught the arts of war and soon will know if I will fight in Europe or in some other battlefield in foreign lands.'"

He remained silent for a few seconds, walking like a tiger in a cage, showing Frank's diary to everyone, until in a given moment, he advanced toward Frank, screaming, "What are you trying to do, Private Farrow? Do you want to kill us all? This is not a diary. It is a storehouse of secret information. Can you imagine if it falls into the hands of a German? You'll be telling him exactly where to attack us."

Dixon then walked back to the center of the dorm, to a place where everyone could see him and continued his tirade.

"Let this be an example to all. This diary is being confiscated and will be destroyed. If someone else has a diary, it is to be delivered immediately, so it will have the same fate. And it's important that everyone knows that in my camp, just one kind of reading is allowed, which are books about war, the great battles, the major strategies, the great generals. Nothing else!"

These last two words came out of his lungs with such energy that echoed the four corners of the dorm. Finally, looking at Frank, he screamed, "Congratulations, Private Farrow. You just got a punishment for your whole group. Everybody must be ready at five in the morning to run ten kilometers and for a long day of exercises. I will make soldiers out of you, even if this is the last thing I do in my life."

He looked down at Frank with superiority, knowing that he had humiliated him and made an example out of him, then turned to the right and stomped out the dormitory.

Frank felt dizzy and still trembling, fell seated on his bed. While he was trying to recompose himself and understand what had just happened, he felt a hand on his shoulder and heard someone tell him, "Thank you so much, Farrow. You put us all on this. What a beautiful way to introduce yourself."

Frank then looked around, and all he found were angry looks of disapproval. He had made quite an impression on his arrival. It would not be easy to make friends after that.

Later that night, when he laid his head on his pillow to sleep, he felt depressed and insulted by Dixon. He was carrying innumerous bad feelings toward his superior, and they did not help at all to legitimize him as his new leader, and that was not good. Then he tried to relax as Benedict had taught him, but before he could even take a moment to pray, he fell asleep. He was just too tired from the trip and from the stress that he had just gone through. Little he knew that his difficulties with Dixon were just beginning.

The First Days

As announced, at 5:00 a.m. the next day, the wake-up call rang loudly, and everyone quickly rushed to present themselves for the run and the scheduled exercises. Frank did everything he could to keep pace with others, but invariably he would stay behind and would have to cope with Dixon, always a few feet behind him, shouting in his ear to keep up and telling him all kinds of offensive and humiliating words. In the afternoon, they went through the first set of military exercises, and Frank felt that the sergeant was always watching him closely, hoping that he would commit a mistake so again he could make an example out of him for everyone. The obvious persecution legitimized by a position of a higher rank would revolt him and would leave no room for any reaction. This situation was very different from the kind of authority exercised by his father, his teachers, or even by the church priests. There was no room for argument; for a difference in opinions, there was no negotiation. He had to submit himself, and that was it. Unaccustomed to such brutal reality, Frank was nurturing inside of him a mortal hatred for Dixon and all that he stood for.

At night when he finally got to his bed, he began to remember the teachings of Benedict. He remembered his warnings about him having to go through many difficulties and how things would worsen before getting better. To increase his distress, he had had no time to tell his family about his move to the new camp, and probably the letter he had sent them would be answered to the wrong destination. But he trusted that the mail service could still find him, even if it would take a while.

His body was exhausted, and he felt pain everywhere. He could not remember ever feeling a physical fatigue to such extent before in his life. Realizing he was nurturing within himself such negative feelings, he decided to do the only thing he had left as a resource in these situations. He started to pray.

Then he sought in his briefcase the Bible that had been given to him by his mother and tried to read a chapter in the New Testament, but his fatigue was such that he fell asleep with the book open on his chest, even before reading the first paragraph. Suddenly, he was abruptly awakened by someone shouting his name in anger.

"Private Farrow!"

As he opened his eyes, still dazed, Frank recognized Dixon's figure exactly at the same place that he was the night before. Apparently, this time no one bothered to provide any warnings about this new surprise visit. Before he could even get up, the sergeant took the Bible from his hands and started checking if it was not a false cover. When he was finally convinced that the book was really the Bible, he turned to Frank and said, "Have you learned nothing from yesterday, Farrow? What kind of reading did I say was allowed in this dorm?"

Frank, at this point, although still a little dizzy, was already up and at attention and remembered the rules set out the previous day. He knew he had been caught breaking one of Dixon's rules, and once again he began to tremble, feeling as if he was about to receive another punishment. Then he tried to elaborate a response that could soften the situation and argued, "But it's the Holy Bible, Sergeant. Can't I read the Bible?"

"Wrong answer, Farrow. Do you classify the Bible as a book about war? You seem to be a little slow to learn your lessons, soldier, so I'll help you. I will have you cleaning the latrines of this dorm the next seven days. On the eighth day, I'll ask again the kind of reading you can do in this dormitory. Let's see if by then you will have memorized the correct answer. I will not confiscate your holy book, but I do not want to see it again in this dormitory, is that clear?"

Frank said nothing. His indignation and outrage at Dixon's arbitrary decisions were growing to unbearable levels. His hesitation to answer angered Dixon, who shouted using his entire lungs, "Is it clear, Private Farrow?"

With a low voice and a knot in his throat, Frank replied, "Yes, sir" in a tone that did not appear to convince Dixon, who demanded, "Louder, because your colleagues across the dorm did not hear you."

The revolt grew within Frank, who then filled his lungs and shouted, "Yes, sir!"

Satisfied, Dixon took the Bible in his right hand, walked to the center of the dormitory, where everybody could see him clearly, and once again, spoke as done the night before.

"Soldiers, we are about to get into war. My mission is to prepare you for the worst of all worlds. I do not want anyone in my group softening and losing focus, weakening the desire to defeat the enemy. If anyone wants to read things like these, read them on your days off. Not here."

He walked back toward Frank, threw the Bible on his bed, and repeated, "I will not confiscate your holy book, but I do not want to see it again."

He looked at Frank one last time with despise and went out the door, stepping firmly.

Again, Frank collapsed, sitting heavily on his bed. This time he did not hear laughter and jokes from his roommates. Everyone seemed to carry some level of outrage at what had just happened. He then took his mother's Bible, thanked God that it had not been confiscated, and put it carefully back in his bag.

He then realized that someone was coming. He looked up and saw one of his roommates asking permission to sit beside him. Frank hesitantly agreed. With no introductions, the other soldier quickly said, "Don't get upset. Dixon is an idiot. He's a guy with no religious faith and obsessed with war. He cannot wait to be in combat, but to his dissatisfaction, they sent him here to prepare new recruits, so he projects his anger on us. He always chooses someone to be his punching bag for a while, but then he gets tired and chooses another target. I know well about it because I was his punching bag until you got here. Hold on and stay strong. Soon he will forget you and choose another one."

The boy got back up, gave a pat on his shoulder, and left, afraid that Dixon would return and see him comforting Frank, which inevitably would lead him back to the sergeant's punching bag position.

Frank was desolate. His body ached in fatigue, he had no news about his family, he could not vent in his journal, and now, he could not even read the Bible. And to further increase his level of frustration, he had just discovered that, in fact, he had been chosen by Dixon to serve as an example for the rest of the group and would be persecuted by him for God knows how long. Nobody would be willing to be his friend while this lasted. He was completely alone.

Finding no other remedy except going to sleep, he went to bed and when the lights went off, allowed a few tears to run over his face. However, before falling asleep, he remembered one of the phrases of Benedict's list: "What does not kill me makes me stronger."

He filled his lungs with air and repeated to himself, "I will go through this and will get out of it stronger on the other side."

And with this encouraging thought, he fell in deep sleep.

Going Too Far

After a week of cleaning the toilets, Frank was surprised by an order of Dixon extending his punishment for another week, which made him furious at first, but he ended up fulfilling his duties with resignation. After all, there was no alternative.

In order to ease his hatred toward the sergeant, Frank resumed his daily relaxation exercises, which were now taking place soon after he would finish the toilet cleaning. He also would take advantage of the time that Dixon and the other soldiers were away to read his list of phrases from Benedict and would try to memorize three of them a day, as his grandfather had recommended.

Upon reaching the fourteenth day of punishment, he realized that it was already the second half of December, and he was yet to receive any news from his family, which greatly distressed him. Despite not having made a single friend, since no one wanted to be caught with Dixon's punching bag, he overheard his colleagues' conversations about the possibilities of a Christmas leave and the chance to visit their families. He figured he should do everything to please Dixon in order to get such time off and be able to return to London, where he could rest a few days and visit the people he loved the most.

The act of cleaning the toilets was not all negative in the end, since he had learned the hard way to appreciate his mother, always taking care of the house impeccably. Quite selfishly, he had never appreciated her efforts and realized that such hard work was in fact an act of love that he was never thankful for. He could hardly wait to be able to hug his mother again and fix that mistake. He felt also much humbler and somehow strengthened by the daily reading of Benedict's phrases.

After dinner, he lay down on his bed and started thinking about life and the abrupt changes that had happen so unexpectedly. Six months ago, he was disdainful of his school, his church, and his family, and now he would give anything to have them back. He remembered one of his grandfather's gems saying that we should always expect the unexpected, because it always comes and turns our lives upside down. Suddenly he heard the usual flurry of his colleagues communicating that Dixon was on his way. After almost three weeks there, he had learned to read the signs. He then stood up and calmly awaited the arrival of the sergeant, as he most likely would go through some kind of humiliation before he was released from his punishment.

Dixon came through the door in a hurry. As usual, everyone saluted him, but he did not pay them much attention. Wasting no time, he went straight to Frank and asked, "Private Farrow, which readings are allowed in this camp?"

Already thinking about the possibility of getting a Christmas break, Frank did not hesitate to scream with all his strength, "Readings about the art of war, sir!"

Dixon looked at him triumphantly. The rookie had learned his lesson.

"Very well, Private Farrow. You have finally given me the correct answer with the proper energy. You are released from your punishment. Soon, we will find someone else to clean the toilets."

Dixon then started walking to the other side of the dorm, and Frank sighed in relief. He had achieved his objective, and it was not as hard after all. He thought that this could also be the end of his time as the punching bag of the sergeant. His chances of visiting his family at Christmas had just increased significantly. Lost in his thoughts, he did not realize that Dixon had turned and made his way back toward him.

"Private Farrow, other than the Bible, what other readings do you carry in your suitcase?"

Totally surprised by the return of the sergeant, he did not answer immediately, leaving Dixon suspicious. Dixon then insisted, "Soldier, I asked you a question, and I demand an answer. What other readings do you carry in the suitcase?"

Caught off-guard by his question, all that Frank could answer was, "I don't bring anything else, sir."

"Oh really? So you won't bother if we make a little inspection, right? Open your suitcase, soldier."

Frank could not believe what was happening. With his jaw clenched, he bent down and sought the briefcase that was beneath his bed. Although taken by surprise, he was at ease since the only book he was carrying was really the Bible. He took the briefcase, placed it over the bed, and opened it, showing the sergeant his few clothes and the Bible of his mother placed in a corner. Dixon observed the open briefcase, and as he did not find anything there that bothered him, he looked at Frank without hiding his frustration. When he was ready to leave Frank alone, he looked at the suitcase one last time, and suddenly his expression changed. Looking a bit closer, he frowned and extended his arm, pulling the corner of a piece of paper that was folded inside the Bible.

"What is this, Private Farrow?"

Frank said nothing. He had no idea how he could possibly explain Benedict's list. Finally he managed to stammer a reply, "N-nothing important, sir."

Dixon then opened the list and began to read it, sentence by sentence, in silence. His expression was changing by the second, apparently getting angrier and angrier. Suddenly he let out a hearty laugh, then turned to the center of the dorm as he had done on other occasions when he wanted to humiliate someone, and said, "Listen to this, soldiers," and began to read the list aloud for all to hear it.

At the end of every sentence read, he would laugh and turn to Frank, humiliating him more and more. Within seconds, the whole dorm was laughing in a loud sound, and everyone was making fun of Frank, who felt his humiliation reach a level never before experienced. He began to sweat, and hatred started to grow more and more in his chest. This was going too far. He could hardly control himself.

When he finished reading the whole list aloud, Dixon raised his right hand, and immediately everybody stopped laughing and became silent. He turned to Frank with a look of someone who had found what he wanted for another display of power. His expression was of superiority and arrogance. With the voice full of mockery and irony, he said, "'Better human being'? 'Help others'? 'Exercise forgiveness'? 'Better world'? 'Love your neighbor'? Where do you think you are, soldier, in a seminary? This is a preparation for war, Private Farrow!"

Frank did not know what to say, because there, on Dixon's left hand was his last link with his grandfather and also his only resource to strengthen up and go through the difficult times that he was experiencing and the ones that were yet to come. His breathing was altered, his body slightly bent forward, and his fists were clenched tightly. Without realizing it, he had entered into attack position. As his anger was coming to unbearable levels, what he feared the most happened. With a condescending smile, Dixon raised Benedict's list and ripped in half, then into four pieces, then eight, and tore it again until it was in tiny pieces. To end his demonstration of power and superiority, he flung it into the air, and bits of paper flew everywhere. He turned to Frank and said, "Find the broom and sweep it, Private Farrow."

That aggression was all that was needed to push Frank beyond his limits of patience and subordination. In a thoughtless act of hatred and despair, he rushed violently toward the sergeant, who was already slowly making his way toward the dormitory door and with a cry of rage coming from the core of his being, struck Dixon with a strong push that threw him far away. Dixon had no time to react and fell to the ground sideways, unable to protect himself from the impact. As he was trying to recover his balance, he ended up propelling himself further and hit his head hard on the foot of one of the beds that was next to the exit door, falling to the ground unconscious. Quickly a small puddle of blood began to form.

The whole dorm was silent for a few seconds, and everyone looked at Dixon lying there on the floor and Frank, standing ten feet away, still breathing heavily.

Finally, one of the soldiers came out of the trance and realizing that Dixon needed immediate medical attention, went out the door screaming for help.

Frank still did not quite understand the gravity of what he had just done, but in his heart, he knew that he had made a mistake that would cost him a lot. Little he knew that such a thoughtless gesture would determine his fate for the rest of his life. Nothing else would be as it was before.

Elizabeth Opens Her Doors

ELIZABETH STOPPED WALKING FOR A moment and kept staring at Frank with her mouth wide-open. She could not believe the story she had just heard. Frank, who was walking two steps ahead, also stopped and looked back with an expression of slight embarrassment, mixed with a plea for understanding.

Elizabeth then resumed walking, and in searching for the key in her purse, she said, "Let's go in. You tell me the rest of this story when we are inside."

During the entire train ride, as well as during the walk to her apartment, Elizabeth had listened attentively to what Frank was telling her, and little by little, things started to make sense. After all, he had gone from one extreme, where he had his parents' care and Benedict's guidance, to a hostile environment where he could not find any friends and had a leader who was the worst kind that anyone could find. It was only natural that he had difficulties in adapting. But that last act had totally surprised her and certainly would have serious implications that she was yet to find out.

When they reached the front door of the apartment, Frank could not hide the smile of satisfaction on the corner of his lips, though the anxiety in his eyes was evident. The most intimate world of Elizabeth was about to open up to him, and that made him feel elated.

Elizabeth could read all this easily on Frank's face, but she kept such awareness to herself, without making any comment that could make him feel exposed or intimidated.

Opening the door, she made a sweeping gesture and said, "Welcome to my kingdom."

Frank went in slowly, and as he took off his coat, he took notice of a place that was perfectly kept. It had a small table with four seats to the right of the door, with a vase without flowers on top, and it was inevitable for him to think that the bouquet he never bought would fit perfectly there. In the center of the room, there was a love seat that was paired with an armchair that seemed to be quite comfortable and a small coffee table. The whole set made the room symmetrically harmonious and cozy. At the corner of the living room, there was the radio, a device that was indispensable for anyone to be informed of what was going on in those days. On the right from the entrance, there was a small but spotlessly clean and tidy kitchen, and ahead, just across the room, there were the bathroom and the bedroom, both with doors closed. The scent of a well-kept house was everywhere. The atmosphere was so pleasant that Frank couldn't hold back on his compliments.

"Congratulations, Elizabeth. Your home is lovely. Now this is a home, not that hole where I hide."

Elizabeth's face lit up, and she could not hide her satisfaction from what she had just heard. Frank then realized that, inadvertently, he had done well with his comments and that such topic was very important to her.

"Have a seat, Frank. I want to know exactly how this story ended." She then took Frank's coat and hung it on the back of one of the chairs and did the same with hers. To Frank's surprise, she then took off her shoes and sat sideways on the couch, folding her legs beneath herself. She put her left hand under her chin and looked at Frank, awaiting the closing of his story.

Frank looked at that beautiful scene and felt intoxicated with her movements, which were harmonic and charming at the same time. He was so hypnotized that it took him a couple of seconds before he could continue talking.

"Well, Dixon was taken to the infirmary, where he was medicated and taken care of and ended up just fine. I was immediately arrested for assault of a superior and spent two weeks waiting for a decision on what would happen to me. I ended up spending Christmas and New Year's Eve inside of a prison cell they had in the camp. An investigation was opened to evaluate the case, and apparently someone ended up giving a testimony in my favor. A punishment was imposed on Dixon, and he was left in the icebox for some time without any chance to go to the battlefields. Apparently, this was not the first incident in his career. That was the reason he was being kept away from where the action really happened. They feared he could more likely become a source of problems than of solutions in a high-pressure environment."

Frank briefly paused to breathe and thought for a moment before resuming the story. "While I was in prison, I finally received a letter from my parents telling me they were now alone, because shortly after I had joined the army, Benedict decided to return to Bread & Joy, taking all his belongings, claiming difficulties in adapting. Although upset, my mother had passively accepted his decision because deep inside, she knew the old man felt like a useless weight there. At least at the farm he could continue working and living with people he had known for decades."

Elizabeth was looking into Frank's eyes attentively. Taking advantage of Frank's pause, she asked, "And how did you feel when you received such news?"

"I was sad, Elizabeth. Very sad indeed. I still had lots of hope that I could meet him again when the war was over. So I wrote to the farm looking for him, but the response I got you already know. I felt I still had much to learn from him, and besides, I got attached to that old man during the months we spent together. He was one of the few people who heard me, understood me, and helped me understand myself. As you are doing right now."

This last observation made Elizabeth stop talking for a moment. She suddenly realized how her attention to Frank was important to him. A heavy feeling of responsibility filled her chest for a moment. In order not to make such feeling grow bigger than it should, she immediately went for one more question, "How did you feel about losing the year-end with your family and spending two weeks in the military prison?"

"It was really bad at the beginning, and it made me very angry. As you can imagine, spending the holidays behind bars was not exactly part of my Christmas plans. But then I began using my days in the cell to find myself emotionally. There, I had plenty of time to read my Bible and do the relaxation exercises taught by Benedict. In the last days, I began to mentally visualize a more positive attitude for me, for when I get out. When I was finally released early January of 1940, I was much more focused and balanced."

Elizabeth was surprised by Frank's answer and looking for a closure for those difficult times, commented, "And I bet it was a relief to get rid of Dixon, right?"

Frank could not contain an ironic chuckle. Elizabeth then opened her eyes and mouth wide in amazement and questioned, "Don't tell me that—"

Before she could even finish her question, Frank interrupted, "He was the first person I saw when I came out of prison. He was waiting for me on the way out, because we had to go through a meeting where we both received clear orders to leave our differences aside and work together for a greater purpose. If we had any other kind of problem with each other, we would suffer even more severe punishments. In short, I would follow under the tyranny of Dixon still for a long time."

"And did he continue to pursue you?"

"Oh yes, of course. But in a different way, more veiled. We started fighting an undeclared war with each other. He hated me because he had lost opportunities to go to the front lines. In retaliation, he also would not release me to fight. For as long as he would not be sent to where the action was, he would not release me for that either. Every time a request would come for new soldiers to be sent to the front lines, I was never on the list. He would say I was not ready yet. And so the months went by. Thanks to Dixon, I was spared from the defeat in Norway and even worse, from the evacuation of Dunkirk in France in May of that year."

Starting to understand why Frank had never fired a shot in the war, Elizabeth was increasingly anxious to know how that dispute between Frank and Dixon ended. But suddenly, she realized that such anxiety made of her a terrible hostess to her own standards.

"Frank, I am so sorry for not offering you anything. I'll make tea with some toast so we can continue with our conversation. While I am heating the water, will you tell me how all of that ended?"

Frank followed her to the kitchen in silence and waited for her to put the water to boil. However, his intentions on following her were not exactly to immediately proceed with his story. Their kiss while together at the park was still in his memory. He could still feel the taste of Elizabeth's lips on his and felt as if he was addicted to such pleasant contact. He approached her and winning over his fears, put his hands on her tiny waist. She welcomed the approach by placing her hands on Frank's arms, who immediately took action to get another kiss, which lasted longer and brought along more affection than the first, making his heartbeat speed up quickly. They embraced each other one more time, and Frank could feel that unique sense of peace that bravely challenged those times of war. When he was in the arms of Elizabeth, nothing else mattered, and that feeling reigned absolute. They stayed like that for a few minutes until the water boiled.

With tea and toast readily set on the coffee table, they accommodated themselves again in their original seats, and Frank resumed his story from where he left off.

The War Intensifies

THE TWO WEEKS SPENT IN a cell had been like a small roller coaster for Frank. Initially, he felt extremely depressed for not going home and having spent Christmas isolated from everything and everyone. But once this malaise had passed, he slowly recovered his high spirits and emotional balance.

He began to recall his conversations with Benedict and understood that the fact of being in a totally new environment and with extremely different routines had hindered his attempt to impose any discipline to apply his grandfather's teachings. He could also remember clearly that his grandfather warned him that he would go through some difficult times, and that since he was so young, it would be hard for him to apply the things they spoke about, which would only happen later in his life. God only knew when such moment would be.

Several times in his moments of solitude, he caught himself closing his eyes, wishing that when he opened them, he would see at his side the wise old man that his grandfather promised he would find. He would then ask him many things, including what to do with Dixon when they met again. But in those moments, he would open his eyes, only to find himself alone, and would laugh at himself, remembering that his grandfather also said that this meeting would only happen when he was ready for it. Not when he wanted.

He also took such time to put to date his correspondences with his parents, but he preferred to omit the real reason why he was not able to visit them for Christmas, simply saying that he had not been released.

Only when he was about to get out of his two weeks of reclusion did he reengage in the meditations and prayers as his grandfather had taught him. That helped him focus on his return to the military routine, so much so that when he finally came out of his cell and faced Dixon waiting for him in a meeting room, he was surprised, but not intimidated.

He was even more surprised when he learned that both of them had been punished, and they would have to prove to their superiors that they could work together seamlessly before being sent to any combat. They were forced to shake hands, which occurred icily from both parties and without eye contact.

When this handshake occurred, Frank could feel from the cold energy and the pressure of Dixon's hand that this dispute was far from over. It would only gain a new shell.

Upon returning to his dorm, he met his colleagues and received some sort of recognition for having done something that many of them would find pleasure on doing, and began to experience some level of respect from them.

Dixon ceased to harass him directly in front of everyone and this helped him toward cultivating greater emotional stability and clarity of thought. He was able to focus on preparing himself to fight and sought whenever possible to do his prayers, even if it was when showering or when he was closing his eyes to sleep. He knew that soon he would need a lot of faith to face armed battles.

The beginning of 1940 brought along the first signs of war to the British people, with rationing of food and some German submarines attacking civilian and military vessels.

Meanwhile on the European continent, the Soviet Union and Germany followed their expansionist race. After the split of Poland, they turned their guns to the north toward the Nordic countries. The Soviets invaded Finland, and Germany did not hide its plans to invade Denmark and Norway. Due to the strategic location of the latter, France and England were already prepared to defend it. The direct confrontation between the two blocs was now a matter of time.

Despite knowing he was in a sort of probation period and that he was not likely to be sent to this first battle, Dixon maintained an intense rhythm of preparations. In fact, in his head, he had different ambitions. Everyone had the expectation that sooner or later, Hitler would also invade France, and it was there that he wanted to fight, as his father did before him in the Great World War.

To achieve this goal, he had stopped harassing Frank publicly and directly, but he would use every physical activity and military exercise as an opportunity to test Frank's endurance and patience and would do everything to harm him, putting him always on the weaker side or where the exercise would demand more physical effort. Frank, in turn, noting the veiled type of persecution Dixon imposed on him, strived even more to make sure his team would win the simulations or that he got to the end of the exercise physically well and with his head held high.

At the end of each day, both would exchange heavy and provocative looks. Frank seemed to say, "I survived you another day." To which Dixon would answer, "Tomorrow is another day, and then I will catch you."

At the end of March, Frank began to feel the positive effects of his intense efforts. His physical condition had reached levels that he had never experienced before. Little by little, he was also beginning to feel ready for action in battle.

When April arrived, Germany finally went on the offensive and invaded Denmark and Norway. As promised, England and France immediately went out to defend the invaded nations, and the first battles then took place on Norwegian soil and waters, with favorable outcomes to the Germans.

With clear indications that the Nazis would soon make similar movements against the Low Countries and France itself, the British and French quickly abandoned the idea of defending Norway. At the end of May, they came in retreat and focused their efforts on defending Paris, repositioning troops in northern France.

Denmark and Norway would then fall and became part of the list of countries annexed by Hitler, along with Austria, Czechoslovakia, and half of Poland. The Norwegian government added itself to the list of those who settled in exile in London.

Frank and Dixon did not seem to be very disappointed with the fact that they were not sent to these early battles, since the result was very negative for their country. But both had high expectations of being called to defend France. And Frank had hopes, albeit small, that he could find his brother, Peter, and fight side by side with him.

But each week, more and more troops were sent to the European continent, and Dixon's time seemed never to come. This gradually increased his level of frustration. As a result, whenever he was asked for a new contingent of soldiers, he would never include Frank, who would also be left behind.

The outcomes in Norway caused a serious debate in the English government on how the country was articulating itself and how it was making use of its resources and troops. Significant changes were inevitable. In early May, the prime minister Neville Chamberlain resigned and was replaced by Winston Churchill, a veteran of the First World War, who came to power with the mission of giving a different direction to the role of England in the combat.

But the month of May brought more than just administrative changes. Mercilessly, Germany invaded Belgium, Netherlands, Luxembourg, and France in only one stroke. Within days, the first three capitulated, and France quickly became the next target.

Frank was following all this through newspapers and radio, and his anxiety was growing day by day. He thought of his brother, who was already on the battlefield, and also of his parents, in worries that if Hitler was not detained in France, he would soon be targeting England. A sense of panic began to take over those who had not yet been sent to fight in the continent.

For everyone's despair, by late May, the Battle of France seemed already lost, and the allied war command decided on a radical move, which was to drawn from the mainland the entire contingent that had been sent there via Dunkirk in France, including the French army itself. The idea was to save the largest possible number of soldiers and bring them to England, where they could then be reused in future fronts, including a possible invasion of Great Britain.

This operation, called Dynamo, finished early June and later would prove to be crucial to the future of warfare. But at that moment, it was humiliating. Frank and his colleagues' morale could not be any lower. Germany was winning.

Frank then wrote to his parents, seeking news of his brother. Frank wondered if he had managed to escape and return to England. A few weeks later, he was relieved to receive a positive response. Peter was back in British lands in another training camp, waiting for the next orders.

On June 4, Churchill made one of his most passionate speeches, calling the English people to prepare to fight against a possible invasion, if necessary for years and alone. He also stated that they would fight at sea, in the air, and on the ground and defend their land until the end, saying in a threatening tone to the Germans, "We will never surrender." Along with a huge group of other soldiers, Frank heard the retransmission of the speech of his highest leader on the radio, and at its end, he felt a patriotic shiver up and down his spine. He was ready to fight. *Let the Germans come,* he thought.

During the month of June, the Nazis marched sovereignly through Paris and the northern half of France joined the Nazis. England was now alone, and quickly became the next target for Hitler. The directive now was to prepare for a possible invasion. Dixon and Frank were not going anywhere anytime soon.

Resigned to his fate, Frank concentrated more and more on improving his physical conditioning. Little by little, he completely abandoned his meditation exercises and prayers. Now all he wanted was to be in the best shape to fight. He began to cultivate a patriotic pride that would grow every day, which motivated him more and more. His fitness was such that he quickly began to call the attention of other superiors besides Dixon, who, in turn, started to feel bothered, knowing that soon there would be no more excuses to hold back the soldier that, without him taking notice, had become one of the best prepared.

Frank saw his body gradually change. Now he was proud of his fitness and would spend long minutes in front of the mirror after showering.

One day he waited for everyone else to leave the showers and was left alone, gazing up. Without realizing it, he had allowed his ego to highly inflate. He liked to look at his well-defined abdomen, swollen biceps, and rounded legs. He felt invincible.

Hypnotized by such narcissistic exercise, he did not realize that Dixon had entered the place and was watching him in silence. Noticing that they were alone, Dixon approached and let out a huge mocking laugh. Caught totally unprepared, Frank was at a loss on what to do. He tried to hide what he was doing and quickly wrapped himself in his towel.

"Private Farrow, what are you doing here all alone admiring yourself in the mirror? Are you finding yourself all strong and mighty?"

Frank did not know what to do or say, and he started retreating to where his clothes were. Dixon followed him and continued talking. "Then be aware that you are nothing, and as long as I am kept here, you do not leave either. Do you hear me, Farrow?"

Frank remained silent, still embarrassed by the position he had been caught in. Dixon continued his harassment. "You can train as hard as you can. You may become the fastest and most prepared soldier of this camp. I will only release you whenever I want. And that moment is only going to come when they send me to fight. If I am not going to fight, you are not going to fight either."

Dixon released another laugh and stomped away.

There it was then, clear and declared, what deep inside he already intuitively knew, but that had never been told in such direct words. Dixon was really still after him. But this kind of persecution bothered him differently. He wanted to defend his country. More than that, he felt he was fully ready and prepared for it. But thanks to the frustrations and weakness of character of his direct leader, he could not. What was the good of being in the best shape? What was the good of all those muscles and lungs if he could not use them?

At that moment, he again felt hatred for Dixon. Something needed to be done. He clenched his fists, punched the locker that was in front of him, and with his mouth in a grim line, he promised himself that he would engage so much in training that Dixon would not be able to hold him back. Sooner or later, he would have to leave.

And he was right, because in a few weeks, he would get out of there. However, his leave would not happen the way he imagined. Soon the unexpected would pay him another visit and would again change the course of his life.

Two Extremes

THE TEACUPS LAY EMPTY ON the coffee table, and the plate with toasts no longer grabbed Frank's attention. Tired of talking, he paused for a moment while observing the clock on the wall. The afternoon was quickly ending, and he began to worry about the possibility of being there longer than he should. As he prepared to say something about the time, he noted that Elizabeth had her right hand under her chin while staring at some point, but she was not looking at any particular object. In fact, she seemed to be far away, as if her thoughts were focusing on something she wanted to decipher. Her gaze was steady, brows furrowed in the manner of someone who was thinking hard about something and reaching deep conclusions.

"What's the matter, Elizabeth? Would you like to share with me what is going through you head?"

Snapping out of her trance, Elizabeth looked at Frank in a sharp way, as if knowing she was about to share with him a somewhat different perspective of his own story, a perspective that probably only an outsider who was free from any emotional attachments could provide.

"Frank, have you realized the extremes that you lived through during that year of your life? Precisely within a twelve-month period, you came out of a situation of total inactivity to another of intense agitation, from the absence of goals to another where you had a focus, a target to pursue. You went from the depths of spirituality to the lack of prayer and to physical body worship. You went from a family environment to complete loneliness and from no routine to the stiff schedules of the army. But none of this compares to the fact that you were exposed to two completely different types of leadership in such a short period of your life. One seems to be the exact opposite of the other. Have you stopped for a moment to think about all this?"

Frank remained silent looking at Elizabeth, totally surprised by her observations. Since Benedict, he had not found anyone else who would hear him with such care and devotion. She not only had listened attentively to every word that was said but had also thought about it and now questioned him, making him think about his own life in a way that he had not yet done, looking at his experiences from an entirely new angle. He was amazed at her intelligence and articulation.

"No, Elizabeth, I had not thought about it that way. Only now, with your comments, do I realize how my life had swung to extremes in so many ways and in such short period of time. And actually I cannot draw very well what kind of effect this may have had."

"Of course not. That's usually the case. We are so emotionally involved with things that happen to us that we just don't think about them. Would you like to explore that a little more?"

Elizabeth's question sounded almost like an invitation to dance, and Frank did not hesitate to accept it. Elizabeth then asked, "Okay, let's talk a little about the issue of goals and objectives. It is impossible not to remember the exercise that Benedict did with you, with the stones being thrown into the bucket. What correlation can you make between the exercise and this period of your life?"

Frank made a brief silence and mentally transported himself to that moment and tried to make the analogy that Elizabeth was asking.

"Well, I seemed to know exactly where the bucket was. My goal was to get into the best physical shape as possible to get rid of Dixon and be able to fight for my country. I would go to sleep and would wake up thinking about it. That was the only focus of my life."

"Hm…only focus…you slept and woke up thinking about it. If you hear someone else saying these words, what would you think about such person?"

Frank was surprised again. What Elizabeth was trying to do was very clear. She already had her perceptions, but she was seeking to have Frank coming to his own conclusions. Frank did not have to think too long to respond and with a low voice and an expression somewhat ashamed, said, "That this person is obsessed. It is very clear now. I had an obsession."

"Exactly. This leads me to the next pair of extremes. Before going to the army, you lived a moment of deep spirituality, but apparently that changed radically. Was there any influence of your obsession on this change?"

Again the answer was obvious. Frank felt like someone was turning on the lights of a dark room.

"Yes, Elizabeth, of course. By allowing such obsession to take control of me, I left space for nothing else in my life. After a given point of this obsessive quest to get rid of Dixon, I quit praying, quit meditating, and ended up totally drifting away from God, to the point of never reconnecting. I never again went to a mass, never again opened my mother's Bible, and never again took care of my inner garden."

Suddenly the energy was heavy in the room, and now Frank was the one who had his eyes fixed, staring at the wall. Without thinking too much about the words out of his mouth, he said in a low voice, "My God, how could I allow Dixon to affect me like that? I was such a fool."

Elizabeth allowed silence to endure a bit longer, since intuitively she sensed that Frank needed it. After a few more seconds of thinking, Frank turned back to Elizabeth with an expression that was still somewhat heavy, but encouraged her to keep going. She then proceeded with her questions.

"Now think a little about this bucket of yours, I mean, on those goals and objectives that had become an obsession. I remember that Benedict had said that you should be aware and make sure that the goals were really yours and not external goals of someone else. Were those goals really yours? Did you really feel aligned with them?"

"No. Not at all. I had and still have a real disdain for the war. This damn war that took all I had from me: my family, my health, my peace. I had never cared much for my fitness, and at that time it was all I wanted. In the end, to be in the best of my shape and to have a beautiful body in front of the mirror proved to be great illusions. Now both of those things are gone, and I am not even in good health conditions. After being dismissed from the army, I stopped caring about not only my spirit, but my body as well. This means that I have abandoned myself completely. And it is all because I pursued the wrong goals and objectives. How did I allow that to happen?"

Elizabeth was curious about the reasons for his dismissal, which he hadn't yet clarified, but did not allow that to distract her. She stopped for a moment to think about Frank's questioning and then answered his question with another question:

"When you think about Dixon and the kind of leadership that he exercised over you, what words come to your mind?"

In thinking about the sergeant and his persecution against him, Frank's expression changed, becoming even more serious, and his tone of voice became full of resentment.

"*Imbalance, foolishness, selfishness, arrogance, indifference, authoritarianism, lack of spirituality*, and of course, *obsession*."

"Yes. I felt the same about him. And when you think of Benedict, what comes to your mind?"

"The exact opposite: *balance, humility, spirituality, integrity, empathy*, and *dialogue*."

"And what did each of them bring to you?"

Frank's answer took a few seconds to come, but when it did, it came out slowly, as if it carried along many important conclusions.

"Exactly the same things. And that means I let myself be influenced by Dixon in the same way that I let myself be influenced by Benedict, and the results were also two extremes. With Benedict, I felt at peace, centered, connected with God. With Dixon, I felt unbalanced, disturbed, far from anything resembling spirituality. The more he hunted me down, the more obsessed I became, gradually forgetting everything else. I'm beginning to think that I have no personality."

Both laughed at the joke, but Elizabeth intervened quickly. "That's not it, Frank. I believe that each of them brought to you exactly what you needed in their respective times. So that's probably why you allowed the two of them to influence you so much. When Benedict came into your life, you were lost and in need of someone to help you find your own self. But when Dixon came, you needed a goal in life, and the goal of fighting in the war quickly occupied this space. As Dixon would not allow that to happen, you started competing with him and went on seeking your target with all your energy, and the result was that your goal became an obsession, unbalancing everything else."

Elizabeth was right. Benedict and Dixon had filled the emptiness that existed in his life in their respective moments.

Suddenly, he had a new thought that scared him. The same thing seemed to be happening with Elizabeth. Quickly she had occupied all the empty spaces of his life, and he should be careful so she would not turn into a new obsession. How to do that, he had no idea. But at that moment, he felt very happy to be there and to be having a deep conversation with her.

In need of some time to breathe, he excused himself to use the bathroom and left the room for a moment.

Leadership Is Learnt

When he returned, Elizabeth was in the kitchen and seemed to be moving in a flow, as if she was preparing something for supper. On the table, there was a notebook and a pencil. Frank looked at it and then to Elizabeth, with a face of someone who did not understand what was going on. Then she explained,

"I think you may have already realized of how a leader can positively or negatively influence his followers, right? While I'm preparing something for us to eat, I would like you to do a little exercise. I remember that Benedict said that there was a leader inside of you."

Frank had a small ironic smile on the corner of his lips, clearly demonstrating that he no longer believed in it. Elizabeth reacted to it immediately.

"Frank, don't laugh at it. I don't think he is wrong. You just haven't had the opportunity to exercise it yet, but you never know about tomorrow. One day you may be in this position, and you already have two very rich experiences in your luggage. Use them to your advantage. I would like you to use that paper and pencil and write down all that you have learned from the two forms of leadership you have just identified. This list can be very useful in the future. Write at the top of the sheet, 'To be a good leader, I…' and complete the sentence with things that you will do, or not do, so you become a good leader."

Frank looked at Elizabeth in disbelief. He really did not see the value in making such an effort. She then used the only argument that would apparently work at that time.

"Will you do this for me? It's all I am asking for."

Frank then replied with a smile of someone who knew he was being adorably manipulated. He sat down, took the pencil in his right hand, and began to write. When he finished, he had the following list in his hands:

To be a good leader I will…
- be humble and treat others with respect, never with arrogance.
- praise publicly and point out errors privately.
- seek to empower people by praising and reinforcing their qualities and strengths.
- treat other people's limitations as an opportunity to improve.
- constantly use dialogue as a way of understanding and helping people to progress.
- seek to be a great listener.
- always avoid the attitude of Mr. Know-It-All and being the only one to have all the answers.
- seek to serve and support people so they grow and become more than they were when I met them.
- try to always inspire through goals, objectives, and a vision of the future.
- admit to my mistakes and learn from them, so I can become better each day.
- never be indifferent to what is important for those around me.
- put myself in the shoes of other people to better understand, serve, and guide them.
- make people's success the biggest reason for my personal success.
- not expect perfection from anything nor anyone, for we are all imperfect.

- seek to be an example of ethics and morality, and above all, a good human being.

Rereading what he had just written, Frank could easily identify the points that came from the bad influence of Dixon and those who came from the good influence of Benedict and realized that Elizabeth was really right. Both experiences were very rich, but he still didn't see much value in preparing such list.

"Done. Shall I read it to you?"

"No, it's not necessary, Frank. Keep this list carefully, because I'm sure that one day, it will serve you. Your life will not be forever as it is now. I'm more interested in knowing if the exercise helped you."

"I think so. I can now understand more clearly how each of these leaders influenced me. But honestly I don't see how I can apply these principles in my life."

The pleasant smell of the hearty vegetable soup that Elizabeth prepared was already filling the air and sharpened Frank's appetite. While serving a generous portion in two bowls, Elizabeth asked, "Do you want to get married someday? Have a wife and children? Raise a family?"

Frank immediately forgot the pleasant smell of soup and stared at her, surprised by her question.

Elizabeth laughed at his expression and immediately clarified, "Relax and do not be so presumptuous. I'm not asking you to marry me. Just answer yes or no."

"Oh, what a disappointment, I thought you had finally made up your mind."

Both laughed at the unexpected situation that the question had created. Frank then thought for a moment and replied, "Yes, I believe so. Although this possibility seems so remote at this moment, after this bloody war is over and life returns to normal, I would like to start a family. Why do you ask?"

"Well, a family hold also needs to be a leader, don't you think? If you reread this list putting yourself in the role of a husband or father, would it help you in any way?"

Frank reread the list and could not stop thinking about his own father and how a simple list like that could have been useful to him, for he had fallen short in so many topics. He also thought about his mother and how she had played several times a leadership role in his life, guiding him and making sure that he would evolve in the best directions. He had never realized before, but his mother had been a great leader in his life. He looked at Elizabeth and consented, nodding with his head. She then asked another question:

"And when you return to work and have a social role, can this list be useful?"

"Elizabeth, even if I get a job, I don't think I would be in a position above other people anytime soon."

As she put the soup plates on the table, Elizabeth smiled and made a negative nod with her head.

"Frank, you don't need to be above anyone to be a good leader. Dixon was above you and had no idea what being a leader is. People confuse being a boss and being above someone with leadership."

Frank read his own list a third time and saw that Elizabeth was right once again. None of the attitudes and behaviors on the list required him to be in a boss position to be exercised. Gradually he came to the conclusion that being a leader was much more a matter of attitude toward life than a position or hierarchical ranking.

"And finally, Frank, let's talk about the most important of all leaderships, which is the leadership over your own self. As we concluded, you have easily allowed both Benedict and Dixon to have influence over you, for there was a great void in your life. Wasn't there also an absence of self-determination? Have you ever stopped to think that maybe you have to be your own leader? That you have to be the first person to watch your thoughts and give a direction to yourself? Just think about it, Frank. Benedict provided you with real treasures of wisdom and spiritual teachings. Why would it be that you did not apply them on a more permanent basis in your life? It certainly wasn't because you couldn't remember them, since you just repeated them to me in detail. The perception I have is that you do not put them into practice in a definitive way simply because you refuse to take responsibility over your own life and in being your own leader. As you allow others to occupy this space in your life, it causes other priorities to eventually prevail. Do you understand what I mean? If you add the principles and philosophies that Benedict taught you with the personality traits of the leader in you and apply them for your own benefit, God knows how far you can go. In addition, all the people who are around you will benefit—children, wife, friends, co-workers. Yes or no?"

Frank looked at Elizabeth with utter bewilderment. He had never thought about it in such perspective, nor had looked at himself as his first and most important leader in his life. He had always looked outside, to others, seeking guidance and direction. First to his parents, then to his teachers, then to the priest, to Benedict, and sad to say, to Dixon himself, being at the mercy of their limitations as leaders and of their somewhat short-sighted, and many times biased, views of the world and life itself. And when these leaders presented themselves as imperfect, he would get frustrated and would put on them the full responsibility of his own mistakes and limitations. This attitude was almost an excuse to avoid taking responsibility over things that would happen to him.

He reviewed his list a fourth time and realized he was doing a lame job as his own leader, never praising himself or seeking to strengthen himself mentally, treating his limitations as if they were incurable diseases, never seeking to inspire himself or defining targets and personal goals.

While savoring his first spoon of soup, Frank turned to Elizabeth and asked, "Okay, and all this knowledge about leadership, where did it come from? It could not be learned by caring for the wounded soldiers in a crowded infirmary."

Elizabeth chuckled and replied, "You would be surprised to know the number of times one has to exercise leadership in a crowded infirmary. But obviously it was not there. It was not only you who had your own gurus in life, good or bad, my dear Frank. My father taught me many things, including leadership. He was the kind of man who took the lead at everything—at the school where he taught, at the neighborhood associations, at book clubs, at church. He always made sure to tell me that, contrary to what many people think, a person is not born a leader. Leadership is something you learn, mainly through exercising it. The key things to be a good leader is taking care of people and treating them with respect, being a good example, being a good listener, being reliable, having an enthusiastic and supportive attitude towards life, and those are all things that can be learned and are not necessarily born with us. He was a good man. He did not deserve an end as tragic as he had."

A gloomy silence fell at the dining table as Frank realized that Elizabeth's eyes were watering. The war had also been hard on her. He then made an effort to change the direction of the conversation and said, "I have not yet told you how my story with Dixon ends. Do you want to know?"

Wiping the tears that barely came out with the tips of her right index and thumb, Elizabeth changed her expression, and as she normally did for the moments she was listening to Frank, she also changed position, turning herself to him. She not only heard with her ears. She literally listened to him with her whole body.

"I'm all ears."

Hearing her response and noticing such level of focus and attention, Frank thought, *Of course, you are.*

The Great Opportunity

THE MONTH OF AUGUST 1940 brought a significant change to the stages of the war. With the Soviet Union annexing Estonia, Latvia, and Lithuania, and Germany finalizing its occupation of France, everyone wondered which would be the next moves of these two great powers. Meanwhile, Italy seized the moment of weakness of the enemies and invaded southern France and the British territories in Africa, such as Somalia. Although it was quite clear that the invasion of England was the next step on its expansionist plans, Germany could not find a favourable situation to make such a bold move. The weather in the English Channel did not help, and the British supremacy in the air and at sea was a definitive factor for the Nazis to postpone the invasion plans indefinitely, so they decided to change their strategy for air strikes. Later that month, they began an aerial blitz, bombing London and other major cities in Britain, bringing panic and despair to all.

During the months of September and October, the bombings continued almost daily, and Frank couldn't sleep peacefully anymore. He was too far from London to truly know what was happening, but from that moment on, he no longer received news from his parents, and that would get him in agony. The information that would get to him was limited and distorted, and nobody could tell for sure the neighborhoods and localities that were impacted the most, but everyone spoke of thousands of civilian casualties. All Frank wanted was to talk to his parents on the phone and know if they were well, but unfortunately, it was impossible at that time.

In Africa, the situation kept deteriorating each day, with Italy invading another English territory, Egypt, and from one moment to another, all that could be heard through the corridors was that this would very likely be the next destination for the soldiers in training. For Frank, that seemed like a fresh breath of air. He would fight after all. It would not be in Europe as he had imagined and dreamed, but at least he would get away from there and probably from the unpleasant company of Dixon, who was not happy with the change of plans at all. His ambition to fight in France like his father was far from being fulfilled.

By late October, the confirmation came. New platoons were being selected to head to Africa. The target in particular was yet to be announced, as it was considered to be confidential information. But Frank did not care. He could hardly wait for the chance to show his great physical condition, get selected, and be able to get out of the paralysis he was in.

On October 29th, Dixon then announced that there would be a selective exercise that night. It had to be in the dark, because the plan was to train soldiers who could be launched with a parachute at strategic points in night attacks. As other officials from the paratrooper group would also be looking at the activities, the selection would not depend only on Dixon, making Frank very motivated. This was a great opportunity.

The exercise would be a kind of competition in a course of obstacles, where a group of soldiers would have to race against time. Those who finish the circuit with the best times would be selected.

When nightfall came, the temperature dropped significantly, and a strong wind began to blow, followed by a light rain. That would make the exercise more difficult and dangerous, since besides being made in the dark, the obstacles now would be wet, and the wind would destabilize every movement.

Frank had already put his uniform on and had just tied his boots when Dixon entered the dorm, walking at a slow pace toward him. Seeming to know exactly what was going on in the mind of his soldier, Dixon approached Frank, bowed, and said in his ear, "You will not pass this test. You will make a mistake, and I'll be there to point it out to the other observers."

He smiled ironically, turned his back, and walked away, whistling out the door.

Frank felt a surge of anger, and an even greater anxiety began to take over him. His heart rate rose, and his breath got wheezy. Soon came the call for everyone to gather at the exercise field, and he could barely control his nerves. Dixon's provocation had had its impact, and he no longer felt so sure of himself.

The wind was strong, and the rain, now more intense, soaked his face, his uniform, and his boots. Everything seemed to weigh twice as much. Darkness had dominated the exercise track, making it an even more frightening scenario.

Dixon and other observers were gathered beneath a tent and were ready with their watches, clipboards, and notepads.

Then they called the first group of soldiers, and the competition began. At each group that ended the circuit, the observers would gather, compare notes, and give the command to the next group.

Frank gradually realized that the sequence of soldiers being called didn't make any sense. It did not follow an alphabetical or a registration number order. Apparently someone had prepared that list in order to leave him to the end.

As time went by, the exercise track was getting in worse condition, and Frank's uniform was getting heavier with so much water.

Finally the last group of soldiers was called, and Frank was in it. He had waited almost an hour in the rain, which was now stronger than ever, and his legs were already feeling somewhat tired.

He aligned himself with three other soldiers and looked straight ahead to the obstacles that awaited him. He had already gone through this circuit many times before, but never at night. He ran the whole sequence in his mind and planned every action. He would have to crawl under wires, cross through poles, constantly alternating directions, climb ropes, go through tubes, scale a wall, and at the end, run to the finish line through a field that was now pure mud because of the heavy rain.

As he walked the circuit in his mind one last time, he got distracted and missed the starting gunshot, leaving half a second behind his competitors.

Frank arrived at the first hurdle three steps behind the others and then began a desperate race to catch up. He crawled under the wires, jumped over obstacles, ran around the poles, and when he reached the middle of the circuit, thanks to his excellent physical condition, he was already fighting for second place.

He followed a maddening pace, knowing that he would have to finish first if he wanted to leave no doubts behind that he gathered the conditions to be selected. He arrived at the final hurdle just a step behind the first place. He would now have to climb a wall about fifteen feet tall and come down on the other side by a rope. From there on, he would only have to run through the mud up to the finish line. Frank reached the top of the wall at about the same time as his competitor. He placed his body on the other side of the wall and sought the rope with both hands while he threw himself down in the darkness. However, the speed at which he launched himself over the wall was a little beyond the ideal, and the rope, being very wet with the rain, slipped through his fingers. Frank felt a shiver down his spine when he saw himself in free fall. The fifteen feet to the ground took an eternity, and in a desperate attempt to break the fall, he tried to place his right leg in a less unfavorable angle, but it was too late.

What was heard then was terrifying—a tremendous crack, a strong fall, and a cry of pain echoed throughout the training camp.

Frank, still dizzy from the impact of his body against the ground, only had time to take a breath to scream in pain a second time. Again, that agonizing sound was heard by all, and several soldiers started searching where the screams were coming from amid the darkness.

Finally, the first flashlights of the officers who watched the exercises began to approach Frank, who was still screaming, feeling the worst pain that he had ever known. Lying with his belly up, he looked at the dark sky and felt the heavy rain drops on his face. He had the feeling that something really bad had happened. When the first flash of light finally reached him, he raised his neck and looked at his leg to see his tibia split open, hanging at an angle of ninety degrees. Then he looked desperately at the person holding the flashlight to ask for help. That was when he saw the face of Dixon with an ironic smile on his lips. It was the last thing he saw before losing his consciousness.

Grounded for a Long While

When Frank opened his eyes, he could not recognize where he was. He could only notice through the window located on the other side of the room, a typical light of early morning hours. It seemed that the day was just beginning. Slowly he regained consciousness and gradually could better assess where he was and how he was.

The first thing he noticed was his right leg casted almost to the groin, being sustained upward by a huge support. He also had a bandage on his right arm and one in the head, just above the right eye. He could then remember the fifteen-feet-high fall, the unbearable pain, and the terrible picture of his leg hanging by meat and skin, with a bone stretched out from it.

He looked around and saw that he was in a huge hospital room with three other empty beds. His bed was the closest to the door, and at the other extreme of the room, there was just one window, which in that moment, allowed the light of the pale autumn sun to bring a heavy melancholy to the scene.

Little by little, he was also becoming aware of other pains in his body. The fall was worse than he imagined. But of course the main concern was his leg, since surely the recovery would not be quick. His hopes of going to Africa were slowly fading, which also meant that once again he would not get rid of Dixon. He then remembered the expression of victory on Dixon's face when he saw him there, lying on the mud, writhing in pain. He felt a deep hatred and was afraid even to think of seeing him again. Then he began to imagine the moment the door would open and Dixon would come through it in triumph to tell him that he had won and that he would not be going anywhere.

Just when he was nurturing these hateful thoughts and his teeth were beginning to press on each other with rage, the door opened. Frank looked at it with an angry expression, ready to send Dixon to hell, but was caught by surprise when a short and quite rounded female silhouette entered the room.

The nurse, a woman already in her fifties, was shocked to see Frank awake and with such expression on his face. "Good morning, you should still be asleep. The amount of anesthetics and tranquilizers that you got injected for the surgery on your leg was a dose enough to put an elephant to sleep. But you seem quite restless. Is everything okay?"

Frank was now beginning to understand everything. He had to be sedated so they could operate his leg. Calming down his feelings, which were obviously out of context, he replied, "Yes, nurse, I'm fine. Could you tell me where I am and what happened?"

"Of course. You should feel a bit disoriented since you've been asleep for quite a while. Right after your fall, you were taken, still unconscious, to the infirmary of the training camp, but due to the severity of the trauma, they soon realized that they would not have the required conditions to take care of you there. Then they brought you here, to the military hospital in Exeter where a specialized medical team was called to assist you. When the medical team finally arrived yesterday morning, you started to wake up, so you were sedated and fell asleep again. After much analysis and discussions on how to fix your leg, you were operated last night, and the surgery was a success. It will take a long recovery, but your leg will be fine. It was a long and very complicated procedure, so that is why we gave you such a strong dose of anesthetics and tranquilizers, which made you sleep so much. Actually, I expected you to sleep even more. You must be very hungry and thirsty, aren't you?"

Frank had not yet noticed, but now that the nurse mentioned water and food, he realized he had a quite dry mouth and a disturbingly empty stomach. He made a positive nod with his head, and soon an apple juice was offered to him. The nurse said she would get some food and would soon return. Before she left, in fear of receiving the uncomfortable visit from Dixon, Frank asked her a favor, "Nurse, if any soldier or officer from my squad comes to see me, could you please say that I cannot receive any visitors? At the moment I'm still not feeling well enough to receive anyone."

The woman looked at Frank and agreed to the request, but before leaving, she said, "If I were you, I would not worry much about that. I learned from the general practitioners who assisted you with first aids in your training camp that after the completion of the exercise you participated in, the selected soldiers and the sergeant in command received immediate orders to depart to Africa. They left at dawn today. At this time, they must be at sea. I'll be back soon with your food."

Frank could not believe what he had just heard. Dixon was gone after all and had left him behind immobilized, alone, unable to fight for his country, and still with a long recovery to go through.

When he saw himself alone in the room, he thought of his parents and brother and felt again the desperation of not knowing if they were alive or dead. He also thought of Benedict. Where was that old well-intentioned man who tried in every way to prepare him for the difficulties of war and adulthood? His teachings today seemed so far away. He thought about himself and how his life had changed so much in such short period of time. He was about to celebrate another birthday, it would soon be Christmas again, and everything led him to believe that he would spend it alone and in a hospital bed.

He could not avoid the tears from dripping down his face. Not even the wise words of Benedict about how we never know where the rock bottom really is could have prepared him for such a setback.

When the nurse finally arrived with his food, his crying was already intense, and she had to take a moment to calm him down before giving him something to eat.

Frank then received the doctor's visit, which confirmed his suspicions. It would take sixty days of immobilization before they could start the physiotherapy work, which could take another two months. They gave him more drugs that knocked him out again. Before falling asleep, he thought one more time about his family and Benedict. He would look for them as soon as he was able to.

The Rock Bottom

As expected, Frank spent his birthday and the year-end holidays in a hospital bed, which he only left in January 1941. While he was there, crippled, he had the opportunity to pay closer attention to the news of the war and could follow the disagreements between Russia and Germany take shape until the Germans decided to break relations with the fearful neighbor. The bombings in major English cities continued almost daily, but the immense destruction caused by them seemed to do little harm to the morale of the British people, who followed their daily lives as best as they could, determined to overcome their difficulties and their enemy.

The fracture healing took a little longer than expected, and the physical therapy work only began by late February and went through the months of March and April. During this time, Frank could follow the Germans regain the territories lost by the Italians in Africa and dominate Eastern Europe, occupying Yugoslavia and Greece. The Nazis were now almost sovereign in continental Europe, with only the Russians left to be conquered.

The bombings into the main British urban centers continued, and London remained the main target. Frank was now six months without any news from his parents, and his concern grew greater each day.

When the month of May arrived, Frank could already walk with ease and was discharged to resume his work at the training camp.

There he received the welcome of a new sergeant, who seemed to be quite young and inexperienced, and underwent further tests with the same doctor who took care of him six months ago, when he had suffered the fall and the bone fracture. Both seemed quite skeptical about Frank's recovery and would frequently talk in low voices, as if they already had an opinion on what they should do.

During the first exercises, Frank was always behind the new recruits, since he was short of breath and a little over his best weight. The six months of inactivity began to take its toll. To make matters worse, he still limped of his right leg while running, which only reinforced the opinions of the new sergeant.

After a month of training, his situation had not improved much, and he then received the information that he would be dismissed. The training camp physician gave the news himself.

"Sorry, Private Farrow, but I do not think you will be able to survive in the battlefield against the Germans. We are doing this to protect you. In order not to let you completely helpless, I was able to approve a small salary, a kind of pension in reparation for the physical damages you have suffered during training. It is a very rare exception that shall last as long as the war lasts or until you get a job. We hope this will help you to keep up for a while. You are required to report whenever you get a job, so that the pension can be discontinued. In a few days, you will receive some coupons to withdraw your pension once a month."

The doctor looked at him sympathetically and gave him a pat on the shoulder as if trying to say that this would be the best for him. Then he turned to Frank again and said, "If I could give you one last piece of advice, stay away from large urban centers for a while. The Germans seem to be losing steam, and the bombings are decreasing, but they still exist. Everything suggests that they will be turning their attentions to Russia and then the situation should improve. You have the sergeant's permission to stay here until your first coupons arrive. Use this time to decide where to go. Then advise us of your new address to receive the coupons."

Frank felt desolate and disoriented with the dismissal and gladly accepted the time to think about what he would do. He needed to return to London to search for his parents, but feared the bombings. While waiting his coupons, he was told that the Germans in Libya had decimated all his former squad, including the officers. All were reported killed in combat, including Dixon.

On June 22nd, the Germans invaded Russia, and their attention would turn almost entirely to the battle fronts of Eastern Europe, no longer bombing Great Britain with the same intensity. The time for Frank to return home had arrived.

Taking advantage of a military convoy, he made his way to London and after almost a day's trip, changing from one method of transportation to another, he finally arrived at the south of the city. While passing through it, he struggled to hold back his tears. It was one thing to listen to the radio or read in the newspapers about the devastation of the bombings. It was another to see his semi-destroyed city with his own eyes.

When he finally arrived at Croydon, as he was passing through known streets and places, he began to really fear the worst. His old school was in ruins. The church that he used to attend was in pieces.

The more he approached his home, the worse it would get.

When he turned the corner of his old street, tears were already running down his cheeks. Few houses were still standing. When he finally arrived at his block, he could see that unfortunately his house was not one of them. It was totally destroyed.

He walked through the wreckage in search of some sign, some known object, but found nothing. Then he sat down on what was left of the wall of his room and wept copiously. He remembered the childhood games with his brother, Peter, in the backyard, the several birthday parties, his difficult adolescence, the disagreements with his parents, and finally the arrival of Benedict, which seemed now something so far away.

Then he noticed that someone was watching him from a distance and recognized an old neighbor. He went to her and asked about his parents. "I'm so sorry, Frank, but they were caught by surprise in one of the first bombings in October last year. They had no chance. The house has been left in ruins like this ever since. The looters have taken everything of use and value. There is nothing else left. I am so sorry, boy, but there's nothing for you here."

The hit was so hard that Frank sat down again on what was left of a wall. He did not have a home, he did not have a family, he did not have an occupation, nor did he have the health he used to have. He had nothing and no one and had no idea what to do from then on.

The neighbor, taking pity of the scene she witnessed, gave him the address of her sister who had a boardinghouse that was still working, located further north, near the center of London.

Armed with his first coupon and without any other option in sight, Frank then followed her advice and decided to temporarily rent a room, until he could figure out what he would do with his life.

After a few days cloistered in his room at the boardinghouse, he began to gradually feel depressed and decided to go out to think and to get to know the new neighborhood. That was when he found the Great Lion, a nice pub with friendly people where he would numb his pains with a lot of beer for the following year and a half. Without realizing it, he allowed his adverse situation to depress him more and more, taking control of him and totally dominating his life. He never looked for work, never made room for new friends except Albert, the owner and bartender of the Great Lion. He gave in to drinking and to loneliness in a definitive way. He had hit rock bottom.

A Matter of Point of View

In finishing his narrative, Frank felt relieved. He had finally had the opportunity to share with someone his entire story. He had shared with Elizabeth all he had lived through for the past four years—how he had gotten where he was now, how he had gone from one extreme to another in his life, how he had lost the thread, and how Benedict's teachings were lost along the way.

Then he turned to Elizabeth and saw that she had a look on her face that expressed both understanding and compassion. But until that moment, she had just listened to him. She had not shared with him any of her thoughts and opinions, which made him feel a little uncomfortable

Trying to get something out of her that could make him feel better about himself and his personal drama, he commented, "Do you understand now, Elizabeth, why I am where I am? Do you understand how life has been hard on me until this moment?"

Elizabeth remained in silence for a few more seconds, pondering over the best way to react to Frank's observation. He was obviously looking for some sympathy for all he had gone through, and this could not be denied to him. However, she also didn't want to be complacent with him, to avoid the risk of endorsing the fact that he had clearly given up fighting to improve his own life. After pondering for a few seconds, she replied, "Yes, Frank, I perfectly understand. Remember that I also lost my parents in the same way and had a hard time moving forward. But after a few weeks, I realized that, for some reason beyond my understanding, I escaped. I was not home at the time of the bombing. I was spared. That's when I realized that I could still be useful as a nurse, relieving the pain of others. God had spared me for a reason. I still had a purpose in my life."

That last remark reminded him one of Benedict's favorite quotes. "The purpose of life is a life of purpose." However, Elizabeth's response was not exactly what he was looking for. He expected her to feel pity about everything he had gone through, but her reaction made him somewhat bewildered. Thus, he argued, "Well, lucky you, my dear, for having a profession, a job, a purpose. After being discharged from the army and losing my family, I was left with nothing. I do not know what to do with my life. I was not so fortunate."

"Hm, you were not so fortunate. So that's how you see everything you went through. Would you allow me to offer you a slightly different angle?"

Frowning and not understanding what other angle could there be, he consented, making a slight nod. Elizabeth then continued, "Amongst all the various training centers that the army could choose for you, they ended up sending you to the furthest one from the major cities of England, cities that were being bombed almost daily. How many bombings have you experienced, Frank?"

"None. I only got to know about them through the radio and newspapers."

"Okay. So when the time came that you felt prepared to fight, you had a serious disagreement with your superior, who had decided to boycott you and did not send you to be defeated in Norway, nor to be humiliated in France, two situations in which you could even not return alive, correct?"

"Yes, I was not sent to these two battles, battles in which we were shamefully defeated."

Realizing that she was beginning to make her point, Elizabeth continued, "And then when you had your big chance to escape the tyranny of Dixon and go fight in Africa, you broke your leg and could not go. Soon after, you learned that the Germans exterminated the whole squad in battle, including Dixon. Isn't that true?"

"Yes, they were decimated. There was no one left."

"And finally, after drinking a few mugs more than you could handle, you fell, hit your head on the curb, was knocked unconscious in a temperature below zero, which certainly could get you killed of hypothermia, and was saved by the owner of the bar, then treated in one of the best military hospitals."

"Yes, I was saved by Albert and treated by you."

"Well, by my count so far, your life has been spared by divine intervention four times. On top of that, the army opened a rare exception that I've never heard before and decided to indemnify you for the broken leg in training, giving you a pension that allows you to pay a room, food, and each consumed beer at the Great Lion. Would that be a good summary of your situation?"

By this time, Frank gave up answering the questions of Elizabeth, who nevertheless wasted no time in continuing. "Look, Frank, we can always choose to see a glass of water filled up to the middle as half full or half empty. The decision is ours. From the perspective that I have just shared with you, God is actually protecting you from many things. We cannot understand his methods, but the fact is that God brought you here, safe and sound, in position to help many people who are in worse situation than you. I understand all your drama and how your path up to here was not really a bed of roses, but I believe that you have allowed this tragedy to become even bigger than it is and take control of everything. Most of the times in our lives, we have a choice. We are our decisions, Frank. One way or another, after all that happened, you chose to enclose yourself in your room at the boardinghouse. You have chosen to hide from life behind a mug of beer. One day you will also need to make the decision of unhide yourself from behind the beer mugs and begin to change all this, don't you think? For me, it is very clear that God has a plan for you. If he didn't, he wouldn't have saved you from a tragic fate on four occasions. You may not know yet what your major purpose in life is, but I am pretty sure that it exists."

Frank, now a little upset, silently listened to everything that Elizabeth was saying. As he was getting prepared to argue back to her once again, Elizabeth kept talking.

"Between the time that things happen in our lives and our reactions to them, there is a moment when we make our choices, Frank. If we choose not to react to adverse situations, we are not being responsible for our lives. If I could give you some advice, I would say that what you need is to take some responsibility for your own life. The word *responsibility* is actually the combination of two other words. To have responsibility is to have the ability to respond. Stop to think for a moment and analyze how is your ability to respond to all that happened to you and start getting out of passivity. Resume action, Frank. Everything could begin to change. Start, for example, with the decision to stop drinking. That alone will make a big difference."

That last comment hit him differently. Not only she did not show pity over him, but she was also asking him to start reacting and touched the wound of his addiction. He wanted to tell her that since the day he met her, he hadn't had a single mug of beer. He had only returned to the Great Lion with her to eat and drink tea. But he was too baffled by the things he had just heard. He preferred then, as usual, to escape from the uncomfortable situation. He looked at the wall clock, stood up, and said, "Thank you, Elizabeth, for the great day we spent together, the food, the tea and the advices. But I think it's getting late, and I must go."

Realizing what was happening, Elizabeth also rose. But instead of walking toward Frank or to the exit door, she went the other way, to the door of her bedroom. Frank followed her with his eyes, not really understanding what was happening.

She then stopped at the bedroom door with a seductive expression, a warm smile, and a look in her eyes that Frank until then had not seen and which sprung on him a strange sensation, as if there was a cold feeling in his womb.

She then said, "We're talking about choices, Frank. Are you sure that leaving is the best option at this time?"

She then went into the bedroom and left Frank alone in the living room.

Open-mouthed and with his heart rate a bit altered, he chuckled nervously and looked at the two doors, one to the apartment exit and the other to Elizabeth's bedroom. He didn't have to think much to come to the conclusion of which door he preferred in that moment.

He walked slowly toward the bedroom where he found Elizabeth lit only by the light of a lamp. She was sitting on the bed leaning on her pillow, with arms at her sides and bent legs crossed at the ankle height. He needed to control his breathing and his emotion, for that was one of the most beautiful sights he had ever witnessed in his life.

He closed the bedroom door quietly and thought, *Well, Frank, apparently your luck has finally changed.*

Back to the Great Lion

When Frank awoke the next day, Elizabeth was no longer at home, but she had left a note on the table saying, "I was happy with your choice. It was a wonderful night. I left some tea and bread for you. Eat something before you leave. I have to work. Take good care of yourself."

He then returned to bed and relived in his head every moment of the night before. He could hardly believe what had happened and had difficulty understanding the sudden change in Elizabeth, but regardless of what had made her change her attitude, one thing was clear in his mind: February 28th would never be a day like any other in his memory.

After a few long minutes in trance, he decided it was time to go home. He took a quick shower, had a bite to eat, and went out toward the train station. He decided he should return to Elizabeth's house that night because he needed to better understand what was going on, since he could not make sense to such a sudden change from one day to the other. When he arrived at his boardinghouse, he began to empty his jacket pockets as he always did. That was when he found in the inner pocket an envelope with a letter. Quickly, he recognized the handwriting of Elizabeth.

The letter read,

Dear Frank,

I know you must be confused by everything that happened from yesterday to today; after all, I went from one extreme to another in such a short period of time, but soon you will understand me.

However, before explaining it all, I want to ask something of you. Please remain calm, because I'll make you a promise. I will be back! I swear that I will be back.

With the decreasing of the bombings in London, we almost don't get injured people in my hospital anymore, so my services are now needed elsewhere.

Three days ago, I was called on an emergency basis to serve as a nurse in a medical camp of the army in Africa. I will leave on a flight today. I will no longer return to my apartment. I waited in a cafe in front of my house for you to go, so I could return, pack my bags, and leave.

I'm going because I need to follow my purpose, which is to serve the wounded and the sick. That's my mission in life. That's what moves me forward. That's what makes me wake up every morning. But I go with a divided heart. I felt attracted to you from the first day we talked at the infirmary, and as the days went by, I was infatuated not only by you but by your life story, by all that you learned from Benedict, and by this complicated time of yours. I'm sorry if I'm going to complicate things a bit more.

If at first I rejected you, it was out of fear. I thought I should not get attached even more to you and should not allow you to get attached even more to me. But when I was alone in my apartment that night, I realized that it was too late. I was already attached. So I decided to allow us to have that moment of love, which should serve us not as a reason for suffering due to our temporary separation, but as a motivation. For me, it will serve as such, since I now have someone to return to. And for you, I hope it will serve as an incentive to get out of this moment of paralysis.

Rebuild your life, Frank. Turn this game around. And wait for me, for I will be back. I promise.

Forgive me for communicating this to you by letter, but I feared that if I were to do it personally, it would be impossible for me to leave. I was a coward, I know, but it was the only way I found to be able to continue with this mission. Before saying goodbye, I want to give you one last suggestion. Try to recover all Benedict's teachings. You still have in your gifted memory the things you learned from him. And though I feel a little insane to suggest you this, continue with your search for the wise old man. You never know what Benedict actually meant by that. And while you don't find him, do the following exercise in times of doubt and distress. Always ask yourself, "What would Benedict do in this situation? What would he say to me?" Maybe this will help you to improve your ability to respond to the surprises that happen to us in life, such as this one that presents itself in this very moment. And please, Frank, stop drinking. I want to find you sober and healthy when I return, do you understand?

See you soon, Frank.

From someone who cares deeply about you,
Elizabeth

Once he finished reading Elizabeth's letter, Frank felt a sharp contraction in his stomach and had tears in his eyes.

He looked at the clock and thought that maybe it was already too late to try to stop her, as she did not even mention when or from where the flight would leave.

Even so, he decided to give it a try. He ran back to the station and took the first train back to Elizabeth's apartment, looking at the watch every minute. The tears no longer flowed, but the contraction in the stomach was still there.

He got off the train as a madman and ran as fast as his legs could carry him.

When he arrived at Elizabeth's apartment, he knocked at the door hastily and with a little more strength than he should. His heart was filled with hope when he heard footsteps and saw the doorknob turning. He then shouted, "Elizabeth!"

However, his face turned to disappointment when a lady opened the door and said, "No, sir. She has left for more than an hour. Can I help you with anything?"

Amid the disappointment and the lack of breath that he was still trying to recover, he asked, "Do you know where she went?"

"Yes, to the hospital where she works. From there, she will go straight to the airport with the other nurses. I am the owner of the apartment, and I came to do the inspection. It is a shame to lose Elizabeth. She has always paid me on time and is a great person."

The woman kept talking, but Frank was no longer listening. He said a quick thank-you, turned his back on her, and rushed back to the station, taking the first train toward the hospital.

When he arrived there, he discovered to his dismay that she had left half an hour before and that the plane was already waiting for them. He would never catch them.

Little by little, he accepted the fact that his efforts to reach Elizabeth were useless. She was gone. And by the recent experiences he had with Africa, he feared the worst. He feared she would never return, as it had happened to Dixon and his platoon mates.

He slowly made his way back home, upset and heartbroken. He had finally found someone who brought a new meaning to his life and that had motivated him to stand up again, to rebuild himself. And now she was gone.

He walked the streets of London for hours aimlessly, not caring where he was, until he felt weak, hungry, and thirsty. At that moment, he realized it was beginning to get dark. He had moved adrift almost all day.

He then returned to the boardinghouse, but as he got off the train, he took another direction. The Great Lion awaited him.

Time for a Life Change

As he opened his eyes the next morning, Frank had a tremendous headache and could barely remember how he had gotten back to his bed.

He tried to recap the previous night in his memory, but he could not. He didn't even remember paying Albert for the beers he had consumed.

While sitting on the bed, he could see Elizabeth's letter on the floor where he had left it the day before. He took it once again in his hands and reread it a few times, paying closer attention to the final paragraphs.

"Rebuild your life."

"Continue your quest for the wise old man."

"What would Benedict do in this situation?"

"Stop drinking."

These words continuously spun around in his head, especially the last request, because he would have already disappointed her on the first night.

He placed the letter over the desk and thought Elizabeth was right. If he wouldn't do something to change his life, he was soon to have a tragic ending. But he didn't know what to do. He didn't know what the first step should be. He no longer knew anyone who could offer him help, a job, and a chance to start over.

And then, as if by magic, a thought crossed his mind. What would Benedict do in this situation? He laughed at his thought and of how Elizabeth would still influence him, despite being already so far away. Then he tried to put himself in the place of his old grandfather and think with a calm and balanced mind. He tried to see the world as if he were old Benedict. But his head hurt so much, and his body felt so intoxicated that he could not go very far in this first attempt to fulfill Elizabeth's request.

He then missed Benedict's list of positive affirmations and his mother's Bible. The latter he still had, stored somewhere, but he could not remember where.

In desperation, he put his hands over his face, cried some more, but his head started to hurt even more, and he had to hold back his tears. He could not even cry at this point. Almost without thinking, he said, "God, where did I lose my path? Help me out of this hole. Get me out of this dead end."

He took a deep breath and remembered living a similar moment in an already distant past. He laughed at the irony of his remembrance and decided to get out of bed and take a long shower.

Coming from the bathroom, he noticed that a sealed letter had been thrown under his door. He found that to be quite odd, since he did not use to receive anything from anyone by mail except his army coupons. He asked himself, "Another letter? The one from yesterday wasn't enough? What other emotions would this one reserve for me?"

He bent down and saw that the letter was a stamped envelope saying, "Bread & Joy Farm."

"Bread & Joy? My God, I haven't heard of that name for so long. Could it be news from Benedict?"

He opened the envelope hastily and saw that the letter had been typed. The sender and the content could not be more surprising. The letter was from his brother, Peter.

When he realized that the letter was from his brother, he could not hold his excitement and screamed in joy, "He is alive. My brother is alive."

Although his relationship with his older brother had always been somewhat distant, he was still his brother. The joy he felt was indescribable.

In the letter, Peter told that he had been severely wounded in Africa, and therefore he was dismissed. He had returned home, but found only ruins and learned that their parents had died. Peter also said that he came to know of his whereabouts through the same neighbor who had suggested him the boardinghouse, but had no luck in finding him there.

Of course, I am always at the Great Lion, thought Frank.

As he did not find anyone else, Peter decided to return to the farm where he was born in search of relatives who could support him. For the lack of available labor, as all physically fit men were at war, he had managed to get an administrative job at the farm, and he was happy there. Finally, he said they still needed help and invited him to also go to Bread & Joy, as he could work and be away from possible bombings that could still occur. He said goodbye by saying that he prayed to God that the letter would get to Frank's hands and that he eagerly awaited him.

Frank held the letter in his hands for a long time and pondered the invitation. He no longer had anything that would keep him there, and the departure of Elizabeth had left him in a deplorable state. He thought for a moment of the possible return of Elizabeth, but he dodged that thought. This could be months away, if it would ever happen at all. And even if she would come back, what guarantees were there that she would really look for him? The fears of suffering and disillusion were simply enormous and unbearable.

He then looked around him, and all he saw was a humble boardinghouse room, a tiny desk with a few papers all messed up, a closet with a few pieces of clothing already well-worn and poorly maintained, a bed that smelled of sweat, and a nightstand with an old alarm clock that he rarely needed to use.

He did not have an occupation that could make him feel useful, and with the absence of Elizabeth, chances were that later that same day, he would be back to the Great Lion.

He then looked at the small suitcase, which rested forgotten on the top of the wardrobe. The same he brought with him since the day he left home to present himself to the army. Then he remembered that his mother's Bible was still in there, from where it had never left since that episode with Dixon. That suitcase represented the only link he had to a past that today, did not seem so bad. In there, all his belongings would quickly fit, and he would be ready to go in a few minutes.

Frank then took both letters, one in each hand. One represented to him a painful loss with a promise of an unlikely return to be fulfilled, and the other waved with the possibility of a new beginning with a family member in a place where no one knew him. No one there would know of his failures, his addictions, and his shames.

But beyond all this, he had a strong feeling that his move to Bread & Joy would bring back the right environment to rebuild himself emotionally and spiritually. He could again focus on his spiritual development and rescue Benedict's teachings. He would have the opportunity to try to be centered again, to balance himself, rebuild his self-esteem, and get rid once and for all of his drinking addiction, which was evidently leading him to a sad end. And deep inside, he nurtured a small hope that he could still find old Benedict, who would certainly help him in all these objectives.

The move to Bread & Joy suddenly took the shape of a great opportunity, a perfect new beginning.

After a few minutes pondering, it did not take him long to come to the conclusion that this was what he needed—a fresh start in every possible way.

He stood up abruptly, threw into the small suitcase all that he still valued, including the letter from Elizabeth, took one last look at his humble little room, and stepped out.

He paid to the landlord of the boardinghouse the month he still owed and also left with her the envelope he had received from his brother with some extra money, asking her to forward him the next army coupons as well as any other correspondence that would arrive, and left.

But before going, he decided to pass quickly by the Great Lion, where he paid the beers from the night before and said goodbye to his only friend Albert, sharing with him the address of his destination.

How ironic. When your only friend is the bar owner, this is really a sign that it's time to change your life, he thought.

Then he left the Great Lion and paused for a moment on the sidewalk. He took a deep breath and began his walk toward the train station, saying, "Bread & Joy, here I come. I'm going back to my roots."

His new journey into the unknown had begun, and new surprises awaited him.

Part III
Paths That Meet Again

Welcome to Bread & Joy

THE NIGHT WAS FALLING ON the dusty roads of the county of Lincolnshire when Frank finally could see the entrance of the farm. Despite leaving relatively early from London, it took him all day to get to his destination, first because he had to wait a few hours for his train to depart and then for the fact that his unannounced arrival had surprised Peter. Although quite happy with the news, Peter was a bit embarrassed over the phone when he asked Frank to be patient until he could get someone to pick him up at the station.

Frank still didn't fully understand why Peter wasn't able to personally welcome him. After all, they hadn't seen each other for a few years, but he decided to put that aside and not create resentment right upon his arrival. He would try to understand his reasons later when they meet.

When the small truck that fetched him arrived at the main entrance of the farm, Frank could see an imposing gate about twelve feet high, made of shiny and twisted metal with a coat of arms in the center of each side carrying symbols not familiar to him. Above it, connecting the two huge pillars that supported the gates, he could see a large arch with the words, "Welcome to Bread & Joy."

A strange feeling invaded his chest, since despite being born there, he did not feel any kind of identity with that place. He had no memory of his childhood that would help him create some sort of connection to it. He really felt in strange lands.

Lost in his thoughts and almost without noticing, he muttered, "Bread & Joy, what a name for a farm."

The driver, a man already of some age, who until that point was fulfilling his task in complete silence, decided to explain. "It's a name that comes from a distant past. Almost a century. They say it was given by the grandparents of the current owners. Or better said, the ladies who now own it, since the only ones left are their granddaughter and her two daughters. They believed that in this farm, they would work to earn their daily bread, but they would also live in joy and would be very happy. Hence, the name."

Only at that moment, Frank realized that he had not been very courteous with his traveling companion. He had spent over an hour in silence thinking of Elizabeth, as he had done throughout the entire trip, trying to suffocate in his chest a terrible pain. He had only experienced something similar before when he left home. A pain of separation and loss that was almost unbearable. He sought to alleviate such pain by distracting himself with the conversation.

"That is quite interesting. Now that you explained it to me, I've come to like the name. And my apologies if I haven't properly introduced myself. I'm Frank, Peter's brother, and I'm coming to Bread & Joy by his invitation for me to restart my life. I was dismissed from the army after breaking my leg and could not find work in London. What about you, what is your name?"

"My name is Carl, and I've lived here for many years. I do all kinds of light duties. Due to my age, I can no longer deal with the heavy lifting. Welcome, Frank! And I'm sorry for your leg. At least it wasn't something more tragic."

Frank didn't quite understand such comment. After all, for him to break a leg so violently was tragic enough, but he decided not to question it.

"Carl, thanks for picking me up at the station. I still don't understand why Peter wasn't able to meet me there personally. Was he too busy?"

The truck was already approaching the huge mansion that served as the main farmhouse, and Carl chose not to answer Frank's question.

When they finally parked, Carl turned to Frank and said, "You'll soon understand why he wasn't there personally. I'll take you to him. Come with me."

Frank picked up his suitcase from the back of the truck and followed Carl, who would already show some difficulty in walking as he made his way around the side of the mansion. Apparently he was looking for a door located at the back.

The sun had already set, but despite the low light, Frank could see in detail an old dark painted house with peaked roofs. By the number of windows, it appeared to have many rooms, but for the lack of a better maintenance, it also showed that it had lived better days.

As they passed by the kitchen window, the smell of food being fixed made Frank remember he had not eaten much all day and was very hungry, but the anxiety of meeting his brother again soon made him forget his empty stomach.

When they reached the back of the mansion, Frank noticed a second building, separated from the first by about twenty meters. It was a smaller house with only one floor, also of angular roofs to avoid the accumulation of snow in the winter, and with four or five windows, all much smaller than the ones he had seen in the big house.

Upon entering the front door of this second house, Frank could see that it was a combination of workplace and lodging, since what could be called the entrance room was actually a kind of a reception, having to the right side two half-opened doors that exposed two bedrooms with beds and wardrobes, a door further down that seemed to lead to a bathroom, and to the left, a larger and more imposing door that was wide open showing what seemed to be a huge office.

When he entered through this door, he could then confirm his suspicion, as he passed by a large hall with four desks, two on each side, which only one seemed to be in use. At the back, near the left side, there was another door that was closed. Hanging at its center, there was a small sign saying, "Management."

Carl stopped about five feet from that door in the back, pointed to it, and extended his hand to say goodbye to Frank, who returned the gesture and thanked him for his services.

When he was finally by himself, Frank turned to the closed door, took a deep breath, raised his right hand, and knocked three times very lightly. The familiar voice of Peter responded immediately and asked him to come in.

On opening the door, Frank saw his brother, who was well dressed in formal attire sitting behind a huge desk positioned almost at the center of a spacious office that had two chairs for visitors. Behind him there was a huge bookcase that went from wall-to-wall and from the ground to the ceiling.

Impressed, Frank opened his mouth and eyes in utter amazement and not holding his excitement, strolled around, saying, "Look at all this. This is amazing, Peter. I never thought you were doing so well!"

Then he turned to his brother and asked, "Aren't you going to get up and give a big hug on your little brother?"

Then with some effort, Peter made a motion with his arms, turned his wheelchair sideways, and came out from behind the desk, exposing the right leg amputated to the thigh height. He then moved toward Frank, stopped, opened his arms, smiled wide, and said, "I'm glad you came. Welcome to Bread & Joy, Frank."

Peter's Story

FRANK TOOK A FEW SECONDS to absorb the shock from what he had just seen. Suddenly it was clear to him why Peter did not pick him up personally. He did his best not to express pity, but he lacked words to say what he felt at that moment. The only thing that he could elaborate was, "I'm so sorry, Peter."

Noticing Frank's embarrassment and the sadness in his eyes, Peter tried to ease the situation, "I'm fine, Frank. At least I'm alive. Sit down and tell me a little bit about you."

In settling down in his seat, Frank gave Peter a summary of his life story since he had left Croydon to join the army, but he preferred to omit Elizabeth. He was not ready to talk about her yet.

When his turn came, Peter said he fought on several fronts of the war, first in France until the retreat from Dunkirk, then in Egypt, Algeria, and Libya.

In all these fronts, he had not only fought but had also helped in carrying out administrative functions such as control of stocks of ammunition, food, uniforms, medicines, and coordinating logistics activities so they could receive more supplies of such important items in times of war. The fact that he had finished high school and had worked in a factory in such functions had helped to differentiate him from the others and to win the preference of the high commanders to perform such selective tasks.

When he was in Libya at the end of the previous year, his camp was attacked by surprise by the Germans, and a grenade fell close enough to throw him far away, destroying his right leg and really hurting the other, which could be saved but still wasn't strong enough to hold him standing so he could move around using crutches.

He was saved by a few soldiers who were leaving in retreat and took him to another English camp. After receiving first aids, he was taken to a small village where the Allies kept a secret hospital so he could be properly medicated and cared for. Given the severity of his injuries, they put him on the first convoy available to the nearest port and from there, he returned to England by ship with other injured soldiers. During the whole trip, he was between life and death. He could not remember his arrival as he was completely unconscious and keeping himself alive by a thin thread. He remembered only regaining consciousness when he was already in a hospital in the region of Dover.

It took him three months to recover and get out of bed. He was then released from his military duties and returned home, but there was nothing left waiting for him in Croydon. He asked about his family in the neighborhood, and then he discovered that Frank had been there and someone had recommended him a boardinghouse. The rest, Frank already knew.

Peter had decided to return to Bread & Joy not only to find work, but also for the sake of safety, in order to escape the bombings that had already taken his parents, but when he arrived there, he found the farm in complete decay. It was being cared for by a few women who did not know much about management and with the support of a few skilled laborers. His knowledge came in handy, and he was immediately admitted.

"Impressive, Peter. Your management skills must be excellent for them to put you in the position of farm manager."

Peter reacted to the remark with a somewhat ironic smile. Apparently there was something else there that had not yet been revealed. As he was opening his mouth to continue his narrative, a female voice echoed from the entrance of the house.

"Peeeter! Peter, where are you?"

Peter then winked at Frank and said, "I was only responsible for inventory, purchasing, and transportation. Prepare yourself to meet the real reason for my promotion to the position of farm manager."

He then directed his voice to the door and yelled out, "I am here, my love."

Within seconds, a woman appearing to be about thirty-five, somewhat overweight, and not at all attractive walked through the door. Her high-quality clothes, although stylish, were already showing evident signs of wear and tear.

She saluted Frank somewhat hastily and went straight to where Peter was. She kissed him passionately on the mouth to the point of making Frank feel a bit uncomfortable. She then finally began asking, "Honey, aren't you coming for dinner?"

Peter then went on to make the introductions.

"Barbara, this is Frank, my brother whom I have already mentioned to you a few times. I'll hire him on the farm to make the functions that were once mine: purchasing, inventory, and transport coordination. I'll train him so soon enough he will be performing these tasks smoothly. Frank, this is Barbara, the youngest daughter of Amanda, the owner of Bread & Joy, and therefore, one of your bosses."

When both realized who they were, they finally saluted each other properly, and Frank heard another "Welcome to Bread & Joy." Barbara then said that dinner was served and they were all waiting for them.

Peter said they needed a few more minutes, and that after eating, they would all go to the village pub to celebrate Frank's arrival.

She then left, and Peter was able to continue with his previous explanation.

"As soon as I started working here, I gained the trust of the farm owners, and I noticed that Barbara was always very affectionate towards me. I approached her, and we quickly started dating. Our relationship is getting very serious, and I am really considering marrying her. I know she is much older and not very beautiful, but considering the state I'm in, I cannot expect much more than that. Who else will want a cripple like me? We can be perfect for each other."

A quite uncomfortable silence hovered for a few seconds. Frank clearly noted that his brother was seeking a marriage of convenience but tried not to judge him. Peter was always more practical and objective with things, and the fact that he had overcome such a trauma and achieved a good position managing a farm, although it looked like it had once seen better days, was something one had to respect. In some ways, he even admired his brother, since Peter had adjusted to a quite hard new reality and discovered a new direction in his life, while he, with a much less serious accident, had surrendered and let himself be dominated by alcohol. Peter then broke the silence.

"You start tomorrow, my little brother. Your table is that one that seems to be occupied. It used to be mine. The others are empty, since at this moment, the work is little. Maybe together we can put this farm to work and grow again. I'm using the bedroom to the right. You can take the one to the left which is empty. I'll get bedding for you. Are you hungry?"

His brother's question made Frank change his expression, and the answer came promptly.

"Starving. I have barely eaten all day."

"Great! So let's eat. Then we can all go out and celebrate your arrival."

Everything seemed perfect for Frank. A place to sleep, eat, work, with the company of his brother. He could finally stop relying on his army pension. The only thing that bothered him was the idea that there was a pub so near and that they would already be going there after dinner. He wanted to be away from drinking, and this would not help much. *Only this time,* he thought. After all, he did not want to insult his brother, who hosted him so kindly.

The meal was served in the mansion's dining room where Frank met Amanda, the owner of the farm, a sixty-year-old presumptuous woman of few words, but who seemed to be happy with the fact that her youngest daughter was apparently finding someone to take care of her. Thus, she treated Peter very well. He also met Victoria, the eldest daughter who was a widow with no children. Her husband had died of an illness at a young age, and she evidently still carried a deep sorrow for it.

During dinner, Frank asked about Benedict. Nobody seemed to know much about him, but Peter gave him a wink, and with a slight gesture using his right index finger, suggested that they would talk about it later.

After dinner, Frank, Peter, and Barbara went out to the pub. Amanda and Victoria retired to their rooms. The three passed long hours drinking and telling stories. Frank, in the beginning, resisted the beer and was proud of it.

At one point, Peter talked about Benedict. "Frank, you asked about our grandfather during dinner. I also wanted to know about him when I got here, but Amanda and her daughters did not know much, as he returned to the village and stayed there for some time. I believe I don't have good news for you. The story I heard from Carl, the man who brought you and who also lives in the village, is that on a cold morning Benedict went for a walk through the woods as he always did, but he never came back. They made several searches, but he was never found. Apparently it was very cold that night, and a person of his age would hardly survive at such low temperatures. Sorry, Frank, but our grandfather is also no longer with us. We only have each other, my dear brother."

Despite having little hope of hearing something different, the confirmation of the disappearance of his grandfather added to the pain he felt by the departure of Elizabeth. That was too much for Frank's resistance, so he ended up asking for the first beer. And it would be the first of many.

Later, when he arrived drunk to his new room, he was still sober enough to notice that his huge double bed was already made with sheets somewhat old but clean and fragrant. He could not help but remember the humble boardinghouse room that he had slept in for the last year and a half and thought of how it would not be missed anytime soon, if ever.

However, he felt very bad about being weak once again. Elizabeth's request for him to stop drinking would still echo in his mind, and it made him promise himself that it would end at that moment. He had gone there to rebuild his life, and that was not a good start.

However, the routine at Bread & Joy would soon surprise him, showing that the win over old vices would not be something so simple.

The New Routine

AFTER NEARLY A MONTH LIVING at the farm, Frank was beginning to better understand his new job and was no longer intimidated with the new tasks, which at first seemed very difficult to him. Doing daily inventory checks, filling up orders, buying all sorts of supplies, getting transportation at a good price, everything had been new to him. But for his luck, the activity was little, and the pace was slow, giving him more than enough time to learn and at the same time explore the farm and the peasants' village, which was not far away.

The month of March brought the promise that little by little, the weather would turn milder. Spring would soon arrive, which would gradually change the landscape.

In the war, the Allies continued imposing consecutive losses to the Germans and Italians. Russia was slowly regaining the territory that had been taken by the Nazis, but not without heavy losses, and Stalin once again demanded France and England to open another front in Europe to split the attention of the opponents.

Attentive to the news on the radio, Frank followed the battlefront in Africa with a heavy heart, hoping that Elizabeth would not suffer the same fate as others that from there, never returned.

Despite the new environment and occupation, Frank had not ceased to think of Elizabeth for a single day. He felt her absence deeply, and the memory of their last moments together still haunted him like a ghost. He could still feel the sweet taste of her lips in his mouth, the texture and softness of her skin on his hands, and the wonderful feeling of their bodies glued to each other. He relived those moments in his mind innumerous times, and it would always take his breath away.

On the other hand, he began to adapt to his new routine. He was totally unaccustomed to the habits of waking up early, observing a time for everything and having discipline. Peter was showing a lot of patience, but little by little, he was demanding more and more responsibilities from his little brother.

But the responsibilities and schedules were not bothering Frank. What really had surprised him negatively was the routine after work, since almost daily Peter and Barbara would go to the village pub for a few rounds of beer and would drag him along.

Gradually Frank realized that there at the farm, they had a dynamic not much different from his back in London. Although Peter had found a great job and was about to get a quite convenient marriage, he also suffered. He also carried the pain of the loss of his parents, of the unexpected and undesired life changes, of the complete loss of a member of his body, and he probably also suffered because deep inside he knew that his relationship with Barbara was something superficial and based on interests.

On her turn, after a few mugs, Barbara always went down to complain about the decline of Bread & Joy, the bitterness of her sister, her mother's coldness, the premature death of her father, and would insistently demand Peter declarations of love and praise, which he wisely never denied. But deep down, she probably knew that those were kind words that carried little sincerity.

Frank, little by little, understood that each of them had their own pains, carried their own crosses, and he was not really different from anyone else. He was nothing special. He was not the only one to suffer. On the other hand, he could become someone different and special if he would only have the strength to overcome his adversities without self-corrupting and giving in to addictions.

But the fact was that he had not had such strength to resist and had accepted this new routine, getting drunk almost every day since he had arrived at the farm, and this was having a devastating effect on him, as he felt that in the end nothing had changed. He would go on without doing any exercise, without reading a book, without taking care of his relationship with God. Body, mind, and spirit were still abandoned to their own luck and were, little by little, getting rusty.

Adding to this the effect of the constant intake of alcohol and the nonstop hangovers, Frank felt his body slowly deteriorating at all levels and aging prematurely. His self-esteem was so low that he no longer adequately looked after himself; he'd even stopped shaving.

During his wanderings through the village, he found the church and came to know that there was a mass offered at nine every Sunday mornings. However, on Saturdays Peter and Barbara would go even earlier to the bar to get heavily drunk, leaving the bar singing on the streets with bottles in their hands, and on Sunday they would sleep until late. For four consecutive Saturdays, he had accompanied them, and that Saturday in particular did not seem to have a different ending in perspective.

As he was getting ready to go out with Peter and Barbara, a very heavy feeling of guilt filled up all the empty spaces of his chest. He thought of Benedict and everything that he had tried to teach him. He thought of Elizabeth and the things she had said about choices. "One way or another, after all that happened, you chose to enclose yourself in your room at the boardinghouse. You have chosen to hide from life behind a mug of beer. One day you will also need to make the decision of unhide yourself from behind the beer mugs…"

Choices, he continued to make bad ones. Alone in his room, he looked at the mirror and told himself, "You are destroying yourself, lad. I don't even recognize you anymore in the mirror with this beard and these sunken eyes. Who are you? Oh, Benedict. Oh, Elizabeth. Why did you have to go?"

That was when Peter's voice brought him out of his trance, calling from the outside of the house.

"Let's go, Frank. We're getting into the car. You don't want to let your dear brother and your lovely sister-in-law die of thirst, do you?"

Frank looked again into the mirror and not knowing exactly who that person was that he saw reflected, got up and said to his brother, "I am coming!"

He put on his coat and stepped toward the door. Then he looked at himself in the mirror one last time with a bizarre eye to eye, as if he was talking to another Frank that he did not really know and said, "I'm sorry."

And off he went, toward the car.

Once again, he had made a bad choice. Once again, he had been weak. Once again, he would not go to the Sunday mass. Once again, he would get drunk.

However, this time the ending would be quite different.

Surprize at the Riverbank

THAT SATURDAY EVENING, FRANK WAS quieter than usual. While Peter and Barbara were getting more and more cheerful and outgoing by each mug of beer they had, singing and telling jokes to some friends who had joined them, Frank was becoming more and more silent and withdrawn. He was in a corner of the table leaning on his chair and only uncrossing his arms to get his mug and drink in large gulps. In fact, as he was not participating in the conversations and in the singing, he was drinking at a faster pace, and unlike the others, the more he drank, the more depressed he felt.

When he realized that he was not having fun and that he did not want to be there drinking, Frank asked Barbara to take him back to the farm. He wanted to put an end to that undesired situation and get some sleep; after all, it was already quite late. The village pub did not have time restrictions as the London pubs did and would only close when the last customer walked out the door. And today, everything suggested that the drinking was going to last long.

Noticing what was happening, Peter intervened and said, "Frank, don't be an inconvenience. Can't you see we are having fun? Stop being a crybaby and have another beer."

Peter raised his hand to the waiter and ordered another one for Frank, who was caught by surprise and did not object, accepting it.

A few more minutes went by until Frank could not drink anymore and could no longer deal with that situation. Then he ran in his confused mind the way back to Bread & Joy and decided to return to the farm walking. That walk, made in a slow pace, would probably take him a bit over half an hour, but at least he would end that torture. He excused himself to go to the restroom, something that he had already done a few times, and without anyone noticing, staggered into a different direction.

He figured it was already past midnight, and with some luck, before one o'clock he would be in his bed.

As he walked through the village streets, he passed in front of the church and feeling embarrassed, lowered his head and continued walking without making any reverences.

As he left the village and took the dirt road leading to the farm, the light began to become increasingly scarce, and he began to have difficulty seeing the way.

After a few minutes of walking in the dark, feeling totally dizzy with the effects of the alcohol, Frank began to realize that he had made a mistake. He looked around in the darkness and noticed that he had left the road and had also lost all references, since he could no longer see the village hidden behind a hill nor the farmhouse, which seemed to be behind some woods, the same ones that Benedict used to go for his walks.

With confused thoughts, he decided that the best thing to do would be to go through the woods as a shortcut to the farm.

Slowly and staggering, he began to walk on a completely uneven terrain full of holes, stumbling and falling several times. When he finally reached the woods, he was already very tired and even more disoriented.

He rested for a moment leaning on a stone and continued his walk into the woods, dodging trees and bushes, looking for something that could look like a path, with no luck. It didn't take him long to admit that he was totally lost, not knowing where he had come from and where he should go to. The effects of the alcohol were becoming more and more present, and Frank realized he could not go on for much longer. Luckily, that night the temperature was relatively pleasant, but bringing his coat along proved to be a wise decision, as it would be enough to bundle him up under open skies.

He walked a little further until he found a glade and heard the sound of running water. He then identified a water stream and a small area of grass in its margin.

Since he could no longer remain standing, he lay down slowly on the grass with his liquid-filled belly facing up, as it seemed to be the most comfortable position at that time. He was then able to observe a beautiful starry night with no moon.

Little by little, he closed his eyes, but before he fell into a deep sleep, he said to himself aloud, "May God protect me, wherever I am."

After a long while in deep sleep, Frank was awakened by the touch of a hand on his face. Despite the feeling of the touch, it felt like something other than that, very soft and distant was slowly and gradually bringing him back to his consciousness.

Little by little, Frank started waking up. He listened to the stream, feeling the grass, the bitter taste in his mouth, a strong dizziness, and an affectionate touch on his face that would not cease. He felt the velvety texture of a hand that at the same time seemed to be quite callous, as if it had suffered the ravages of time.

When he finally tried to open his eyes, he realized it was already day. The sun was high in the sky, and its intense light blinded him for a moment, in a way that he could not identify who was there, waking him up so tenderly.

With great effort, he tried to put himself in a sitting position and covered the sunlight with his left hand. While still struggling with the brightness trying to open his eyes, he heard a familiar voice saying, "Hello, son. I'm so glad you came. We have to finish what we started."

Frank was completely scared and supporting both hands on the ground, pushed his body backward. He looked again at the person who was there and could finally identify who it was.

"Benedict? Is that you?"

Yes, it was his grandfather, who as usual calmed his grandchild down with silence and a calm and serene look. But there was something different about him. His skin was whiter than ever to the point of slightly reflecting the sunlight. His hair and beard were much longer than before; his eyes seemed to have rejuvenated, carrying an even more intense glow. He wore white trousers and shirt that seemed to be brand new, which also seemed to reflect the sunlight.

Still struggling to open his eyes and see his grandfather clearly, Frank got to his feet and feeling scared, said, "No, it cannot be. You died. They told me you died. It cannot be you."

Benedict said nothing. With a smile and tender look, he opened his arms and gestured with his hands, asking Frank to hug him.

Frank was reluctant at first, but soon he left his disbelief aside and ran into the open arms offered by his grandfather. While there, wrapped around by his grandfather's arms, he felt a peace that he had never experienced. But little by little, the sense of peace gave way to emotions that had been held for quite some time. It seems that his grandfather's embrace offered the necessary protection for such emotions to emerge.

Frank fought back the tears that seemed to be repressed for a long time. He wanted to cry for everything that he had been through until then: the death of his parents, the humiliations imposed by Dixon, the loneliness of his boardinghouse room, the destruction imposed by such an odious war, the loss of Elizabeth, for the crippling of his brother, for his addiction to alcohol, and finally, for his own weaknesses.

Realizing Frank's effort to contain his emotions, Benedict slowly broke the embrace. He looked into Frank's eyes and said, "Come, my grandson. We have a lot to talk about."

With a gesture, he pointed out two large stones by the river that Frank had not noticed before, since he had arrived there in the midst of total darkness. With his eyes already adjusted to the brightness, Frank could finally see the scenery around him. The view was simply paradisiacal. The clear river moved slowly, and beautiful trees on both sides leaned over it. The sounds of different birds could be heard, and the grass was so dazzlingly green that it almost looked like a carpet. The sky had an incredible variety of shades of yellow, orange, and red, which reflected in the few clouds that were present and brought up the surreal perception of being part of a Claude Monet painting.

    Both finally sat down and positioned themselves face-to-face. A long and revealing dialogue was about to begin.

The Long-Awaited Conversation

Benedict crossed his arms, stood in a more serious manner, and said, "You must have a lot of questions for me. But keep in mind that our time is short. I cannot stay long. So I suggest you use our time together the best way possible."

Frank still felt confused by all that was going on and actually didn't know where to start. It took him a few seconds to recompose and to reflect until he finally asked his first question.

"Grandpa, where are you living? Why did you disappear for all this time?"

"I live here, my grandson. In these woods, on the banks of this river where I find the peace that I couldn't find in the world of men. I disappeared because my time had come, and we have to accept that in peace."

"But why hasn't anyone found you before?"

Smiling with the corner of his lips, Benedict replied, "Well, to begin with, that's not exactly true. Some people in fact have crossed paths with me here in the woods. But the only ones to find me are the ones I want and when I want them to. And these are precisely the people who know how to keep a secret, as you will keep about our encounter."

Outraged and puzzled, Frank asked, "So then you are not coming back with me to the farm?"

"No, Frank. As I said, my time in the world of men is over. Where I am now is my place."

Disappointed, Frank thought about arguing, but something in Benedict's eyes made him understand that it would be a waste of time. He seemed to be happy where he was, and he would hardly change his mind. He decided to take the conversation into another direction.

"Grandpa, I have so much to tell you and so much advice to ask. I don't even know where to start."

"When time is short, we have to give attention to what is really important. So I ask you, if we had time to talk about just one subject, what would you talk about? What is bothering you the most right now?"

Frank did not take long to identify what was his greatest pain at that moment.

"Benedict, I left London to escape from the war and to change my life, since I had become a drunk. I came to Bread & Joy to get away from drinking and to start a new life. However, the same night I got here, I was already drinking again. I am getting drunk here as much as I used to in London. Despite having moved from one place to another, nothing has changed. I cannot escape. I cannot rebuild my life. I feel like I'm destroying myself and sinking deeper. I need to do something to change that, but I don't know what to do."

Frank then covered his face with his hands, ashamed of what he had confessed and showing a deep degree of despair. Benedict held his position of folded arms, but his look was now sharp and penetrating.

"My dear grandson, you need to understand something that is quite serious. No matter where you go, no matter how far you travel, there is someone who will always come along, and that someone is you. The temptations will always be around. Everywhere in the world, there will be people suffering for one reason or another, with all forms of physical and emotional pains, and there will always be reasons to appeal to all kinds of anesthetics, alcohol being just one of them. You can run away from the conflicts that exist on the outside of you, but you will never be able to escape from the conflicts that exist on the inside. If you do not solve those conflicts, no matter where you go, the result will always be the same."

Frank thought for a moment and said in a low voice, "The storm is within me …"

"Yes, Frank. And please do not feel less than others for that. You're no different than anyone else. We all bring pains and internal conflicts. We all bring our storms. What sets us apart is how we deal with them. The attitude you took to come here looking for a fresh start has been a great step forward, but by itself, it does not solve anything. If you do not make peace with some pains you carry, the motivation to drink will always be there." Sensing that his grandfather was starting to touch the real problem, Frank asked him to continue, "Can you tell me more about that?"

"Frank, alcohol or any other chemical substance that alters your state of consciousness is nothing but an anesthetic for an emotional pain, but it does not cure the pain, just relieves it for a short period of time. If you do not treat the pain itself, soon you will need more anesthetic. What pains are causing you to seek an anesthetic? Think before you answer that question and let's talk about each of them."

After a few moments of reflection, Frank replied, "My parents. The death of my parents."

"Perfect, Frank. I see that you are willing to face your greatest pains, and this is very important. Talk about it without fear. Come on, face it." Frank struggled with his emotions and took some time to express himself. Benedict remained silent until Frank started talking.

Finally giving way to a restrained cry, Frank said with difficulty, "I always expected more of them. I always wanted them to be more attentive and caring with me, that they would not impose so many rules on me, accepting me more as I was. When I finally gave value for what they had done for me, when I could finally better understand them and accept them as they were, when I was finally ready to embrace them and tell them that I loved and forgave them, they were gone. I never had the chance to say any of this to them."

Frank paused and then said, "I miss them, Benedict."

Benedict allowed a moment of silence so that Frank could breathe, then he spoke calmly in a low voice, but in a firm manner, "What if I told you that they can hear you now? What if I said it is not too late and that you can have that conversation with them now?"

"How can that be, Benedict?"

"Frank, the vital energy does not cease when the body dies. Close your eyes for a moment."

A little reluctant, Frank obeyed his grandfather, who continued, "Imagine your parents right in front of you. Think they're here now. What would you like to say to them?"

Frank was becoming increasingly emotional as his grandfather guided him in coping with his pains. Then he went on imagining Frederick and Charlotte in front of him. The tears could no longer be held and flowed over his face. With great difficulty, he began to talk to them.

"Father, mother, I never took the proper time to say this to you, but I love you very much. Today I understand that you are people of humble origins, with limited resources, who worked hard to make me a good man and that you also loved me. I forgive you for not being as I expected you to be, as the problem was not you, it was me and my misguided expectations. So I also want you to forgive me."

Benedict then intervened, "Well, Frank, they heard you perfectly. Now imagine that they are forgiving you too and the three of you are embracing. It will be a long quiet embrace, a healing embrace."

Frank then could imagine his parents approaching him and embracing him tenderly. Everyone forgave and cured each other with that hug. Frank could feel the strong arms of his father and the loving hands of his mother. The experience was so real he could feel the texture of their clothes and the usual smells of their bodies. It felt as if they were really there.

Benedict allowed the hug to take a few long seconds until his next intervention.

"Very well, Frank, now finish this embrace and let them go in peace. You and they are now at peace with each other. There are no more reasons for resentment or pains that cannot be understood and managed. Let them go."

Frank slowly finished the hug and left them. They moved away slowly and with tender and loving glances, said goodbye.

"Okay, Frank, you can open your eyes now. How do you feel?"

Frank slowly opened his eyes, and once again the brightness of the day reflected on Benedict and bothered him for a moment. He little by little stopped crying and replied, "Lighter. It was as if they really were here."

Benedict stared at him with a sideway glance, somewhat questioning his last observation. Frank soon realized his own lack of faith and completed, "I'm sorry, Benedict. In a way that I still do not understand, they really were. Thank you. I already feel much better."

"That's great, but we are far from finished. We still have lots of work to do."

Surprised by his grandfather observation, Frank made lateral movements with his head, as if he was seeking to relax the tense muscles of his shoulders and neck.

The grandfather then asked, "What other great pain is bothering you?"

Frank began to search inside himself. Leaning against the stone with his hands on his knees, he had his body slightly leaning forward as if resting and taking a breath before the next emotional battle. Soon he would identify his next great pain.

Gradually his facial expressions started changing. Suddenly one could see anger in his eyes, which was fixed on a lost point on the ground, as someone who is looking but not seeing. But his lips would not move.

Realizing what was happening, Benedict broke his grandson's trance.

"Speak, Frank. Put that anger out. What is it that raises so much hate?"

Frank began to breathe intensely and angrily until he finally spoke in altered manner. "War. This damn senseless war that took everything from me—my house, my family, my health, the health of my brother, and…"

Frank paused for a second. Benedict remained intact, and noticing that little by little the features of his grandson once again swung from anger to pain, he decided to help him once again. "Come on, Frank, let it out."

Frank shouted and once again began to cry. "Elizabeth. This damn war also took Elizabeth from me."

Again, Frank covered his face with his hands as he cried. And again, Benedict gave him a time to take everything off his chest. After a few seconds, Frank continued, no longer shouting, but speaking loud as if expelling from his chest the bad feelings that he sheltered. "I'm disgusted by Dixon. That idiot just finished with the little balance and serenity I still had. He ripped your list of phrases, stole my diary, forbade me to read the Bible, made me wish to go to war just to get rid of him, so much that I destroyed my own health to reach that stupid goal. I hate this war and all these idiots who promote it without thinking about the human lives they destroy, and Dixon, who represented them so well, executing their orders and destroying what was left of my physical, mental, and spiritual health."

After having finished his outburst, Frank still had his breathing rhythm altered. He dried his tears and pulled his hair back. Then he turned to Benedict and with hurt in his eyes, came to a close by saying once again, "I hate them. All of them."

Benedict stood there in silence, listening to every word from his grandson. His gaze was now full of compassion. He then asked him to relax and to once again close his eyes. After allowing a few seconds for Frank to breathe, he said, "Once again we will have to exercise your ability to forgive, Frank. And now it will be even more difficult, since you will have to forgive people you do not know or love. First, think of the warlords, some known to you, some not, but all with one thing in common, an insane desire to conquer and control the world. Something they will never be able to do. Unfortunately they will only understand how futile and impractical their desires and aspirations were when it's all too late. When they are closing their eyes on their deathbed, giving account of how wrongly they lived their lives, how much evil they have done to millions of people and that they will be the reason of infamy for generations and generations to come."

After a brief pause, Benedict continued, "Frank, understand that the warlords hold nothing personal against you. They are just people who, for the most wrong reasons in the world, such as greed or the belief that one religion, race, skin color, or ideology is superior to all others, think they should change the lives of people by force. They believe that their tribe is superior to all others. And they will only understand that we are all equal before God when it is all too late. Their ignorance is their cross. They will have to go through many spiritual trials to understand, acknowledge, and repair their mistakes. And for this to pass, they will suffer as much or more than you. So, my grandson, make an effort and forgive. Let this pain go away."

Little by little, Frank was processing everything that his grandfather was saying and realized that he did not control any of that. That all he could do was understand and seek to make the best of his life, given these circumstances. He also understood that people who are in power often have distorted understandings of how the life of a person shall be lived. And that war was part of a long and painful process of spiritual learning that was still far from over.

Making an extreme effort, he forgave the warlords and inside his core even felt sorry for them and for all the spiritual weight they would carry once they leave this life.

Seeing that his grandson's face was calmer, Benedict decided to continue, "Do not open your eyes yet. Let's talk about Dixon now. This has already been told before by someone else, but apparently the message has not yet been captured by you. Dixon saved your life. He was only an instrument of God to get you out of a lost battle and certain death. Your time had not yet come, and you were not supposed to be on that boat to Africa. As much as you hate Dixon, think for a moment. Where is he now? Would you like to trade places with him? Remember that everything that poor man knew was the military life. His family prepared him only for that. Nothing else had any value for him. And when he could finally experience a taste of being in battle, it did not last more than a few days, and he had a tragic end. Now answer me, my grandson, is Dixon more worthy of your anger or of your compassion?" The words of his grandfather seemed to have had the desired effect.

Frank still had his eyes closed, but he seemed more relaxed and had a very calm semblance. He did not seem to be feeling angry or hurt. Benedict went on, "Still with your eyes closed, stand up, Frank. This will not be easy, but imagine that Dixon is here now, right in front of you."

Frank moved away from the stone and stood up, but his face changed a bit, as if rejecting the request of his grandfather.

"Come on, Frank, trust me. Stay with me just a little longer."

Frank made a gesture with his head allowing Benedict to proceed. "Now look at his face and see the disappointment of having lived a short and vain life and the guilt of having done harm to you and to so many others for such futile reasons. Feel his pain."

Little by little, Frank's face changed, going from disgust to compassion.

"Now go to him, hug him, and forgive him. And again, thank him for indirectly saving your life."

Still a little reluctant, Frank obeyed his grandfather. He embraced Dixon, and through it, he could feel the suffering vibrations of his former tyrant and understood he suffered as much as him, or even more. He stepped away, looked Dixon in the eye, and said, "I forgive you, and I'm thankful to you."

"Excellent, Frank. Now as you did with your parents, say goodbye and let him go. Be at peace over this pain, for now everything can be understood and emotionally managed."

Frank obeyed his grandfather. Moving away from Dixon, he watched him as he walked away. He waved and gave him goodbye.

"And finally, Frank, so we can turn this page, forgive yourself. Forgive yourself for willing to go to war, something you despise, just to get rid of Dixon. Forgive yourself for having hated him so much. And forgive yourself for allowing this hate and this desire to get rid of him lead you to obsession and to the accident that broke your leg. Remember that all this actually saved you from a more tragic fate."

Frank took a deep breath and allowed his grandfather's teachings to occupy all his thoughts, and little by little, he freed himself from this other guilt.

"Great, Frank. One less pain in your life. I believe from now on, even your leg will hurt less, and you will soon be able to exercise again without any problem. The leg broke so it could save you from bigger pains. Now open your eyes and breathe a bit, my grandson."

Opening his eyes, Frank was surprised to see that the sunlight was no longer as strong. A thick fog seemed to be lowering and taking over the woods and the river. Benedict looked around and said, "Let's keep going, Frank. Unfortunately my time is running out. What other great pain is bothering you?"

Tired, he supported himself once again on the stone behind him, sat down, and leaned back against it. Then he turned to Benedict and with his eyes already red and exhausted, almost begged for that exercise to end there and then. Benedict immediately reacted and in a tender but firm manner, encouraged his grandson to continue, "Come on, Frank, there is not much left. Soon it will be over. Tell me, what else is bothering you?"

With almost no more tears to be cried, Frank sought for strength deep within his soul. He had been running away from this last pain for a few days. In fact, that was the main reason he was there. When searching within him on what would be the next big chain that he was carrying, Frank could only find one single word, "Elizabeth…"

Sitting at the riverside and leaning on a stone, Frank had his gaze fixed on the ground. The increasingly thick fog was taking over everything, and Benedict once again rushed his grandson.

"Close again your eyes and tell me, Frank, how do you feel about Elizabeth?"

Frank took a deep breath and closed his eyes, looking within himself for an objective answer to his grandfather's question, but many things came from his chest at the same time. He then proceeded to say them one by one, "Pain of a loss, rejection, nostalgia, abandonment, bad luck, injustice, revolt."

"Great, Frank, it's coming out. Keep your eyes closed. Answer me one question. You talk about loss, but did you actually ever have Elizabeth as yours at any moment?"

Frank thought for a second and realized that the answer was obvious.

She was never really his.

"No, never. But I still lost her presence in my life."

"Very well. And is this loss permanent? Or could it be something temporary?"

Frank then remembered Elizabeth's letter and her promise.

"I don't know. There is a possibility that it's temporary, but I believe it's definitive."

"Okay, Frank, now think about what you just said. You chose to believe that the loss of Elizabeth in your life is something definitive, and therefore you feel treated unfairly and abandoned. But then I ask, are these all beliefs or facts?"

His grandfather's argument had an amazing and disturbing logic. His question had caused Frank to understand that he had created that reality. He, Frank, had decided that the loss of Elizabeth was final, and therefore, things were unfair and he was unlucky. His revolt was gradually losing strength. Finally, he found himself only with feelings of rejection and the pain of missing her.

"She rejected me, Benedict. She traded me for a lot of sick and wounded people God knows where."

"No, Frank. She traded you for a purpose. For a greater cause. We must never question a person with a purpose. Her decision had nothing to do with you, son, but with her cause to help the sick and wounded in a situation and place where people with her talents are really needed. You are seeing this situation in a very self-centered way, Frank."

Finally, Frank found himself face-to-face with the last stronghold of pain, and as he faced it, he started crying again. Almost in a whisper, he said, "But I miss her so much…"

Taking a deep breath, Benedict paused briefly, allowing the last tears to come out. With a firm voice, he said, "Now that's legitimate and true, Frank. Nostalgia. Missing those we love. And this pain, my grandson, you will have to learn to live with, because it is part of life. It is part of love, for we will never have all the people we love with us all the time and everywhere we go. People come and go. But nothing ends until the circle is closed, and this one in particular is still an open circle. Now let's get to the moment you need so much. Embrace Elizabeth mentally and forgive her."

Frank then imagined Elizabeth before him. He could feel her presence, her smell. She wore the same clothes and the same perfume as on their last meeting in the park in London. And she smiled fondly at him, as if saying, "This is not over." Crying a lot and feeling a lot of pain in his chest, Frank held her and forgave her.

"Very well, Frank. Now I leave it up to you to choose what you are going to say to her. Goodbye or see you soon."

Frank then looked at Elizabeth, who stopped smiling and had her hands together in front of her body. She looked back at Frank and waited for his final words. Frank hesitated for a moment and finally said, "See you soon, my love."

Elizabeth then smiled tenderly, turned the other way, and at a slow pace, also left.

"Very good, Frank. Now I want you to forgive yourself as well, for not having believed in Elizabeth's promise and for running away from your pains coming to Bread & Joy. Do not blame yourself, because this decision will be a determinant factor in your life. You have a reason to be here."

Making a positive nod, Frank consented and forgave himself as well. When he opened his eyes, Frank got scared. The fog was so thick now that he could hardly see the other side of the river, and Benedict had some sort of urgency in his eyes.

"My grandson, my time with you is ending. Is there something else bothering you that you want to talk about?"

Frank was exhausted and could no longer continue. But indeed there was one last issue to be dealt with his grandfather.

"Yes, Benedict, you. Why can't you stay with me? Why do you need to stay here hidden from everything and everyone in these woods? Why is your time with me running out?"

Benedict then changed his features and looked at him with a mixture of pain and tenderness. He patted the side of his grandson's face and said, "Believe me, Frank. This is also painful to me. But as I said, my time in the world of men is over. We do not control that. It is for us just to accept. But do not worry, because you will no longer need me. You will always have the wise old man at your disposal."

Frank was confused with Benedict's response. What did he mean when he said that his time was over? How could it be that he did not control it? But actually, what had ended up winning his attention was the last sentence of Benedict.

"Grandfather, when will I see this wise old man? Are you sure he exists?"

Benedict smiled at Frank and surprised him with his answer, "Frank you've actually already found him. You simply did not recognize him. You must beware, son. Now I want you to accept the fact that we cannot be together. We will still see each other, but we cannot be together. Be at peace with that, son. Otherwise, I will also suffer."

Closing his eyes, Frank lowered his head and heavily felt the words of Benedict, but he no longer had tears to cry. He made a positive nod and asked the grandfather to embrace him.

After a few seconds, Benedict interrupted the hug and looked around. He could no longer see anything but fog. Then looking at his grandson, he said, "Congratulations Frank. What you have just done is not easy, and not everyone is capable of doing it. People usually see forgiveness arrogantly, as if it were an act of superiority. They cannot overcome their pride and do not understand that forgiveness is actually an act of humility. But that's the only way to leave the past in the past. If we do not forgive and accept the imperfections of others and our own imperfections, we go through life turned backward, always looking back, not allowing ourselves to look forward and start over. With this act of bravery and humility on your part, you proved yourself to be noble and worthy of a new beginning. You are ready to look ahead and start over."

Frank opened a relieved smile. Indeed he felt as such, ready for a new phase.

Benedict then ended, "Now I want to make you a request. Seek Carl. He has something important for you that will help you go forward in your much-desired personal transformation."

Frank then remembered the old man who had fetched him at the train station a few days ago. But he felt exhausted. A strange tiredness began to take over him, and he couldn't even stand up.

"All right, Grandfather, I will go after him. But in another time, for now I am very tired."

Benedict looked at his grandson as if he already knew that this would happen and ordered him to lie down a bit on the grass, to what Frank consented immediately. He then moved about two or three meters away and watched his grandson getting down on the grass at exactly the same place where he was sleeping before. Frank rested his head on his hands, and as he was closing his eyes, he could see the figure of Benedict being shrouded by the mist, gradually disappearing.

Before disappearing altogether, Benedict said one last time, "Remember, seek Carl."

Powerless to react, Frank watched Benedict's image disappear completely in the mist and fell deep asleep.

A New Awakening

The sun was shining strong on his face when Frank awoke again on the riverbank.

He slowly stood up and gradually opened his eyes, which were struggling to adapt to the brightness. The perception was that he had slept for a very short while since his conversation with Benedict, but where would be all that mist that had evolved them just a few minutes ago? And besides, his impression was that the sun was lower on the horizon, as if the day had just begun.

Once his eyes were finally open and used to the light, he looked around in search of Benedict, but there was no sign of him. He was gone. In the same mysterious way that he had appeared, he had also disappeared, leaving no trace behind him.

Frank then stopped for a moment and thought about the things he had talked about with his grandfather and realized that he felt incredibly lighter and with an overwhelming sense of peace. He had elaborated and processed each of his greatest pains and guilt, and that made him feel really well.

But there was one thing that intrigued him. Many of the things they spoke about had happened after he and Benedict went on separate ways—the months in the army and the difficulties with Dixon, his involvement with Elizabeth and its sudden and surprising end. And yet Benedict seemed to know about everything. How could this be possible?

He pondered for a moment if what he had just lived moments ago was a dream or reality, but everything felt so real that he abandoned such considerations quickly.

He then realized he was very thirsty and began to look for a place at the river where he could drink some water. A few feet away, he noticed that the river had a bend in which the margin stretched out, creating a sort of pool where the water almost stood still. There he could serve himself at will.

He took off his shoes, rolled up his pants to the knees, and went into the water, which was really cold and brought a chill through his spine. Then he stopped for a moment to watch the scenery, to listen to the birds and again felt a deep sensation of peace.

He then crouched down to quench his thirst, and in doing so, he was able to see on the cold water the reflection of his face, which once again impressed him in a negative way.

The combination of his longer than usual hair all tousled around, since he had just woken up, with a beard that was already creating some volume, taking over his whole face, borrowed him a look worthy of the beggars from the streets of London. Added to this set, he had the bulging eyes of someone who had a hangover from a tremendous drinking. Embarrassed, he put his hands in the water, shuffling the image he was seeing and that disturbed him so much. After relieving his thirst, he observed his image slowly taking shape again and said out aloud, "You look like an old man, Frank. You are getting old before your time. If you keep down this path, you will not live long. It's time to change this."

He stopped for another moment and stood there, crouched and static, allowing his image in the water to finish taking shape. He looked again deep into his own eyes and went into a kind of trance.

He thought about the words he had just said, "I look like an old man, and I'm getting old before my time."

Then he remembered what Benedict had said to him. His words echoed in his ears, "Frank you've actually already found him. You simply did not recognize him. You must beware, son."

Suddenly a crazy thought crossed his mind, *The wise old man? Could it be? I may be getting old before my time, but wise?*

It could not be. He thought he was having a reverie. Then he dismissed this hypothesis from his head and decided it was time to go back to the farm. Peter was probably very concerned by now.

Out of the water, he put on his shoes and left to finish his walk. In broad daylight, he had no difficulties on finding his trail.

On the way, he found the railway and crossed the train tracks. Seeing the tracks that brought him to Bread & Joy, he paused for a second and had a brief moment of nostalgia, but quickly decided he was better there than in London.

After half an hour of slow and quiet walk, he reached his destination. When he finally got home, he realized that his absence hadn't even been noticed, since Peter had the bedroom door half-opened and could be seen deeply asleep. At his side was Barbara, who had apparently decided to spend the night there. Frank closed the door, allowing them to keep resting and went to his room.

There, he once again faced himself in the mirror and saw his semblance disfigured by self-imposed mistreatments and the consequent lack of health. The figure of the old man was, bit by bit, getting clear to his eyes.

He began to laugh at himself and at the discovery that little by little was sinking in, since he had sought the wise old man everywhere, but everything was leading him to believe that such person was right there, in the mirror, closer than he ever imagined. It was just hard to understand where such wisdom would come from.

Then he remembered the last words of Benedict. "Seek Carl."

That's what he would do as soon as possible, since he was very curious to know what that quiet old man would have for him. Little he knew that with Carl, he would find the answers to all his questions.

The Unexpected Legacy

After a good shower and putting on clean clothes, Frank left his room and met with Peter and Barbara, who were on their way out.

Surprised to see him, his brother turned and said, "Good morning, little brother. I am relieved to know that you found your way back. For a moment, I feared that you could have gotten lost in the woods. What a night, huh? You are proving to be a great company for our night outs. Shall we have lunch? Carl should be bringing Amanda and Victoria from church at any moment now."

Yes, it was almost noon, and he was feeling really hungry. But the opportunity to talk to Carl was something that could not be missed.

"Of course. I'm starving. I will join you in a few minutes."

Frank waited for Peter and Barbara to get away and instead of heading toward the main house where lunch would be served, he went the other way, to the side of the road and waited for the truck driven by Carl bringing Amanda and Victoria to pass. He was positioned at a safe distance where he could not be seen and waited for the two ladies to enter the house. When he saw the opportunity, he ran to the truck and approached Carl, who had already started his procedure to park.

Carl was surprised by the sudden appearance of Frank and in an impulse, asked, "Are you crazy, lad? What a scare you gave me. What can I do for you?"

Frank looked him in the eye and said, "Benedict. He asked me to look for you. He told me that you had something for me."

Frank's words made old Carl's features change immediately. He looked at the road and took a quick inspection at his pocket watch. Then he turned back to Frank and said, "Hop in. We don't have much time. Lady Victoria needs my services after lunch."

Frank quickly came around the truck and got in. He had hardly settled into his seat when Carl took off at high speed. Not having a clear understanding of what was going on, he asked, "Where are we going?"

"To my house. He requested me to deliver the package to you only when you asked for it and far away from here, where we could be alone, so I kept it in my house in the village. But I have to get back quickly before anyone notices my absence."

"Why didn't you tell me before that you had a package from Benedict for me?"

"Because I didn't know. He just told me to deliver it to the person who would ask for it. And you just did. Only now I found out that it's for you."

"And what is this package?"

"I can't tell, because it's closed. It has always been. But you will soon understand."

"But why did he leave it with you?"

"Well, I'm not sure, but I believe he had no one else to leave it with. When he came back from London, he could no longer find work at the farm. Maybe because of his age and also because the farm was already not doing too well. As we were friends, since we had worked together for a long time, he came to me. He asked to stay with me for a few months, and as I have no one else, I accepted gladly. It's always nice to have company. But he did not stay very long. He seemed to be very tired and in poor health. One day, he told me that his time was running out and that it was time to go."

"And where did he go to?"

"He didn't tell me anything, Frank. And by knowing your grandfather, I decided not to ask too many questions. But by the way he left, I believe he went somewhere far away to die in peace and alone. He took nothing with him except the clothes he was wearing and left me with the package, only saying that I should give it to a man who would one day come to me and claim for it."

From then on, there were no more questions. Frank remained silent, thinking about what Carl had just said. How could it be that Benedict would have left to die? He had seen him only a few hours ago and he seemed to be quite healthy.

In a few minutes, the truck approached the village, where few people walked the streets still returning to their homes after the morning mass. The urgency of Carl and Frank's anxiety contrasted with a Sunday morning that was dragging slowly and lazily.

Carl's house was far on the outskirts of the village so they had to cross it entirely to get there. When they finally parked, Frank could see a humble cottage with only a few rooms.

Without even looking at Frank, Carl said, "Follow me, lad. Please ignore the simplicity of my house. I am alone and do not need much to live."

To Frank's surprise, Carl did not enter the house. He walked around by the side and went straight to the back where there was a separate room from the rest of the building. Carl opened the door, and Frank followed him. He then could notice that there, old Carl kept all sorts of old stuff. Work tools covered in dust, old auto pieces and parts, and a huge carpentry workbench that obviously had not seen any kind of action for many years, as spiderwebs were everywhere.

Carl then pointed to the table and said, "It's there, lad, underneath this table, but you will need to pull it out, because I no longer have strength for that."

Frank then crouched to be able to look under the table, and what he saw left him awestruck. There, under that old table, covered by a thick layer of dust, was Benedict's treasure: his chest of books and personal notes.

Frank then turned to Carl and with a totally puzzled expression, said, "I cannot believe it. He left his treasure for me."

He then stretched out to reach the chest and with difficulty, pulled it out toward himself until it was in the middle of the room, between him and Carl.

Carl then looked at Frank a little worried and said, "Lad, if this is a treasure, I believe I have bad news. Benedict never opened it while he was here with me, and after he was gone, I got curious and I tried to open it. Unfortunately it is locked, and he forgot to leave the key. If you want, I have some old tools here, and we can try to open it by force, but I think we would waste our time because this lock seems to be one of the strong ones."

Frank's face then lit up, for he remembered the envelope he found in his suitcase the day he reported himself for services in the army.

"The key. Of course. The key. That Benedict is a genius. Let's go back to the farm, Carl. I believe I know where the key is."

Immediately they took the dust off the chest, carried it to the truck, and headed back to Bread & Joy. Frank had a sort of silly smile and from time to time, would start laughing and say aloud, "Crazy old man, this is typical you."

When they finally arrived, they benefited from the fact that everyone else was inside, probably having lunch, and carried the chest to Frank's room unnoticed.

Anxiously, Frank sought his old suitcase that was on top of the wardrobe and opened it. Then he began to search for the key in the pockets located on the sides of the bag, but he found nothing. Then he raised the old Bible of his mother, and there it was. Benedict's key, still inside the same envelope.

He then turned quickly to the chest and inserted it into the lock easily. He then made a slight movement to the left and heard the distinctive click of a lock opening. He opened a huge smile and said to Carl, "Your work is done, my dear Carl. Benedict's package is delivered. Thank you for keeping it safe and for risking yourself to drive me there to get it."

Carl smiled back at Frank, and although a bit frustrated since he could not satisfy his curiosity on knowing what the treasure was, he was glad, for he had fulfilled his old friend's will. The chest had found its owner after all. Before getting back to his duties, he said, "You are welcome, my boy. Make good use of your treasure, whatever it is."

Benedict's Treasures

FINALLY ALONE WITH HIS CHEST, Frank summoned the courage to open it. As expected, there were all Benedict's books and personal notes. Frank took the books out, one by one, reading their covers and back covers and noticed that each of them offered him the chance to discover new horizons, ideas, and thoughts all different from what he knew. There, he could find information about a variety of religions, teachings about how to develop spirituality, meditation and thought control practices, personal development, and a variety of other interesting topics about many cultures of the world that Benedict had the opportunity to experience.

But what caught Frank's attention the most were Benedict's manuscripts, which were separated into two blocks, both tied with a piece of red ribbon.

The first block brought together a series of thoughts and philosophies of life. Frank flipped through them one by one and could see that they gathered the content of most of the conversations he had had with his grandfather. He found notes that were true gems. There were manuscripts about the habit of cultivating the garden of the soul. There was one about the sponge attitude, absorbing everything that happens to us, either good or bad, as learnings. There was another about the spiritual path as being something unique and individual. He also found writings about how to benefit from religion as a means and not an end, making use of what they bring that is good and discarding their humanities. There were others about the lessons that our pains teach us, about the relationship between what you give to the world and what you get back from it, about expecting the unexpected, and finally, about the benefits of keeping alive, loved and cared for, the child that each of us bring inside.

When he reached the final manuscript of the first block, Frank then had the most pleasant surprise of the day. It was a draft of the list of thoughts that his grandfather had given him on the eve of his departure to the army. There were the fifteen thoughts of Benedict. The list that was destroyed by Dixon, in a totally unexpected way had returned to him. Frank held it fondly and said aloud, "Thank you, God. Thank you, Benedict."

After rereading carefully one by one the fifteen phrases of the list, Frank put it in the drawer of the nightstand next to his bed and promised that from that day and on, he would read three sentences every morning and would let them govern his actions throughout the day.

Frank then opened the second block of manuscripts and was happy to find a series of lists of exercises and activities that one could practice. They taught how to do relaxation and meditation, how to pray surrounded by the divine light of an imaginary sun, how to set personal goals, and how to draw action plans to achieve them, and other things that could be applied in everyday life.

Little by little, Frank realized that there, in Benedict's chest, was all he needed to return to the path he had once started with his grandfather nearly four years ago. Or almost everything.

He got up and rescued from inside his suitcase the Bible that had been given to him by his mother, and the list of attributes of a good leader that he had built with the help of Elizabeth.

Now the arsenal to fight his personal war was complete.

Standing in the center of his room, Frank looked around and saw the books and Benedict's manuscripts scattered all over the place and said to himself, "The wisdom. Here is the piece of the puzzle that I was missing. But I will take years and years to conquer it."

Closing his eyes, Frank began to imagine how he would be if he had read all Benedict's books and manuscripts and if he had practiced the exercises countless times. He imagined himself as an old man who knew everything that Benedict knew.

Positioned right in front of him, his older version was watching him with a look in his eyes similar to the one his grandfather used to carry, conveying infinite affection, patience, and wisdom.

Keeping his eyes closed, Frank then asked his imaginary older version, "Hello, old Frank, will I ever be wise as Benedict?"

And the old Frank replied, "Of course you will, lad. You still have plenty of time. But if you want wisdom, you have to earn it through a lot of reading, experiences, and practical exercises. And you will have to face every life experience as a lesson to be learned. There is no other way. It will take some time, but with effort and determination, you will get there."

Continuing this imaginary and surreal dialogue, Frank said, "Okay. I see it clearly now, and I promise you that I will make the necessary effort. I have already made peace with my past, and I am committed to write a new future. What else is there to do?"

The old Frank thought for a moment and said, "Focus on your work, my boy, and blossom where God has planted you. Exercise your leadership potential, since your brother will need you very much here. Stop drinking once and for all, because alcohol is harmful to your body and your spirit. Reengage in developing your spirituality, praying, and meditating every day. Pray whenever you feel like and allow God to grow within you again."

Frank quietly listened to the words of the old Frank, pondered over them, and nodded in approval. Blossoming where God had planted him seemed to be a very powerful thought. The old Frank seemed to know what he was saying.

Then he decided to make one last question to his older version, before ending that imaginary conversation that began to seem something very close to insanity.

"Okay, old Frank. Do you believe that when I finish reading all these books and Benedict's manuscripts and practice the exercises several times, I'll be ready to find the wise old man?"

The old Frank then remained silent and smiled at the young Frank, looking at him in a tender and loving way. His eyes seemed to say, "You will not have to wait that long."

Frank then smiled broadly, as his suspicions had been confirmed. The wise old man, which often seemed just a daydream of Benedict, really existed and was closer than he had ever imagined.

As Benedict would, the old Frank remained silent for a few seconds, waiting for that moment of discovery to be completed and then finished, "You just accessed the light that exists within you, Frank. Use it to illuminate your way. We bring this light within ourselves, but we prefer to ignore it and waste often a lifetime seeking such light in the outside world. Whenever you want or need, isolate yourself for a few minutes and sit comfortably in a quiet place. Relax and summon me, and I'll be here for you. As I am very old, I have lived all the experiences that an entire lifetime can bring. On the other hand, I have very little time left to live. Thanks to this powerful combination, I do not let myself be blinded by ego or by pride, and I can help you see every situation in a broader and less self-centered way. I can separate what is only the result of a moment from what is really important. And as my time is running out, I don't leave for tomorrow the things that need to be done today, simply because I don't know for sure if that tomorrow will exist. I am here for you, Frank. Summon me, and I will always help you to make wiser decisions."

Frank then opened his eyes and felt a plenitude that he had never experienced. He was at peace with himself and with his past. He had forgiven everyone and himself. Around him, he had at his disposal a multitude of resources that Benedict had left him to develop as a person and as spirit. And most importantly, he had found in a surprising way the wise old man that Benedict announced so long ago.

With feelings of self-assurance that had long been lost somewhere in time and space, he said to himself, "I'm ready. Today I start a new life. Today, a new Frank is born."

Starting Over

THE MONTH OF JULY HAD brought along not only pleasant temperatures and beautiful sunny days, but also good news about the war conflicts, which although were happening so far from the routine of Bread & Joy, would affect the lives of everyone directly or indirectly. In Africa, Italians, and Germans had surrendered, bringing to an end the war in that continent. The Allies then went to the offense and invaded Sicily, starting from there what appeared to be a slow and gradual recovery of Italy. This state of affairs led Mussolini to be dismissed from power, and the Italians started giving every indication that their position in the war would be reviewed soon and that Germany would be abandoned to their own luck.

Frank and Peter followed the daily news on the radio and celebrated noisily when they heard about the victory in Africa. Peter shouted, "We will win this war, my brother. And it will not take long."

"Do you really think so?"

"Of course. Soon Italy will also surrender. The Russians continue recovering their territory, and now it is us that are bombarding Germany and not them bombarding us. It's a matter of time before Hitler surrenders and seeks an agreement to escape alive. You'll see. I believe that this war will not last beyond this year."

Frank pondered over his brother's predictions and allowed himself to get excited by them for a moment, but he had his doubts about the end of the conflict being so near.

It was inevitable that he would also think about Elizabeth and question where she would be at that moment, since in Africa the conflict was over. He had been feeling worried and frustrated for quite some time now, for not receiving any letters from her. The lack of news caused a fear that something bad might had happened, or that she had simply forgotten him.

But his last conversation with the wise old man had helped him leave his ego and his fears aside and hear the voice of his heart, which said that Elizabeth was fine and that there should be a reasonable explanation for not receiving letters from her yet. Then he calmed down and stopped feeding his fears and frustrations, which, after all, were just a figment of his imagination.

"I wish they would not surrender so we could kill them one by one, until the last one. Damned people. They destroyed my life, my family, and had me end up here in the middle of nowhere. I hate them all."

Peter's words took Frank away from his thoughts. He looked at his brother and saw him paralyzed, with a glazed look into some corner and a closed mouth, his jaws pressing hard against each other. There was hatred in every corner of his face. For the first time since they had met again, Peter externalized to Frank how bitter and miserable he felt. Frank considered talking to his brother about forgiveness and making peace with the past, but he sensed that it would be a waste of time, at least at that moment. Peter then wiped the frown from his face and said, "But today is a day of joy. Let's celebrate this important victory with a lot of beer. Come with us tonight. Would you do it for your older brother?"

Since the meeting with Benedict at the riverbank and the rescue of the chest with his books and manuscripts, Frank had fulfilled his own promise rigorously and had not returned to the pub with Peter and Barbara. Feeling ready for the challenge that was being presented to him, he replied, "Of course I'll go with you, Peter. But I'll ask you something in return."

"Tell me. I'll do anything for you to come with us today."

"I want you to accept the fact that I will not drink, only accompany you."

Peter looked at Frank with an expression as if he did not understand and said, "You have really changed a lot since arriving here, Frank. You have been going to the mass every Sunday now and are always praying. You are working hard as I never thought you could. You are reading a book after another and going out every day for your solitary walks late in the afternoon. And besides all this, you do not drink anymore. I don't know what happened, but you're becoming a really boring guy."

Peter then pushed the wheels of his chair toward his office and before going through the door, said without looking back at Frank, "If you are not going to participate in the drinking, you don't need to come. Stay home with your prayers and your books."

Frank decided not to respond to his brother's bad mood and frustration. He knew that his choices would have its cost and expected that sooner or later, Peter would understand.

His change of attitude had been noticed by everyone—firstly by Carl, Amanda, and Victoria, who had won a new companion for the Sunday masses, then by Peter and Barbara, who, in their turn, had lost a companion to the almost daily drinking.

But it was on the day to day of Bread & Joy that Peter had felt his changes more intensely. The more Frank would learn his new job, the more he would dedicate himself to it. Peter gradually gained confidence and began delegating to him more duties and responsibilities and started to rely on him for nearly everything. However, if on one side Frank had become his right-hand man in what was related to work, on the other, he no longer accompanied him to the night outs and that bothered him.

In the solitude of his room, Frank's change went far beyond from what other people's eyes could see. There, he would make his relaxations, pray, and meditate. He would revise Benedict's notes daily and reread his sentences every morning before leaving for the day.

That morning specifically he had read, "To understand my neighbor, I will put myself in his place and will feel his pains and joys." He practiced it with Peter at that time and had no difficulty understanding his revolt with the Germans. He felt his pain of being limited to a wheelchair, his eagerness to numb himself with alcohol, and his frustration to see his younger brother well and balanced while not having the strength and tools to do the same.

He forgave his brother for his aggressive response and decided not to accompany him, since he would surely not drink and this would further frustrate Peter.

As the end of the afternoon was approaching, he decided to put a close to his workday. He put on more comfortable clothes and shoes and left for his daily walk.

As Benedict had anticipated, the act of freeing himself from his emotional chains had done well not only for his soul, but also for his body, and the leg that had been broken no longer bothered him as before. Every day he exercised with more ease, and his health was improving consistently.

Among the several manuscripts of Benedict, Frank had found one that had been especially useful, as it taught him to draw specific goals and action plans for personal development in different aspects of life.

On a personal level, the manuscript segmented us into three dimensions: physical, intellectual, and spiritual, and asked that for each of these dimensions a goal and a plan to achieve it would be stablished with well-defined dates and activities.

Frank had defined as his first goal, to read all the books in Benedict's chest at a rate of two per month to develop his intellect. He would seek inner peace and closeness to God through daily meditation and prayer, and he would go to Mass every Sunday, thus developing his spirituality. And finally he drew another goal, to get back in the same shape he once was during his time at the army, even if it was slow and gradual, and for that he would exercise and walk every evening to restore his physical health.

The manuscript also requested the definition of goals and activities related to social aspects such as work, family life, personal finances, and the exercise of charity.

For these, Frank had defined that he would learn something new every day and would devote himself to work hard to master all the activities of the farm, he would keep what he would have spent on beers as savings and would participate in the church's charitable works. In the family, he had a goal to get closer to his brother, but this last objective had proven to be more challenging than initially imagined, since Peter seemed to be full of defenses and the fact that they had always been so different and far apart was not helping.

With the exception of this last goal, all others were being fulfilled to the letter, and Frank felt like a new person. Since he had started this new routine, he was experiencing feelings of fulfillment that he had never known.

That Saturday night, as he was getting ready to go to bed, he thought about the difference that the last month and a half had done in his life and how much better he felt. He thought about how he had been blessed with that last reunion with Benedict and was grateful to have all those resources left for him so he could work on his personal development. And finally, he had a sense of fulfilment with the fact that he had found the wise old man, summoning him already a couple of times to consult his infinite wisdom.

Closing his eyes that night, he decided it was time to seek Benedict again to thank him and to let him know of his findings. *Tomorrow I will return walking from church, and I will find him,* he thought to himself before falling asleep.

Ready to Move On by Himself

As it had already become routine on Sunday mornings, Carl had left Frank, Amanda, and Victoria at the village church door fifteen minutes before the beginning of the mass. While Amanda and Victoria would head for the front row, Frank would position himself at the back and always used that time to close his eyes, relax, and tune his thoughts and vibrations with the divine energies. He would listen to the children's choir and allow those heavenly sounds to elevate and prepare him for the messages that were to come.

Since returning to his meditations and prayers, he had gotten closer to God again and felt more and more harmonized with the Sunday services. He had learned from Benedict to separate what belonged to men and what belonged to God and to carry with him only what was food for his spirit, discarding what did not suit him.

It was also increasingly clear to him the differences between religion and spirituality, and he knew that he was there so one could be a vehicle to the other. Therefore, the imperfections of his religion no longer bothered him. He was aware that they were the result of the imperfections of the men who governed it. They no longer served as a distraction in his objective to grow spiritually.

This attitude, besides being less conflictual, allowed the needed opening for him to read and study without guilt the Buddhism, Hinduism, Taoism, and so many other "isms," filtering from each of them what served him, without feeling limited by the walls of a unique dogma. He was harmonized and at peace with all that.

When the Mass was over, he decided to put into practice his plan elaborated the night before. He searched for Carl and told him that the day was wonderful, neither hot nor cold, perfect for a long walk. He would return to the farmhouse walking and eat alone later.

Carl looked at Frank suspiciously and said, "A wonderful day, hm? Perfect for a long walk. Yeah, I get it. If by any chance you find him, say hello for me, will you?"

Carl winked at Frank and went in search of Amanda and Victoria so they could return to Bread & Joy.

Frank laughed at the cunning of old Carl and began his long lonely way toward the woods. As indeed the day was particularly beautiful, he was easily distracted with the landscape and could see things that by car he had never noticed in this abundance of detail. He saw leafy trees, beehives, birds' nests, and could closely admire the potato plantations, which were about to be harvested.

After some time walking down the dirt road, Frank sighted the woods where he got lost a few weeks before and then changed direction, making his way toward it. Within minutes, he went into that small forest and began to pay more attention to his ears, trying to listen to the sounds of the creek. Every step he took, he looked around him trying to find Benedict behind some tree or bush.

After a few minutes, he could finally hear the sound of running water and continued until he found the stream. Then he went down by the riverbank until he got to the exact location of the last encounter. When he arrived there, he could recognize the whole scenario—the lawn where he leaned back to rest, the stones on which he and Benedict sat down to talk, the trees leaning over the river, and the place where the margin stretched, creating a sort of pond where the water almost stopped.

Everything seemed to be exactly equal to the day of the meeting with Benedict, except for the fact that at that moment, Benedict wasn't there. Frank drank some water and sat down to enjoy the view, hoping that his grandfather would soon appear.

After a long wait, Frank started to get impatient. He got up and started screaming his grandfather's name the loudest he could, "Benedict! Benedict!"

All he had as an answer was the sound of the river and the hummingbirds.

Frustrated and resigned to the fact that he would not find his grandfather that day, he started to take at a slow pace his way back home.

After a few minutes walking, Frank saw the railroad, at about the same point where he crossed it the previous time and felt assured that he was in the right direction. He would soon be home.

However, as he made his way toward the rails, he heard the distinctive sound of a train. Raising his head and looking to his left, he could see at the distance the locomotive coming toward him, pulling its cars at high speed. Then he measured the space between him and the tracks and the speed at which the train was coming and realized he would not have time to cross the railroad before it passed. He would have to wait for it.

He walked with his head down toward the railroad, and as he approached it, he raised his head again. At that moment, he got a big scare and could not believe his own eyes. There, across the railroad, just a few meters from the track, was Benedict, watching him quietly among the bushes. This time he was wearing gray clothes and had long loose hair over his shoulders.

Frank looked once more to the train coming toward him reevaluating the distance and started running toward his grandfather. When he got just a few meters from the tracks, he realized that he would really not be able to go across before the train passed. Soon it would be between him and Benedict.

He looked at his grandfather and not containing his anxiety, shouted, "It happened, Benedict. I found him!"

Before the train positioned between them two, Frank could read Benedict's lips, which opened into a wide smile, "I know."

Soon the train came between them, and Frank approached the rails as much as he could. As each car would pass, their eyes would meet for a split of a second. Both had smiles full of tenderness on their faces. Frank could hardly wait to hug his grandfather again.

But as the last wagons approached, Benedict raised his right hand and waved to his grandson, giving him a goodbye. Frank changed his features immediately, surprised by his grandfather's gesture and looked left to see how many more wagons were still missing to pass. There were only three. Soon he would be able to go through and talk to Benedict more calmly. But when he looked back to where his grandfather was, he did not see him anymore.

The last car finally passed, and there, across the railroad, there was nobody. Benedict was gone.

Frank crossed the tracks immediately and went on to look for his grandfather on all sides, but could not find him. After a few seconds of frustration, he wondered why Benedict would have done what he did, and little by little began to realize that most likely, that last visit was a farewell. His grandfather's mission with him was finally over. He could now count on his wise old man and all his infinite wisdom, and the presence of Benedict was no longer necessary. He would be in good hands.

From now on, Frank would have to go his way alone, but he felt good about it, confident that he had everything he needed to take care of himself.

He thought about the sentence of Benedict's list that he had read earlier that morning, before leaving to church. "All that is good or bad, one day will pass. I will take the best from each experience and move on."

Then he said quietly, almost as if to himself, "Goodbye, Benedict. Be with God, my grandfather. And thank you for everything."

Peter Has News

On a cold night, already at the end of November, Amanda asked for her daughters, plus Peter and Frank, to gather in the living room to set up together a beautiful Christmas tree. Before the work started, she gave a glass of champagne to each one and headed to the center of the room. With her usual matriarchal and aristocratic way, she raised her glass and said, "I know that for many years we have discontinued this tradition. With the loss of your father and Victoria's widowhood, along with this damned war, we quit celebrating Christmas with the joy it deserves. But I want this year to be different. We are gradually winning the war, and with the latest news received, I think it's just a matter of time now for it to be over."

Everybody was quick to agree, since they knew what news she was referring to. Italy had changed sides and now supported the Allies. Germany was isolated in the center of Europe and was suffering defeats on all fronts. A few days before, Russia had regained Kiev, a city of strategic importance in the east, and in Italy, the Allies were little by little coming upward to the north. Everything led to believe that the war would actually not last much longer. Amanda then continued, "But we have other reasons to celebrate Christmas in a special way this year, for God answered my prayers. Alone I had many difficulties in managing this farm, and things were not going quite well. There were times when I came to fear that we would lose everything, and we would eventually be in poverty. Then Peter came and changed all that. He put the house in order and then brought Frank to help him. Thanks to you both, Bread & Joy already lives better days. Besides, I do not remember seeing my daughter Barbara so happy in her life, and this is also due to you, Peter. You two are now much more than my employees, you are part of the family. I want to propose a toast to all this."

Everyone then raised their glasses, but before they had the first sip, Peter raised his arm and began a toast himself, "Thank you, Amanda, for your kind words. But before we drink our deserved champagne, I want to say two things. First, I owe a lot to my dear brother, isn't that right, Frank? Since he arrived here, I've been delegating more and more responsibility to him, and he has exceeded my expectations. Today he practically takes care of this farm by himself."

Although what Peter said was the absolute reflection of the truth, his words took Frank completely by surprise, as he would expect from his older brother everything but that sort of public recognition. In recent months, Peter had more than delegated powers to him. In fact, he had almost abandoned all the management of the farm in Frank's hands and had been living a life increasingly promiscuous with Barbara, getting up late and drinking every night. When he was not going to the pub, he would give himself up to the whiskey bottles that were always abundant in the house.

But what would disappoint Frank the most was Peter's change of attitude. He was becoming more and more aggressive and bitter, complaining about everything and everyone, but especially about Frank, always depreciating the things he did and the decisions he made. Frank really could not understand why Peter was treating him so aggressively, keeping a distance between them that would not allow any deeper dialogue. Although trying very hard, he could not break his brother's defenses.

But Frank would be even more surprised by what Peter still had to say, "And secondly, but not less important, Barbara and I have something to announce. As it seems that the war is heading towards its end, we decided to get married in the summer, in July of next year. By then we believe that we will be living in times of peace."

Everyone cheerfully responded to the announcement, at least in a first moment.

Amanda said, "Finally you two have decided. I don't know what took you so long. I bless you, my daughter."

She embraced the two, followed by Victoria, and finally by Frank. Everyone then raised again their glasses and drank champagne, except Frank, who pretended to wet his lips, but then put his glass aside and began working to set up the Christmas tree.

Everyone had fun with the task except Peter, who preferred to watch it all from a distance in his chair, drinking glasses of champagne one after the other.

Frank couldn't help noticing his brother's isolation and his devotion to the champagne, forgetting the assembling of the tree. He thought about talking to him the next day. He would try a more direct approach, for he felt he needed to help him somehow.

But something else caught Frank's attention. Victoria had a worried look on her face. When she went to the kitchen in search of more champagne, Frank followed her on the pretext of helping her. When they were alone in the kitchen, he took the opportunity and asked, "What's with you, Victoria, aren't you happy for Barbara and Peter?"

"Frank, do not misunderstand me. I'm happy for them, but I'm also worried. I love my sister very much, and I do not like to see the direction she and Peter are taking with the drinking. My mother pretends not to notice, because she wants to get a husband to Barbara at any cost. But he seems to be getting more depressed and bitter each day. I believe that if we don't do something about it, it will end badly. As his younger brother, please try to talk to him."

"All right, Victoria. I've been trying to address the issue for a long time, but he doesn't give me any room. I will try again tomorrow. I promise."

After a few hours, the tree was finally all decorated and transformed the entire living room. It seemed that the Christmas spirit was really coming into that house after years of absence.

But not everyone was happy. After many glasses of champagne, Peter was totally drunk and asked Frank to take him to his room.

Frank apologized to the women of the house and told Barbara not to worry because he would put Peter in bed.

Once in the bedroom, Frank helped Peter to move from the wheelchair to the bed and to change his clothes. When he rested his head on the pillow, Peter mumbled something like, "The tables have turned, right, my little brother?"

Not really understanding what his brother had just said, Frank approached and asked, "What did you say, Peter? I did not understand."

Peter then turned to him and with his eyes wallowing said, "The tables have turned. Previously I was the brother with the head over the shoulders. I was the good example. You were the troubled son, the misfit, the rebel. Now you are the one that works, that doesn't drink, that goes to church, and I became the misfit and the depressive drunk."

"Peter, there are no tables being turned. This is all in your head. You are going through a difficult phase. Soon it will all pass. Soon you will get married and will be very happy."

Peter then began to laugh at what Frank had said and answered, "Frank, you know I do not love her and that I'm getting married just for interest. I will never get out of this wheelchair, and I have no motivation to work anymore. If it wasn't for you taking care of everything, I would be doomed. I'm proud of you, my brother. But I am very ashamed of myself. I am a useless cripple, a failure."

Peter then began to cry like a child, and Frank was able to better understand his brother. He not only had difficulties accepting his condition, being condemned to live the rest of his days in a wheelchair, but he also felt guilty for marrying for interest. But the greatest discovery of that dialogue had been that his brother resented the fact that he, Frank, had become the better example of the two. Now he could understand why he had so much aggressiveness and so many defenses. Deep inside, Peter loved him, but he also envied him, and this would put him in a very difficult position to help his brother directly.

Comforting Peter the best way possible until he fell asleep, Frank then decided to try to help his brother in a different way. And he already had an idea on who to turn to.

A New Purpose for Frank

On Sunday after the mass, Frank sought for the priest and waited until he had a chance to talk to him alone. When he finally got his attention, he described to him the drama of his brother, the difficult situation that existed between them and asked if he could provide some advice.

Father Donovan was young, not yet into his forties and was full of energy and enthusiasm. He put his hand over Frank's right shoulder and said, "First I want to congratulate you for being capable of winning over the addiction alone, lad. This is not an easy thing to do."

Frank thought, *It wasn't exactly alone, but better not try to explain it.*

"And also for showing such love and concern over your brother. I fully understand why you would not be the best person to help him directly at this time. But I think I have good news for you. What's happening to him and that also happened to you is more common than you might think. Many parents have lost their children for this war. Many others returned mutilated as Peter. And most of them do not bear the pain of these losses without an anesthetic such as alcohol or something worse. Unfortunately some even commit suicide before help arrives, and we don't want that to happen to your brother. We have a group of people in the community that offers help and support to these suffering souls. They talk to them, pray for them, and seek to help them in every possible way. It will be a pleasure for them to offer this support to Peter."

Frank opened a smile of relief. There was hope for Peter to get help after all.

"Look for Mr. Ferguson. He is the pharmacist of the city and also the leader of this group, and I'm sure he will help you."

Frank thanked the priest for his reference and hurried out of the church. Outside he met Amanda, Victoria, and Carl waiting for him, already impatient. He apologized and asked them to go ahead and leave to Bread & Joy, since he still had one last conversation to have in the village.

As he walked toward the pharmacy, Frank started to develop other ideas that went beyond his original purpose, since he saw in this group something more than an opportunity to help his brother.

Frank knocked on Mr. Ferguson's door and quickly was welcomed by a tall skinny gentleman, already in his fifties, with a huge nose and little hair. Frank introduced himself and let him know that he had been referred by Father Donovan, which provided him immediate access to the living room.

Again, Frank told the whole story of himself and his brother and asked for help from Mr. Ferguson, who promptly explained to him that the group used to meet in the school cafeteria every Tuesday evening at seven. There, each person had the time to talk about their addictions, dramas, fears, losses, feelings of guilt, and they would receive the support not only from the group leaders, but also from other people who were in a similar situation. Ferguson finished by saying, "We not always succeed, but in most cases we can help people get through their addictions or at least control them in a way that they would stop destroying their lives. When necessary, we act also individually, talking and supporting a person who has difficulty speaking in a group. Don't you want to come this Tuesday to see how it works and decide if this is the sort of thing you are searching for your brother?"

"Yes, that sounds perfect. I'll be there. I just have one more question. What is needed to be part of this group of people? I really wish I could help."

Ferguson looked at him with a smile and said, "Only the will to help and lots of love in your heart, lad. Are you interested? Your personal experience would be of great value to these people. It is through successful stories and examples like yours that they understand that it is possible to overcome addiction and start over."

Frank pondered for a moment and said, "Let's talk more about this on Tuesday. Have a good day."

While making his long journey back to Bread & Joy, Frank felt not only happy to have found what appeared to be a very interesting alternative of help for Peter, he also felt highly energized by the idea of being able to help others with his personal experience and remembered the sentence from Benedict's list he had read that same morning, saying, "I will use every opportunity that life gives me to help others. I will treat others as I would like to be treated, even when I am not." Apparently, there was a great opportunity that life was offering him, and he could not let it slip away.

When it was Tuesday, he got permission to use the farm truck and went to the village to attend the meeting.

There he could witness the drama of many people who had lost loved ones or possessions due to the war. But also he met people who, like Peter, had been mutilated or had poor health as a result of an incident during battles. All of them, in one way or another, filled their emptiness with some kind of addiction and sought help.

At one point in the meeting, Frank was taken by surprise when Mr. Ferguson invited him to tell his own story.

A little hesitant at first, Frank spoke about having left home so young, the difficulties encountered with Dixon in the army, about the accident that fractured his leg in such a violent way, the subsequent dismissal, the loss of his parents and the destruction of his neighborhood, the solitude in the boardinghouse room, and the alcohol addiction that nearly destroyed him.

Without elaborating much, he also spoke of the positive influences of his grandfather and Elizabeth and how it is so necessary to have the support of people who care about us and who want to see us well.

When asked about what he had done to overcome alcohol, he simply replied, "I have forgiven. I forgave everyone who hurt me, I forgave life for being so hard on me at times, I forgave God for taking me through paths that back then I did not understand, and I forgave myself for being weak and imperfect."

Frank then mentioned one of his favorite phrases in Benedict's booklet. "I will always exercise forgiveness towards those who do me wrong. I will use pardoning as an act of love towards those who hurt me and towards myself."

Everyone agreed, and some even took note of the phrase. Frank then continued, "When I was able to forgive everything and everyone, I was able to cease looking back and began to focus on the present. I sought new horizons and new occupations and began to rebuild myself."

Using another of Benedict's sentences, he said, "I decided to make the best out of my present time, because it's all I have. I will make of my past a source of learning experiences and of my future a sea of possibilities."

Once again he received the approval of all, and again some people noted down his words full of wisdom. Finally, Frank completed, "But I still need to help my brother and the others who are in the same situation. I believe that only then I will reach my total redemption."

Everyone then applauded Frank's words, and the people who were part of the group embraced him and said he would be very welcomed there.

That night while driving back to the farm, Frank felt renewed, full of energy and good vibes. Helping people going through the same drama he once had elevated him and made him feel closer to God.

He had learned that the purpose of life is to live a life of purpose, and he had found another one.

"Elizabeth, you would be proud of me, because I learned to develop my responsibility. Or the ability to respond as you had once taught me." He spoke aloud as if she could hear him.

That last thought brought along some pain, since he missed her and wished deeply that his friend and lover would still be with him at that moment.

Arriving at the farm, he needed to keep away those thoughts from his head, for he remembered that he still had an important challenge to overcome. Get closer to his brother and try to help him.

To his frustration, he would soon find out that it would not be so easy.

Peter's Wedding

THE MORNING OF JULY 2ND, 1944, had arrived gloriously to Bread & Joy, with pleasant temperatures and plenty of sunshine. It was a perfect Saturday for an outdoor wedding.

But unlike Amanda had wished, the wedding of her daughter Barbara would be nothing more than a simple ceremony with few guests, since unfortunately the times were still difficult. The German resistance had surprised everyone, and those who had bet on a quick surrender of the Nazis now understood that the war would only be over when the Allies would get to Berlin, and no one had the slightest idea of how long that would take.

Several times Peter and Barbara considered postponing their wedding to the following year, but the uncertainty about how long the war would last made them reconsider. It could be a useless wait, so the wedding date was kept.

The news received at the beginning of June had reinvigorated the hopes of victory. Although everything was taking much longer than expected, optimism was back.

Rome was the first enemy capital to be conquered by the Allies, sending a clear message to Hitler that his defeat was a matter of time.

But the most important achievement of that historic June happened further north, on the beaches of Normandy. In the biggest war operation that the world had witnessed so far, the Allied forces crossed the English Channel and landed more than a hundred and fifty thousand soldiers in occupied France. In a few days, they entered into Europe opening the long-awaited front of the west, required by Stalin for nearly two years.

Now the Germans had to divide themselves into three different fronts, and rather than attacking, they were forced to focus solely on defending their territory. To the east, they were fighting the Russians, who were gaining ground day by day and already occupying part of Poland. To the south was where soldiers from various nationalities had joined together and little by little were driving the Germans off of the Italian peninsula. And finally to the west was where the Allied soldiers began freeing French cities from the Nazi domination.

Although they kept the day of the ceremony, Peter and Barbara postponed the honeymoon for when the war would be over and the situation more favorable for it.

Alone in the living room of the house in the back of the farm, Frank looked at his watch for the third time in less than two minutes and began to feel unrested with Peter's delay, not wanting his brother to be late for his own wedding.

Uncomfortable with the silence coming from the bedroom where Peter was getting dressed, he decided to knock on the door.

"Peter, are you okay? Do you need some help?"

All he got as a response was more silence. He decided to insist and knocked again.

"Peter, are you okay?"

Finally his effort was rewarded, and he heard the door unlock from the inside. Not showing himself, Peter then opened the door for about an inch, giving a quiet signal that Frank could come in.

Frank hesitated for a few seconds until finally he pushed the door slowly and found his brother almost ready, already with his pants and shirt on and the jacket of the suit extended on the bed. But he was still missing the bow tie that stretched over his shoulders to be tied.

Sitting in his wheelchair, Peter peeked through the bedroom window with a blurred look in his eyes, as if he was looking but not seeing a thing. With a low and unemotional voice, he said, "Yes, I need help with this damn tie."

Frank smiled at his brother, came closer to him and took the tie in his hands. "Let me help you."

Frank wrapped the tie around Peter's neck and arranged it with ease. "Ready. There you go. My dear brother is ready to really hang himself."

Frank's joke stole a brief smile from Peter's mouth. Frank then took the opportunity and tried to cheer him up.

"Peter, you need to make a better face. You can't go out for the ceremony like that, as if you were going to a funeral. Barbara is crazy about you. Amanda is extremely grateful for everything you did for Bread & Joy and is also very fond of you. You will become the heir of a beautiful and productive property that is sure to live much better days when the war is over. One day you'll have kids that will fill this house with joy. Cheer up, my dear brother, because many men who went to the battlefields never returned, or returned to a life and future much less promising than yours."

Peter listened in silence to each of Frank's words. Then he turned to him and asked him to come a little closer and bow so he could give him a hug.

After a long embrace, Peter asked Frank to sit on the bed and said, "You are right, Frank. In fact, for more than a year now, you are the only voice of reason between us. You have been taking care of everything and of me, and all that I give you in return are grumbling, complaints, and impatience. You have already tried innumerous times to help me get out of this depression and of my dependency on drinking, and I did not allow the slightest space for this to happen. Sometimes I feel that my biggest addiction is not drinking, but self-pity instead. I feel sorry and ashamed of myself, and I cannot look at my face in the mirror."

Both were silent for a few seconds—Frank for being caught totally by surprise by his brother's words and for not knowing yet how to react, Peter for being a bit lost, doing something he wasn't used to. Seeking the best way to continue, he said, "I think I should apologize for being this torment in your life during all this time. I want you to know that I am very grateful to you and admire you very much. You stopped drinking and take care of your health in an enviable way. You read all the time, always trying to learn something new. You take care of your spiritual life in a way that I do not quite understand, but at least you do it. And this year you have become a beloved leader to everyone in this farm. No employee wants to talk to me anymore, since I became this grumpy man who forgot how to deal with people. Everyone seeks for you to receive orders, direction, and often, counseling. Not to mention this wonderful work you are doing in the village with the people who suffer with the war and seek support to deal with their traumas and losses. And all I did was to refuse your invitations, one after the other, to go with you to at least one session. Sorry, Frank. You have been an incredible brother, an admirable person, always trying to help me, and I have not done anything to ease your task. You turned your life around by yourself, and today you are an example of a great human being. It really makes me very proud of you. I would like to have the same strength."

Frank was totally surprised and still did not know how to react. During the last six months he had tried to help his brother in every way, without finding the slightest room to do so. All he received from Peter was a cold and distant treatment, even rude at times. As hard as he had tried, he had not succeeded in breaking his brother's defenses. And suddenly, perhaps motivated by the emotions of the important moment he was living, Peter opened up so unexpectedly.

Thrilled, Frank hesitated for a moment, long enough for Peter to get closer to the door and start his way toward the exit, saying, "Could you help me with the jacket?"

In a split of a second, a thought crossed Frank's mind. "You cannot miss this opportunity." He got up quickly, positioned himself between Peter and the door and said, "Wait. I have some things to tell you as well."

Perceiving what was about to happen, Peter tried to escape once again. "Frank, I'm already late. Can't we talk another time?"

"No. This will only take a few minutes."

Peter took a deep breath and realized he was not going to get away this time. He moved back a bit in order to better face Frank and crossing his hands in front of his body, made a signal for Frank to continue.

"Peter, first let me say that I am very moved by your words and recognition. It really wasn't an easy journey to get to this point. But there are a few things that need to be clarified."

Frank sat back in a way that he could look his brother in the eyes and at the same level. With a serious attitude of someone who is about to reveal something important, Frank continued, "I will share a secret with you, Peter. This perception you have that I changed my life by myself is wrong. I didn't do anything alone. I needed help to get out of the situation I found myself in. I had mentors who opened new perspectives to me and who supported me in the process of finding myself and to win the hardest of all battles, which is the battle against our own selves. We are our own worst enemies. And without these mentors, I would have never found the way. One of these mentors taught me that for us to become better human beings we must seek this goal every day, until we convert ourselves into a role model for those around us. It's a choice, Peter. It doesn't happen by luck or chance."

Now Peter was the one surprised, and then he asked, "Mentors? You had mentors? And who were they?"

Frank felt he had gotten the attention of his brother. Then he continued, "Very well. Are you ready for a big surprise? My greatest mentor was Benedict, our grandfather. He helped me from the moment he arrived at our home in Croydon, and in a way he is still helping me. All the books you see me reading were his. And he left me many things beyond books. He left me many manuscripts and guides to live a fuller life. Without him, I would have never reversed my situation."

"That's amazing, Frank. But I do not understand. How did these books and manuscripts get to you? And how has he helped you after you got here?"

"Well, these answers will indeed need more time, but I promise to tell you everything in detail later."

Recognizing that Frank was right, Peter resigned to wait until the whole story was told at another time. But he remained curious. "Okay, no problem, but you mentioned mentors. Who else helped you in your transformation?"

Frank hesitated for a moment, smiled at his brother, and said, "A woman."

Surprised, Peter reacted immediately. "What? You had someone in your life? How come you never told me? Who was she?"

"Well, sorry, Peter, but I did not tell you because you never asked me anything."

Embarrassed, Peter recognized that what Frank said was right. He had never been interested in the life of his brother. He just assumed he had achieved his comeback alone and that he never had someone in his life. He felt bad about it and did not know what to say.

Realizing the discomfort his remark had caused, Frank continued, "It doesn't matter, Peter, I'm telling you now. Her name is Elizabeth, a great woman who made me see the world in a more positive way and who taught me to be my own leader. With her, I lived the most amazing week of my life. But she had to leave because of the war. At this moment, if she is still alive, she is serving at the army as a nurse somewhere in Europe, and I hope one day I will find her again. I still love her, and I think of her every day."

"Incredible, Frank. Now I understand."

"Understand what?"

"Why you never paid attention to Victoria and the way she looks at you."

Surprised, Frank began to laugh, and for a moment the conversation went into a different route.

"What? Victoria sends me looks? Peter, she is at least ten years older than me. Stop kidding around."

"It is not a joke, my dear Frank. She has been observing you for a long time. But do not let it get to your head, okay? After all she is a very lonely woman, and she hardly leaves the farm. Your only competition is old Carl."

"Yes, just like you inviting me to be your best man. Who else could you invite?"

They both laughed at their own jokes and suddenly felt a friendly atmosphere among them that hadn't been there for a long time. Frank then continued, "Peter, my point is that no one overcomes a difficult moment such as the one you are going through on their own. Everybody needs help, and to act based on pride at times like these will not help you at all. But there's something even more important than to be humble and let others help. In these months that I've been working with this support group at the church, I have noticed something very important that would suit you very well. The people that come to us and reach their personal transformation objectives bring within the sincere desire to change their lives, and they want to be helped. No one can help a person who doesn't want to be helped. Do you understand me? If you don't open up to this, nothing can be done. You need to help yourself first. Do you understand what I mean?"

Peter weighed Frank's words for a moment and then responded to them, "Yes, Frank, I understand. But I feel ashamed of my failure as a soldier, ashamed to be in this wheelchair, and I cannot talk about these things in public. Joining your group is out of the question."

Realizing that public exposure was probably not the best direction to go, Frank tried a different path. "Okay, I understand your perspective. But allow me to say that your failure as a soldier is all in your head. As I told you, we are our own worst enemies. Such failure is a fantasy of yours. You defended your country with great honor for a long time. Your brother here didn't even make it to the battlefields. I propose the following: during these months working in the group, I learned a lot, and I have been sharing with the people who come to us, many of Benedict's teachings and Elizabeth's philosophies. What would you say if we talk just the two of us, every day for half an hour after work? There is no need for commitments of drastic changes in your life. Let's start talking and then you do whatever you want. If you want to go to the pub, you go to the pub. If you want to lock yourself in the bathroom and cry for half an hour for self-pity, go ahead. But at least give yourself the opportunity to talk and listen to what I have to say. You have absolutely nothing to lose. What do you think of the idea?"

Peter thought for a moment and finally made a positive nod. Frank had managed to break through his barriers after all. Then he decided to leave one of Benedict's nuggets for Peter to reflect on;

"My dear brother, we all have a past, but we also have a future. Your future is a blank page, and the pen is in your hands. Write the most beautiful story that you can create. And you can start by making Barbara a very happy woman."

Frank embraced Peter, who hugged him warmly in return. A new bond between the brothers had been created. Frank then looked into Peter's eyes, gave him a pat on the shoulder, and said, "Ready to hang yourself up?"

"Yes. I just forgot that I will need some help to push my chair across the lawn to the altar. Would my best man help me?"

"It will be a great pleasure."

And the brothers went together to the ceremony.

Paris Is Free, and Peter in the Right Path

TUESDAY, SEPTEMBER 26TH, BROUGHT BAD weather and the first signs that summer had really ended. Frank was in the village, with Carl buying groceries, and as they were paying, they heard on the radio of the small shop the announcement of more achievements of the Allied troops. During the previous month of August, everyone had celebrated enthusiastically the recovery of Paris. The City of Light was released from the Nazi domination on the 25th with minimal destruction of its unique architectures.

Now the whole region of Belgium, Netherlands. and Luxembourg had just regained their freedom, and the Russians were quickly advancing through Poland toward Berlin. In the European front, the Germans were retreating on all sides, and in the Pacific front, the same was happening to the Japanese, who were losing island after island to the Americans.

But there was something new in the bulletin received that day. Something that symbolized a significant change and a signal that the end was really near. For the first time in the war, the Allies had entered German territory, invading and controlling the city of Aachen, on the border of Belgium.

Carl and Frank were really happy with what they heard and returned to the farm eager to celebrate the news with the others.

As they made their way through the dusty roads of Lincolnshire, Frank was thinking about the small but significant progresses made by his brother. Since the wedding, he and Peter had managed to keep a good frequency on their late afternoon conversations, which little by little were bringing some results.

During those talks, Frank had told Peter on how Benedict and he had gotten so close and had tried to recap the long conversations they kept before the war. He spoke of his teachings about the weeds we let grow within our souls and that we should cultivate them as one cultivates a garden; about the sponge attitude making the most of every life experience; that we receive from the world what we give to it; of the need to pursue our spiritual path and evolution; and the need to fill our lives with purpose and objectives, among other things. Peter was no longer as depressed, and his trips to the pub had significantly decreased as he had restricted them to only Fridays and Saturdays. During other nights he wouldn't visit the whiskey bottles with the same frequency as before, and there were very few situations where he would be noticed with a hangover the next day. But he still had a long way to go.

But there was something new comforting Frank's heart. Gradually he had gone from disciple to master. His fellows at the support group for soldiers returning from the war would now recognize him as someone very wise for his age. He gradually had become a reference point. Many wanted to consult with him and would seek him for advice.

However, what everyone ignored is that to be well prepared for this responsibility, Frank kept a strict daily routine of meditation and intense counseling sessions with his wise old man.

The interactions with his most wise and elderly self had begun as something casual and opportunistic, since Frank would only summon him when an important decision had to be made. But with the need to advise his brother and the ones seeking support in the church group, consulting his old wiser self had become almost a religion. With the responsibility undertaken to help people in difficulty, Frank now would be advised almost daily, in a ritual that would take him to the depths of his own being and that would give him access to a wisdom that seemed to be unlimited.

He did not quite understand where such wisdom came from, but this little detail didn't matter much to him. What really mattered was that through it, he would be in the position to advise and help many people.

The expectations that the war was nearing its end also made him think of Elizabeth. Would she still be alive? And if she was, would she be in good health? And where could she be at that moment? Italy? France? Belgium? Obviously, these and many other questions would remain unanswered.

Arriving at the farm, Frank sought eagerly after Peter to share with him the good news, while Carl would carry with difficulty the groceries through the back door.

To Frank's surprise there was already a celebration going on in the farm living room. Peter, Barbara, Victoria, and Amanda hugged and congratulated each other warmly. Apparently he had arrived too late with his news.

"So you already know the news? Finally we entered into German territory. Isn't that great?"

Everyone looked at him with amazement and began to laugh. Without understanding what was going on, he made a signal to Peter seeking some kind of explanation. Peter then satisfied his curiosity. "Forget the war for a few minutes, Uncle Frank, and come celebrate with us, because soon this family will receive a new member."

Frank took a split second to understand his brother's response.

"Uncle Frank? What do mean? How?"

Everyone laughed again until Frank finally understood what all that celebration was about. Barbara was pregnant. Soon he would be an uncle.

Frank couldn't hold his emotion and knelt to embrace his brother. "I am very happy for you, Peter."

While Peter reciprocated the hug, he whispered in his ear, "I want to talk to you later, okay?"

When he finished his hug, Frank made a positive sign showing that he had understood his brother's request and then began walking toward Barbara to also congratulate her.

"Congratulations, my sister-in-law. And take good care of my nephew. Now you carry one more responsibility. Do you need anything? A tea? A snack? Are you hungry?"

Everyone laughed once again, this time over Frank being overly concerned with Barbara. And then, one by one, they started getting back to their daily duties.

Peter then asked Frank to help him return to the office and was attended promptly.

There, Peter closed the door and turned to Frank. His semblance was mild, and he carried a spark in his eyes, one that hadn't been there for quite a while.

"Frank, this news will change many things in my life. I never thought that the prospect of fatherhood could shake me so much. Our conversations have been very helpful and are making me look at things through a different perspective. But it will no longer be sufficient. I need to change in a more radical way, now that I will be a father. I want to be an example for this child. I do not want him to be a child of an alcoholic."

Peter paused for a moment and Frank thought it would be better to remain silent, realizing that he still had something important to say.

Peter finally took a deep breath and continued, "I want you to take me with you tonight for the meeting with the support group. I want to quit drinking once and for all. I know that if I quit drinking, Barbara will follow. As you taught me, we all need a purpose in life. I have just found a huge purpose in mine, which is being a father."

Frank once again embraced his brother and congratulated him for this decision. By divine intervention, Peter had found something greater than himself to motivate him to stop drinking—being a father. And with this decision, he would begin to transform his life permanently. Frank was ecstatic, as one more personal goal had been achieved. He had rebuilt his relationship with his brother, who in his turn was taking an important step toward rebuilding himself.

When he was finally alone, Frank thought that life was really full of surprises and asked himself, "What else is there to come?"

And the Unexpected Always Comes

FIVE MONTHS OF SESSIONS IN the support group were needed for Peter to finally be able to announce himself sober for thirty consecutive days. During the months of October and November, he had had good progress, drinking only occasionally and always alone, since Barbara no longer accompanied him. The sickness feelings that were typical of pregnancy had brought as a benefit the rejection of alcohol.

However, during the festivities of Christmas and New Year, Peter had gone back to feeling depressed and had some serious relapses, drinking until losing consciousness. Everyone had lost faith that he would quit drinking, except Frank, who stayed by his side the whole time, and in the days following the drinking, he would always motivate and encourage him to keep fighting and to continue attending the support group meetings. He would always repeat the same phrase:

"No matter how sad, disappointed, or frustrated you are, keep moving forward."

Peter would listen to his brother, would thank him for his encouragement, but seemed deeply frustrated each time he would succumb. He had to start all over again, and that weakened him.

But as the year of 1945 started, Barbara's belly finally took shape. Everyone who passed by her would comment and would give their opinion if it was going to be a boy or a girl. This had a powerful effect on Peter, and something changed inside him.

Another fact that motivated them all, and consequently Peter as well, was the imminent end of the war. In the month of February, Germany was invaded on all fronts, Warsaw had also been freed, and the Russians were now less than a hundred miles from Berlin. American, French, and English soldiers on one side and Russians on the other were now on a veiled dispute of who would arrive at the German capital first. The Nazi surrender was expected at any time.

Fatherhood and the end of the war were now palpable situations for Peter. He could feel his son in Barbara's belly, and preparation for the postwar life was already a trivial topic in conversations. Life was changing around him, and this apparently had a definitive impact. He seemed much more determined to eliminate drinking once and for all.

The announcement of the thirty days sobriety came at the meeting of the support group that took place on Tuesday, February 27th. Everyone in the group applauded and congratulated him.

At the end of the meeting, many came to shake his hand and say, "Keep going, Peter. One day at a time. Soon it will be a thing of the past."

Peter thanked each one for their greetings and at the end told them all that this achievement deserved a celebration at the pub. He raised his hands up and asked, "All right! Who is coming? The first round is on me."

Everyone laughed at his joke and started making their way back to their homes.

On the road back to the farm, Frank was very happy and said to Peter, "I'm proud of you, my brother. I believe there is no turning back now. I see you with a different look in your eyes."

Nodding his head positively, Peter agreed, "You know what? I feel the same way. It's as if something changed inside of me. I feel much more emotionally stable and motivated to take good care of my son. I want to be a good example for little Frederick."

Frank reacted immediately to Peter's news. With a big smile, he said, "What did you say? Little Frederick? Will you give the baby the name of our father?"

With a glowing expression of satisfaction, Peter confirmed, "Yes, my brother. I really miss our parents and want to honor them. If it is a boy, he will be called Frederick."

"And if it's a girl? Charlotte?"

"No. If it's a girl, Barbara will have the privilege to choose the name. And she hasn't made her choice yet. But it doesn't matter, because it will be a boy."

They both laughed at Peter's optimism.

They sat silently for a few moments. When they were approaching the farm, Peter changed the direction of the conversation and said, "Frank, there is an issue I have to talk to you about. It's kind of a delicate matter."

Frank was driving, and the change in Peter's tone caught his attention, so much that he took his eyes off the road for a second. When he was about to respond to Peter, asking him to go ahead and start talking, a sudden curve came, and two car lights coming from the opposite direction completely blinded him.

In a quick reflex, Frank pulled the car to the right and went into the bushes, avoiding the collision. He pushed the brakes and gradually managed to control the car, but let the engine die, quickly putting out all the lights.

In total darkness, Frank still had time to look into his rearview mirror and see the taillights of the car that he almost collided with disappearing down the road toward the village.

He looked at Peter and said, "Are you okay?"

Fixing his hair that now was falling over his eyes, Peter nodded and said, "Good maneuver, my little brother. You saved our lives. What a madman. How can someone drive in the middle of the road like that? He is certainly not from here."

"Yes, you are right. And he was coming from the farm. Who could it be?"

"I don't know, but we'll soon find out."

Frank started the car again and began to slowly return to the road, until he was back to the original route. While finishing the drive toward Bread & Joy, Frank completely forgot about the conversation Peter had started and began a quick reflection on what had just happened. He had the sensation that he had just been close to dying, similar to what had happened to him two years ago, but this time the feelings were completely different.

When he was lying on the street near the Great Lion, he felt like he would die in a pathetic way, drunk and abandoned, without physical or psychological strengths to react. He was done, ready for the cold London night to bring a closure to his destiny. He was a miserable man who would not leave any legacy to anyone. Probably he wouldn't even have someone to claim his body and would be buried as an indigent. Dying at that moment would be almost a relief, putting an end to that meaningless existence.

Today he felt fulfilled. He was living a life without vices, was working, and had a stable home with people he cared about around him. He was helping many people with his acquired wisdom through the interactions with Benedict and also because of his own experiences. He would leave his message and good memories to lots of people, and certainly many would be present at his funeral. He felt he was close to plenitude, in balance, and a leader of himself, as he had sought for so long. Dying now would be something disastrous.

He thought then about the difference that two years had made in his life and about Benedict's wisdom when he taught him that to live is a blessing in itself, and therefore one should choose to live life to its fullest. Yes, there was a lot about making choices on this.

While he was getting out of the car and helping Peter to settle into his wheelchair, he could not help the feeling of deep pride for changing his reality. He was stabilized and in love with his life. He was happy as he hadn't been in a long time, and he didn't need accidents or sudden changes in his route like the one he had just experienced on the road. He just wanted to move on without major changes. He had controlled his internal storms.

Frank and Peter entered the main room of the farm still a little scared and eager to tell the others what had just happened. They found Barbara, Victoria, and Amanda there, the three standing in the same corner of the room, and Frank was quick to announce, "You will not believe what just happened. We almost got killed on the road! A car came at full speed in the middle of the track in the opposite direction and almost drove right into us."

Peter continued, "Yes. He was such an irresponsible driver. If it wasn't for Frank's quick reflexes in avoiding the collision, we would be in pieces right now."

The three were silent without showing any reaction, until Amanda pointed to the opposite direction from where they were, showing two bags that were there on the floor.

An old voice, familiar to Frank, made everyone look to the other side of the room.

"It must have been the taxi that brought me here. That guy really drove like a madman."

Frank felt a chill running up his spine and a shiver through the nape of his neck. His eyes could not believe what they were seeing. His mouth suddenly went dry, his heart raced, and his legs felt slightly strained.

There, in the corner of the living room of Bread & Joy, sitting quietly in an armchair with her legs crossed, was Elizabeth.

Gradually all eyes turned toward Frank. Everyone waited for his reaction, but one would not come. He was awestruck, but completely silent and static, as if he had been completely frozen.

For a moment, he seemed to hear Benedict whispering in his ear, "Didn't I tell you to expect the unexpected?"

Part IV
Paths That Diverge

The Return

Silence reigned sovereign in the living room of Bread & Joy for a few moments, until Peter decided to break it by turning to Frank and saying in a low voice, "I want to see you maneuver out of this one, little brother."

Everyone laughed at Peter's comment. This proved enough to get Frank out of his trance and eliminate the feelings of discomfort that was created by his lack of reaction. Elizabeth stood up and said, "I thought you'd be a little happier to see me."

Frank then realized that his fright had frozen him longer than ideal and that he needed to break away from it immediately. His impulse was to run to Elizabeth and embrace her with all his strength, but his British essence restrained him. He neither wanted to go to the opposite extreme and create another kind of embarrassment for himself.

He then smiled tenderly at Elizabeth and began to cross the room slowly, showing a calmness that he didn't really feel, for in reality his heart was pounding so strongly that one could almost see it from the distance. Without saying a word, he positioned himself right in front of her, took a moment to admire her from head to toe, and extending his right arm, touched her soft tender face for a moment. His eyes were heavy with emotion. No longer able to resist his impulses, which had been restrained until that moment, he took another step forward and embraced her tightly and ardently, being reciprocated immediately.

All others smiled and exchanged glances of approval, as if they were sharing that moment of great tenderness.

"Welcome to Bread & Joy, Elizabeth," said Amanda, and making a sign with her right hand, asked all others to exit the room, leaving Frank and Elizabeth alone.

When finally the embrace was interrupted, they looked around and didn't see anyone else. Then they sat side by side and admired each other for a while, until Frank decided to speak.

"It's so nice to see you again. Many times I doubted that this moment would happen. I missed you so much. Are you okay? You look thinner."

"Yes, I'm fine. I'm just tired. These were two very difficult years. I know you had your doubts that I would return. But I promised, didn't I?"

Frank agreed by slightly nodding his head. They smiled at each other, and Frank then reached out and wrapped Elizabeth's hands in his. She then continued, "I hope you do not hate me, and forgive me for choosing—"

Returning a gesture she had made two years ago, Frank gently placed his hand on her lips, asking her to stop talking.

"Shhhhh. Let's not talk about the past. I understood, and I forgave you a long time ago. Now I'm just happy to see you. Many times I thought something bad had happened to you by the lack of news, since you never wrote me. What are you doing back in England, and how did you find me here in the middle of nowhere?"

Elizabeth then took a large bag that until this moment was by her side. She opened it and took out a pack with about ten letters, all held together by a red ribbon.

"I was released from my duties two weeks ago. The Germans are in retreat and are now offering little resistance. There is no longer as many wounded people as before, and the need for doctors and nurses has reduced considerably. As I was about to complete two years of uninterrupted services, they sent me back home. During that time, I went from Africa to southern Italy and from there to France. In the recent months, I was on the border with Germany. I stayed there for a while until the Germans withdrew and we started the offensive. In my last weeks, I was in Paris, caring for recovering soldiers until I was discharged and released to return home."

Elizabeth then showed the letters to Frank and continued, "I wrote you several times, but I never got any answer. With time, I stopped writing. I did not understand your silence and was also quite worried, thinking that something bad could have happened to you. The first thing I did when I returned to London was to look for you at your boardinghouse. There, a young girl told me that her mother, the owner of the boardinghouse, had died shortly after you left, and she did not know where to send your letters. But she had kept each one of them. Take them. They are yours."

Elizabeth handed the letters to Frank, who held them in his hands and admired them fondly. He then looked at Elizabeth and asked, "So how did you find out where I was?"

Elizabeth smiled and said, "I am not the kind of woman that gives up easily, Frank. From your boardinghouse, I went to the Great Lion, and Albert told me where you were."

Frank smiled for a moment and thought, *Albert, always finding a way to help me. And to think I almost didn't stop there before leaving London.*

"I was alone in the world, momentarily without an occupation and extremely tired. I thought then that a farm would be the perfect place for me to rest after all I went through. Do you think they would allow me to stay here for a while?"

Frank felt a great joy to know that she came to stay and nurtured the hope that "for a while" would mean "permanently."

"I'm sure they will. They are very good people and will certainly appreciate the benefit of having an experienced nurse around. I will talk to them about it."

"Thank you, Frank. And you, how did you end up here? You look great, very healthy, and also well cared for. Did you find a girlfriend, by any chance?"

Frank laughed and shook his head making a negative sign.

"No, my dear. I'm the one who's been taking care of me. When I found your letter in the pocket of my jacket, I went out like a madman through the streets trying to reach you. I wanted to talk to you before you left. I wanted to ask you to stay. But I arrived just moments after your departure."

"Thank God you did not find me, Frank. It would have made everything much harder. I hate goodbyes. I know I was a coward, but I cannot handle such moments."

"I understand. Then I went back to the boardinghouse, but before, I went to the Great Lion and drank all the beers I could."

Elizabeth laughed at Frank's comment, but her gaze was of compassion and a hint of concern. Understanding the message, Frank tried to reassure her, "No worries. I stopped drinking almost two years ago."

Elizabeth's eyes widened, and she smiled broadly.

"That's great, Frank. I am so happy to hear this. And indeed I'm noticing you quite different. Something seems to have changed dramatically within you."

"You have no idea, but that's a long story that I will tell you tomorrow. The day after your departure, I received a letter from Peter inviting me to come and help him managing the farm. It was an invitation sent by God, because I really didn't know what I would do with my life from that moment on. I grabbed my things and came. Luckily, I passed by the Great Lion to say goodbye and to pay the beers from the night before. If it wasn't for that quick visit to Albert, we would have lost each other forever."

They looked at each other tenderly, and without knowing, both had the same thought. Fate had orchestrated a quite magical and surreal moment to keep them connected, so they would not lose each other. It was like a little divine intervention, a string so thin that it was almost invisible, but it was enough to rescue them. Thanks to this thin thread, they were there, face-to-face, eye-to-eye, heart-to-heart, and soul-to-soul.

Without much thought, their mouths slowly began to approach as if there was a magnetic field between them, irresistible and impossible to be contained. They kissed for a long time while their hands held and caressed each other.

When the kiss finally broke and their eyes opened again, they noticed that there was someone else nearby. They turned immediately and found Amanda standing in the center of the room. Blushing, they tried to compose themselves and apologized.

"There is no need to apologize, I am the one who owe you excuses as I did not imagine that…well, never mind. I just came to tell you that your room is ready, Elizabeth. We have also prepared a bath for you if you want. When you are ready for bed, I'll take you there."

"Amanda, I cannot thank you enough. You don't even know me, and I was even impolite enough to arrive unannounced. And yet you welcome me in such a hospitable way. Please accept my apologies for the unexpected visit."

"No worries. A friend of the Farrows is also our friend. Besides, life here at the farm can be quite boring at times, so a novelty always helps to break the routine. When you are ready to go to bed, let me know. I'll be reading in the library next door."

"There is no need for you to wait. I'm exhausted, and I'll go with you right now."

Elizabeth then turned to Frank, brushed her hands over his face, and said goodbye. "I will take a bath and get some rest. Tomorrow we'll talk more. I'm sure we have a lot to tell each other."

"I'm sure we do," said Frank, returning the affection and wished her good night.

Frank remained in the living room, watching Elizabeth go, carrying her two suitcases, which probably carried everything she owned. He could barely believe his eyes. When he saw himself alone in the room, he looked at the letters and thought, *It will be a long night.*

When he got to his bedroom at the house in the back, where he now lived alone, Frank took off his shoes and settled into his bed. He took the first letter in chronological order and began a long journey in time and space. Elizabeth had written to him exactly one letter a month during the first ten months of absence, and two more, already spacing in time.

The first letter from March 1943 came from Tunisia and began with an apology for having abandoned him like that and also asked him not to misjudge her. She confessed being in love with him, but explained that the decision to go to Africa had already been taken a month before they met and that she could no longer decline. She said that this was her life, and she could not fail to comply with her mission.

The letters that followed came each from a different location, always showing some kind of advancement of the Allied troops. First in Tunis, preparing to leave for a dangerous crossing of the Mediterranean, then already on the other side on the west coast of Sicily. Then later, when she was about to leave the island and enter Calabria and from that point and on, going on a slow and gradual rise toward the center of Italy. Elizabeth shared with Frank moments of fear and loneliness. She said she was missing him, that she was homesick and also missing a hot shower and good food. That she had been the witness of too many deaths, pain, and suffering, but she was determined to stay until the end.

In one of her last letters, already in Anzio, south of Rome, Elizabeth mentioned the fierce German resistance to avoid losing control of the Lazio region where the Italian capital is located and described a moment of fear and despair when they were counterattacked by surprise. The medical camp where she was, which is usually located in a safe and secure point from the direct combat, had also been the target of enemy attacks. A stray bullet had grazed her left shoulder and had her immobilized for a few days.

The last letter, dated June of 1944, described a more optimistic scenario with the news of the Normandy invasion and the victorious offensive to conquer Rome. But the letter ended saying she would no longer write, since she had not received any answers and did not know if her letters were even being read.

When he finished reading Elizabeth's last message, Frank placed each letter back in their respective envelopes, wrapped them again with the red ribbon, and stored them in Benedict's old chest. They were now a part of his treasures.

He then lay down again, closed his eyes, and opened his usual channel of communication with the divine energies. As Benedict had taught him, he imagined a beautiful light in front of him and thanked God for that moment in his life. His loved one had returned.

With an immeasurable feeling of plenitude, he fell asleep. Only the next morning he would realize that he had fallen asleep without even changing his clothes.

Rediscoveries

THE SUN WAS ALREADY HIGH and the clock pointed ten thirty in the morning when Elizabeth finally came in through the door of the office that used to be Peter's and that now was occupied by Frank. He smiled with her appearance and soon left the pen aside and rose to greet her with a kiss on her forehead.

"Good morning, sleeping beauty. I'm here in anguish. I already went twice to the main house to ask about you."

"I was very tired from the long trip, and the bed they gave me is wonderful. It was almost impossible to leave it. Then I had a long breakfast and interesting conversations with Peter and Barbara. I loved learning more about your brother. I thought I would find him here, working with you."

"He usually comes only in the afternoon to check how things are, stays for bit, and goes. It's been some time now that I've been taking care of everything."

"I'm impressed, Frank. I had created several possibilities in my mind on how I would find you, but seeing you behind a desk like this, managing a farm, was certainly not among them. How did this happen? What a transformation!"

"Yes, dear. A huge transformation! And I still have more to tell you. Why don't we take a walk around the farm while I tell you everything?"

"It sounds like a wonderful idea."

Frank and Elizabeth then went out for a walk hand-in-hand through the farm while he told her in detail about his path until that point. He spoke of the long trip to Bread & Joy, the sad surprise to find Peter in a wheelchair, and the initial difficulties in maintaining his intention not to drink, due to the negative influence of his brother's habits. He narrated to her with enthusiasm the reunion with Benedict and the moment of redemption that he had experienced with him. He explained to her how that moment had transformed him from inside out and that he had since ceased to look at his past with pain and resentment. He concluded by saying that to quit drinking after such moment had been a peaceful and uncomplicated process.

Elizabeth then understood why he didn't keep any resentment for her decision of leaving him. As Frank was narrating his personal transformation process after that encounter and how he was able to rescue Benedict's chest with all his books and manuscripts, Elizabeth also understood that she was in front of a different Frank and that she needed to rediscover him and adapt to this new person who now stood before her.

Interrupting Frank's narrative, Elizabeth asked in curiosity, "What about the wise old man? Have you found him after all?"

Frank hesitated for a moment, not knowing for sure how to best answer her question. After meditating for a few seconds, he said, "Yes, Elizabeth, I found him. And whenever I need him, I summon him."

Before Elizabeth could ask her next question, he pointed to the railway and continued, "It was here that I last saw Benedict. He waved his hand as if he was saying goodbye, and when I shifted my attention for a few seconds to see how long it would take for the train to pass, he was gone."

Elizabeth decided not to ask any more questions. That was exactly what Frank wanted, since he didn't feel that it was yet the right time to talk about the wise old man. One day he would, but not at that moment. "Come, I'll show you where Benedict and I met in the woods. It is a very beautiful place, and it's not far."

While walking to the river, Frank finished his narrative. He talked about his rapprochement with God, his participation in the church support group, and his commitment to help Peter to stop drinking, until he reached the previous night, when they attended the meeting together, and the progress that his brother had made until then. At that moment, Frank remembered that Peter wanted to tell him something before Elizabeth's taxi suddenly shifted in front of them, forcing him off the road. He needed to ask him what it was.

Finally they reached the river, and Elizabeth marveled at the sight of the crystal clear water, the grass surrounding the riverbanks, the trees leaning over the stream, and the soothing sound emanating from the water making its course.

Frank pointed to the location of their encounter and invited her to sit on the grass in the shades of a large tree.

Once seated, Elizabeth locked her eyes on Frank, still surprised with everything she had heard. While looking deep into his eyes, she could recognize the boy she had found in a hospital bed, only more mature and focused.

"I am pleasantly surprised with everything you told me. But I need some time to get used to this new Frank. I need to get to know you again."

Frank extended his right hand toward her with a playful smile and said, "Nice to meet you. My name is Frank Farrow, manager at Bread & Joy and counselor in the church support group for addicts and depressed. At your services, beautiful lady."

Elizabeth laughed at his joke, and this was like music to his ears. He remembered at that moment how much he had missed seeing and hearing her laughter. Then he caressed her face and completed his introduction, "And I have never forgotten you, Elizabeth. I still love you." He approached and kissed her tenderly.

Intoxicated by that moment and the beauty of the landscape, it was no longer possible to stop the caresses. Within seconds, they were making love as they had done in Elizabeth's apartment exactly two years ago. Again the last day of February gifted them with an unforgettable moment.

Then they rested together for a few brief moments by the river, enjoying the beautiful landscape. Elizabeth was wrapped in Frank's arms and legs, while resting her head on his chest.

As Frank ran his fingers through her hair, he said, "I am so happy that you came back to my life, Elizabeth. I don't want to lose you anymore."

The silence that followed left him restless and insecure. From experience, he knew that when Elizabeth was silent like that, there were things happening beyond his understanding, and it made him wonder if there would be something that she was yet to share. Not wanting to ruin the moment, he decided not to ask any questions. He would seek to understand this enigmatic silence later. Besides, it was past lunchtime, and they still had a long walk back to the farm.

The Real Intentions

After a few days at Bread & Joy, under Frank's request, Amanda allowed Elizabeth to move to the house in the back so she could stay with him. Victoria was the only one to oppose for the sake of religious values, since they were not married. However, Amanda already knew that it wouldn't make much of a difference to keep them in separate rooms, as she had witnessed every now and then that Elizabeth did not sleep in her own room, and that in fact, what her daughter felt was pure jealousy of the one who had become her only object of admiration, although supposedly a secret one.

Living with him, Elizabeth could then observe Frank more closely and witness his routine of readings, meditation, prayer, exercise, work, and participation in the support group in the village.

As the days went by, she began to cultivate a growing admiration toward the Frank she had found on her return, and even started adopting some of his habits, such as the relaxations and reading some of the books from Benedict's chest.

On his side, Frank seemed to be living a dream. He had rebuilt his life, and to complete his great moment, the woman he loved had returned and was there by his side all the time. He was so inebriated with this state of things that he preferred to avoid any questionings about Elizabeth's plans for the future, but he knew that sooner or later, he would have to deal with this subject.

On the first Sunday of April, Elizabeth accompanied Frank and the others to the mass as she had done every Sunday since her return. Frank proudly introduced her to everyone, but couldn't help noticing that, although courteous, Elizabeth would not bother to approach anyone else there. She seemed to intentionally avoid creating any kind of deep and lasting bond.

As they returned to the farm, everyone sat at the table to eat, as it was typical of every Sunday when a family gathering for lunch was almost an obligation.

At one point, Amanda turned to Elizabeth and asked, "So tell me, Elizabeth, how do you feel after a few weeks of rest at Bread & Joy? Are you feeling better? At least you seem healthier. When you arrived here, you looked pale and really thin."

A little embarrassed, Elizabeth replied, "That's true, Amanda. I feel much better, thank you. I think I have even gained a few pounds more than I should. You treat me like a queen. I am very grateful for your hospitality."

Victoria then did not let the opportunity pass and asked, "Do you feel ready to resume your work activities? We know all the important people of the village, and if you plan to stay permanently, my mother could easily find a job for you. There is always a need for an experienced nurse."

A somewhat uncomfortable silence took place on the table, but Frank allowed the conversation to continue. He was wondering what the answer would be. Elizabeth finally reacted.

"Well…uh…I think I still need a few more weeks to feel completely ready to resume my activities. We'll talk about it soon. I appreciate the offer."

Elizabeth's vague response provoked an exchange of questioning looks, and that was enough for Frank to understand that the time had come. He needed to talk to Elizabeth and understand what was really going on.

He waited for lunch to finish, and as the weather was unusually mild for that early April, he invited her for a walk.

When they were far enough from the house, Frank stopped in a shade, turned to Elizabeth, and said, "I think we need to talk. Since you arrived, I've been observing some reactions of yours that worry me. First, it was your silence when I said I no longer wanted to lose you, then the fact that you don't make friends with anyone in the village, apparently keeping your distance from people intentionally, now this vague answer, declining Amanda's offer to find you a job. I understand your postwar stress, but this is not typical of you who love your profession so much."

As Frank was talking and developing his line of thought, Elizabeth's face started to change. She could no longer look at him face to face, and her eyes were saddening. Realizing that his words were having such an impact on her, Frank changed the tone and sought to be more understanding.

"I wish I could help, but I need you to open up. Now that you came back to me, I need to understand what is really happening."

Elizabeth remained silent for a few seconds, contemplating the horizon, apparently formulating the best way to respond. When she finally spoke, she looked at Frank with tearful eyes charged with emotion, since she knew that what was about to be said would break his heart.

"Frank, I actually have something to tell you, and I only haven't done it before because I still carry a lot of doubts in my head. I don't know what to do yet. The fact is that I did not come back to you, Frank. I came back for you."

Confused, Frank looked at her with an expression of someone who was completely lost, asking for further explanations. She then continued, "I didn't come back to stay with you, Frank. I came back to fetch you. When I was in Paris on my last duty during the war, I joined the Red Cross in order to continue with my life mission. I want to keep helping people in need around the world. I have no one else in England, Frank, only you. And in my understanding, you also had no one else and could benefit from a fresh start. Therefore, I asked permission to take you with me as another volunteer, and they agreed to it. All you need to do is to accept it, and you can come along with me. I could never imagine the turn of events that took place. My only hope was to find you alive and rescue you from your situation of abandonment and loneliness, so you could rebuild your life with me. I swear that my intentions were the best possible."

Elizabeth paused and thought for a moment on how to continue. Frank's mouth had dropped open, but at the same time he was eager to understand the rest of her story. Elizabeth then went on, "When I was released to come home, it was just to rest for a while. Soon I will receive a new mission and be sent to any place on the planet to take care of needy people, going through some kind of deprivation or suffering. Maybe they will send me to Asia, Africa, or Central America. I don't know yet. They are just waiting for the end of the war to decide. I heard on the radio yesterday that the Allies are demanding the Germans to surrender. The war will end any time now, Frank. Soon I will receive my mission and two ship tickets, mine and yours, to a new destination. But seeing your new reality during this past month while by your side, witnessing how you rebuild your life and how happy you are, I lost the courage to ask you to come with me. I cannot take you out of here. I do not feel I have such right."

Frank was paralyzed. He did not know what to do or what to say.

When he spoke, it was in a disappointed and frustrated tone.

"Why didn't you tell all this before? Why did you allow us to live this month of absolute happiness, only to destroy it all this way? Why did you make me believe on this illusion that what we were living would be forever?"

"Please forgive me, Frank. But first I needed to see what your new reality was. Then when I realized your new situation, I got lost. I've been looking for the best way to say this to you for days. And I'm suffering as well, because I am also happy to be living this moment with you."

"Then why don't you stay? Why do you need to leave? Stay with us, Elizabeth."

Frank paused for a moment and then made the ultimate request, the one that he really wanted to make: "Stay with me."

Elizabeth then could not hold her emotion and in tears, she replied, "This farm life is not for me, Frank. I could not bear it for too long. I'm sorry."

Elizabeth then turned and left running, heading back to the house with tears on her face.

Still numbed by the news that he had just received, Frank took a few seconds to react, and when he screamed asking for Elizabeth to wait and return, it was already too late. She was too far away to consider such request.

Alone, Frank then said to himself, "Very well, Frank. You wanted to find out what was going on. You just did. And now, what are you going to do about it?"

After a few minutes there, pondering on what had just happened, Frank realized that Elizabeth's intentions were the best possible and that they still had some time left until a final decision had to be made. Maybe if he could make the following weeks a positive experience for her, he could convince her to stay at Bread & Joy.

Slowly he went back to the house to look for her and to try to calm her down. He found her alone in his office, apparently doing the same as him—reflecting on what had just happened. She was no longer crying but still had a grieving look on her face.

When Frank came through the door, she tried to anticipate him and said, "I'm so sorry Frank. I think I was extremely presumptuous to think that I could plan your future, to think that you could not find your own path in life."

Frank smiled and replied calmly, "And didn't I do the same thing to you? How could I imagine that a woman like you wouldn't already have a plan? I've been around you long enough to know that your head doesn't work in such way. I think that in the end, we are guilty of the same crime. We both thought that we would be the solution for the each other's problems."

Elizabeth nodded her head in agreement.

Frank then approached and bowed down in front of her, took her hands, and looking into her eyes, he said, "There is still some time before this war is over. We don't know if it will last for another day or another year. What if we leave this matter aside? Let's try to make the best out of this time together, until comes the day for decisions to be made. Can we do that?"

Once again, Elizabeth nodded her head in agreement with Frank's proposal, knowing that there really wasn't a better alternative at that moment.

They embraced, and again without knowing, they thought exactly the same thing:

I hope that the little time we have left will be enough to convince you to stay with me.

Hope Is Born at Bread & Joy

IN THE WEEKS THAT FOLLOWED, Frank and Elizabeth tried to please each other as much as they could, secretly seeking the same objective. One wanted to convince the other to rethink life and guide it to a different direction. However, they avoided at all costs raising the issue of the decisions that soon would have to be made.

But as April came to its end, it was becoming clear that the decisive moment was approaching. The battle for Berlin had begun, and the Russians were already engaging in combats street by street to take the German capital. It looked like it was a matter of days for Hitler to surrender, and that made their anguish grow more and more.

On May first, Elizabeth awoke with a strong tightness in her chest, even greater than the ones she had experienced in recent days, intuitively knowing that they had very little time left.

As she finished getting dressed to leave the bedroom, her thoughts were interrupted by the sound of a heated argument coming from the office.

She stepped out of the room slowly without making a sound, and as she approached the office, she could hear Peter and Frank arguing over some administrative decisions of the farm. Both seemed to have different opinions, and she could hear Peter saying, "Frank, you need to get me involved in these decisions. Although you have taken my assignments, I'm still in fact the administrator of this farm. Remember the night when Elizabeth arrived? While we were in the car I wanted to talk to you about this, but the taxi that almost hit us interrupted me. What I wanted to say that night is that I already feel in conditions to once again assume my responsibilities here. I'm doing all right. I no longer feel depressed. I don't drink anymore. I didn't bring it up again because of Elizabeth. I didn't want to divert your attention, but I cannot let things continue as they are, Frank."

Elizabeth then heard strong, quick-paced footsteps. Victoria walked through the door pale and worried, screaming, "Peter, Peter, come quickly!"

Elizabeth followed her, and both entered the office, interrupting the discussion of the two brothers. Victoria was afflicted and still catching her breath, said, "Come, Peter, it's time. Barbara's water just broke."

The four then moved hastily toward the main house, Frank pushing his brother's chair so they could move faster.

When they reached the bedroom Barbara was in bed writhing in pain, and Amanda was sitting next to her holding tight to her hand. Peter got distressed to see his wife in such situation and hurried to demand for some action to be taken.

"Let's get her in the car immediately. We need to take her to the village, so a doctor can take care of her."

Amanda then interrupted in a worried tone, "I'm not an expert on the subject, but from what I could see, I don't think we have time for that. I think the baby is already being born."

In an even more desperate tone, Victoria cried, "My God, what do we do?"

Then a calm and secure voice echoed in the room, "Have you all forgotten that there is a nurse in the house?"

Everyone stopped for a moment, looked back, and there was Elizabeth, standing at the door witnessing the whole scene. She then entered the room and said, "I've done everything in my life, including a few deliveries. Can I examine her?"

Amanda answered quickly, "Please, Elizabeth."

Elizabeth then asked for the men to leave the room.

Peter and Frank left their work-related differences aside and gathered in the living room, both with quite concerned faces.

A few seconds later, Amanda and Victoria passed by running through the room, and Peter screamed, "What's going on? How is she?"

Victoria returned and hastily replied, "Please keep yourself calm, Peter. Your baby is coming. Elizabeth will make the delivery and asked us for a basin with water and some towels."

She barely finished the sentence and quickly made her way to the kitchen.

The brothers looked at each other with their mouths open, and Peter leaned back in his chair. Frank smiled, put his right hand on his brother's left shoulder, and said, "Try to calm down. She is in good hands."

The hours that followed seemed days to Peter and Frank. Both moved from one side to the other in the room, taking turns in front of the window. Occasionally they would hear a louder scream of pain from Barbara, and every time this would happen, Frank would have to hold Peter's impulse to urge in his chair toward the bedroom.

The sun was high, and it was already past noon when finally a baby's cry echoed through the four corners of the mansion. The two brothers then made their way down the hall and waited for someone to come out through the bedroom door.

After a few long minutes, Amanda came out of the room with the baby wrapped in a sheet and placed it in the arms of Peter, who had his face illuminated by a smile that conveyed both relief and joy. Frank then approached, and while looking at the child, touched his brother's arm and said, "Congratulations, Peter. I am very happy for you." He was soon followed by Amanda.

"Yes, Peter, she is a beautiful baby. She seems to be in very good health."

Peter had his eyes hypnotized by the sight of having his offspring in his arms, but immediately reacted to Amanda's observation.

"She?"

"That's right Peter, it is a girl."

Frank then said, "Apparently we might have to wait for little Frederick a bit longer." And Peter then continued, "And it seems that we are more and more a minority in this house, my brother."

Everyone laughed at Peter's observation, just as Victoria was coming out of the room. With a worried face, she put her finger in front of her mouth, asking for silence.

"Shhhh, come down. Barbara went through a hard delivery and is exhausted. She needs some rest."

"Can I see her for a moment?" asked Peter.

"Yes, but it has to be brief. She needs to rest and recover to be able to start breast-feeding."

Everyone then slowly entered the room with worried looks.

Elizabeth was in the corner of the room and carried a face of someone who had fulfilled her duty, as she wiped her hands with a white towel. She had a lot of blood in her cooking apron, which had been improvised for the occasion.

Peter passed the baby back into the arms of Amanda and approached Barbara. She seemed to be almost unconscious, making a great effort to keep her eyes open.

Worried, Peter looked at Elizabeth, hoping to get more information.

She understood immediately and said, "Don't worry. She just lost a lot of blood and is exhausted. She will need some time to be in good shape again, but she will be fine. I'll take care of her for the next days."

Now feeling calmer, Peter thanked Elizabeth for all she was doing. Then he reached for Barbara's hand, held it tight, and while looking into her tired eyes, smiled and said, "Congratulations, my love, you did it. We have a beautiful baby girl." She smiled back at him, holding his hand tight. He felt at that moment something different, which until then he had not yet felt and realized he had learned to love his wife.

Suddenly, behind them, the half-opened door creaked while being opened slowly, breaking the magic of the moment.

Everyone looked back and saw Carl stretching his head into the room.

"I apologize to everyone for interrupting. First of all, congratulations for the baby."

Amanda knew Carl, and she was quite aware that he would rarely go into the most intimate areas of the house, even when invited, and thereby entering unannounced like that was not of his making. Sensing that he would have an important reason to be there beyond congratulating Barbara for her baby, she made a sign with her right hand, giving him permission to enter and said, "Thank you, Carl. But come in and tell us, what brings you here?"

"Well, Mrs. Amanda, I just heard something on the radio that I think is of everyone's interest, so I came. It has just been confirmed that Hitler committed suicide yesterday. With his death, the expectation is that it will not take long for Germany to surrender. I think the war is over. At least there is a big hope that it is."

There was a great commotion in the room, and everyone celebrated the news. But while celebrating with others, Frank and Elizabeth looked at each other in a somewhat worried way. They both knew in their hearts that the decisive moment was approaching.

In the midst of such turmoil, a tired and shaky voice was trying to say something. It was Barbara, who after a few seconds was finally able to get the attention of Peter, who raised his hand and asked for silence to all.

"Everyone quiet, please. Tell me, Barbara, what do you need, darling?"

"Hope. I want our girl to be called Hope, so we never forget this moment and may look at the future with new eyes and hearts longing for better times."

Peter then asked Amanda to hand him back the baby, and once he had it in his arms, he looked at Barbara and said, "So welcome to this new world, Hope Farrow."

At that moment, the emotions in the room were widespread, and some tears were inevitable on the faces of Amanda, Victoria, and Elizabeth.

Victory Day

THE DAYS THAT FOLLOWED BROUGHT a world of excitement to Bread & Joy.

While everyone followed anxiously on the radio the ramifications of Hitler's death and the fast disintegration of what was left of the German resistance, Elizabeth, Amanda, and Victoria were taking care of Barbara and Hope, making sure that both would get the appropriate food and rest.

Peter alternated his time and attention among three activities: helping on the recovery of his wife, adapting to his new role as a father, and following the news on the radio.

With so many things happening around him, Frank had no other choice but to postpone his plans of having two important conversations, the first one with Peter, about what to do with the administrative responsibilities of the farm going forward. His brother had made it clear that a review of their tasks and responsibilities was needed. And the second important conversation would be with Elizabeth, to try to convince her to stay with him at Bread & Joy.

Both conversations would have to wait for a few days, until the war was over and Barbara was fully recovered.

On May eighth, Barbara finally woke up feeling more invigorated, and as she got out of bed, soon began to argue in favor of a ride around the village.

"I want to see people and a little agitation. After a week cloistered in the room, I need to distract myself a bit."

Her concerned mother immediately manifested herself against the idea, but stopped arguing after hearing Elizabeth's opinion.

"An infection would have already shown after so many days. Let her go. I think it will be good for her."

Amanda consented, but asked Elizabeth to accompany her. As she also needed to catch some fresh air after taking care of Barbara and Hope for so many days, she gladly agreed to it.

So Carl, Barbara, Peter, Victoria, and Elizabeth left toward the village. Amanda stayed behind, taking care of Hope, and Frank followed with his routine at the office.

When they arrived at the village, they noticed that something odd was going on, as everyone seemed to be inside the shops or their homes. Few people walked on the streets.

They got out of the car and decided to head to the main store, as they also needed to pick up some groceries. When they entered, they could finally understand what was happening. Several people were huddled around the radio. They were announcing something important, and everyone had stopped to listen. They joined the others just in time to hear the last words spoken by the broadcaster:

"It's confirmed. Germany has just surrendered unconditionally. We repeat, unconditionally. The war in Europe is over. We repeat. The war is over."

This announcement was soon followed by shouts of celebration and relief. Many were crying with joy, others of anxiety, since they could hardly wait to see their sons, nephews, grandchildren, siblings, and friends returning home.

Within seconds, the street was filled with people embracing each other and celebrating the victory after nearly six years of fighting.

Carl pushed Peter's chair out of the store so that he could better witness the celebrations on the street.

Barbara seemed to be one of the most agitated and celebrated the news effusively. To each person she embraced, she would say, "My baby will live years of peace. Thank God."

The stirring after days in bed seemed to be too much for her, and she suddenly felt a little dizzy, and her legs buckled. Supported by Elizabeth, she returned to the store where they were before and was quickly given a glass of water. Elizabeth then tried to reassure everyone, "It was only a slight pressure drop. Didn't you want a little excitement, Barbara? It seems that you got a little more than you could handle."

Everyone laughed and decided unanimously that it was better for them to return to the farm, as the celebrations would throttle any possibility of a peaceful walk at the village.

Carl had some difficulty driving through the streets, which were filled with people and other cars honking their horns frantically, but after a few minutes, they made it to the dirt road.

When they finally arrived at Bread & Joy, they soon realized that the news of the end of the war had also been heard there, as they entered precisely when Amanda carefully danced and sang a waltz with Hope in her arms, while being watched by Frank, who was enjoying the scene. Everyone then gathered in the living room, opened a bottle of champagne, and toasted with enthusiasm the beginning of the new times.

Proving that he had overcome his addiction, Peter behaved very well, controlling his actions and taking only a sip of the tasty drink.

Frank and Elizabeth took part of the celebrations with the others, but whenever they would look at each other, there was something of concern in their eyes.

After everyone calmed down, Frank whispered in Elizabeth's ear, "I have something for you."

Leading her to the library, he reached into his pocket and pulled out a letter with a sealed envelope that was addressed to Elizabeth. It was from the Red Cross. He then said, "They really didn't waste time."

She looked at the letter with a bit of sadness and said, "I was expecting it. They needed me urgently since they do not have many volunteers at this time because of the war. I believe that as soon as they learned of Hitler's death, they took action."

Elizabeth sat down, opened the envelope, and began to read the letter in silence. When she finished, she folded the letter, put it back in the envelope, and with her eyes turned to the floor, told Frank about its contents.

"They're sending me back to Africa, but this time to a different place. I'm going to South Africa. The ship departs from Liverpool to Cape Town on May 12th in the early afternoon. I have to be there the day before to get the tickets, so I shall leave in three days, Frank."

Silence filled the library for a while, until Frank finally broke it. "I really want you to stay here with me. But I do not feel in the position to ask that of you."

Elizabeth stood up, looked him in the eyes, and answered, "I really want you to come with me. But I don't feel in the position to ask that of you."

The two hugged and kissed intensely. When they finished their kiss, still embracing, Frank whispered, "Please stay."

To which Elizabeth replied, "Please come."

The Moment of Decisions

THE DAY FOLLOWING THE RECEIVING of the letter from the Red Cross, Elizabeth announced to all that she would be leaving in two days for her new mission, which generated a great commotion, especially on Peter, Barbara, and Amanda, who were very grateful for all she did when Hope was born and for taking care of both mother and daughter during the days that followed. She decided not to comment on the fact that she had an extra ticket for Frank, in order not to cause any influence on a decision he could eventually make.

Then she began to pack her bags for the trip, hoping to see some reaction from Frank that would suggest a preparation for him to go with her. But she was frustrated in noticing that such thing did not happen.

Frank, in turn, did not change his routine, trying to show that his decision was to stay in Bread & Joy, hoping that Elizabeth would change her mind.

Frank stayed reading until late that night, trying to distract himself from the anguish that was gradually growing in his chest. When he finally decided to retreat and try to get some rest, he found Elizabeth already deep asleep.

In the corner of the room, he saw her bags that seemed to be almost ready. The door of the closet was open and revealed only two sets of clothes hanging, one for the next day and another for the eleventh, when she would leave.

He lay down carefully so as not to wake her and closed his eyes, thinking, *She really is determined to leave. If you plan to do something about it, Frank Farrow, it has to be tomorrow. This will be your last chance.*

Frank woke up the next day at six in the morning as usual to do his meditation and prayers, but as he looked to the side, he was surprised to see that Elizabeth was no longer in bed. A chill went through his back up to his nape when he looked at the corner of the room and didn't see her bags anymore. He then turned to the closet and noticed its doors closed. As he opened it, he saw that the two sets of clothes were also no longer there and in desperation, screamed, "Noooooooo."

Frank ran out hoping that he could still reach her, but once outside the house, he no longer found anyone. The sun was slowly rising in the horizon, and all he could see were the truck's tire tracks on the dirt road, certainly left by Carl only a few hours ago.

Dismayed, he went back into the house and in passing through the living room toward his bedroom, saw a letter lying on the table. Not controlling his emotions, he said aloud, "Not again, Elizabeth. Please."

He stood there looking at the envelope, building courage to take the few steps toward it and open it. When he finally did, the letter simply confirmed his suspicions. It read,

> My beloved Frank,
>
> As you already know from experience, I have no tolerance for goodbyes and thought it would be best to leave a day early. It would be too painful to say goodbye not only to you, but to everyone who welcomed me for the last two months. I left with Carl another letter of thanks to Peter, Amanda, and her daughters.
>
> I think you have plenty of reasons to go on in your current course. I have never seen you so happy and fulfilled, so I cannot take you out of

this great moment in your life. I want to see you thriving and growing more and more.

Forgive me, but at this point in my life, I do not see myself settling in a farm permanently. Maybe one day, when I have lived what I have to live, I may reconsider. But now I carry strong in my heart the feeling that I still have plenty to see and live. I also need to feel that I am making a difference in this world full of injustices and suffering. That's why I must take this ship and be on my way.

Then I took the initiative to ask Carl to take me to the station before dawn, so I could take the first train to Lincoln, leaving at six thirty in the morning. From Lincoln, I follow to Liverpool and will be there at the end of the day. I asked Carl to keep it a secret, and being the gentleman that he is, he attended me. Do not scold him for that, please.

Tomorrow I will get the tickets, and I will communicate your withdrawal.

Your ticket will be returned without losses, so do not worry.

When I get to my destination, I will write you again. As I said, I am not of farewells, so do not see this as such. It is only a "see you soon." I'm sure our paths will still cross again one day.

May God be with you and please take good care of yourself.

From the one who loves you very much, enough not to mess with your life,
Elizabeth

When he finished reading the letter, Frank looked at the wall clock and saw that it marked six ten. By the time that Carl would be back, it would be too late for him to get to the station in time to catch her. But even if time was enough, what would he do? Ask her to stay? She had been very clear in her letter.

Resigned and convinced that Elizabeth once again had done the right thing, he began to wonder if he had made the best decision himself.

Days of Suffering

Frank went through moments of much pain and suffering that tenth of May. Everyone tried to console him, but their efforts were in vain.

Even good old Carl apologized, saying he had no idea that Elizabeth was leaving permanently. He thought it was just a short trip. Frank obviously forgave him at once.

At the end of the day, he went for a walk and passed by the sites where he had met Benedict, hoping to find in vain someone that could comfort him. As he did not find what he looked for, he mumbled to himself, "Yes, Benedict, I know, I already have my wise old man, but at this moment, I'm in such pain that what I seek is a little bit of comfort, not advices."

He went back to the farm, and as he got to his room, his pain turned even stronger. Two months had been enough for him to get used to the presence of Elizabeth. Her scent was everywhere. But most of all, Frank missed her energy, her positive vibe, and the delightful feeling that he had someone to devote himself to and seek to impress. Have Elizabeth as his audience had proved to be incredibly motivating. During those two months, he had done everything with greater enthusiasm. Work, reading, exercise, prayer—everything seemed to have more flavor because he had someone he loved observing him.

He realized then that an old acquaintance was paying him a visit—the desire to drink. He felt an incredible urge to go to the main house and invade the cellar seeking for a wine or whiskey that could numb such pain and realized that until that moment he hadn't gone through a real test in his life without addictions. Here was the moment of truth. Would he be strong enough to overcome the pain without the subterfuge of drinking?

He then got himself into his knees and began to pray, asking for help to gather strength and serenity to overcome that moment.

After his prayer, he began to search for something in Benedict's chest that could relieve him. He checked the books and manuscripts one by one and realized that he had read all of them at least once, and none would serve as comfort in such times.

He woke up the next day surrounded by books and pieces of paper scattered around the room and with the terrible feeling that he had slept less than he needed.

The eleventh of May dragged on. The minutes seemed like hours, and the hours seemed like days. Nothing seemed interesting. Everything he did appeared to be harder and tedious. His power of concentration was almost inexistent.

Everyone noticed his mood and decided to leave him alone for a while. At that moment, nothing could help him. They believed that after a few days, he would be back to his normal.

On retreating rather late to his room that night, Frank realized that it was only a few hours until Elizabeth would be gone, and he had no idea when he would see her again. A multitude of questions began to spin around his head. What if she decided that after South Africa she would go to Australia or New Zealand or India? And what if her missions would follow one after another and she never came back? And what if she found someone else in her missions?

He could not bear the pain that some answers to such questions would bring him and once again wondered if he had made the right decision.

Then he concluded that the time had come to seek some advice. He would make a supreme effort, and despite all the emotional turmoil he felt at that moment, he would try to have a conversation with his wise old man.

The Balance between Bread & Joy

BEFORE SUMMONING THE WISE OLD man, Frank realized he needed to try to calm his emotions down. He sat in his favorite armchair, crossed his legs, rested his hands on his knees, and began to relax every member of his body. Once he had achieved a deep level of relaxation, he started to work on controlling his thoughts and emotions.

After a few minutes of struggle, he felt calmer and in control and began to imagine his older and wiser version in front of him.

Soon the imaginary old Frank appeared with his usual calm and smiling feature and looking at him with tenderness and compassion, initiated the dialogue. "Hello, young man. I feel your heart is really distressed. How can I help you?"

Frank thought for a moment and answered, "I made a decision, but now I have doubts. I don't know if I did the right thing."

"Hm, I see. Why don't you tell me what you see that is good and bad in your decision?"

"Well, what I see that is bad is easy to say. I feel I'm about to lose in a definitive way the woman I love. I believe she is the woman of my life. But to be with her, I would need to give up everything I've conquered so far and go to unknown distant lands, not knowing what I would do with my life. Today I have my work, I regained my self-esteem, I feel balanced, I've quit drinking, I help people. What I see that's good in my decision is that I will keep all this."

"Very well, Frank. I understand your moment of doubt. Let's talk about the things you said you have today, that you are apparently reluctant to leave. Let's talk about your work. How did you get to be employed at Bread & Joy?"

"Well, my brother, Peter, invited me to work with him and taught me everything I know. When he failed to perform his duties because of his drinking and the depression he was going through, I ended up temporarily taking his place, and today I take care of everything."

"I see. You used the word *temporarily*. Can you explain that to me?"

"It's just that I'm occupying the farm manager position until…"

Frank remained silent for a few seconds as if he had reached the first important conclusion of that conversation. The old Frank then asked, "Until?"

"…until he feels better and is able to occupy his position again. And I believe that it's been a while that this already happened."

"Is that so? And why do you think this transition hasn't happened yet?" Again there was a brief moment of silence until Frank replied, "Because I did not allow it to. I gave him no space. He tried to talk about it, but I did not listen."

The wise old man then decided to intervene;

"Put yourself in his shoes for a brief moment. He now has a family to care for and wants to be a good role model to his daughter, correct? How do you think he feels about this situation, Frank?"

"Terrible. Surely this is troubling him a lot."

"Could we come to the conclusion that this state of things will have to change sooner or later?"

Frank lowered his head and consented, "Yes. Soon he will take back his position, and I will return to being just his assistant."

"One more question about your work and the things you learned in this job. Can they only be applied here?"

"No, not at all. I learned how to buy and sell, how to plan and take care of finances, how to get transportation and storage for the harvest, to lead people. In short, I learned things that I can certainly use anywhere."

"Ah, then we could come to the conclusion that your new knowledge is not only applicable to the farm, it is transferable. This will be very helpful to us. But let's change the subject. Let's talk about your work helping people at the church group. What kind of people does it seek to help?"

"The ones returning from the war and their families. We also help those who have lost loved ones in the war."

"Very well. Certainly an admirable work and it is understandable why you feel so proud of it. With the end of the war, how do you believe this work will proceed?"

This question was followed by another moment of reflection. Once again the wise old man made him notice that one of his pleasant occupations would probably have short life.

The wise old man allowed silence to have its turn, until Frank replied, "I don't know actually. Probably it will continue for a while, but we will have to adapt to a world without war, perhaps seeking other objectives."

"Of course it will. What this group does will always have a demand. And what you learned to do there can also be applied elsewhere, with people seeking other kinds of support, isn't that so?"

Frank then asked, "Where are you going with this?"

The old Frank smiled and helped him get to the conclusions. "Frank, remember that I am you but much older, with little life to live, and being so, I have the ability to look back and see the decisions that made me happy and those of which I regretted. Being in this position, when I look back, I see this time of my youth as a decisive one in my life, since in those days I learned things that can be applied anywhere. I stopped being a boy and became a man, full of talents that could serve me in any situation. When I look at this moment in isolation, I understand how natural it is for you to be enchanted by it, because you have really lived a thrilling turnaround. However, I also see that you are making the mistake of falling in love with this temporary situation and getting attached to it. Moments pass, as this one too shall pass. The time has come to let it go and start looking to the future. Your life is changing, Frank, and you do not control that. Attachment to this momentary situation will only bring you more suffering and frustrations. The most important is that you have learned different ways to conquer the daily bread, and this will be useful for the rest of your life."

The observations of the wise old man brought long minutes of silence and reflection. The fact that he could see things through the eyes of someone who already have a lot of experience and little time left ahead, allowed him to put things in a totally different perspective, and his logic was unquestionable. Whether Frank liked it or not, his life was changing and would be much better if he was part of the change instead of reacting negatively to it.

"Okay, I think I got the message."

"Good, Frank. This gives us space to talk about the bad part of your decision—the possibility of losing the person you believe to be the woman of your life. But instead of talking about the person involved, let's talk about this feeling of loss that you're going through. You seemed to be happy and fulfilled until the arrival of Elizabeth. But now that she's gone, you no longer seem so happy. What has changed? After all, what have you lost?"

Old Frank's question made him think. Actually the situation was exactly the same as two months ago, when Elizabeth hadn't yet returned, but now work was no longer as fun, and helping people in the church group had lost a bit of its excitement. What had changed? Little by little, he started elaborating on the answer;

"I believe that before, everything was new, and each activity was part of a process of rebuilding me. But my routine was dry and had no joy. The arrival of Elizabeth seemed to have fulfilled a void that not even I knew existed. I believe everything I do brings me great self- fulfillment, but I think I was missing something. With Elizabeth here, everything became more colorful. Everything was more fun."

"Oh, interesting. What is the name of this farm?"

"Bread & Joy."

"And remind me again, why does it have that name?"

"Because the first owners believed that we should have both at the same time."

"Precisely. Could we summarize by saying that you learned to conquer your bread, but had no joy of living?"

"Yes, I think you're right. With Elizabeth here, I believe I had both. I felt a plenitude that I had never felt in my life."

"Then allow me to tell you this, Frank. As you know, I am very old and no longer have much time. When I look back and I see my life after the departure of Elizabeth, I see a lot of work, balance, and dedication to helping others. I never again drank and was able to develop myself spiritually. But despite all that, I lived a life with little laughing, with little color, with little emotion. I did not feel that plenitude that I felt during these two months that I just experienced. I'm an old content man, for I have lived a life of purpose, but I lacked something Frank. I earned the daily bread, but I lacked the joy of living. And I bitterly regret never having made the necessary effort to stay with Elizabeth, wherever that would be, because the place doesn't really matter. I will die soon, but I never forgave myself for it. I feel a lot of regret. In summary, Frank, the bread you will be able to earn anywhere, for you have developed the talents for it, but the fun, the joy, the plenitude of being with someone you love, this is something you cannot easily find."

Another long moment of silence and reflection followed. Frank was starting to get to some conclusions, but in considering some alternatives, he felt that he lacked the strength for changes that were a bit more radical.

"I understand what you say. But I feel so safe here. I'm not sure I would have the same courage as Elizabeth, to leave for distant lands that I don't even know how they are or what I would find there. I'm afraid, very afraid."

The old Frank nodded, showing that he understood perfectly.

"I know. And it is this fear that can paralyze you and make you lose Elizabeth. It can make you lose your joy. Fear is not the problem, Frank, but being overcome by it, is. Feeling fear is normal, it is even healthy sometimes. It is a natural instinct of self-preservation that can spare us from many problems and upsets. But it can also generate paralysis, and thereby ruin our happiness. Courage is not the absence of fear, Frank. It is the strength to overcome it. And for that we often need to be a little more adventurous. But I'm not the one who can help you with that."

"No? So who is it then?"

"Where is your inner child, Frank?"

Frank then remembered the dialogue he had with Benedict before leaving for the army. He had learned in that conversation that he should never allow his inner child to disappear. That he should always cultivate and nurture that child, since for many times, it carries us through the most difficult times of life and helps us to venture into others. And he had forgotten it completely. The old Frank then concluded, "Without it, you will never take some risks and will never venture. When I look back and I see my life without risks and adventure, I feel that I have lost many opportunities and lived a life that was somewhat tedious. It was a useful and productive life, but with no adventure and joy. Rescue this child, Frank, and overcome your fears before it's too late."

These last words from the wise old man seemed to have had a transformational power over Frank. He then came out of his trance, opened his eyes, and the imaginary dialogue that he was having with his wiser self ended immediately. He had heard enough.

Before taking any action, he remembered the words in Elizabeth's letter: "Tomorrow I will get the tickets, and I will communicate your withdrawal. Your ticket will be returned without losses, so do not worry."

Despite knowing that he could no longer take the ship, he also understood that he could not allow things to be as they were. He needed to seek one last opportunity to talk to Elizabeth and try to convince her not to go. What they would do after didn't matter at that moment. He needed to try to recover his joy of living with her, however this would be.

He looked at the clock and saw that it was past two in the morning. He had to do something to change his destiny, and it had to be quick. He had only a few hours left.

The Race Against Time

Frank calculated that if Elizabeth's ship was to leave at around two in the afternoon, she would be embarking at around noon. He would thus have about ten hours to get to the port of Liverpool and find her. How he would convince her to stay, he didn't quite know yet, but it really didn't matter at that moment. The most important thing was to find a way to get to her in time.

He concluded that the train would not be a good solution. There would be too many stops, and by the time he would get to the port it would be too late. The only alternative left to him was the farm truck. He then spoke to himself, "Sorry, Amanda. Desperate times call for desperate measures. I will borrow your truck and will soon return it."

He thought of leaving a note for Peter, but figured that there was just no time.

He found the keys to the truck and went out the door. When he started the engine, he realized two things that would make his trip very difficult, if not impossible. First, by being an inexperienced driver as he was, he had no idea how to get to Liverpool. And second, the truck had almost no fuel.

One name and one hope came to his mind and made his heart flutter. "Carl."

He sped off toward the village. He would wake Carl up and ask him for help. Carl would understand.

When he arrived at Carl's house, he knocked on the window until the old man woke up. Carl opened the door, completely surprised and concerned, and went out saying, "What happened, Frank, is everything okay?"

"Carl, I need your help. I need gasoline and some directions."

"Frank, why do you need gasoline at this time? It's three in the morning."

"I am going to Liverpool. Now."

Carl looked at Frank and soon understood what was going on. "You are crazy."

Frank remained silent, looking at Carl with eyes that showed despair and clearly communicated that he was his only hope. Resigned that he could do little to convince Frank to change his mind, Carl pointed to the back of the house and said, "Come. I have gallons of gasoline in the back, but I need your help to carry them."

Frank carried the gallons to the truck. He used one of them to fill up the tank and put the other on the trunk to use later during the trip. Distracted by his task, he lost sight of Carl for a moment. When he finished, he turned toward the front door and found Carl, with changed clothes, walking his way. Surprised, he asked, "Where are you going?"

"You have no experience driving the roads all the way to Liverpool, my boy. I still feel a little responsible for helping Elizabeth to leave. This is my chance to redeem myself. I'll take you there."

Frank felt so relieved with Carl's proposal that he hugged and thanked him profusely.

Then, they left toward Liverpool. Carl estimated that with some luck, few stops, and no incidents, they would arrive at their destination at around ten in the morning, which by Frank's calculations, would give him about two hours to find Elizabeth and convince her to change her plans.

However, they ended up stopping many times to rest and eat, had a flat tire, and in the end the trip took longer than they had expected. They were only able to make it to the port at around eleven o'clock. Frank's time was getting shorter and shorter.

When they got there, they were surprised by the size of the place. Dozens of old buildings, some dating from the eighteenth century, raged for miles and were intercrossed by a multitude of streets of all kinds of width and length that gave access to different docks.

Not too far from them, they could contemplate the River Mersey, which a few miles down would give access to the sea.

Due to the size of the port, it took a while for Frank to find which ship was in which dock, the times of departure, and where the one that would go to Cape Town was located. To his despair, he found at eleven twenty that the vessel going to that destination was scheduled to leave at one thirty in the afternoon. If Elizabeth was supposed to board two hours before departure, she should already be at the dock. That left him very little time, maybe ten or fifteen minutes, but luckily the dock he was seeking was not too far away.

Then he sped off, running through the galleries, deviating from travelers, sailors, and street sellers until he arrived at eleven thirty-five at the dock he was looking for.

As he turned the corner and walked into the dock, he saw that there were not so many passengers waiting to board. Apparently Cape Town was not such a popular destination. Some people were already lined up, showing their tickets to a sailor that would check them, would return the part of the ticket with the information of the cabins to them, and then would grant them permission to walk through a small walkway giving them access to the vessel.

Could it be that she already boarded? he thought.

He looked at the huge ship and realized to his despair that if by any chance she was already inside, he would no longer be able to find her. Then he concentrated his attention at the dock, observing face by face, hoping to find the one he was seeking.

Suddenly, across the agglomeration of passengers and people who were there to say their goodbyes, his eyes met with familiar eyes, which were apparently already watching him for some time. There was a tender and happy smile on Elizabeth's face.

Frank felt the familiar chill in his belly, and a wave of relief mixed with joy ran through his body.

He began to walk toward her, now much slower, making his way with difficulty among the people who were there, until he came face-to-face with her. Then they embraced at length.

Unlike two years ago, this time he had managed to reach her. But a few seconds later, still wrapped in her lovely hug, he thought, *What now?*

After a few seconds embracing, Elizabeth moved back, held Frank's hands, and looking into his eyes, she said, "I never lost hope that you would come. I would be the last person to enter this ship."

"And for a moment I thought I had arrived too late."

"Not this time."

Frank then sought the best possible words to take the next step. It took a few seconds until he could finally articulate what he wanted to say;

"Elizabeth, I know that I no longer have my ticket and that you are determined to get on this ship. I also know that I said I didn't have the right to ask you to stay, but the days that followed your departure were very difficult. I completely lost the joy of living and came to the conclusion that life without you is not the same thing. I need you with me to feel such plenitude. So I am left with no alternative than to ask you to stay. Please reconsider."

The features of Elizabeth changed immediately, shifting from joy and tenderness, to sadness and frustration. She let go of Frank's hands, looked around him for something that she did not find, and then said, "Now I understand why you did not bring any luggage. You did not come to go with me, you came to get me. You came to ask me to stay." Disappointed, Elizabeth kept her gaze directly into Frank's eyes and while putting her hands inside her coat pocket, she pulled something and immediately handed it to him. "I just said that I still had hopes that you would come. That I would wait for you until I was the last person to get on this ship. I said that because I never communicated your withdrawal. I never canceled your ticket, Frank."

Frank was surprised and paralyzed to see his ticket in his hands. Mouth open and not knowing how to react, he looked at Elizabeth and said, "I'm sorry. I had no idea you would keep it. I don't know what to say."

Elizabeth approached him, gave him a kiss on the cheek, and said, "Frank, you know I'm not the kind of person who gives up on things or loses hope. I know I said I did not feel the right to ask you to come. But my days without you have not been at all easy as well. I also have missed you very much. So I also want to ask you to come. Please reconsider."

Frank was totally surprised and disoriented and stood there paralyzed, not knowing what to do. He was not prepared for that. His idea was to convince her to stay. It was to return with her to Bread & Joy and decide together what to do and what direction to take next.

Realizing his hesitation she reached down, grabbed her bags, walked a few steps toward the ship, turned once more to him, and said, "See you inside."

A Sign

Frank stood there in complete perplexity and as if immobilized, watched Elizabeth hand her ticket to the sailor, walk along the walkway, and enter the ship, without looking back.

And there he was, on a dock of the port of Liverpool, face-to-face with the decision that he had avoided taking three days ago.

Life was offering him a second chance, and he could not help but think that the decisions that we avoid taking, sooner or later, pay us another visit.

As he watched the movement of people around him, Frank realized that there was no longer a queue for entry and that there were only a few people who were still busy with their goodbyes. Probably soon they would withdraw the walkway that was giving access to the ship and would finalize the departure procedures.

Pondering the idea of entering the ship or not, once again fear took over him. He thought of Bread & Joy and the quiet life he had there. He also thought about the people he helped at church, in his daily meditations, prayers, and readings. He would have to give up a life that seemed to be so stable and secure.

As much as he wanted to live next to Elizabeth, he could not move toward that walkway, which despite being a small bridge of only a few meters, represented a radical change in his life. To cross that short distance meant that his life would never again be the same.

He put the ticket in the inside pocket of his jacket and began to walk slowly down the dock, looking for the courage he lacked. He looked back at the ship hoping to find Elizabeth and beg her one last time to stay, but he could not find her.

When he reached the street corner that led to the dock, he saw that Carl was sitting in the gutter next to an alley, just a few yards away. He walked slowly over to him and sat on his side. Carl then tapped on his shoulder and tried to comfort him.

"You could not convince her, huh? I'm so sorry, Frank. Maybe it was not meant to be. At least you can say to yourself that you tried."

Frank then took the ticket from his pocket and showed it to Carl. "Look at this, Carl. She still had my ticket and asked me to go with her. But as much as I want to, I can't. I'm in panic. I cannot find the courage to break my bonds. I'm simply unable to. The fear I feel to leave behind everything I've achieved is too strong. I wish I could overcome it, but I can't. I wanted so badly to be sure I will not ruin my life by getting on that ship. I wanted so much that God would send me a sign."

Suddenly they heard a different sound that caught their attention.

Someone was enthusiastically whistling a very well-known tune. They sought to find where such a sound was coming from and saw that there, across the narrow street that led to the dock, an old man, wearing beret and mended clothes, sweeping the floor while whistling. He would occasionally stop to lead an imaginary orchestra. He had his back turned to them and, apparently entertained by fulfilling his task, did not realize he was being watched.

Carl smiled at the scene he was witnessing and said aloud so the old man could hear him, "I love this song, sir. And apparently it brings you very good vibes."

The old man stopped with his whistling but kept sweeping the street and still with his back toward them, said, "Yes, it is the Ninth Symphony of Beethoven, the fourth movement." The old man continued doing his job and went on, turning the corner into the alley, but before he went away, he turned slightly sideways to them and said, "It makes me feel like a child. It is also known as 'Ode to Joy.'" He turned and went his way, disappearing from the view of the two.

They were silent for a few seconds until Carl said, "My goodness, that old man looked so much like…"

And then they both spoke at the same time, "Benedict!"

Frank rose to his feet and ran to the corner looking for the old man. Carl, due to his age did not have the same agility, but came right after. But as both turned the corner, they ran into an empty alley and saw several closed doors where the old man could have entered. Carl then observed, "With his hair cut and no beard, but I could swear it was him. Now we'll never know."

Frank then paused for a moment and pondered, "Feeling like a child…ode to joy…my God, what am I doing?" His face was lightened, and a wave of bravery flooded his heart. He now knew what he needed to do. He just hoped it was already not too late. Overcoming his fears, he turned to Carl and in a rush asked him, "Carl, tell Peter that I will write him explaining everything as soon as possible, okay?"

Frank embraced Carl, thanked him for everything, and sped off.

Turning the dock corner, a shiver ran down his spine since he realized that they were already taking the walkway out. He took the ticket from his pocket and began to run desperately screaming, "Wait, wait, there's one more passenger."

However, the port workers that were performing their task made a sign that it was too late. They would not let him board.

Ignoring them completely, Frank made a lateral move that would cause envy to any rugby player and passing between two men who tried to stop him, entered into the walkway that was already being untied and was almost all loose. Halfway, he realized he still had the ticket in his hand. He turned back and still running, handed it to one of the men who were there. He was awestruck by Frank's determination to enter the ship and had no reaction. Frank put his hands on the man's shoulders and said, beaming with happiness, "I'm going to Africa, my dear friend. Finally I'm going to Africa." He turned back again and ran into the ship, disappearing from sight. Now all he needed to do was to find Elizabeth.

Part V
Paths That Merge

The Letter to Peter

A FEW DAYS AFTER FRANK'S DEPARTURE, a letter arrived at Bread & Joy. It brought a stamp from Lisbon, dated May 14th. It was addressed to Peter but had no return address. Opening it, Peter saw that it was from Frank and read,

My dear brother,

I must confess that I am not too sure on how to start this letter. To explain to you how I took the decision that I did would take too long and would be incredibly complicated. So I'll leave it for another opportunity. The truth is, not even I knew that I was going to take this ship.

First of all, I want you to know that I am well, still finding myself in this new path that my life is taking, but well.

I am taking advantage of our last stop on a European port before leaving towards Africa to send you this message. I hope it doesn't take long to arrive, as I imagine you must be eager to hear from me.

I will start by saying that I will be eternally grateful for everything you did for me and for helping me rebuild my life. Thanks to you, I have learned a profession, and now I can work and earn my daily bread anywhere. I know I had good food, care, and comfort at the farm, but that's only half of what I seek for my life, and I can surely win them back. I'm leaving because I still need to conquer the other half, which is the joy of living and that, I can only achieve beside the woman I love.

The truth is that it was more than time for you to resume your activities as the manager of Bread & Joy, a job that you do as no one else. Today you have your family. You are well in your health and shall reoccupy the place that has always been yours. I am sure that with the end of the war, many young people returning home will soon be looking for work. You will not have difficulties in hiring someone else to help you.

I would like to take this opportunity to ask you a few small favors.

First, at the next meeting of the support group, I want you to tell everyone that I am eternally grateful for taking part of this work, and that thanks to it, I grew, matured, and strengthened myself very much. Today I feel prepared to help people who are experiencing moments of difficulty or distress, and certainly I will keep exercising that duty wherever I go.

I also want to ask you something very important. In my bedroom, you must have found an old chest. It is the chest of our grandfather Benedict. The story of how it came to me is too complicated to explain here, and it will also wait for another opportunity. I promise that one day I will tell you everything in detail, sitting beside a fireplace. The important thing right now is what's inside. There you will find books from the most diverse parts of the world, on the most varied cultures, philosophies, religions, and life stories. Today, looking back and putting things in perspective, I believe that old Benedict always knew that one day I would go wandering around the world, and he was getting me prepared for it all along. You will also find many of Benedict's manuscripts that helped me a lot in the process of rebuilding my life. For that reason, I leave to you a kind of "homework" for you to complete your recovery process. I want you to read as much as possible of the chest's content. And I want you to pay particular attention to a manuscript that carries fifteen thoughts you should read every day. Benedict gave me such list as a birthday gift on the eve of my departure for the army, and it helped me a lot. Today I already have it memorized, so please do not bother sending it back to me. Now it's yours. Read three sentences a day and try to practice his teachings. I am sure this exercise will do you well. Also there, you will find the Bible that was our mother's and my savings. Keep them safe for me please, because one day I'll be back to claim them.

Finally, I want to make one last request. I want you to try to find yourself again spiritually. I know you still have hard feelings for what happened, for being in a wheelchair, and believe that God is not exactly your best friend. But if we think a bit more about it, he orchestrated things in such a way, so that today you have a dignifying work and the joy of a beautiful family. He gave you bread & joy, especially now with the arrival of baby Hope. Always be grateful for that. Try to see the winding paths that he uses for us to meet our destiny. I'm living that right now, putting my life with all my faith in his hands.

And the next time you pray, because if you follow my recommendations I am sure that you will, remember your beloved little brother, who decided to embrace the unknown and go out into the world in search of the unexpected.

Please also thank Amanda, Victoria, and Barbara for hosting me for all this time. They will never be forgotten. Of course, send a fraternal bear hug to old Carl. If it wasn't for him, I wouldn't be here.

I will write again when I get to my destination, somewhere in the countryside of Africa.

Be with God, and I will see you one day.

From the brother who loves you,
Frank

Embracing the Unknown

THE LAST THING THAT FRANK could see as he looked back when entering the ship was the walkway he had just crossed being removed by workers of the port.

A scary thought crossed his mind at that moment. *That's it. Now it's too late to change my mind. There is no turning back.*

With his heart still pounding and the adrenaline pumping through his veins, he paused for a moment to breathe and think about what he would do next. For a moment, he felt a sharp pain in his stomach. The weight of the decision he just took made him a little dizzy and left his mouth dry. He had taken a ship going to a distant place that he didn't know and had only brought with him the clothes he was wearing.

Sitting in the first chair he found, he tried to put himself together again. Now was not the time for faltering, even because it wouldn't change anything. The decision had already been made, and he needed to embrace it with all his soul.

Little by little, he calmed himself down and started remembering the conversation he had the night before with his wise old man. Everything would be fine at the farm. Things would still happen as usual at the church support group. Life would follow its course, and all the pieces would fall in their places. He would certainly find a new role, a new job, and more importantly, he would be with Elizabeth. But beyond all this, there was something new in his life that brought him tremendous excitement, which was the unknown. And his inner child was thrilled with it.

Once he recovered his breath and his thoughts and emotions were better organized, he closed his eyes for a moment and made a little prayer, asking for divine protection on his next steps and for him, along with Elizabeth, to be able to start a new life and find plenitude.

That was when he abruptly went back to the reality of that moment. He still had something very important to do. For his new life to begin, he still needed to find Elizabeth.

He realized then that by getting into the ship in such messy and hasty way, he had not asked back the side of his ticket with the number of his cabin. He would have to scour the four corners of the ship to find her.

He then proceeded walking around the ship and visited all sections, restaurants, and the halls that gave access to the cabins. He searched her for over an hour and found no sign of her.

Suddenly he felt a move and realized that the ship was leaving.

Maybe she would be at the top, watching the departure.

He then climbed to the deck and once again did not find her.

He stopped for a moment and watched the people around him waving to others that little by little were getting smaller on the dock at the harbor. Liverpool was slowly falling behind, shrinking on the horizon. Frank waved as well, saying his "see you someday" to England, to London, and to Bread & Joy.

He thought then on how this transition was difficult to him, how he was rooted and attached to the past, and how he was learning to be different with Elizabeth, who was always looking ahead and toward the future. At that very moment, it became quite clear to him where he would find her.

Now with no hurry, he made a slow walk toward the bow, sure that he would find her there.

And this time he was right. There she was, leaning on the ship's railing looking out to the open sea that lay ahead. While everyone was gathering on the side and stern waving their goodbyes, she was there alone, looking at what was ahead. And he admired her for it.

He approached her slowly, trying not to make any noise until he was about ten feet away, and there he paused for a moment to admire her forms, her strength, her determination, and thought, *My God, how I love this woman*. He was happy with the decision he took. It was then that he realized that Elizabeth had a handkerchief in her hands and was discreetly trying to wipe a few tears running down her face. Despite being there, looking at what lay ahead, she was also suffering, thinking that he had left her. He decided to shorten that suffering immediately. Walking toward her he said, "Wouldn't you, by any chance, have men's clothes in your suitcase?"

She turned surprised and shouted, "Fraaaank! You came."

She moved toward him and hugged him tightly.

After a few seconds, she pulled back and looked into his eyes. Her tears still flowed, but now there was no pain, only relief and happiness on her face.

"What took you so long? I thought you had given up on me."

"And I almost did. I panicked when you put the ticket in my hands. I really didn't expect this and didn't know what to do. But I believe that an old friend found his peculiar way to help me make a decision. I'll tell you all about it some other time, because now I want to enjoy this moment. I am very happy to be here."

They kissed for a while, and Elizabeth then pulled him by the hand to the tip of the ship, where they could enjoy the view ahead of them.

The waves were being broke one by one by the ship, which was already moving at full speed.

There it was, the unknown, right in front of them, looking at them face-to-face, eye-to-eye.

Frank took a deep breath and in relief, once again embraced Elizabeth tenderly.

He closed his eyes and felt the plenitude that he searched for so long. With the sea breeze on his face and embracing the woman he loved, he could experience intensely that intoxicating energy.

Right at that moment, Frank had the feeling they were being watched and still with eyes closed, he was able to feel the presence of his wise old man and his inner child, embracing each other a few feet away, watching and enjoying this beautiful scene.

The wise old man then looked at Frank's inner child and said, "Let the unexpected come."

And Frank's inner child replied enthusiastically, "Yeeeeesss."

Frank smiled at them and thought, *Yes, my dear ones. And you are both coming with me in this journey. To the unknown, here we go.*

Benedict's List

(Practice three of these thoughts a day.)

1. I am becoming a better and stronger human being each day. I will overcome one by one the obstacles that life brings to my path. I will persevere, and I will win.
2. I will convert errors or mistakes made by me into learning experiences, not guilt.
3. I will use every opportunity that life gives me to help others. I will treat others as I would like to be treated, even when I am not.
4. I will always seek to learn something new. I have different qualities and strengths, but many of them are yet to be discovered.
5. I will put focus and energy on the things I can control and in the hands of God, with all my faith, the things I cannot. He'll know what to do.
6. I will always exercise forgiveness toward those who do me wrong. I will use pardoning as an act of love toward those who hurt me and toward myself.
7. I will make the best out of my present time, because it's all I have. I will make of my past a source of learning experiences and of my future a sea of possibilities.
8. I will build a better world myself, being the agent of the changes that I want in it.

9. To understand my neighbor, I will put myself in his place and will feel his pains and joys.
10. All that is good or bad, one day will pass. I will take the best out of each experience and move on. What does not kill me makes me stronger.
11. I will create my own positive thoughts. A positive attitude begins within me and does not depend on what is around me.
12. To love your neighbor is a matter of choice and attitude, not of feelings. I will choose to love, and I will do it through my actions every day.
13. Fears and limitations are generally fruits of imagination. They are not facts, only beliefs. I will not allow these beliefs to limit me. I will seek to be all that I can be.
14. My future is a blank page, and the pen is in my hands. I will write what I want, and I want for myself the most beautiful story that I can create.
15. I will thank God every day for all I have and for all that I don't have. After all, he knows better than anyone what I really need in my life at this moment.

Milton Keynes UK
Ingram Content Group UK Ltd.
UKHW010153040424
440506UK00019B/1105